Robert M Williams
Haydsville Utah
July 3 1993

Jhnd
6/93
Cedrilk, Ut

A Question of Proof

Also by Joseph Amiel

STAR TIME
DEEDS
BIRTHRIGHT
HAWKS

A Question
of Proof

Joseph Amiel

CROWN PUBLISHERS, INC., NEW YORK

Published by Crown Publishers, Inc., 201 East 50th Street, New York, New York 10022. Member of the Crown Publishing Group.

Random House, Inc. New York, Toronto, London, Sydney, Auckland.

CROWN is a trademark of Crown Publishers, Inc.

Manufactured in the United States of America

Library of Congress Cataloging-in-Publication Data

Amiel, Joseph.
A question of proof / Joseph Amiel.—1st ed.
p.   cm.
I. Title.
PS3551.M53Q4   1993
813′.54—dc20
92-27230
CIP

ISBN 0-517-57520-5

10 9 8 7 6 5 4 3 2 1

First Edition

To my children,
Andrea and Jack

A Question of Proof

Prologue

"He's dead!" the woman's voice screamed into the telephone receiver. "He isn't moving. He's dead!"

The 911 operator immediately transferred the call to a dispatcher.

"What's the address, ma'am?" the man's voice asked.

"Send an ambulance—someone—right away! Help him, please!"

"What's the address?" the dispatcher repeated. "Ma'am, we need to know the address."

"The address?" she asked, not comprehending the question and repeating the words aloud to hear them once again. "It's on Walker Drive. In Chestnut Hill.".

"What number, ma'am?"

She told him, and then she cried out, "Come quickly! Peter's dead!"

"One moment, ma'am." The dispatcher clicked off. A few seconds later he was back on the line. "What's your name, ma'am?"

She gave him her name.

"And the name of the victim?" the dispatcher asked.

"Peter Boelter."

"Jesus!"

"For God's sake, hurry!"

"A squad car and ambulance are already on their way."

The woman fumbled the phone back onto the cradle.

The squad car arrived in less than five minutes, the ambulance in eleven. The rescuers were far too late. The body of Peter Boelter, publisher of the city's dominant newspaper, the *Philadelphia Herald,* was already growing cold.

1

1

Five months earlier, on a night in January, Dan Lazar awoke to the sound of a key in his apartment's front-door lock and then Mara's quick high-heeled click along the hallway to the bedroom. Mara worked for Dan and his partner's small law firm and had spent the day at the York County courthouse, about an hour and a half's drive from Philadelphia. She had been defending a shopkeeper charged with burning down his failing haberdashery.

Eyeing the red clock-radio numerals, Dan started to reach for the lamp switch.

"Don't get up," Mara whispered, solidifying into a silhouette against the window light filtering through gauze curtains behind her. He heard her dress rustling and then saw it rise over her head and descend onto the chair like a black parachute.

"It's almost one in the morning."

"Sorry," she said, anticipating his annoyance. "I told you on the phone I was going to be late." Her faintly Eastern European accent curled sensuously around the apology like an intimacy whispered over espresso at a street café. As an adolescent, she had fled with her mother to America after her father died in a Czech prison.

"A *little* late, you said. I phoned the York County prosecutor's office at nine. Everyone had gone for the night."

Her tone conveyed her resentment that Dan had checked on her. "We went out to dinner to hammer out a plea bargain."

3

"You could have negotiated a Middle East peace treaty in less time."

"Almost as good. One count of recklessly endangering another person, and the prosecution will drop the arson charge. Our client is hoping that way he can hang on to the insurance money. Proud of me?"

She slipped into bed against him. He kissed her, fitting his nakedness to hers, inhaling her perfume. Dan was in love with Mara Szarek, and although he had no reason to doubt the explanation for her lateness, he knew he would never be sure. She was like a cat, independent and unbeholden and, as a consequence, fascinating. You took her on her terms. Dan was attracted to that quality in her because he himself was just as autonomous, never depending on anyone and wanting no one to depend on him.

"Actually, I worked late myself," he admitted. "Montano's preliminary hearing comes up tomorrow."

"How does it look?"

"I think I can discredit Feeney's testimony, but I can't be sure. He wouldn't speak to me. On the DA's orders, probably."

Mara's index finger brushed back and forth across Dan's lower lip. "I had a wonderful birthday dinner planned for you."

She kissed his throat, then licked slow loops along the edges of his chest muscles and down the hard furrows forming his abdomen.

"I'll make it up to you," she whispered, pulling back the blanket.

Her long fingernails lightly etched spirals lower down, eventually around the hardness that rose up to them. She kissed the soft skin inside his thigh, provoking a shiver. Then, without warning, she withdrew from the bed.

"One second," she promised.

She flipped a switch inside the bathroom. Light streamed through the crack between the door and the jamb, suffusing the bedroom with dim illumination and spotlighting her as if she were on center stage. Her small, sultry face was set off by her dark hair like a brooch on black velvet.

She's so sensual, Dan thought, so incredibly sensual.

"Why the light?" he asked as she glided back toward him. Mara did little on whim.

Blue eyes glittering with sly intent, she wet her upper lip, a tiny, blood-red Saracen's bow lifted into a wicked smile. "I want you to be able to watch."

She kneeled on the edge of the bed between his feet, her head lowering again toward his thighs.

"Happy birthday, Dan."

"It's already the day after. Come here."

He drew her back toward his face and then moved over her. "It's better to give than to receive."

Early in the morning, dressed to leave, Dan had just brought in the *Herald* from outside the apartment's front door when Mara, sleepy-eyed, emerged from the bedroom.

"You going to work?" she asked. "It's still dark out."

"The health club."

A shade under six feet tall, he had dark, nearly black eyes above a nose that had survived a lot of youthful fights more or less straight. His full head of curly black hair ended a bit below his collar. He wore it long not because he thought it becoming or fashionable, but simply out of inattention to how he looked. At forty-two, he possessed a casual handsomeness that greater care with his appearance might not have achieved.

"I could make us some breakfast," Mara offered. "Is there anything in the fridge?"

"There's milk for coffee." Dan rarely ate home, but he had remembered to pick up milk in case Mara stayed over. She kept some clothing at his apartment.

"I like seeing you here when you wake up," he said. She looked soft and vulnerable swaddled in his blue terry-cloth robe. "It's been a while since we had time for each other."

"I thought this morning I'd catch your cross-examination at the preliminary hearing."

"According to the *Herald,*" he replied grimly, "there won't be much of a cross to watch."

He handed her the newspaper, so she could read the banner headline: FEENEY TO NAME MONTANO AS CO-ED KILLER. The smaller headline just above the story read: DA LAUDS HERALD DRIVER'S ID AS KEY.

Because Dan had been away skiing with his son, Mara had done a lot of the early legal legwork when Ricardo Montano was arrested for Cassy Cowell's rape-murder, the second such crime in a month: representing Montano at the preliminary arraignment, investigating the charges, meeting with people from the district attorney's office, interviewing witnesses. Upon his return Dan took over from her. To his consternation, he soon found confidential information damaging to his case turning up in front-page *Herald* stories. He was convinced the information had been purposely leaked by the district attorney, Gilbert Huyton.

His antagonism toward Huyton went back many years, to a case they had fought early in their careers. The two had taken an immediate and inevitable dislike to each other. Huyton, then a young assistant DA, pegged Dan as a devious wiseguy. Dan, then working for the public defender's office, considered Huyton arrogant and dogmatic. The bitter charges, countercharges, and insults flying back and forth since Montano's arrest had highlighted press coverage of the case.

Mara glanced up from the newspaper. "You probably won't like what I'm going to say. . . . Granted the *Herald* went a little overboard about Feeney because he works for them, but we both know it's a good, impartial newspaper."

"That isn't a very impartial headline."

"Step back a second, Dan. Stop thinking like Montano's advocate. Huyton's got an open-and-shut case here."

"The judge might have a different view of things."

His tone startled her. "Dan, set my mind at rest. Tell me you don't have a chance of getting that killer off."

He shrugged noncommittally, slipped on his overcoat, and bent to kiss her good-bye.

She pulled back. "Feeney identified Montano in a lineup."

"*After* Montano's photo appeared in the paper and on TV broadcasts. My dead grandmother could have identified him then."

"Dan, that bastard Montano is a rapist, a murderer!"

Dan reached for the door. "I'll see you at the hearing."

Dan's visit to the homey sanctum of the health club proved to be a mistake. While jogging on the treadmill, he got caught up in a conversation with two of the other regulars, took a misstep, and twisted his knee. He insisted on finishing the workout and then, after showering and changing, walked fast up Broad Street to his office, where he picked up his briefcase, and then two blocks farther north to City Hall.

With the traffic light against him, he stood staring across the stream of traffic at the late-Victorian, wedding cake of a structure. The largest, tallest building in the country when it was constructed a century ago, City Hall somehow managed to cram beneath its mansard roof the mayor's and City Council's facilities, several other municipal offices, and a jumble of forty-nine courtrooms.

He had first entered the building's ornately embellished splendor to file papers for a lawyer's service he worked for while putting himself through Temple University Law School at night. He had been as dazzled by the building as by the aspirations it embodied for him. Now, a decade and a half later, he was at the pinnacle of the city's criminal defense bar, and the building's attractions had begun to pall on him; each duel wore him down a little more than the last and faded more quickly into the blur of previous matches.

As the light changed and Dan crossed the street, he was struck by the thought that City Hall's architecture perfectly symbolized the building's hypocrisy; its facade bustled with impressive columns and pilasters and innumerable dark windows that masked the self-dealing inside. Atop the building's outlandishly elevated tower stood a statue of William Penn, who founded the city and the commonwealth as a sanctuary where his Quaker coreligionists and others could live in safety. Head among the clouds, gaze fixed idealistically on the horizon, Penn's statue provided a visible symbol of both the Quakers' admirable tolerance for other viewpoints and their pacifism's unfortunate effect of withdrawing them from rough political tussles. That left the field open to hungry, unscrupulous newcomers.

As he walked through one of the archways that led on all four sides to the empty courtyard at City Hall's center, Dan perceived that it exemplified the moral void at the municipality's heart. This city, the birthplace of the nation's democratic institutions, had a long history of electing crooked, incompetent public officials, who were careful to stay on the good side of the powerful families that long dominated the city's social and economic life, but that, for the most part, shrank from dirtying themselves in the muck and infighting of elective office.

Dan halted for a moment to peer up at Penn's statue. Residents had long been amused by the accidental irony that its index finger, held at hip height and pointed at the former red-light district, looked very much in profile like a lustier, more shocking physical appendage. Perhaps to calm old Billy down, prostitution had shifted location over the years and now transpired in good part behind his back. Dan's client, Ricardo Montano, had been pimping for two women working the corner of Thirteenth and Locust on the night Cassy Cowell was murdered less than a block away.

"Dan!" a voice called out.

Dan turned. Hurrying toward him, puffing white smoke in the winter air, was the tenacious figure of Scott Feller, the crime-beat reporter for the *Herald*. A fringe of dark hair hung like an awning over his wire-rimmed spectacles.

Dan remarked curtly, "I'm surprised you didn't shoot me in the back when you had the chance."

"I can't control how my editors rewrite what I turn in," Feller protested. "Just wanted you to know today's ambush wasn't my fault."

"Peter Boelter probably loved it."

"Newsstand sales are up. Boelter recognized the circulation possibilities once Feeney came forward. You have to give him credit for that."

"And for trashing me in print when I took the case?"

Dan had taken offense at a story that implied his success on behalf of notorious clients had somehow tarred him. Although mellower in recent years, Dan possessed a short temper when faced with even small injustices. That innate aversion to unfairness and a distrust of those in authority had steered him toward law school and criminal defense work.

"It's Boelter's newspaper," Feller pointed out. "He gets to play by his rules."

"Including giving his buddy, Gil Huyton, the front page when he shoots off his mouth to win points with the public?" It was no secret that the publisher's and the DA's upper-class families had long been friends and allies; the Boelters had backed Huyton's election campaign editorially and financially. A lifetime's experience had taught Dan that the rich and powerful invariably made such mutually beneficial arrangements.

"I don't think it's personal on Boelter's part, Dan. You just happen to represent the bad guys. This is a big story, and what the DA says about it is big news. Law and order sells papers."

Dan's expression heated into anger. "I never met Peter Boelter, but it's personal, all right. I'm the Jewish shyster who grew up in South Philly, remember? Not on the Main Line with him and his crowd. I didn't go to Yale Law like Huyton or get hired by some firm with names on the door that signed the Declaration of Independence. I don't sit with those guys on the board of the Art Museum or the Orchestra or University Hospital. And I'm sure not a member of their Philadelphia Club or their Fish House. You fucking bet it's personal."

Feller pulled out his memo pad. "Maybe it is. Not on Boelter's part, I mean, but on Huyton's."

"Did Huyton say something?"

Feller nodded. "When I interviewed him on the phone this morning."

"What did he say? Exactly."

"That one of the reasons he ran for DA was to rid the justice system of guys like you, shady lawyers who use all the technicalities and tricks to get criminals and killers off. Any comment?"

"Huyton should try his cases in the courtroom, not the newspaper."

Dan broke off the conversation and stormed across the courtyard toward the south wing of the rectangle.

Gil Huyton had taken office right after the November election; his predecessor had already resigned because of illness. His administration's first important prosecution had been against one of Dan's clients, a major organized-crime figure. His right-hand man had tried the case. Huyton was badly embarrassed when Dan won an acquittal for his client.

By then the two lawyers' animosity had turned into hatred. After Dan agreed to defend Ricardo Montano for Cassy Cowell's rape and murder, Huyton announced that he himself would prosecute.

Cassy Cowell had been pretty, lively, and young, too young to work at a bar. But the good income paid for the college education she was pursuing during the day, and a false driver's license got her the job. At midnight, after finishing her shift, she had left the bar on Twelfth near Walnut to walk the dozen blocks home. Like much of Philadelphia, that part of Center City contained old four-story brick buildings on blocks that were often sliced through by narrow, interconnecting alleys that served as interior streets. She had probably started to zigzag through them to save some walking. Her half-naked body was found early the next morning behind a dumpster on St. James Street, one of the alleys between Twelfth and Thirteenth. She had been raped and strangled, apparently when she struggled with her attacker. No one in the adjacent buildings had heard a sound. Lab tests revealed semen in her vaginal cavity, but could not determine the attacker's blood type. Like fifteen to twenty percent of the population, the attacker was a nonsecreter—his blood type did not show up in his other bodily fluids.

An almost identical rape-murder had occurred in mid-December, when the body of a woman stockbroker who had left work late the night before was discovered only a few blocks away. In that case, too, no clues were found. But this time a policeman who had been driving a patrol car in that sector the night before remembered spotting Ricardo Montano, a local pimp, walking alone at midnight on Thirteenth headed north toward Walnut. Upon seeing the policeman, Montano had ducked into one of the alleys in the direction of Twelfth, but the officer was not sure which one. Nevertheless, Montano was brought in for questioning.

Two days later Tim Feeney, a truck driver employed by the *Herald* who had been delivering copies of the paper to downtown newsstands that night, came forward to identify Montano as the man he had happened to see running out of St. James onto Twelfth a few minutes after midnight.

Dan passed beneath City Hall's western arch to the outside of the building and turned left toward the entrance on the building's northwest corner. He stepped out of the cold morning air and into a medieval keep. A wide circular stairway, hugging the red marble and sandstone block wall but totally freestanding, ascended to the upper floors. The far doorway led to elevators and the ground-floor corridor. To the left, at an angle between the two outer doorways, was a snack bar. Dan had not eaten yet.

"I'm ashamed of myself to be talking to you." Matt Rooney's expression was censorious, at least as much of it as his short stature permitted to be seen over the high top of the glass display case.

"What is it now?" Dan asked.

"This case of yours today. They ought to take the rat out and shoot him."

"You Irishmen are always trying to keep a Jewish lawyer from collecting his fee." Dan joined in Rooney's laughter.

An ex-cop born and brought up in South Philly in the shadow of St. Joseph's, Rooney had retired on disability after a shootout in which he caught a bullet that was still lodged in his head and accounted for a lot of the jokes he made at his own expense. Rumor had it that another cop had shot him when Rooney stumbled onto a drug payoff. The corrupt cop had been killed in the exchange of gunfire. Rooney had kept his mouth shut, and the city had quietly settled with him for a large sum and thrown in the franchise for the snack bar. Since retiring from the force, he had become an avid observer of the criminal court scene.

Dan always dropped by when starting a case, if only to pick up the scuttlebutt Rooney inhaled like a vacuum cleaner.

"Heard anything?" he asked.

"Nobody will talk about the case. With all the sensation, that's strange. Usually everybody's trying to show off how plugged in they are. Maybe they figure the less that gets out, the less ammunition you'll have."

Dan glanced up from the display case. "When are you getting in those chocolate doughnuts I like?"

"Jesus, Dan, you don't want to eat that crap! I keep telling you the fat and sugar'll kill you. Even a guy with a hole in his head wouldn't be caught dead eating that stuff."

"Let me have a package of cheese crackers and a Three Musketeers."

"Fat, sugar, and *salt!* Your veins got to look like sewers. I got bagels, muffins. With margarine, if you want it. Polyunsaturated."

"Did Huyton buy a muffin?"

"Oat bran."

"Figures. I'll just take the junk food."

Dan grabbed the paper bag containing his purchases and thrust two dollars at Rooney's wife, who sat at the cash register eyeing the bag like a sentinel. Forcing himself to ignore the pain in his knee, he took the steps at a run two at a time, a way of stoking his competitive fires for the hearing. He was a man for whom winning had always been an obsession, but had become harder to focus on in recent months.

At the sixth floor, breathing heavily, he jig-stepped through the doors into the gloomy corridor. He halted his progress momentarily while a handcuffed suspect was hustled past him, and then he sidestepped a lawyer whispering advice to a knot of worried family members. He barely noticed either of the familiar tableaus; his imagination was shadow-boxing down a crowded aisle toward a floodlit ring, almost cocky with impatience for the main event to start.

He knew many of the regulars loitering along the wide hall: lawyers, court employees, courtroom buffs. Many were eager to greet him or wish him well this morning, a few to flaunt their acquaintance with him to companions. He chatted with one, tossed a quip at another. A court officer wanted advice for a cousin arrested for drunk driving. A young lawyer asked to borrow a copy of one of his trial transcripts to study. The image he instinctively exhibited in his ritual progress down the corridor—fast-talking, outgoing, kinetic—invigorated him.

Bright lights suddenly came on, and two groups of darkened figures behind them thrust TV cameras and microphones at him. Dan moved past them toward the metal detector guarding courtroom 675. One of the officers slipped him in ahead of the long line of people waiting to enter. Dan's hand pushing through the courtroom door had tightened into a fist.

The Montano case would be the first of the twenty-five or so preliminary hearings to take place here this morning. Defense lawyers, prosecutors, and police officers awaiting their own cases had filled up the front row of the spectator section. Although the jury box was reserved for reporters, most were gathered around Peter and Susan Boelter, whom Dan recognized from newspaper and magazine photos. The celebrity patricians, he thought, have come to watch the gladiators fight it out.

Both Boelters were tall and attractive, and appeared to be in their late thirties. The Golden Couple, one society columnist had dubbed them, and the nickname seemed apt, despite the husband's dark hair. His uncommonly blue eyes were set amid sharp, handsome features. He was animated as he spoke, tilting his head with an ingratiating half smile toward the reporter who was timorously addressing him. However, the rest of his stance, Dan noted, was that of a man used to getting his way; with his hands on his hips inside his open jacket, he looked like a gunfighter ready to draw.

Susan Boelter possessed the silky blond hair and serene good looks customary in old WASP families. Dan could not tell whether she was appraising her husband or happy to stand in his shadow. He had heard she quit working as a reporter at the *Herald* after her marriage, but doubted she could have been serious about her career; he recalled seeing her lauded on society pages for the usual array of benevolent activities—mostly in connection with some kind of family foundation.

As Dan stepped around the group, he caught sight of Mara chatting with Gil Huyton. The two had been hidden from his view until then. She wore the well-tailored black suit with a short skirt she had left in his closet.

When he glanced back again from the front of the room, she was striding toward him with the determined, ambitious walk he knew so well.

"I think I can get Gil to consider a deal on Montano," she said.

Philadelphia's prosecutors were known to be particularly zealous in taking homicide cases to trial—and in seeking the death penalty. The possibility of their agreeing to a mandatory life sentence instead was not to be lightly dismissed.

"Since when are you and Huyton on a first-name basis?"

"You're as bad as he is, Dan. I've known him and his wife for ages. This town ought to be grateful someone like him is willing to roll up his sleeves and try to clean it up."

"And you think I should make it easier for him by pleading a client guilty who swears he didn't do it."

"You don't seriously believe the word of a criminal with Montano's rap sheet. He's already served time for rape."

"*Statutory* rape. He wasn't much older than the girl, and she was crazy about him. The mother was the one who pressed the charges. That's not the same thing as attacking and killing a woman."

"That's *two* women, Dan."

"Nothing links him to that first case."

"He's also got a suspended for pimping."

"Huyton can't get in his priors if I don't let Montano testify."

"I'm not talking about trial strategy," she fumed. "I'm talking about your maybe helping a vicious killer to go free. The women in this city were terrified out of their minds until he was caught. Nobody would criticize you for convincing him to plead guilty and save himself from the death penalty."

"And get life instead. Ice in the winter."

"Dan, you only got involved in this case because the court administrator twisted your arm. He needed a top lawyer for Montano so it would balance out all the notoriety the case was getting. Certainly no one expects you to win it."

Dan refused to reply.

Mara's expression stiffened. "You're not thinking about Montano, only about this personal vendetta you have against Huyton. You're afraid any kind of guilty plea will look like you lost to him."

"I can win it," Dan replied evenly.

"Then God help the next woman Montano meets on a dark street."

She spun back toward the spectators' section.

Dan looked over at Huyton, who was now standing at the head of the center aisle, arranging his papers and quietly conversing with Jensen, his chief deputy and head of the Trial Division.

Gilbert Huyton was a lean man about Dan's height. He had craggy cheekbones and fair hair receding from his forehead in a slow, orderly evacuation. A tight, wide mouth and jaw and a darting gaze disclosed his obsessive energy. He wore a blue, vested suit. Only in the hottest summer, Dan remembered, did he forgo the vest.

Huyton came from a socially prominent family that had produced inconspicuous, prosperous lawyers for generations until it suddenly defied upper-class tradition by entering politics. His late grandfather had returned from the democratizing experience of fighting in the Second World War determined to plunge into public service and reform his city and state's corrupt politics. Switching from Republican to Democrat, he had eventually served three terms in the U.S. Senate; a man of unswerving integrity, his name remained hallowed throughout Pennsylvania. Gil's father had also gone into politics and was still a ranking member of the House and a major power in the city; he had added political savvy to the family wisdom, comprehending that one had to work at politics like a business, making alliances and espousing policies that would win votes. Although Gil had little of his grandfather's majestic presence or his father's practiced affability, he had intently directed his life toward a political career since childhood.

After a short stint as an assistant DA, he had joined an old-line law firm as a corporate litigator, where he made money, built up his political influence, and cultivated potential contributors. Last year, deeming the time right, he had run for DA and was swept into office along with a new, reforming mayor. He had run far ahead of the rest of the ticket, his family name and tough stand against crime and corruption winning wide popular support.

At that moment Peter Boelter approached to say something privately to Huyton. Dan noted the DA's amiable ease with his boyhood friend. How different he was with people outside his social circle: He invariably held himself stiffly, uncomfortably making small talk only because he understood its necessity. He had played football at Princeton, and Dan guessed him to have been the sort of player who made up in ferocious desire what he lacked in natural skill—not overly fast, but willing to risk life and limb to make the tackle or hold on to the ball in a crowd.

Huyton had employed that same fierce certainty of purpose to overcome his natural formality and reserve and to put his principles into practice. What irked Dan was that Huyton's good intentions often slipped over into self-righteous zealotry. Dan was wary of people who believed they possessed an infallible certainty about the truth.

A far door opened. Handcuffed and escorted by two deputy sheriffs who had transported him from Holmesburg Prison in North Philadelphia, Ricardo Montano entered and scanned the crowded courtroom with hooded, sullen eyes.

On the short side and fair-skinned, with a black mustache and wavy dark hair, he had immigrated from Colombia as a young teenager.

After he seated himself beside Dan, the cuffs were removed and the deputies planted themselves right behind his chair.

"All rise," the tipstaff intoned. Appointed to preserve order, guard the jury, and wait upon the judge, he bore a title that harked back to Old England, where his predecessors carried a silver-tipped staff.

Judge Louis Carter entered. He was a round-faced, careful, black man in his forties, a new appointment, beholden to Huyton's party. The spectators may have crowded into the courtroom on account of the Montano case, but Carter had a full schedule of preliminary hearings to work through this morning and immediately began the proceedings. After the list of cases was read, with the lawyers for each announcing either their readiness or their need for a continuance, Carter gestured toward the tipstaff to call the first preliminary hearing, the *Commonwealth* v. *Montano*.

Dan and the two prosecutors, Huyton and Jensen, took seats at adjacent tables facing the judge's bench. Dan's only function would be to cross-examine prosecution witnesses called to tie Montano to the crime and, in so doing, convince the judge that the evidence was insufficient to hold Montano for trial.

Huyton questioned a series of witnesses. First a member of the Mobile Crime Unit who had examined the scene the morning the body was found. Then the manager of the bar on Twelfth, who stated that Cassy Cowell left work there at a couple of minutes after midnight, when her shift ended, having told him that she was going straight home to study for an exam in the morning.

Next was the policeman, who reported seeing Montano at a little past midnight, two blocks away, on Thirteenth and Locust. It was a cold night with few people on the streets. After realizing that he was being observed, the policeman said, Montano had headed into one of the alleys leading to Twelfth. The officer was sure of the time because he and his partner had reported in to their district station a few minutes earlier.

The two prostitutes Montano pimped for were called to testify. The first was a blowsy, overweight blond, who claimed that Montano had left the corner at around midnight, walking north on Thirteenth. The other woman, prettier, thin, and black, was more specific, declaring that she had gotten a terrible migraine headache and was about to go home when a car drove up containing two men who wanted to hire both women. Montano had pulled her aside and slapped her hard several times to force her to take the job. He then stomped off in anger.

Dan's first cross-examination was of Harry Stallworth, a thick-bodied police detective with a neatly cropped mustache and beard, who had arrested Ricardo Montano. Dan tore into him with a series of questions that challenged the basis for the arrest. Stallworth maintained that he was convinced he had sufficient cause to make the arrest, but he was sweating when he stepped down.

"Mr. Huyton," the judge said, "do you have any other witnesses?"

Dan held his breath.

"One more, Your Honor," Huyton said. "I call as the commonwealth's last witness Timothy K. Feeney."

Dan began to breathe again. He lived for moments like this.

Tim Feeney was a stocky man with a pug nose, dark eyebrows and hair, and a mouth that twisted into cocky amusement as he swaggered up the aisle. Under Huyton's questioning, he more or less repeated the story he had given in his front-page interview in the *Herald*. Just after midnight he was driving south on Twelfth Street along his truck route, delivering bundles of newspapers to downtown newsstands. He had just gone through Walnut when he saw a man running out of an alley and onto Twelfth. The man glanced his way for a moment before racing off in the opposite direction and around the corner.

"Is that man present in the courtroom?" Huyton asked dramatically.

"Yes," Feeney replied, with equal drama. He was glorying in his moment in the sun.

"Please point him out."

Feeney raised his arm and pointed to Ricardo Montano, seated beside Dan.

Huyton added, "Let the record show that the witness identified Ricardo Montano as the man he saw running from the murder scene that night."

Amid the murmured comments in the gallery, reporters bent to their notebooks.

Huyton turned again to Feeney. "You're quite sure."

"Yes, I am."

"You have no doubts."

"None."

"Thank you." Huyton glanced at Dan. "Your witness."

Dan stood up and approached the witness box. As Dan had anticipated, although Huyton was a top litigator, he was rusty at doing preliminary hearings. Instead of introducing the barest minimum of evidence needed to establish that enough of a case had been made to try Montano for the rape and murder, the DA was overproving his case with the direct testimony Dan needed to cross-examine.

"Mr. Feeney, do you mind if I ask you why you waited several days before going to the police with your story?"

"I didn't really connect the guy to anything until I seen his picture in the paper."

"You say you had a good view of him when he ran out onto Twelfth and you were at Walnut?"

"Yes."

"There are two alleys that cut through the block. Was it the nearer or the farther one?"

"The farther one, St. James. I went down there a couple days ago just to be sure," Feeney added smugly.

"That would make it—what?—maybe a hundred fifty feet from the corner to that alley?"

"Something like that."

"Saw his face clearly, did you?"

"I sure did."

"Under the streetlight on Twelfth at St. James?"

"Yes."

"Good and clear, was it?"

"Right."

Dan stepped closer. "Would it surprise you to learn that both streetlights on Twelfth Street between Walnut and Locust were out that night and still are?"

Huyton leaped to his feet. "Objection, Your Honor. No foundation has been established that the lights were out, and Mr. Feeney is not an expert in the city's lighting system."

Dan's eyebrows raised. "Your Honor, the witness says he saw the defendant 'good and clear' under the streetlight a hundred and fifty feet away. I have an affidavit here from a supervisor with the Streets Department that says the streetlights were not in working order that night. I'd say identifying my client in the dark wouldn't take an engineer, it would take Superman."

A laugh broke from the gallery. Carter gestured for the lawyers to approach the bench to argue the point more privately.

Huyton began. "Your Honor, the witness apparently had sufficient light to see the defendant."

"At midnight? With no streetlights?" Dan rejoined sarcastically. "Feeney's lying."

"Defense counsel's question already assumes the fact in question— that the streetlights were broken."

Carter appeared relieved to be able to make the ruling on a technicality. "Sustained. Mr. Lazar, please restate your question."

Regardless of the ruling, Dan had already given Feeney a warning that any inaccurate testimony about the lighting would be disputed.

"Was the streetlight out at St. James?" he asked.

"Well—" The teamster's voice lacked its earlier confidence. "—It might have been."

"And the other one on that block?"

"That one, too."

Dan moved close now, blocking Feeney's line of sight to the prosecution's table, where a nod or gesture might lead him out of danger.

"Mr. Feeney, if, as you now indicate, the streetlights may not have been working, how was it possible at midnight for you to see the face of a man well enough to identify him accurately from a hundred fifty feet away?"

The silence in the courtroom grew torturous as Feeney struggled with the problem.

Finally he answered, "I didn't mean that I was sure he was the guy. I mean he kind of looked like the guy I seen that night. Same build."

Dan pounced. "But, in fact, you can't be at all sure he's actually the man you say you saw, isn't that right?"

"I guess that's right."

"In other words, he could be someone completely different."

"Yeah, he could be."

"So you now retract your identification."

"Retract?"

"Take back."

"Yeah. I take it back."

Dan smiled congenially. "Thank you, Mr. Feeney. No further questions."

Enraged and at a loss, Huyton glared first at his lieutenant, whose preparation had failed him, and then at his witness, on whom his case had been built. He had grilled Feeney extensively before trial, and the man had been adamant about his identification. Huyton tried for ten minutes, through redirect questioning, to resuscitate his witness's identification, but the damage had been done. He had to rest his case.

Dan immediately rose and moved that the charges be dismissed because none of the testimony tied the defendant directly to the crime. Gil Huyton was irate.

Carter hushed the angry voices and led them to a far corner of the courtroom, where they could not be overheard.

"Lou," Huyton hotly contended to the judge, "you're going to be putting a dangerous animal back on the streets!"

"There's no evidence that Montano's the killer," Dan countered.

Carter's shoulders lifted apologetically, as if he was about to deny Dan's motion. Dan exploded.

"If you cave in here, Carter, you're going to look like shit. I'll blast you to those TV cameras waiting outside and file a motion to quash. There isn't a snowball's chance in hell that your decision would stand up."

For a moment Carter considered disciplining Dan for the outburst, but then thought better of it. The apologetic look turned on Huyton.

"Sorry, Gil, but I'm having trouble seeing my way clear to charge the guy. None of the evidence connects him to the crime."

Huyton was beside himself. "He's a brutal rapist and murderer! He's a menace. Even his girls want him behind bars. They're terrified. One told us he once raped her and beat her up so badly, she was hospitalized. There's a pattern of conduct here."

Dan shot back, "That testimony's so suspect, you didn't even bring it up when she was on the stand, so don't try to smear him with it here."

"Smear *him!* He's a pimp! He's slime!"

"So far he's only a suspect."

"I'm sorry, Gil," Carter finally ruled, "I've got to agree with defense counsel. None of this is admissible, and it certainly isn't relevant as to whether a *prima facie* case has been made against Montano here. I've got no alternative. I've got to discharge him."

Huyton's eyes on Dan smoldered with the resentment raking him. "That cross-examination of yours smells to high heaven."

"You had a lousy witness to build a case on. Why the hell didn't you do a DNA test on my client?"

"Yes, why didn't you?" Carter asked Huyton, as well.

"We intended to for the trial, but had him dead to rights here," Huyton snarled. "An eyewitness."

"Too late now," Dan remarked to needle Huyton.

He and Dan were nose to nose, neither willing to retreat an inch. "This trick you just pulled sets a killer free and makes me look like an ass in front of the whole city."

"I'd like to take credit for that last part, but you did that all by yourself. All I did was defend my client."

"You're an unprincipled swindler, Lazar. I don't know what happened today, but I'm going to get to the bottom of it."

"Gentlemen, take your seats!" Carter ordered.

Back on the bench, he announced his decision, letting loose tumult in the courtroom.

Susan and Peter Boelter arrived at the elevators as Dan was waiting for one.

"Congratulations," Peter offered. "My wife's been telling me all along that the *Herald* went too far. She said we had no business taking such an aggressive position. Sorry about that." No tone of apology accompanied the words.

"I don't excuse libel that easily," Dan sharply replied. "I understand you're selling a lot of papers at my expense."

Peter offered a self-deprecating smile, refusing to quarrel. "As a matter of fact we are. Not easy to do when you consider the state the newspaper business is in right now."

The polished aluminum doors opened.

"You could lose those impulse buyers just as quickly," Susan pointed out to her husband once they had stepped into the elevators and the doors had closed.

"How to hang on to them? That's the question," Peter mused, and then puckishly asked Dan, "Any more good murders for us on the horizon? Something with a lot of illicit sex? A hot crime of passion?"

Dan laughed despite his animosity. "They don't make murders like they used to."

The elevator doors opened. The three, still laughing, stepped into the lobby.

"I like you, Lazar," Peter said with the congenial smile and ingratiating tilt of the head Dan had noted upon entering the courtroom. "We're having some people over for dinner next week. Next Friday night. If you're free, I'd like you to join us. To bury the hatchet and end any hard feelings."

Surprised, Dan started to decline.

Susan spoke up. "Please come. It will be an opportunity for you two to put any misunderstandings behind you."

Peter said, "Your performance this morning and what I know about you, they intrigue me."

"From Peter, that's a great compliment," Susan commented. "Please join us. It will be wonderful to have someone new."

Dan had intended to ask Mara to go away with him for a long weekend. They had not been away together in a while. "I might have other plans."

"Your wife?" asked Susan.

"A woman friend. I'm not married."

"Please bring her."

"I don't know if we'll be able to make it."

Susan promised to phone Dan's office at the end of next week and, if he could come, give him directions to their house.

"We live in Dellwyne," she added.

I never doubted it for a moment, Dan remarked to himself. Or if not Dellwyne, then Gladwyne or Ardmore or Haverford or Villanova or

Merion or one of the other in the string of Main Line enclaves of large mansions and estates. He decided to tell Susan Boelter when she phoned that he would be unable to make it.

Just what I need in my life, he thought as he watched the Golden Couple depart: the gentility of rich gentiles.

After work Dan went out for a celebratory drink with Cal Patterson, his law partner. He arrived back at his apartment in a jubilant mood. Mara was waiting for him.

Dan tossed his coat on the hall chair and bent to kiss her hello.

She pulled away, her blue eyes as cold and hard as glacial ice. "I spent the afternoon meeting with Gil Huyton. He's offered me a job with the DA's office. I'm taking it."

"You're serious."

Like many of the city's best trial lawyers, Mara had started out in the DA's office. She had left the Homicide Unit two years ago to join Lazar and Patterson.

"Dan, I was repulsed by what I saw in court today. You scared Feeney into denying an ID he was absolutely certain of."

"Hey, nobody twisted his arm."

"You were clever. You reminded him about the broken streetlights, but conveniently left out that there was a lot of light coming from the buildings."

She took a deep breath. "I've had it, Dan. Last month you bamboozled a jury into acquitting the state's biggest Mafia boss of murder and extortion when he should have been sent away for life. Your Boy Scout's good deed today kept a despicable piece of human garbage on the streets, where he can kill more women."

"He's thinking of going back to Colombia," Dan said quietly, his pleasure at the victory rapidly draining away.

"Where he'll rape and kill and exploit Colombian women, instead of Americans. A real triumph!"

"We've already been over this a couple of times today." Dan's voice sounded weary, as if his private doubts these last months had taken on physical weight. "The adversarial system isn't foolproof—we both know that—but it's the best way anybody's found to get at the truth."

"The truth? Is that what we get at? If more than one in a hundred of these slimeballs we defend was innocent, I'd be shocked. How many rob or kill or rape again?"

She already sounded like Huyton, he groused to himself. Why the hell should he have to defend the basic right of everyone to a vigorous detense? The Constitution required it, and he believed in it; it was his creed, his justification.

Dan's tone sharpened. "I'm not responsible for their whole lives, just for trying to see that they get justice in court."

Mara pounced on his statement. "You don't care about justice, only winning. The law isn't just a job to you, it's a sporting event, like one of your poker games. You're a high-priced hired gun. You'll fight as hard for a serial killer as for a corporate looter."

"So will you. That's our job."

"And I hate myself for doing it. What I really want to do is lock up all those lowlifes so the rest of us are safe from them."

Dan stared at Mara, examining her remarks. At their core he discerned fabrication.

"All that's bullshit! I know you too well. Huyton must have offered you a hell of a job."

Caught off guard by the insight, she nodded, unable to summon an appropriate evasion; he would learn the truth very soon anyway. "Deputy in charge of the Trial Division."

"He fired Jensen?"

She nodded again. "Huyton was furious at him. First the Mafia case. Now the broken streetlights. Besides, I told him Jensen's job was what it would take for me to leave your firm and go there."

"A woman of principle!"

"It isn't just the law practice," she said quietly. "I'm ending it personally between us, too."

"Just like that? What about these last few months? What about last night?"

"Dan, let's just say good-bye nicely . . . end it as friends."

"Hey," he angrily shot back, "this isn't about a job you want, about getting ahead, it's about us. For the first time since my divorce, I really cared for someone. I was pretty sure you felt the same way."

"We had some good times. And I have real feelings for you, Dan, I do." Her tone was firm, businesslike. "But it just didn't work out."

"That's it? That's all? 'It just didn't work out?' "

"I've already thought it through."

She handed him his key and moved to the door. He noticed her small suitcase against the wall; she had already packed the few things she kept at his place.

"Good-bye, Dan."

Her purposeful walk carried her out of his apartment and his life. She did not glance back or display even a pretense of regret. He was already part of her past, a curio absently tossed into the back of her memory's storage closet. For her, he realized, love could not abide where ambition no longer resided; the one evoked the other; who and what she lusted for must combine.

But recognizing her self-centeredness did not lessen the distress. Like an amputee's phantom limb, her presence remained—provocative, calculating, confrontational, and always seductive. The grief that had crept into the corners of the room as she spoke now rushed in to fill the huge space her small figure had inhabited.

Dan decided that ending the relationship as she had—quickly, with no time for tears or backsliding—had been the best way. Better now than later, when he might have grown to need her—rather than simply to desire her—or, worse, to trust her. Loving Mara, allowing her—or any woman—to wriggle her way inside him had been a mistake he'd known he was making but could not help. His wariness had been futile, and did not diminish either the hurt or the sorrow. They lingered everywhere, like her perfume.

A few hours later, in the men's room of a bar near where Cassy Cowell and Jane Hopkins were raped and murdered, Tim Feeney was arrested as he tried to buy drugs from an undercover cop.

2

In the days and nights that followed, Dan often felt as if he were marooned on a sandbar lapped by endless loneliness; he could not remember his loneliness depressing him so deeply before Mara entered and then left his life. Even a week and a half later, he was unable to keep his mind on his cards at the regular Thursday-night poker game and came out the big loser.

He slept fitfully that night and, suddenly wide awake before dawn, could not go back to sleep. When he finally gave up trying and got out of bed to go to the health club for an early workout, he discovered that the sore knee had stiffened. Contemptuous of men who consulted doctors for every little ache that nature would eventually cure, he took a hot shower. The knee seemed to loosen up a bit, not enough for him to exercise, but enough for comfort. He went into the living room to read.

Dan was a history buff. His father and a junior high school teacher had nurtured his natural inquisitiveness, and he had majored in history in college. An entire living room wall was lined with history books. The previous year had been the two hundredth since the Bill of Rights had been passed, and this year the five hundredth since the pivotal year of 1492. He had been devoting his free time to studying both, sensing implications that somehow linked those events to each other, to the world's and his own personal histories, and, most pertinently, to the small spiritual dissatisfactions that, like globules of mercury, had been coalescing into a mass within him for months.

23

Settling into an armchair, he picked up the biography of Columbus he had been reading. Dan had come to believe that even stronger than Columbus's quest for wealth had been his religious fanaticism, his hope of gaining "everlasting" glory by conquering new lands for Christianity and converting the natives, at whatever the cost to *them*. A cruel, repressive religious fervor characterized that entire era. On the same early August night that Columbus began his initial voyage into the uncharted western seas, Spain's harbors were packed with ships carrying off the last of that country's Jews, some of whose families had lived in that land for fifteen hundred years. The Catholic monarchs had brutally ordered that any Jew refusing to convert to Christianity who did not leave by that date would be put to death.

The vast majority of "Sephardic" or Spanish Jews chose exile, despite having much of their currency, gold, and jewels confiscated by the Crown. Houses and other property they could not carry were often sold off for a pittance. Hoping to return, many simply locked their homes and kept the keys, which would eventually be handed down for generations. Many of the exiles would die before finding tenuous sanctuary.

Only the Turkish ruler openly welcomed the Jewish refugees, declaring that the Spanish kings were "committing an act of folly" by banishing such an accomplished and industrious people, "as their loss will be our gain." Aboard the sultan's ships were Dan's ancestors, who settled on the coast of northern Greece, then a Turkish possession.

Jews enjoyed peaceful tolerance there for more than four hundred years, until the twentieth century, when Turkey was forced to cede the territory to a now independent Greece and the Jews again faced nationalistic and anti-Semitic repression. During the Second World War, the Nazi occupiers delivered the death blow to what was left of Greece's Jewish community.

God save us from the zealots, Dan thought. He and his people had been fighting to survive them since Biblical time began.

Caught up in the book and having no early appointments, Dan arrived later than usual at his office in the old Fidelity Bank Building on Broad Street. He intended to spend the morning preparing motions for an upcoming robbery trial. The defendant's family would be able to pay him only a minimal fee. That was true of many cases Dan took on.

As he pushed open the outer door that read, "Lazar and Patterson, Law Offices," Dan noticed that Mary Alice, the small firm's secretary, was staring angrily across the reception area and that his law partner, Calvin Patterson, a tall black man, was standing in the center of the room, angrily reading a document. Opening the door all the way, he saw a third person, a small man with a characteristic slouch and oversized ears that jutted straight out from his dark hair like open car doors. He was a police detective permanently assigned to the district attorney's office, named Eddie Grecco, whom Dan had known for a long time.

"I hate to do this, Dan," Grecco apologized. He had a hoarse city accent.

"Do what?" Dan asked his law partner.

Cal's face was grim. "This is a warrant for your arrest."

"What for?"

"Bribing a witness. Timothy K. Feeney."

"Son of a bitch!" Dan erupted in shock. "Huyton can't be serious."

"You can't get more serious than this."

Grecco glumly added, "The DA's really on the warpath. I'm supposed to bring you down to our place for slating."

"The DA's office?" Dan was incredulous. The district attorney traditionally ordered only major criminals brought there for the paperwork, when he wanted to splash the arrest across TV screens and newspaper front pages.

Grecco nodded. "He called the press and told them to expect it."

"Shit!"

Grecco bit his lip. "He's a great one for the press."

"How the hell did he come up with these insane charges, Eddie?"

"Feeney was busted last week on a street buy."

"Coke?"

"Yeah, but a lot of it. A thousand bucks' worth. The cops who made the collar, they figure he's a street dealer trying to deal for some supply. So, he gets scared he'll do a big hit in the joint and tells them that if they drop the charges, he'll give them something heavy the DA can lay on you."

"And they believed him?"

"They called in an assistant DA, who called in his boss, who told Huyton."

Cal handed Dan the complaint. "You're supposed to have paid Feeney five thousand dollars in cash to withdraw his identification of Montano."

Dan read the document and then looked up. "This is horseshit. The guy's lying to save his ass."

Grecco dipped his head regretfully as he produced a pair of handcuffs from his back pocket. "Dan, I hate to ask, but would you mind . . . ?"

Dan glared at him.

"Okay, fuck Huyton!" Grecco growled. "But when we get down to the office, I'll have to."

The phone rang. Mary Alice answered it.

"For you," she said to Dan. "She says her name's Susan Boelter."

Recalling her dinner party that night, he remarked with some exasperation, "Just tell her I can't make it."

Mary Alice was about to convey the message when Dan suddenly changed his mind. "No, wait."

He took the receiver from her.

"Mrs. Boelter, Dan Lazar here." He paused, listening, then said, "I'm looking forward to it. I'll be coming alone." His glance took in Grecco. "I have an appointment that might keep me tied up for a while, but I'll do my best to get free by then."

He wrote down the address and the driving directions.

"By the way," he asked, "could you give me your husband's office number?"

Dan dialed the *Herald*. Peter Boelter took his call. Dan asked if someone could look into the newspaper's personnel file on Tim Feeney. Peter replied that his brother, Midge, who was in charge of the *Herald*'s finances and administration, would be at the house tonight and would bring the information with him.

A police paddy wagon conveyed Dan to the district attorney's office at 1421 Arch Street across from the Municipal Services Building and, beyond that, City Hall. Mobs of press people and cameras were waiting on the sidewalk to photograph the humiliation of his handcuffed entrance. After about two hours of processing and paperwork, he was taken—again by paddy wagon—to police headquarters, known as the Roundhouse, to await his preliminary arraignment.

Sinuously curved in the rear, the Roundhouse was a low, modern, concrete building that curled around in front to form two circular wings on Race Street. Like many things in Philadelphia, the now provocative-sounding names had rather prosaic origins. Horses once raced along Race Street, and police sergeants in the early 1800s were known as roundsmen.

Eyes down, Dan concentrated on retaining as much dignity in his walk as he could muster despite his wrists' being cuffed behind him.

Cal had been in the building all the while, quietly moving from one official to the next as he tried to arrange his partner's release, no easy matter in this city's overwrought justice system. Several more hours went by until he had done so. Although his custom tailoring belied it, Cal had once been a cop and had seen the best and worst of places like these. Finally, locating a police lieutenant with whom he had gone through the academy, he received special permission to descend to the holding cells to accompany Dan back up to the courtroom for the preliminary arraignment.

Swinging back the large steel door and locking it behind them, the guard led Cal past the holding tank toward the smaller cells in the rear. Dan stood in a corner of one, staring at his feet. A fat red-haired man was seated on the toilet, his pants down, loud sounds resounding from the bowl. An emaciated man lay on one of the two steel cots. Eyes closed, arms around his thinly clothed body, he was rocking from side to side and moaning softly.

"Sorry it took a little longer than I figured," Cal called out. He shook his head. "I can't believe they'd put you into one of these!"

Dan glanced up. "I guess the Ritz was booked."

"Miller's the bail commissioner on duty. He agreed to run you through fast and quietly and release you on a fifty-thousand-dollar SOB."

Dan nodded. Before getting named to the post, Lloyd Miller had been a hustling, small-time lawyer to whom they had often referred clients they did not wish to represent. They were owed a favor. This one was to release Dan on a "sign own bond"—his promise, secured only by his own signature, to pay fifty thousand dollars if he failed to appear in court.

The guard relented enough to snap the cuffs in front, not behind, before letting him walk out of the cell. Dan stared at the steel banding his wrists as he waited for the outer door to be opened.

"You okay?" Cal asked, watching him with concern.

Dan's eyes lifted to his partner's. "Cal, every TV crew and reporter in the city was waiting in front of the DA's office. I kept saying, 'I'm innocent. This is a frame-up.' And I sounded about as credible as some cheap gangster on a cop show. Then they hauled me up to the tenth floor and slated me. They didn't miss a trick—fingerprints, mug shots, the works. Just like a criminal, Cal. Just like a fucking criminal!" His voice shook with disgust.

"Hey, don't worry. We'll get to the bottom of this and have it all cleared up in no time."

Dan shook his head glumly. "The district attorney is the protector of law and order, Cal. If he says I'm guilty, that's all people need to know. They'll look at me like I was filth. A thousand acquittals won't wash it away."

At the cloverleaf, Dan exited the Schuylkill Expressway onto U.S. 1, known by everyone for the first five miles as City Line Avenue. He halted his motorcycle at the stoplight and noted the political sleight of hand that had caused the middle word of the street signs to be painted over so that they now read "City Avenue." However, the paint had not erased the very visible division between the shabby, working-class city neighborhoods on the southerly side of the artery and, on the northerly, the affluent suburbs long ago dubbed the Main Line after the old Pennsylvania Railroad route that carried their affluent residents into and out of the city.

"More political bullshit!" Dan fumed. Just paint over the uncomfortable words and ignore the problems.

Vehicular traffic was heavy on this warm Friday evening and progress slow, which added to his irritation. He rarely came out this way. Perhaps to prove to himself that he was not sucking up to the rich and socially enviable Boelters, he had ridden out on his Harley. Exhaust fumes from the cars ahead enveloped him like fog.

After passing the clutch of chic department stores and shops, he cut north on the road Susan Boelter had indicated. Soon he was in woodlands dotted with large houses. Despite his aversion to rural landscapes, he found himself relishing the faster speed and the sweetness of the air; his mood began to lift.

Dan usually felt out of place in the country; the more trees and greenery there were, the more alien and anxious he became. In the city he lived within walking distance of his office, the courts, his health club, restaurants he frequented, and the one he had helped his father buy. He owned a red '66 Mustang convertible that he had restored, which he used mainly for driving to and from his beach house on the Jersey Shore. This motorcycle was his escape, his magic carpet. Sometimes, though, late at night, as he roared along a highway or a deserted road, he found himself turning up the throttle full out, pushing the speed higher and higher, to the point where he finally summoned up terror.

Realizing now, as he flashed past houses and trees and driveways, that during the months he had been with Mara he had not felt the need to outrace death, he twisted down the throttle and applied the brakes. But the brief lightening of his mood had ended.

For all his conviviality in public, Dan was a loner at heart, a man who knew from childhood that he was an outsider. His father had survived the slaughter of Jewish Greeks during the Second World War by joining the partisans fighting in the Macedonian mountains. Afterward he had emigrated to America, knowing no one. He chose Philadelphia only because a family he met on the ship was going there. He fell madly in love with this country, found a job as a waiter, and married the family's eldest daughter. A few years after giving birth to Dan, she died.

Being raised without a mother had toughened Dan early. It had also inscribed on his heart the certainty that any woman he might let down his guard to love would eventually leave him.

Mara Szarek had not been the first to hurt him.

His ex-wife, Hannah, had betrayed the spirit of their divorce agreement right after he signed it by fleeing with their young son to California, where her family lived. He missed the boy intensely and knew that no matter the number of phone calls they shared and the vacations they spent together, the distance was causing him to fail his son in ways that his own father, despite being a widower and having little money, had never failed *him*.

Slowing the motorcycle as he entered the village of Dellwyne, he halted at the stoplight. Handsome retail shops lined both sides of the avenue for several blocks. This could be another planet, he thought; no blacks, no poor, not even anyone poorly dressed. The scent of protected privilege offended him like a stench. Added to his recent misfortunes, it was one outrage too many. He angrily gunned the engine in neutral, shattering the quiet. Heads turned in wild alarm at the sight of the anonymous marauder in the black helmet and conservative overcoat.

Once past the township's local police outpost and the small, dignified supermarket at the end of the village, he shot forward along the tree-lined road and bore right at the fork onto Albemarle, leaning into the turn. Dipping from side to side like a tango dancer, he rocketed up the twisting road past houses set back behind trees and hedges, hoping the wind would rip away the depression that weighed him down like shackles. Gentility, here I come, he said to himself with little enthusiasm.

Catching sight of tall square posts, the entrance in the high brick wall he had been told to look for, Dan slowed. "Boelter" was carved into granite rectangles inset at the top of both pillars. He turned into a long driveway. It meandered through woods to a huge Georgian-style mansion set within a park of shade trees and flower beds. Well to the redbrick building's rear, beyond hedges that seemed to enclose a vast garden, he could see a groom leading a horse from a white-fenced paddock to a stable and a greenhouse brightly lit within to force growth out of its greenery.

Just folks, he decided.

Dan had witnessed in his own lifetime a decline in the ranks of the aristocratic families that once inhabited estates like these. Only in recent decades had this stodgy, inbred, restricted group been forced to make room for rising newcomers in their clubs and on the boards of their cultural institutions, a phenomenon they had resisted over the first half of the century. Their children were now joined by outsiders taken on merit at their once exclusive secondary schools. No longer automatically accepted at Dad's and Granddad's Ivy League colleges, the newer Old Philadelphians were being forced to journey all around the country to gain their higher education, which often led to their marrying unpedigreed classmates and settling down away from Philadelphia.

However, a large body of affluent upper-class families still remained atop the city's social hierarchy, even some who could afford to live on vast estates like this one, the Boelters among the foremost of them. John Boelter, the family's late patriarch, who had shouldered his way into their caste, had seen to that.

Dan recalled what he knew about John Boelter. The son of a shop-keeper, Boelter had had a barrel chest, thick eyebrows, and a belligerent jaw. A dominating man, he had begun at the *Herald* as a reporter and quickly climbed to managing editor. Less than a year after the owner died, John married the man's widow, a woman considerably older than he. She herself died two years later, leaving him all her property, includ-ing the newspaper. Rumors circulated at the time about the unlikelihood of such a healthy woman's dying so suddenly and about possible irreg-ularities regarding her will. The woman's cousins sued, but nothing came of it, and John Boelter turned his energy to making the *Herald* the most powerful newspaper in the city and state.

John Boelter became a towering figure in the newspaper industry and in the city that he loved, engendering awe in some and fear in others, but never less than utmost respect. During the turmoil of the sixties and seventies, acknowledging the need for social justice and reconciling him-self to the emergence of ethnic consciousness, he had used the pages of his newspaper to move the city toward change and, as a result, reduced much of the simmering potential for racial conflict. And yet Dan could imagine him, like his son, capitalizing on a lurid murder case to increase circulation. John Boelter was, first and foremost, a hard-driving busi-nessman.

By the time of his death three years ago, the *Philadelphia Herald* was the city's predominant newspaper, dwarfing the city's other paper, the tabloid *Daily Mirror,* and his heirs were left very rich and socially prom-inent. Following in the centuries-old tradition of Philadelphia achievers, his second marriage had been into an Old Philadelphia family that had fallen on hard economic times. His aristocratic second wife, Margaret, had borne him three sons, two of whom were still living—Peter and Midge. The eldest, Richard, had been killed in a car accident years before, leaving an infant son and a young wife, who was herself a wealthy descendant of one of the region's nineteenth-century iron barons.

Handsome, upright-looking people with gleaming teeth and a princi-pled tradition, Dan thought. Despite his personal pique at the *Herald*'s coverage of the Montano case, all that he had heard about the Boelters indicated to him that they embodied what was best about the Old Phila-delphians: refinement, modesty, cheerful good manners, and suprisingly liberal values. No scandal had ever been attached to any member of the present generation. Even the questions about how John Boelter acquired the *Herald* had long been laid to rest as jealousy-inspired rumor. To Dan the Boelters stood for the sort of old-fashioned moral resoluteness the city so desperately needed.

His hard-knock upbringing made that a grudging admission on his part. He had seen evidence of some not-so-admirable qualities in some of the more tedious of the city's Brahmins: conformity that substituted for morality, materialism, antagonism toward new ideas and change, secret anti-Semitism and racism, and condescension toward all those who had failed to be born into their unearned privilege. Dan wondered whether the infusion of John Boelter's vigor into the family's bloodlines had overcome or been submerged by Old Philadelphian stagnation and decay. Most particularly, he wondered what Peter Boelter was like. Some people maintained that he was the genuine article, a polished replica of his brilliant, overbearing father who would extend the family's glory, increase its finances, and strengthen the newspaper that was the heartbeat of the city. Others had their doubts. Only around the stubbornly determined eyes could Dan discern a kinship between father and son.

Dan drew up beside a black BMW 735i sedan, a long black Lincoln, and a dark-gray Lexus parked in a widened area in the driveway. The evening's other guests, he assumed. He walked stiffly to the white portico at the building's center—the ride had left his knee aching. As he lifted the brass knocker on the door, he heard a chime within the house.

Susan Boelter answered the door herself, a maid hovering in the background. Her eyes widened at the sight of the bulbous blue motorcycle in her driveway, but did not lessen their welcome when they shifted back to him.

"How good of you to join us," she said congenially as the maid took Dan's gloves and overcoat. "Peter and Midge have only just arrived."

Dan relaxed. At least the people here had not yet heard about the charges. That would make it easier to get through what he expected to be a trying evening.

3

The front hall retained the grandeur of an earlier age. Tall white columns supported a high rotunda. Pedestals elevated white marble busts in niches along the circular wall. Dan was about to utter polite praise when he noticed that Susan was still gazing out the open doorway.

A boxy yellow school bus had made its way up the driveway and had stopped to let off a tall, blond girl of perhaps thirteen or fourteen with wet hair and a black shoulder bag heavy with books. Beneath her open coat he could make out a figure that had already begun reshaping itself into a woman's. She waved good-bye to friends on the bus and bounced up the steps and into the house. Susan introduced her daughter, Karen, to Dan.

Dan judged that when the girl's hair was dry, mother and daughter shared the same shade of blond. Her face, too, soft and round-cheeked, appeared to be a younger version of her mother's.

"Sorry," the girl said. "Swim meet ran late."

"How did you do?"

"Okay." She suppressed her pride.

"You won?" Susan's guess was answered by a head bob. "That's wonderful! I'm really sorry I couldn't make it there today to see you."

"That's okay—it's Dad's birthday. Is he home yet?"

Susan nodded. "You'd better hurry upstairs and change."

"Did the store have the present I ordered?"

Susan smiled. "Yes. I left you the gift paper to wrap it."

Karen emitted a relieved sigh. "Thanks. All day I was worried it wouldn't come in like they said it would."

"It didn't, but I found a store that had it, so no harm done."

Karen effusively kissed her mother. "That's so great. Thanks, Mom. I really appreciate it."

She charged toward the stairs.

"Karen!" Susan called out.

Only when the girl reached the landing halfway up to the second floor did she turn around. "What is it?"

Susan laughed. "I was going to tell you not to run."

"Oh, sorry."

Karen continued up the stairs with exaggerated slowness. Her mock restraint lasted exactly three steps, until her enthusiasm got the better of her good intentions, and she bounded upward again.

"She's a very lively girl," Dan offered. "Very pretty, too."

Susan murmured her thanks.

"Do you have any other children?" he asked.

Her smile faded to an impassive expression. "No. She's our only one."

Susan led Dan into the left wing along a hall that rose two stories to a carved ceiling. Oil paintings lined the walls. The indistinct sound of voices grew louder. Susan explained that there was a small party for Peter's birthday.

Dan halted. "Look, I wouldn't have intruded if I'd known. I didn't bring a gift—" And I feel awkward and out of place, he finished silently.

"He wouldn't want you to bring a gift," Susan said, slipping her arm amiably through Dan's to prompt him forward. "Peter would be bored silly with just the family here. He was delighted that you agreed to come."

"I still don't understand why he invited me."

She laughed. "Oh, I think he's genuinely remorseful about how the *Herald* treated you during that rape-murder case."

Dan's expression hardened. "And no doubt concerned about what my legal recourse might be."

"Perhaps," she readily replied. She reflected for a moment, then glanced back at Dan with some amusement. "It might even be that he honestly admires you. Peter works very hard to win over people he admires."

"Or needs?"

"Especially his adversaries," she agreed.

Dan had observed that women in Susan Boelter's class invariably strewed verbal pleasantries along their conversational paths with reflexive cordiality, while carefully letting fall little of consequence. Susan Boelter surprised him.

"I gather he's used to getting his way," Dan said.

"Oh, yes," Susan replied, and the smile broke into a light laugh again. Dan noted the affection in her voice when she spoke about her husband, even when describing what others might consider faults. "He can be like a stubborn little boy sometimes, relentless."

"I imagine he gets that from his father."

"Probably."

"I understand your father-in-law could be a very difficult man."

"Demanding, perhaps. But he was more like a father than a father-in-law to me."

Walking slowly, she explained, "We met when he spoke at Bryn Mawr during my senior year there. I was editor of the paper and was considering an offer to work for the *New York Times*. We didn't know each other—my family's from Massachusetts—but he recognized my family name and, after the speech, took me to dinner. It was around the time of Watergate, and I was really a romantic about journalism. My comments must have made me insufferable. You know: 'A free press is the conscience of the nation, the bulwark of its rights . . .' But he offered me a job at the *Herald*. I was overwhelmed by him. He wouldn't let up until I said yes."

Then, Dan thought with an inner chuckle, you married his son and never had to work again for the rest of your life. Perhaps that was what God had intended for women like Susan Boelter: to do the world's horse-back riding and massage- and manicure-taking and its gracious living. She and her kind all seemed bred for graciousness, as their horses were bred for speed.

In Susan's case, she was endowed with a strong and forthright beauty, as well: thin, straight nose, delicately shaped at the tip; well-formed mouth; high cheekbones; and intelligent hazel eyes flecked with orange highlights. Her face radiated composure and self-assurance, as befitted a woman who had everything.

At the end of the long hall the double doors were open onto a large drawing room that filled that end of the wing. To Dan's untutored eye the chairs and polished wood tables appeared to be in some sort of eighteenth-century style. Here, hanging from walls covered in pale yellow silk, were more paintings in ornately carved gold frames.

Peter's greeting obliterated Dan's hope that the arrest might pass unnoticed.

"The infamous Daniel Lazar, attorney-out-law!" His smile softened the discourtesy into mild teasing, dissipating much of the hostility that had instantly overcome his guest.

"I've had better days," Dan conceded.

Midge was introduced to Dan first. He seemed lesser than his elder brother in every way—a couple of inches shorter, facial features smaller and less distinct, his hair darker and sparser, his manner less outgoing. His real name was Michael, but the nickname Midge had attached to him in infancy. Dan's initial impression was that he had spent a lifetime trying not to grow out of it.

Explaining that Dan had recently cleared the infamous Ricardo Montano of murder charges, Peter introduced him to the two women seated together on a pale-green silk sofa. The elder was the matriarch of the Boelter family, Peter's mother, Margaret.

Peter tweaked her. "My mother refuses to celebrate her own birthdays. If only to remind her of her age, I have to invite her to celebrate mine."

Indeed, the woman looked younger than Dan would have expected, although she had to be in her mid-sixties. She had smooth skin and a clean chin line that Dan judged had probably been surgically achieved. Her pearls, too, differed from what he would have expected: larger than the inconspicuous little strands those with her breeding usually wore. Even the dress was surprising: the neckline a bit too low and the style too young-looking for her.

"Peter!" she replied with an indulgent laugh, as if her son's comment had been a compliment. But her next words were delivered as an admonition. "I don't think your guest is interested in private family jokes."

Dan did not doubt that although she obviously doted on her eldest son, her favor could be withdrawn at any moment.

"This is my sister-in-law, Amelia," Peter said next.

The widow of the eldest Boelter son was a couple of years older than Susan and also a blond. Shorter and with a fuller figure, she had less classic facial features: a turned-up nose, small but lively blue eyes, and a wide mouth. She was smiling at Dan.

"If I'm ever accused of some terrible crime, I shall immediately call Mr. Lazar to defend me."

"A man who goes all out for his client, is that it?" Peter asked.

She smiled again at Dan. "Everyone was so sure Montano would be put on trial and convicted."

Peter was quick to tease Amelia. "Am I wrong or do I detect some personal interest in our guest?"

She laughed, not at all abashed. Like her mother-in-law, she seemed pleased by his attention.

Supporting Peter's drink on a tray, the butler waited unmoving behind his employer like a setter. Peter was in no hurry to take the drink. Instead, still standing, he reached into the side pocket of his jacket and produced a packet of paper that he slyly unfolded with the flourish of a magician creating a paper Christmas tree. It was a dummy of the next morning's *Herald* front page, the center occupied by a photo of Dan, handcuffed, as he was led up the steps into the Arch Street building. The headline read, "MONTANO'S LAWYER CHARGED WITH BRIBING WITNESS."

"Our honored guest!" Peter announced.

"Mr. Lazar is a criminal then!" Margaret declared, her nostrils lifting as if she expected him to smell like something that a dog had left on the carpet.

"Not necessarily," Peter replied, lowering himself into a chair and finally taking his drink.

Barely controlling his resentment, Dan declared, "I would hope that answer means you don't believe the bribery charge."

"Actually, I don't, but what I believe isn't important. Journalists report the facts. We give the news as straight and objectively as we can. That's our job in the democratic process."

"Sometimes it isn't that straightforward. The stories you pick and the way you report them often support your own preconceptions and economic interests. In the Montano case, you wanted to reassure a worried populace that they could go shopping or out to dinner again because a dangerous sex killer had been caught. A Latino pimp was a perfect culprit. The problem was, the evidence wasn't there."

Peter was indignant. "You sound as if we take sides. We don't."

Holding the publisher's eyes with a hard stare, Dan warned, "That would be a very safe policy to stick to."

Susan was quick to dissipate the tension. "I've been waiting days to ask about that clever maneuver of yours at that hearing. How did you know the streetlights were out?"

"I just did my homework," Dan admitted. "That's ninety percent of being a good lawyer. I went over to the crime scene at about the same time of night as the crime occurred. When I saw the streetlamps were out, I checked with the Streets Department and learned there'd been an electrical problem over there since before the murder. Because the body was discovered in the morning, the Crime Unit at the scene had never noticed the lighting problem. The DA or his people went over there, too, I suppose, but during the daytime, their working hours."

Amelia's eyes were bright, her tone a touch flirtatious. "If the criminal had returned to the scene of the crime that night—like people say they always do—you would have seen him."

Dan laughed. "Not without the streetlights, I wouldn't."

"The whole thing's rather sordid," Margaret commented in a tone that banished Dan, his clients, and his profession to eternal damnation.

Peter, however, lifted his glass in salute. "To the cleverness of our new friend here, and to the diversion he provides."

Dan lifted his own glass, willing to meet the publisher in burying their squabble. "And to justice."

This graciousness stuff isn't half as tough as it looks, he decided.

The group was already seated around the dining room table when the youngest Boelter female charged in, still fastening the last button at the back of her light-blue dress. Her free hand held a small gift-wrapped box.

"Karen," Susan reminded her, "after dinner."

Karen eyed her mother, but as her father had already taken the gift from her and had begun opening it, she stayed put, her hope of his approval written plaintively on her face. He lifted the box after unwrapping it to display the contents, a handheld video golf game that he immediately began to play.

"Peter loves electronic gadgetry," Susan explained to Dan. "His study looks like an airport control tower."

Karen dutifully moved to her chair beside her mother at the far end of the long mahogany table, her gaze still on her father.

A moment later, putting the image of the golf ball into the image of the cup, Peter cried out, "Aha! Good gift, Karen."

Karen glowed under the compliment. In a voice loud enough for her father to hear, she explained to Dan, "Daddy's a terrific golfer."

After the butler and a maid had served the appetizers and left the room, Peter unexpectedly asked his guest, "You don't represent any of the newspaper unions, do you? Although, God knows, some of them need a criminal lawyer."

"No," Dan assured him.

Peter then felt free to relate to his family the difficulties being experienced in negotiating a new contract with the newspaper unions. Everyone knew that these were hard times for the newspaper industry. The nationwide recession had caused a drastic, long-term drop in advertising revenue. His lighthearted manner replaced by a burdened expression, Peter explained that the unions were refusing to reduce the *Herald*'s high labor costs by not agreeing to lower their wage demands and reduced staffing and by loosening rigid work rules.

Peter turned to Dan. "You can't believe the featherbedding we're struggling with. We have twice as many pressmen as we need, but union contracts won't permit me to cut a single one. Teamsters, either. Even reporters. Costs are strangling us. We need the savings. But are the unions willing to listen?'' He grimaced. ''Like talking to a firing squad. Do you know Vinnie Briggs?''

Dan nodded. Briggs was both head of the pressmen's union and the most hostile on the council of traditionally hostile newspaper trade-union leaders. He was a thug, whose rivals in the pressmen's local had often ended up in the hospital. They had consulted Dan, but could never provide enough evidence for him to take Briggs to court. Recently, though, they had banded together to present an opposing slate at the next election. Dan guessed that would make Briggs tougher to deal with. The union leader could not afford to be flexible on a new contract because the dissidents would claim he sold them out.

''You know what Briggs said to me this afternoon?'' Peter continued, incensed by the thought. ''He said, 'If there's a strike, Boelter, we'll break you. You don't stand a chance. I eat prep-school faggots like you for a snack!' ''

Peter angrily tossed back the last of the wine in his glass and poured himself another from the bottle in the cooler.

''Do you see what I'm up against, Dan?'' Peter said. ''This country's drowning in debt. Europe and the Japanese are pinning our ears back. And we aren't even free to manage our own businesses.''

As he spoke about the problems facing the company, Peter seemed to include Dan within the circle of his family, as if confiding in him, seeking his advice. He appeared to hold little back. Dan suspected that Peter Boelter was blessed with the prodigal son's naive certainty—or delusion—that he was loved by all and that his confidences would not be betrayed. Although to some degree his openness was doubtless a pose to gain allegiance from others, it also seemed to Dan a natural component of the man's charm.

Amelia started to bring the family up to date on how her son was doing at boarding school, but then halted to focus on Dan. ''Do you have any children, Mr. Lazar?''

''Please call me Dan,'' he answered. ''Yes, a son. He's twelve and lives with his mother in California.''

''That's never easy. You must miss him.''

''I do,'' he answered tightly.

Dan's discomfort among these exotic strangers had been increasing, as had his regret about coming, so he was relieved that the conversation swiftly moved on to other matters: an Art Museum exhibit Margaret was helping to sponsor, Amelia's observations on the latest ballet season, Midge's recent election to the board of the Academy of Music.

Peter suddenly interrupted the talk. "You've said very little tonight, Dan. I had expected more spirited participation from you."

"Actually," Dan replied, "I was wondering what keeps a family like this together when so many of the Old Philadelphia families have crumbled or drifted apart."

Margaret was reluctant to answer, but at Peter's urging, she claimed it was the family's position in the community. "One has to stand as an example to others."

Amelia named the pull of family loyalty on them all, while Midge and Karen named Peter as the glue.

"We look up to him," Midge said.

Susan had a different reason. "The *Herald* is where everything began for this family, and it's the heart of this city. We're bound to it by the obligation that places on us."

Peter's answer was the most cynical. "Dividends. The Boelters are tied together by our cash cow. When we can no longer rely on the *Herald* for milk, poof! The bubble will burst and the illusion of cohesion will end. And right now, old Betsy is staggering."

Peter opened the rest of his presents in the living room. The women guests departed soon afterward, and Karen went to her room. Peter asked Dan to stay on and chat with him and Midge and Susan.

While pouring himself a Glenfiddich scotch at the bar, he remarked that he had been interested in the answers to the question Dan had posed. "It was revealing of all of them."

"And of you?" the lawyer asked.

"Yes, but my answer was also the most factual. My father's will ties all of us together. It's our bread and butter."

Susan was not ready to concede. "But the *Herald*'s position in the community also places a responsibility on us."

"On you, my dear," Peter replied, the undertone sharpened into what sounded to Dan like a caustic edge. "We were left the money. You got the responsibility. You see, Dan, Susan is our official conscience."

"All of us care about the newspaper," she said in a good-natured manner that seemed designed to deflect the conversation from the path she could sense it might take. "But Peter runs it."

"My wife is being too modest," Peter said, as he returned to the circle with his drink. "She has very strong opinions about how to run a newspaper—and the means to be heard. It's common knowledge that my father's will gave fifteen percent of the newspaper to his wife and each of his three children—Richard's share went to Amelia and her son. With the other forty percent, he set up the Boelter Foundation . . . you know, to contribute to charities and cultural groups. Who better for my father to put in charge of all that benevolence than Susan, the daughter-in-law with whom he had such a special relationship?''

"Peter, you're giving Dan the wrong idea," Susan said. "Your father knew I'd have the time to putter around with the Foundation . . . that you'd be too busy running the business.''

Midge interceded, eager to make peace. "We *all* use the Foundation to make donations. It's not as if the job is worth anything. The will forbids her from taking any salary.''

"You see," Peter continued to Dan, who was discomfitted by the personal turn the conversation had taken, "unless my family and I vote together on matters, the Foundation's block of stock controls the Herald Corporation, which owns the newspaper. And, of course, my loving wife controls the Foundation. My father, you see, had more faith in my wife than he did in me.''

Susan moved to calm the sudden squall. "The Foundation's interests are the same as the family's, you know that. The better the paper does, the more funds are available for the Foundation.''

Peter eyed her fixedly. "My father was so impressed by you: your lineage, your intellect, your shining rectitude, and so much else. He trusted you always to do the right thing.''

He turned back to Dan. "You see, one of Susan's ancestors, who happened to have interests in this state, was an original investor in the *Herald* over a century ago. The paper changed hands several times over the years, but my father, for all his forcefulness, always considered that having a Winstead among us"—Peter gestured grandly toward Susan— "added validity to the rather questionable circumstances under which he inherited the newspaper.''

"Peter, that's silly," Susan said.

"But then, everyone is impressed by Susan." Peter's glance fell now on her. "We *all* trust Susan to always do the right thing. We have to.''

He glanced at his watch, then asked Dan, "Do you shoot pool?''

Dan nodded. When he was a teenager, his pocket money often came from winnings at the neighborhood pool hall, and on lonely or boring nights, he still occasionally wandered over to the all-night pool hall at Front and Oregon to lose himself in the game's angular strategies.

"Fine. We can shoot a game of pool while we chat." Peter stood up. "I have a phone call to make, but Midge and Susan can entertain you for a few minutes.''

Peter left the room, and Midge followed to use the bathroom. Alone with Susan, Dan took the opportunity to apologize.

"I'm sorry if I was the cause of, well, contention between you."

Once again, she surprised him with a forthright reply. "It wasn't your fault. Lately Peter has been drinking too much and saying and doing things he ordinarily wouldn't. Actually, beneath what might seem like openness to you, Peter's a very private man. I didn't understand that myself when I married him."

"Would it have made a difference to you?"

She laughed. "I was head-over-heels in love with Peter Boelter from the moment I met him. I still am. And I like that there are parts of him that are still a mystery to me." She changed the subject. "I gather you're divorced."

"Yes."

"You said you were dating someone?"

"Not any longer."

"Oh, good!"

Laughter returned as she realized how inappropriate her exclamation must have sounded, and she confessed, "Amelia asked me to find out. I'm sure I wasn't supposed to tell you that. Or perhaps I was—to intrigue you. I'm very inexperienced at this sort of thing."

"Your sister-in-law wouldn't be interested." A pairing between him and Amelia Boelter seemed absurdly surreal. "We'd run out of things to say five minutes after I walked in the door."

"Oh, I doubt that."

"I'm Jewish, Mrs. Boelter." Irritation at his increasing discomfort in these surroundings and with these people topped Dan's tone. "I grew up in South Philly, between the Irish and Italian districts. My father's an immigrant. I don't go to museum openings, and I'm sure as hell not a patron of the ballet company. The only horse I ever rode was on a carousel at a church bazaar. I figure I'm lucky to have gotten through dinner tonight without half my meal in my lap. A lousy match for her to pick."

"Perhaps, but there's no cause for you to be angry with her. She's a good woman. My best friend, actually. She's just lonely."

"Sorry, but there's a lot of that going around lately. Besides, I've just been charged with bribery. Not the most elite social credential."

"You said you were innocent."

"I claim a lot of my clients are innocent, and very few of them are. No, I don't think there's much chance she'd want to date me once she really thought about it."

Dan would gladly have departed had he not come here for a reason.

When Midge returned, Susan went down the hall to find her husband, but the door to his study was closed. She, Midge, and Dan conversed desultorily for a few minutes until Peter reappeared and led the men downstairs.

Side by side in the center of the room stood a pool table and a billiard table, both brightly lit from above and ornately carved, as if rescued from a Victorian saloon.

Midge begged off on playing and sat down on one of the tall chairs at the room's dimly lit periphery. Throughout the evening his gaze had rarely strayed from his brother. When drinks were offered, he had glanced at Peter, seemingly for approval, which had not been forthcoming, and he had declined. That had not stopped Peter himself from drinking, however.

Now Peter retrieved a bottle of Glenfiddich scotch from a bar concealed within a cabinet and poured himself a glass. His tone had grown more aggressive, his eyes narrower.

"Billiards is more my game," he asserted, "but no one plays it anymore."

No one from my neighborhood, you mean, Dan thought. If a billiard table had ever shown up at the local pool hall, Maxie, the owner, would have sent it back, complaining they forgot to drill the holes.

Dan rejected Peter's suggestion that they put money on the match, sensing that the liquor was provoking the other man to macho combativeness. They began to play leisurely, not keeping score, concentrating more on the companionship the activity afforded. Peter soon relaxed. His unsipped-from glass remained on the bar.

"You said you'd look into Tim Feeney's record for me," Dan reminded him.

Surveying the table as he chalked his cue stick, Peter called out, "Midge?"

The younger brother took a folded note out of his pocket, which he opened and studied for a moment. "This is all confidential, you understand. Timothy K. Feeney started working for us as a truck driver last summer."

"Why did he get a Center City route?"

"To keep the supervisors' eyes on him. There were some absences, particularly the last several months."

"But he was working the night Cassy Cowell was murdered?"

"Yes. And he made his delivery to the next newsstand more or less on time."

Dan's interest quickened. "What does 'more or less' mean?"

"Six minutes late."

"How can you be sure?"

"That happened to be one of the newsstands we were checking that night. You know, to be sure a driver isn't sneaking off for a drink along the way, that sort of thing."

"You seem to be saying his supervisor was looking for a way to dump him. Claiming he spotted Montano must have saved Feeney's ass."

"That's one way to look at it."

Peter scratched. Dan retrieved the cue ball and placed the ten ball on the spot.

"Three ball in the far corner," he announced. "Any financial information?"

Midge glanced over at Peter, who waved a hand to indicate that his brother should dispense with such petty compunctions as concern about privacy laws. "Dan can always subpoena all this from us anyway."

Midge peered down at the information. "He was paid biweekly at teamster scale. An appliance store attached his wages a month after he started working for us. He had missed two installments on an 'entertainment center.'" Midge looked up. "I gather that's a TV and a stereo together."

Dan made the shot and drew back into good position for his next one. He asked, "Do you have any idea how a guy who was broke could have suddenly gotten hold of five thousand dollars in cash?"

Midge shook his head. "He had no access to company funds, and there's no report of any money stolen or missing."

"That's it?"

Midge nodded. "Except for a hundred dollar good-citizenship award we gave him after he came forward."

Dan lined up a shot. "Seven ball in the corner pocket. I'd like to speak to people at the *Herald* who know him."

"I'll arrange it. Nothing easier," Peter assured him. "I'm curious. Do you take just any client who comes along if he can pay?"

"We take a lot who can't, too. More than we should, but there are too few experienced criminal defense lawyers around. Sometimes the court pays us, sometimes they don't. We usually end up losing money on indigent clients."

"But the guilt or innocence of these clients, it's irrelevant to you?"

Dan nodded.

Peter pressed him. "No moral hesitancy? Never a qualm that you might set a dangerous man free?"

"Like Montano? Everyone else seems a lot more troubled by that than I am." Mara's harangue was fresh in Dan's mind.

He stepped back from the table and, leaning on his pool cue, looked directly at Peter. "I'm not the prosecutor. That's not my job. But just between us, yes, sometimes I think about it."

Peter replied philosophically. "If anyone ought to have qualms about guilt, it's the criminals."

"Not the kind I represent."

The cue ball hurtled the length of the table, smashing apart a combination that sank the seven ball. Dan looked up at the other men.

"So, I guess one of us has to."

The door suddenly snapped open. Susan stood in the opening, her mouth pressed tight with fury, her gaze seeking out her husband.

"I'd like to see you alone."

"Dan and I are in the middle of a very important match—for the championship of the known universe."

"This is personal, Peter."

"It's getting late," Dan said. He put down his cue stick and reached for his jacket. "Thanks for a nice evening. I'll see myself out."

"Me, too," Midge agreed. "It's getting late."

"I'll see you out," she said.

When she returned, Peter was idly practicing pool shots. She confronted him, her expression as angry as before.

"You left your guests and me in the drawing room for quite a while. Your study door was closed. That's very unlike you. And it set me to thinking. Later, I went in there."

Peter smiled, finding the idea funny. "Dusting for fingerprints?"

"Actually, I was appalled at myself for contemplating an invasion of your privacy, even for doubting you. But you've been so erratic lately, so angry and removed that I finally swallowed my scruples. I'm not proud of it, but I went over to your telephone, picked up the receiver, and hit the redial button."

Peter stared at his wife in astonished admiration. "How resourceful!"

"A phone number came up on the little screen that I didn't recognize. A woman's voice answered. I didn't recognize that, either. I kept quiet. After a few seconds the woman laughed and said, 'Is that you again, darling?' "

"What happened then?"

"I said to her, 'This is *not* your darling, it's his wife!' And I slammed down the phone."

Susan waited, her eyes imploring her husband to deny complicity.

Instead, Peter leaned over the table and stroked the cue ball into a corner pocket.

"I'm so very bored," he said.

4

Confused by his arrest and shamed by the disgrace, Dan barricaded himself into his apartment high up in the apartment tower at the edge of Society Hill, overlooking the Delaware River. He spent the weekend brooding and reading, while ordering in from a local Chinese restaurant.

In the course of his career he had questioned hundreds, perhaps thousands of witnesses and had argued many prominent cases. No whisper of impropriety had ever stained his reputation. Suddenly this one witness, a shifty, undependable man, whom the district attorney should have distrusted from the start, claimed Dan had bribed him to change his testimony. Simple courtesy, if not common decency, should have dictated that the DA grant Dan the time and opportunity to refute the charges before taking the shocking step of arresting him, a fellow officer of the court.

Dan reasoned that, mortified by the collapse of Ricardo Montano's prosecution, self-righteous and incapable of conceding fallibility, Gil Huyton had ascribed his defeat to his opponent's deceit. Eager to cast off the blame, Huyton had rushed to announce the charges to the world.

Now Dan could look forward to long months spent amassing evidence to disprove the charges and to save what little would be left of his name. He was convinced that even after he was exonerated, people would always whisper, "Look, there's Dan Lazar. The guy was charged with bribing a witness once. I think maybe he beat it. Slippery bastard."

*   *   *

On Sunday morning his father showed up at his door with containers of Sephardic Turkish dishes cooked at his restaurant. Jacob Lazar had phoned his son after reading about the arrest for bribery, but Dan had already taken the phone off the hook.

"I just ordered Chinese," Dan said.

"*I'll* eat the Chinese," his father declared, after noting the proliferation of white containers that filled the kitchen garbage pail.

Jacob Lazar began to set the dining room table and lay out the food he had brought. He was Dan's height and only a few pounds heavier. His hair was mostly gone, and he wore glasses, but he had the bearing of a younger man, of the uncompromising warrior he once was. He had once been a scholar, too, but by the war's end, too much time had passed, too many people had died; the habits and ease of mind that could take pleasure in ideas for their own sake had fled. Just living without the threat of imminent death seemed future enough for him.

America was heaven. What others might have considered problems in this new, wonderful land, he shrugged off. Because he'd grown up speaking Greek and Turkish in the streets, French in school, and Ladino, an ancient form of Spanish, at home, developing fluency in yet another language was simple. He asked no favors in life, merely tolerance.

When the Chinese food was delivered to the apartment, Jacob set it out on the table, but neither man had much interest in eating.

"Why are you hiding in this apartment all weekend?" Jacob asked.

"Why go out? Everyone I run into will be sure I'm a crook."

"They will if you hide like one."

Dan shrugged.

Jacob stared at his son for a long while. "There are confusions in your heart I'll never understand."

"The first time I remember your saying that was when I got back from Vietnam."

"*I* fought a war, too. Longer and tougher. *All* the prisoners ended up missing, not just some."

"But different."

"So you tell me."

"Huyton's not a Nazi, if that's what you're thinking, Pop."

"Why should I think that?" Jacob asked.

"It's not that simple, I mean."

Jacob rose to leave. "You make *everything* complicated."

At half past ten that night, unable to bear staying in the apartment any longer, Dan walked the few blocks to a piano bar he frequented on

Second Street near Lombard. Most of the regulars, who would ordinarily have welcomed his customary liveliness, had heard about his arrest. They offered mumbled hellos and then chose to keep to themselves. But the piano player, sensing Dan's sadness, slid off the seat so Dan could take his place.

As a boy, Dan had dutifully, unenthusiastically studied the piano to please his father. Music finally came alive for him the day he first heard ragtime. This was music written and played by blacks at the turn of the century in clubs and whorehouses along the Mississippi, and he could hear their melancholy beneath the honky-tonk brightness. His soul had cakewalked atop the outcasts' syncopation. He went home and taught himself to play it. Ragtime was what he began to play now, but so slowly and sadly that a young blond waitress he used to date ignored her customers and sat down beside him, so he wouldn't be alone. She asked if he wanted to go out for drinks afterward, but he said no and went home alone around midnight.

Concerned about Dan, Cal Patterson arranged to meet him for breakfast at Hi, Johnny's, a luncheonette in the City Hall area. Dan, a creature of habit, particularly regarding food, was a frequent customer and generally ordered the same things.

After he and Cal slid into the booth he favored, he briefly recounted the sparse information about Tim Feeney imparted to him at the Boelters' on Friday night. He soon digressed into observations about the people he had met there.

Cal interrupted him. "What did they serve for dinner? I've read that their cook is incredible."

Dan shrugged. "Some kind of chicken, I think."

"A gourmet!" Cal grumbled. "To you, there are only two kinds: the Colonel's regular and extra-crispy."

Calvin Patterson was three years older than Dan and, unlike Dan, who gave little thought to his appearance, was always immaculately dressed. The gray pinstripe suit exposed just enough shirt cuff to reveal handsome gold cuff links and was set off by a red silk tie. His suits and shirts were handmade. "Bespoke," as he put it. Dan was occasionally amazed that at the end of a long day in which his own clothing was as crumpled as a discarded phone message, Cal looked as if his had just come off a hanger.

It had been the same at law school, where they met and became friends. Cal, a policeman, might have just completed a twelve-hour patrol-car shift, but always somehow managed to shower and change into fresh civilian garb and get to class on time. Dan eventually realized the reason for such care. There were few blacks in the law school. Cal wanted to be sure that nothing would provide people there with an excuse to malign him.

Cal went to work as an assistant DA, and Dan, who found the idea of working for the prosecution abhorrent, went to the public defender's office. Figuring a black and a white would have the criminal defense field covered, they eventually left public service to start their own firm. As a happy family life, prosperity, and the passage of years brought Cal greater contentment, he had become increasingly protective of his old friend and partner, whose personal life was falling apart.

"First Mara, then this arrest," Dan muttered, as if expecting the logical third in the series to be world destruction.

"That reminds me. Rick Moss accepted our offer."

"Moss? Oh, the kid you had me interview to replace Mara. The private investigator."

Cal nodded. "I know we're not getting an experienced trial lawyer, like Mara. But he'll be finished with law school in May, and I like the PI work he's done for me. Thorough. Smart. He's pulling good grades. With some trial experience, he'll make a good lawyer."

"Can we still use him for investigations?"

"That's the idea. He can earn his keep while he learns."

Johnny approached to take their order.

"How about trying a sourdough walnut raisin roll?" she asked the men. When the place was crowded, as now, she helped cover tables herself.

"Great," Cal said.

"The usual," Dan told her. A chocolate doughnut and coffee.

The young woman was the restaurant's most recent owner. At night, she attracted young professional couples with her *haute cuisine* cooking and the Formica tabletops and Naugahyde booths that for them were retro-fifties reminiscences of "Happy Days." Dan refused to go near the place after three in the afternoon, when the menu changed.

"Sourdough . . . walnut . . . raisin . . . roll." Dan repeated after Johnny left to fill their order, pronouncing each word with exaggerated contempt. "Jesus! You really jumped at the chance to join the trendsetters. Ciao, baby."

"If it was up to you, we'd all be ordering at some drive-through."

Dan chose not to continue the bantering. His gaze grew distant. Cal waited out the long silence, until Dan finally voiced his thoughts.

"Cal, it seems to me that if I were Gil Huyton, I'd be really wary now about anything that Feeney told me. I'd figure that the guy burned me once, so he could burn me again. Huyton would need a lot more than just the word of a witness who got caught lying on the stand to be confident enough to go for an arrest.''

''He'd probably have something in writing or an eyewitness, maybe both.''

Dan's tone turned harsh. ''And you want to know whether there's a chance he might have them? In other words, whether I did it?''

''You know that's the last thing I'd ever believe.''

Johnny appeared with the order. She waited for Cal to try the sourdough walnut raisin roll.

''It's really good,'' Cal told her.

''Do you think it needs cinnamon?''

''No, it's just right the way it is.''

Pleased, the young woman retreated. Cal turned back to Dan, ready to be ribbed about the exchange, but Dan was lost in thought again. Cal finally asked, ''Do you want me to act as your lawyer in this?''

Not gaining a reply, he asked the question again.

''I guess so,'' Dan finally answered.

Cal sat back abruptly. ''Look, if there's someone else you'd rather—''

''What? Oh, no. Come on, Cal, you know it's not that. Sure I want you to be my lawyer. Thanks.''

The tightness left Cal's expression. ''Okay. Then I suggest we put Moss to work on tracking down the facts to clear you.''

Dan silently fumed a long while before he blurted out, ''That fucking headline! You want to know what Boelter served for dinner Friday night. Chopped Dan Lazar flambé.''

Dan spent the rest of the morning closeted in his office with Carlo Paoluzzi, the Mafia don the press called Casanova Carlo because of his good looks and the stories of women who had fallen for him. Dan had managed to keep Paoluzzi out of jail through two trials in state court, the most recent only a month earlier. Right afterward the FBI arrested him on federal charges. Intent on gaining for themselves the glory of convicting Paoluzzi, the feds had withheld from a now infuriated Gil Huyton that they had been able to install a bug in the back of the Italian restaurant off Washington Avenue where Paoluzzi often held court, and had taped several conversations. Carlo was expecting Dan to pull off another miracle.

Only one tape contained incriminating dialogue, and the U.S. attorney had turned over a duplicate to the defense. Listening to it with Paoluzzi and his bodyguard on a Marantz variable-speed cassette player, Dan found the sound clear and the wording fairly unambiguous.

"Carlo, there's no doubt that that's your voice saying, 'We got to kill that fucking Fischetti.' "

The other man thought a moment. "The waiter must a brought me an uncooked fish for lunch. I'm not one of them Japanese guys who eats raw fish. I was saying, 'You got to kill that fucking fish.' Eddie was prob'ly the name of the waiter."

"The only waiter you trust to serve you there is Vito. Three days later Bad Hand Billy Fischetti ended up in Emergency at Jefferson with three bullets in him."

Carlo winked. "So, nobody killed him. That proves I wasn't involved."

After the tape was heard in full, Dan declared that Paoluzzi's ingenious interpretations aside, he would keep trying to come up with a more reliable defense.

"Whatever you say, counselor," Carlo remarked as he stood up and buttoned his jacket. "If I get sent up, maybe we can share a cell."

Whoops of laughter trailed Carlo and his bodyguard like a wake as they cruised down the hall and out to the elevator.

A moment afterward Mary Alice entered to inform Dan that his next appointment, with a former bank president about to be indicted for embezzling tens of millions of dollars, had been canceled.

Dan observed, "He thought it wouldn't look good if a white-collar criminal was defending him from charges of white-collar crime, is that it?"

"He wasn't that blunt, but that's probably it."

A woman in her forties with two teenaged sons, Mary Alice displayed a maternal interest that spilled over into Dan's personal affairs. Her curiosity went far beyond him, taking in the lives of an extraordinary telephone network of friends scattered throughout the infrastructure that supported the city's legal and administrative system.

"Reporters have been calling like crazy," she informed him. As usual, her expression was serious, but her tone implied immeasurable levels of irony. One of the few times he could remember seeing her smile was when she learned Mara had left the firm.

"What did you think when you heard about the charges against me?" he asked her now.

"Gutter scum."

Cal and Rick Moss, the new associate, entered at that moment and saved Dan from asking whether that characterization referred to the charges or to him. He decided to give himself the benefit of the doubt.

Rick Moss was on the short side, with brown hair and open, regular features. He had a feistiness that Dan remembered liking at the interview.

For his part, Rick had been eager for a job with Lazar and Patterson.

A law professor had once sent the entire Criminal Law class to the courthouse to observe one of Dan's cross-examinations. "I don't expect you to be that good," the professor had told them, "but at least you ought to see how it should be done." By the end of that afternoon Rick revered Dan Lazar.

He was amused to find the difference in the partners' personalities evident in their office decor. Cal's office was austere, with elegant modern furniture; Dan's had large, old, comfortable pieces. Rick settled into one of the red leather armchairs and placed the Montano files atop the heavy mahogany desk. During his interview Dan had confided that he bought the desk because it had served lawyers in the city for more than a hundred years, so it had probably picked up a lot of wisdom. Rick had been unable to tell whether Dan was joking.

Yet the firm's electronic equipment—computers, telephone, fax, copier—were state-of-the-art. Rick would be doing much of his research through a computer linked by phone lines to Lexis, a data base packed with legal information—cases, statutes, law review articles—and to Nexis, its sister data base of newspapers, magazines, and other publications. Days would be required, he knew, before he felt comfortable with the high-tech phone system that bristled with all sorts of elaborate features: an LED readout of the dialed number, conferencing, speed dialing, and, for after hours, both message answering and remote forwarding of incoming calls to an outside number.

"Whatever gives us an edge," both Dan and Cal had told him separately.

Cal gestured toward the door. "Paoluzzi sounded like a happy man."

"Carlo seems to consider my arrest a sign of my trustworthiness," Dan joked. "What's up?"

"I thought we all ought to touch base on where we're going on Feeney's charges."

"There's only one starting place: Feeney."

"He's not going to talk to us. Even if he wanted to, he can't. Huyton has him locked up tight as a drum on the drug charge."

"My good old buddy Peter Boelter has offered to let us interview his coworkers. That might give us some leads."

"And Rick spoke to a lawyer he knows with a bank that has a branch near the Herald Building. He figured a lot of *Herald* employees probably bank there."

Rick said, "The DA's office hit them with a subpoena Friday afternoon for Feeney's records. My friend says we should, too."

"Did he say what we'd learn?" asked Dan.

The younger man hesitated an instant. "Off the record, yes. Feeney made a large deposit into his account the day before he testified in the Montano case.''

''How much?''

''Five thousand dollars. Cash.''

''Oh, shit!'' Dan said in a soft sigh. ''On the nose.''

''Well,'' Cal reminded him, ''we figured Huyton had to have some hard evidence. But a bank deposit by itself doesn't necessarily link *you* to the payoff.''

Dan leaned back and stared at the ceiling. ''The timing looks really bad.''

Cal shook his head. ''It means nothing if they can't connect you to the money.''

Dan quickly added, ''And you want to check my bank statement for that month just to be sure, right?''

''Jesus, Dan!''

''Well, you ought to. Huyton'll certainly subpoena it. Ask Mary Alice for it.'' His tone hardened. ''And, no, you won't find a five-thousand-dollar withdrawal on it.''

Cal grew angry. ''Hey, we're on your side, remember.''

''Chances are you're the only ones.''

5

After seeing Karen off on the school bus Tuesday morning, Susan rode her new filly for an hour through the woods behind the house, then showered and dressed and drove her dark-green Jaguar sedan into the city to the Foundation.

Sharing offices with her father-in-law's old accountant, the Foundation primarily contributed to individuals, groups, and activities that improved the city in some way. For much of the morning, she studied grant applications from the opera and orchestra, both longtime Boelter family causes, but decided not to increase their grants. They could draw on wealthy individuals eager for the prestige. She was more interested in small, struggling, and invariably controversial arts programs and social-welfare organizations, like the Anti-Drug Coalition.

At eleven she drove to a newly opened shelter for homeless families, the Foundation's second. The six-story tenement building was located in a rundown part of North Philadelphia, where drugs and random shootings were rife. Because the streets were dangerous, a playground was being built in the building's rear courtyard.

Several mothers were seated there, chatting together and watching that their playing children did not stray too close to where concrete was being poured by the workmen. She talked with the mothers for a while and then went inside for a discussion with the director about how to prod the authorities into reimbursing the shelter more quickly for the residents' living costs and whether to initiate programs to teach parenting skills.

As the time neared twelve-thirty, she hurried to her car. Every month, before the Herald Corporation's directors meeting, Margaret invited her daughters-in-law to lunch at a good downtown restaurant. Afterward the three would proceed to the meeting. Luncheon was invariably a waste of Susan's time, but she knew that absenting herself would convert her mother-in-law's careful courtesy into active dislike.

Today's lunch was at Le Bec-Fin, and Susan picked sparingly at her salad in order to splurge on the calories in one of the sinfully rich desserts. She managed to keep track of her end of the conversation only by exerting a lot of effort. She was thinking about Peter.

Unconcerned and unflustered after she had confronted him in the billiard room, Peter had explained that the last phone call he had made from his study had been a wrong number. He had put off redialing the call until Monday, when he would be in his office and could verify the correct number. He was so nonchalant about the matter and so loving in bed that night, she felt assured the call had indeed been an innocent wrong number. The rest of their weekend had been pleasant and relaxed.

Yesterday morning, though, a disagreement had flared up between them. Peter was about to leave the breakfast table for the drive to 30th Street Station, where he would take the Metroliner to New York City for an overnight stay. The previous night he and Susan had discussed a party to which an older teenaged friend had invited Karen. Susan's inquiries had disclosed that there would be drinking and little, if any, parental supervision. Because she was almost invariably the disciplining parent, she had asked Peter to forbid Karen's attending.

At breakfast, though, Peter had turned to Karen and bluntly declared, "Your mother doesn't want you spending time with this girl Heather, so you can't go to her party Saturday night."

Karen had glared at her mother and stormed from the breakfast room.

Susan was aghast that Peter had placed the blame on her. "Not allowing her to go was both our decisions."

"Damn it," he exploded, "I've got a lot on my mind. Can't you handle something as simple as this without bringing me into it every time?"

In his tone she thought she heard something worse than irritation, something more than the distractedness or shortness of temper she surmised business problems had lately been provoking in him. She thought she heard disinterest. She loved him so much, and she was suddenly afraid that he no longer loved her.

He had pushed himself away from the table and left for the station. She had not spoken to him since.

*   *   *

The Herald Building was actually a pair of adjacent nineteenth-century industrial buildings with high windows and thick floors located on a full block north of City Hall. The newspaper's operations had spread into every corner of the combined structure over the years. From the city, the surrounding counties, the commonwealth, the nation, and the rest of the world, information flowed into it to be digested, analyzed, and then organized into articles that were printed into four daily sections and more than twice that number, as well as ad inserts, on Sunday.

The conference room where the board of directors met was located on the top floor of the taller building, at the hub of the senior business executives' offices. Peter had gone straight from the train station to the *Herald*. Susan tried to hide her apprehension about his mood behind a welcoming smile.

He surprised her with a warm kiss hello.

"I hope you missed me," he said.

She kissed him quickly again and felt an arm briefly hug her before he turned to greet his mother and Amelia. Midge was already seated at the conference table. Peter was in a good mood and laughingly related a funny mishap with his suitcase. Susan relaxed, her hope rising that his long period of irritability had finally passed.

"Wonderful trip," Peter told them. "Wait till you hear."

After agenda items were disposed of, Peter dismissed the company's employees attending the meeting. Only directors were allowed to remain in the room. All were Boelters: the three women, Midge, and Peter himself.

"Now for my news," he announced, smiling broadly, still standing at the head of the table. "Totally confidential, you understand. I spent all day yesterday, until late at night, in a secret meeting in New York with Oren Lawlor."

No one emitted a sound. Oren Lawlor had built an empire of newspapers, magazines, and book publishing houses. He was a publishing mogul on a grand, international scale. Most significantly, he had purchased Philadelphia's other daily newspaper, the *Daily Mirror,* two years earlier. Much money had been spent on upgrading the tabloid's look and content and, with less success, on increasing its circulation. It remained the city's second newspaper, appealing mainly to the working class, but was far less popular and prestigious than the *Herald* and, rumor had it, still losing money. The recent recession in the newspaper industry had hit hard, but the worst hit had obviously been newspapers that competed with each other for readers and reduced advertising revenue.

Peter explained, "Lawlor hasn't made a firm bid, but he's ready to pay four hundred million dollars for our company. Sixty million dollars of that would go to each of the stockholders, one hundred sixty to the Foundation."

Margaret sought clarification. "You're talking about selling the *Herald* to him?"

"Yes, of course." Peter was smiling broadly. "Times are tough, but I think I can get him to go for it and get us off the hook."

Susan spoke up. "I take it he would liquidate one of the two newspapers, fire half the employees, and have a monopoly in the city."

"Exactly. That's why he's willing to offer us this kind of money. With the newspaper business so poor and the friends we have in Washington, the Justice Department won't object to the merger. He intends to stick with the *Mirror,* which has a newer printing plant and a more advantageous contract with the unions. He'd probably keep on some of our reporters and editors and kill the rest of the *Herald.*"

Peter looked around the table for approval, but no one appeared pleased.

"Susan?" he inquired, looking toward her for acceptance that would tip the others toward the proposal.

Susan started at the sound of her name. Anyone else, she had thought, when he was searching the faces about her, anyone else, but me. For months she had been tactfully lobbying him to make fundamental changes at the *Herald.* She contended that hard news, particularly local news, had to be covered more deeply and features made livelier and more relevant to readers' lives, particularly to the young adults who were not yet regular readers. The writing had to be better, too, and the layout more readable and attractive. Separate zoned sections should be developed that were targeted to individual outlying counties, so as to win readers there and stop the encroachment of the suburban papers and the penny savers. And she had urged Peter to consider buying new, more efficient printing presses that could also print color, although that would mean lowering the company's already sharply reduced net profits. But despite her tact, he had resisted her advice, sometimes listening stonily, sometimes arguing about the tiniest points, regardless of their relevance.

His intransigence had increased her concern about his mercurial leadership. He would become taken by a scheme to improve something and then lose interest and leap toward another. But this latest plan permitted no retreat.

"Susan," he repeated.

She chose her words carefully. "I hope you don't think I'm trying to be negative, but I don't see the advantage in a sale, particularly to someone like Oren Lawlor. Our daily circulation is still over half a million readers, and we're turning a profit. Not a week ago the *Wall Street Journal* said Lawlor's business empire was struggling. He's strapped for cash and heavily in debt. The *Mirror* is losing millions each year for him. No wonder he's willing to eliminate a rival by buying out the *Herald*. That would turn the *Mirror* into a bonanza.''

She leaned forward to exhort Peter. "A concerted effort by the *Herald* could put the *Daily Mirror* out of business."

"That isn't the issue before us," Peter responded. His expression had remained unemotional while she was speaking. Now she could hear his cold anger. "We can get a good price from Lawlor and get out!"

Midge had been doing some quick calculations. "In normal times the *Herald*'s probably worth twice what he's offering, maybe more."

"These aren't normal times."

"But the economy has begun to turn around," Susan pointed out. "More advertising dollars will be coming in. Why sell?"

Peter scowled at her. "The newspaper industry may never recover. Besides, I have other plans for my life. You should want a sale, too. The damned Foundation would be flush with cash for its projects."

Not only the price offered, but the very fact of selling the *Herald* upset Susan deeply. " 'Without fear or favor.' That's been printed on top of every front page since the first day. But that isn't what Oren Lawlor stands for. He doesn't care about this city or the people here. He's been to Philadelphia maybe twice in his life. He's just desperate to save his investment in the *Mirror*. Buying us out makes that investment a gold mine."

Peter's voice was harsh. The muscles in his neck and jaw were drawn tight. "That isn't our concern."

Her fervor gripping her, she addressed herself to everyone in the family. "In his will John Boelter said he wanted all of you to carry on as he did. We have an obligation to him and to the people of this city to do that."

Peter's face had turned red, and he still had not resumed his seat. He hated this periodic circus where he was expected to parade his decisions before a coffee klatch of addled-brained women for their uninformed inspection. Damn it, he was in charge of running this newspaper, and he bitterly resented the threat that such prying, hormone-driven, unfathomable creatures posed to his authority. Just having to submit matters to their vote every month or two undermined him with the staff; it humiliated him.

Now, instead of having the feminine good manners to defer gracefully, his own wife was disputing him on the most important issue he had ever raised. Hands on the table, Peter thrust his face toward her and was about to attack her argument as maudlin and unbusinesslike when his mother suddenly spoke up.

"Susan is quite right to wonder what John would have thought of such a proposal. I'm sure he would have rejected it out of hand. None of us is starving. The *Herald* is doing well enough, despite the difficult economy." Her head, already high, lifted a fraction higher. "What would this city be without the *Herald,* and, just as important, what would *we* be? Peter, we're the Boelters not because we have money, but because we own the *Herald.* I see no pressing reason for you to have entered so precipitously into negotiations that would force us to relinquish that."

Peter slowly sank back down in his chair. Hints from his mother had encouraged him that she might support a sale. Now, after he had committed himself in conversations with Lawlor, she had reversed herself, as if it were a game to occupy her empty time, as if he were still the child she manipulated by alternatively smothering him with attention and then withholding it, freezing him out for weeks at a time, refusing to talk to him, so as to teach him some lesson comprehensible only to her.

Peter forced himself to ponder what might have caused his mother's change of heart about selling the paper. "We're the Boelters," she had haughtily declared. His mind's eye recalled the countless times she had marched into the Academy of Music or a charity ball or the country club dining room, nodding to left and to right, like the Queen of England proceeding through London to open a new session of Parliament. The *Herald* endowed her with prestige and power. And control over him. Acquiring additional funds was a pallid replacement.

Amelia spoke next and said she wanted time to think about the proposal. Peter's sense, however, was that she probably sided with Susan but saw no reason to offend him by saying that.

Midge did not venture an opinion, but Peter detected worry in his eyes. He worked here. The *Herald* gave him a purpose in life. What would he do all week without the *Herald?*

Peter's plan had been repudiated, and everyone knew it.

Fuck you all! Peter silently growled to himself. He was so tired of being shackled to the problems of this paper, of having to answer to his own relatives. He sensed that the others had been undecided until Susan spoke, that he might well have won them over without her presence here. But when he offered her a chance to endorse his aims, she deserted him—and after the affection he had shown her in his greeting.

How could he have so badly misjudged her willingness to comply with his judgement? She always affected such a caring, accommodating attitude in public that he had ignored her frequent nagging about the paper, certain that she would yield when he advocated action. Instead, she proved to be a viper in the weeds, striking from concealment when he most needed her support.

It occurred to him now that she had an urgent reason to reject the sale. If the *Herald* were sold, she would lose the power that the Foundation gave her over him. The woman had her jaws clamped to his throat and would never voluntarily let go.

"Well," he said, with as much composure as he could, "I think the consensus is that we shouldn't rush into anything. I'll just continue the conversations with Lawlor from time to time and report back if anything develops."

The meeting ended with none of the usual small talk as people filed out of the room. Susan was loath to leave without stitching closed the rip gaping open between her and Peter.

"You must be tired from all the travel," she said. "Why not come home early and relax. I'll have Jenny prepare something special." Jenny was their cook.

"I have work to do here."

Dan had arranged a four-o'clock appointment at the *Herald*. He and Cal were walking down the executive-floor corridor when he came upon Peter and the other Boelters standing around the open door of the board-room. None was speaking. They all appeared tense.

"Dan!" Amelia exclaimed, recognizing him. "How good to see you."

"Hello," Susan quickly added. "I hope you're holding up all right under the strain."

"I'm fine," Dan replied, sensing that his unexpected appearance provided them with a welcome excuse to veer away from contention among them. "Just here to track down facts and put this all behind me."

"I'm sure you will," said Amelia solicitously.

He introduced Cal to the others, noting how diplomatically the Boelters hid their astonishment that he had a black law partner. Just as diplomatically, he and Cal failed to mention that all weekend the front page of the newspaper's city section had featured follow-ups to the bribery story about Dan. The fact that Feeney, his accuser, who had confessed to taking the bribe, was a *Herald* employee had been mentioned in only one of the stories—after the jump to an inside page. Dan had once heard that only ten percent of readers generally bothered to make the jump to a story's continuation.

Peter explained to the others, "I'm showing Dan—and Cal here—around the paper. They want to meet some of that Feeney fellow's co-workers."

Midge and the younger women wished Dan luck as they departed. Although Margaret nodded good-bye, she did so with a disdain that reflected her sincere belief that his incarceration would make the world a better place. At that moment Dan decided that of all the Boelters, he probably respected her the most. The others feigned a congeniality toward him he was certain they did not feel. Given present circumstances, he could not blame them.

To most people Dan appeared to be his old self: dynamic, quick-talking, funny. But he knew that he was assuming his customary manner out of habit, forcing himself back into the motions, using his gregarious exterior like a shield to deflect the voyeurism of people he was sure regarded him with contempt. Margaret, at least, did not hide it.

Distracted by his thoughts, Peter silently led Dan and Cal down a flight of stairs to the newsroom. The novelty of running the newspaper had exhausted itself long ago. The problems were stubborn and difficult to solve. He felt trapped between the unions' intransigence on one side and the blockade his wife and mother and the others had erected across his escape route on the other.

Peter guided his guests onto a large open space covering almost the entire floor, which was divided into areas for the Foreign Desk, the National Desk, and the State and City Desks. The designations were a holdover from the time that editors sat around U-shaped desks editing stories rushed from reporters by eager copy boys. Separated by shoulder-high partitions, reporters were now linked to editors by computers. Peter explained that nearly everything was done by computer, from a reporter's writing the article to an editor's calling it up on the screen to edit and write headlines for it.

He entered a walled office at one end of the newsroom and introduced the two lawyers to Leo Kucaba, the newspaper's managing editor, who oversaw the news content of the paper. Kucaba was a middle-aged man who would not have looked out of place at a tabloid in the 1930s. Overweight and jowly, he had wary eyes and gripped a cigarette between thumb and index finger. A pile of butts filled his ashtray. A sign on his desk that read "SMOKING SECTION" dared visitors to object. His tie was pulled down and his shirtsleeves rolled up.

The *Herald* had given Kucaba his first job out of high school. His father had been a pressman here. John Boelter thought him bright and energetic and made him a copy boy. Now, almost four decades later, he had been running the news operation for several years.

"How's the defense going?" Kucaba asked Dan. Seeking a possible story was instinctive with him.

"Trying to find out more about Feeney. Did you deal with him at all?"

Kucaba shook his head. "My job is to put the news together. Pressmen print it. Paper handlers collate it. Drivers deliver it to newsstands and distributors. He's a driver. Only met him once."

"When was that?"

"Right after he identified Montano. We gave him a hundred-dollar check in the newsroom. Photographed him for the front page."

"Good citizenship award," Dan commented sourly.

"Sounded good at the time."

"How does it sound now?"

"I'll let you know after your trial."

Peter enlisted the managing editor to show his guests around the newsroom. Kucaba nodded and stubbed out his cigarette.

He walked them past the various departments, pointing out the Picture Desk, which had its developing and printing facilities elsewhere in the building, and several stand-alone departments: Arts, Books, Science, Lifestyle, and Editorials, which were fitted into niches at the far reaches of the floor. Sports and the Sunday supplements were on a different floor, as were the support operations: Marketing, Finance, and Human Resources.

"I think you know Scott Feller," Kucaba said as they moved past one of the partitioned pens where a thin young man was peering at a computer.

The latter murmured greetings.

Kucaba asked Feller to explain what he was working on and used the time to draw Peter into a far area for a private conversation about some matter that had just come up.

Feller pushed up his wire-rimmed spectacles and pointed to the monitor. An old story from the *Herald* filled the screen. He explained that any story appearing during the last decade could be called up by computer. For pre-computer-age material, one had to go to the "morgue," a library of old newspaper clippings filed by subject matter.

Dan interrupted him. "Have you learned anything new about Feeney?"

Feller shook his head. "They won't let anyone see him. And nobody at the DA's office will spill anything."

"What do you think?"

"Same thing I thought all along. That he lied about seeing Montano running from the scene. For a while I thought he was going to get away with it. Good going."

"Be nice if Huyton felt the same way."

"My hunch has always been that Feeney killed both women. His route also took him near the street where the Hopkins woman's body was found. But Fred Moore—he's the deputy managing editor—put a clamp on any digging around that might upset the promotion bandwagon they had rolling. It's a shame. Would have been a hell of a story. But I guess his hands were tied, too." Feller frowned. "Not that they loosen the purse strings much for investigative reporting other times."

He paused and then admitted, "That's not completely fair to them. Money's tight, and I've got more than enough work pounding out my share of words on breaking stories."

"Does Boelter have much to do with the editorial side of the paper?" Cal inquired.

"You didn't hear it here, but people walk on eggshells around him. Maybe he knows the business end—I'm not qualified to judge—but he thinks he's got that sharp editorial instinct his father had. So far I haven't seen it. But Kucaba's no fool, so when Boelter tells him how he wants a story covered, Kucaba kisses ass and agrees."

Dan asked, "Could I meet Moore?"

Feller stood up. "Come on."

Fred Moore stood behind a desk in a large open area at the center of the grid of partitioned spaces. Leaning over several pages, Moore and another man were discussing a story.

"What's he like?" Dan whispered to Feller, their backs to the row of enclosed offices along the wall.

"Smart, outspoken, compulsive workaholic," the reporter whispered back. "Also a compulsive womanizer. Two wives have divorced him. Great newspaperman. Not just good, great. He won us a Pulitzer last year for a series he wrote himself about a welfare mother. That's the only thing the news operation's won around here since John Boelter died. When it looked like he might leave unless he got a promotion, Boelter made him deputy managing editor under Kucaba."

As soon as Moore was free, Feller introduced Dan and Cal. They chatted a bit about Dan's legal problems. Dan felt an instant kinship with Moore, a man about his own age, who bristled with energy. Moore rarely sat, but rather, as he himself often did, paced as he spoke. An inner-city accent revealed that his motivation to succeed in this respectable white-collar profession was as much socioeconomic as journalistic.

Asked why Dan and his client had received such rough treatment during the course of the Cassy Cowell case, Moore replied, "Do my guys ask you why you used a certain tactic in court?"

"Yes."

"Okay," Moore admitted with a laugh.

"Orders?" Cal inquired, noticing Moore's attention to Peter and Kucaba's conference on the other side of the newsroom. "The circulation boost they were getting from Feeney?"

Moore reflected for a moment and then admitted, "Let's just say some people around here thought that the way crime was plaguing this city, the paper had a civic duty to give the new DA a breathing spell for a while. You know, let him get up to speed on the job without being distracted by criticism."

The answer nettled Dan. "So you made me the whipping boy?"

"Lazar, there's a rapist-murderer out there, and people are scared sick. With no clues available, the only thing they have to worry about is whether your client Montano might really be the culprit."

"In other words, whether I bribed Feeney to get Montano off?"

"Did you?"

Dan glared at him. "No!"

Moore laughed again. "Hey, trying to get a story is like trying to get laid. It never hurts to ask. You'd be surprised how many times they say yes."

Feller observed Peter separating from Kucaba and guided the visitors back to him.

Taking Dan and Cal through a lower floor, Peter pointed out the Advertising Department, which was responsible for soliciting, booking, and often designing large ads, and the bank of operators who took calls for Classified. He explained that the latter term originated with the idea of classifying ads into categories like "houses" or "boats," so buyers could find them more easily in the paper.

He showed how the computerized text and artwork layouts were formed into printing plates from which the newspaper would actually be printed.

The immense offset printing presses were located in the building's high, vaulted basement. Ribbons of newsprint paper unwound from huge rolls fed into them to be printed on at high speed and then combined in the correct order. The individual newspapers were then cut, folded, and conveyed on belts to be bundled by the paper handlers and loaded onto trucks for delivery. The *Herald* was a morning paper. The late edition would not begin being printed until well after midnight, which would allow for a late deadline, but still permit copies to land in front of doors and in honor boxes and on newsstands in time to greet early risers.

The presses were now turning out the Sunday Arts Section, which would not contain last-minute news. Rotogravure printing of the Magazine Section and ad inserts were turned out at another location and brought here for inclusion in the Sunday edition.

"We could do without half those guys," Peter grumbled, gesturing toward the pressmen. "And we ought to have color. But the old *cojones* are caught in a vise."

Several drivers who knew Feeney well had been asked to come in during the day to speak to Dan. They had congregated at the truck-loading dock, waiting to be questioned, and were talking to a large man with ham-size forearms below his rolled-up sleeves. Peter introduced Bill Nelson, who headed the Delivery Department. He had the look of someone who had worked his way up from the ranks and would fight to keep his hard-earned place.

Dan began by asking, "When Feeney came back here the night Cassy Cowell was murdered, did he tell you or anyone else that he'd seen a man running from the alley?"

Nelson shook his head. "The first time I knew about it was when I read it in the paper a few days later."

"Did you believe him?"

Nelson answered bluntly. "I told Mr. Kucaba he was making a mistake making a hero out of the guy. You couldn't always be sure Feeney was telling the truth. He's the kind of guy who's always making excuses. Besides, you knew the publicity would go to his head."

"Did it?" Cal wanted to know.

"Did it? He was swaggering around here, telling me he ought to be moved up into management. Began turning up late, looking like he was on something. I sure couldn't let a guy like that out in one of our trucks, no matter how much he swore he was okay. So, I'd have to put on a substitute driver."

Peter bristled, displaying an irritation the subordinate could not mistake. "Bill wanted to fire him. He didn't understand that was something we just couldn't do—for public relations reasons—while the trial was pending."

"How about firing him now?"

"I'd like to," Nelson said, making up his mind to be frank with Peter. "I'm talking to the teamsters' union about it. The guy's trouble."

It turned out that none of the men in the department was particularly close to Feeney, but what they knew of him they didn't like.

"He could get kind of violent," one said. "Took offense at something and right away he'd want to fight. This isn't that kind of place. We're all family men here."

"He probably owes a ten or a twenty to every guy he works with," said another. "We'll never see a penny."

Then one of the men remembered, "His wife was friendly with Ed Malloy's wife. Maybe she still is."

"I didn't know he was married," Cal said.

"Might not be, but they came to a couple of events together, and he called her his wife. I guess after a while it's the same thing."

Cal wrote down Ed Malloy's address and phone number. Then he and Dan followed Peter upstairs to the lobby. Peter was pleased at how well the interviews had gone. Better to cooperate with Lazar and defuse his resentment toward statements about him that appeared in the *Herald* during the Montano hearing than to chance his suing for libel. That would entail heavy legal fees and the risk that some crack-brained jury might award him millions in damages. You could never be sure what kind of embarrassing light a guy like that could put you in.

By now many day-shift workers were leaving work and their night-shift replacements were entering, the opposing streams flowing through each other between the front doors and the elevators.

"Fascinating place," Dan observed.

"Like any place," Peter replied. "After a while you want other challenges."

"Like what?"

"I don't know. I'm still here."

Ordering his secretary to hold all his calls, Peter slammed his office door shut behind him and allowed the anger he had constrained since the board meeting to break into his brain like a pillaging horde. He poured himself a drink and brooded on the defeat he had suffered.

Even before his initial conversation with Lawlor, Peter had made up his mind to sell the *Herald* and get out. He was not a man who changed his mind, only his tactics. He would have to figure out how to win over the others in his family. Of one thing he was sure, however: He would not tolerate a moment more of Susan's defiance.

He had always believed that when his father died, he would finally be totally free. He would control the *Herald*. He could do anything he wanted. It had not worked out like that.

After his marriage and certainly after Richard died, Peter had anticipated becoming his father's eventual successor and being absorbed into the intimacy his father and his wife shared. But he had never succeeded. Their bond—whatever it was—proved too strong. His father was still trying to dominate him even after his death, Peter was convinced, through his surrogate, Susan. Although, seeking to found a dynasty, his father had not bequeathed Susan stock in the company, he gave her control of the Foundation—and virtual control over the company: the right to vote forty percent of the stock!

Today her obstinacy had barred his way and contrived to win over his family into an alliance against him. She had stopped him in his tracks, wrapping herself in his father's memory as if she, and not he himself, were John Boelter's child.

Admittedly, in many ways she was an admirable wife, who had brought impeccable social credentials to the marriage, despite not having a dime to that fine name of hers. He was proud of her good looks, that she could be charming in company and amusing and had a top-notch mind. But her steadfastness in maintaining her own views in opposition to his had always annoyed him. Her prodding and interference, however diplomatically conveyed, had become tedious, and he was tired as well of her stubbornness or character or whatever it was that kept her urging him to do things he had no interest in. Now, when the time had come for her to prove her wifely loyalty, when he had counted on her allegiance to him to supersede her sentimental attachment to the *Herald,* she had betrayed him.

Sleeping with her had also become tedious to Peter. She was an ardent lover, but the sex had become predictable. His exploration of her and her possibilities was years in the past. Often when they had sex now, he had drunk too much, and as he sometimes privately mused, What the hell difference did it make then who I put it into? The sad truth was that she would never be new for him. Over the last few months he had realized that he was forcing himself to be with her, to go home to her, at a time when he was eager for new things in his life.

Susan always insisted on telling him that she loved him. Well, now he would see just how much.

Peter arrived at his Dellwyne estate later than usual and was met at the door by George, the butler. Peter had been drinking, but his walk was straight, and he was filled with a cold intent.

He found Susan writing out checks for household bills in her small study next to their bedroom. Her smile froze at the sight of her husband's expression.

His voice was a low hiss, laced with acrimony. "That's the last time I ever allow you to humiliate me in front of my family! In front of anyone! I'm through being your employee. I'm leaving."

He strode through the side door into their bedroom and began to pull shirts out of his bureau. A moment later George entered from the other door with the suitcase Peter had taken to New York. Opening it on the bench at the foot of the bed, he emptied it of laundry and began to place fresh clothing into it, enough for a week, his employer had told him. Peter intended to send for the rest later.

"Peter, please," Susan implored him. "I'm sure George doesn't want to listen to this. Let's go back into my study, where we can talk privately.'' If she could get him to put off the decision, she was sure that by morning, when he was sober, he would come to his senses.

He ignored her.

"Peter, don't go. Whatever's wrong, whatever's happened, we can work it out.''

"You will never, ever, humiliate me again!''

This was not mere pique, she suddenly realized, or a performance to win her capitulation. He truly intended to leave her.

She began to cry. "I love you.''

"Not enough to vote my way this afternoon!''

"That shouldn't have anything to do with our personal life. I'd hoped you'd understand. I . . . I had no choice.''

"I *have* a choice. I'm leaving you.''

Peter quickly reviewed the items being placed in the suitcase, handed George the book on his night table, and strode from the room. He had thought through his departure thoroughly. Rather than doing so when he reached his hotel, he even stopped at his study on his way out of the house and programmed his phone to forward incoming calls there. At the front hall closet, he chose a raincoat and, for weekends, a windbreaker.

Stunned, her life in collapse, Susan had followed him downstairs. As he turned to leave, she stepped in front of him.

"Peter, I love you, and I know you love me. Please don't walk out like this.''

"Get out of my way!'' he shouted.

His arm swung violently outward, flinging her against the wall. He seemed about to smash her face with a raised fist when he caught himself and charged out of the house. George followed and put the suitcase into the trunk of Peter's car.

Susan stood sobbing and shaking. She had been unprepared for Peter's abandonment of her. Their relations had been strained for a while, to be sure, but she had never considered that he might be so disaffected as to leave her.

He was drunk. That was it. He was so drunk that he had almost struck her. In a day or two, when the unreasoning mood had passed, he would be back. She wanted to believe that. She loved him. She and Karen were his family.

Finding her still there when he came back inside, George guided her to a chair. Comforting her did not seem proper. Perhaps some tea, he thought, and hurried to the kitchen to prepare some.

Karen! she remembered; she would have to tell Karen. The child adored her father. But Peter could change his mind by morning, when he came to his senses. Why upset her unnecessarily?

Susan decided to wait. If by tomorrow night Peter had not returned, that would be time enough to tell Karen that her father had left them.

After checking into the Rittenhouse and tipping the bellman to bring the suitcase to his room and put away his clothes, Peter realized that he had not eaten since breakfast. He had already made plans for later tonight, but he was hungry and getting queasy from all the liquor on an empty stomach. He went to 210, the hotel's somberly elegant restaurant overlooking Rittenhouse Square.

"Phone call for you, Mr. Boelter," the captain informed him, just as Peter was ordering. Peter was about to ignore the call, thinking it might be Susan with a plea to come home, when the man added, "He said his name was Donaldson and to tell you it was urgent."

Chet Donaldson was the *Herald*'s executive vice president, the man in charge of the business side of the newspaper. Peter realized that the phone call to his study had been automatically forwarded here to the hotel.

Peter took the call at the captain's desk.

"It's a wildcat walkout, Peter," Donaldson informed him. "A supervisor said something to a pressman that they all took exception to, and they just walked out of the building. Machinists, too."

"I'll be right there," Peter told him.

The crowd of shouting workers on the sidewalk rushed up to Peter as he was stepping out of the taxi in front of the Herald Building. At their head was Vinnie Briggs.

"Did I interrupt your dinner, Boelter?" Briggs inquired with a broad grin. "How about half my egg salad sandwich?"

Briggs extended an object wrapped in wax paper.

"I always thought you ate shit, Briggs."

Peter angrily pushed past him and into the building.

Most of the *Herald*'s business executives had already made it back and were waiting in the boardroom when Peter arrived.

The facts were quickly reviewed. Although the pressmen and machinists had walked out first, the teamsters and paper handlers, who were not scheduled to start work yet, were already gathered on the sidewalk. This walkout was clearly a show of strength and solidarity to back the union coalition's demands in the contract negotiations.

A staff lawyer pointed out that if the unions struck now, while the old contract was still in force, management could declare that labor had broken the contract and could then legally hire new people at lower wages to replace the strikers.

Peter's head had cleared, and he had never felt more focused, more ready, or more capable than he did at that moment; he intended this fight to be his vindication. He and his senior executives had foreseen that the unions would try something like this and had been secretly training management people to take over the presses and trucks.

"This is the moment of truth," Peter declared. Briggs and the pressmen had challenged him, and he was going to grind them into the dirt. "If we stand tough now, we'll get everything we want. I'm ready to issue a statement calling it a full-fledged strike. Management mans the presses and trucks tonight. Tomorrow we begin to hire permanent replacements."

Just then, however, a security man guarding the presses from possible sabotage rang up with some news. As if having guessed perfectly what they could get away with without losing their leverage, the pressmen and machinists had just returned to their jobs.

Peter went to the window. Down below, Vinnie Briggs now stood alone on the sidewalk across the street, peering up at Peter. He was laughing.

6

Dan and Cal took a taxi up to that part of the Frankford section of the city where white lower-middle- and working-class families lived in blocks of row houses. Ed and Fran Malloy's house was one of those. Ed had already left for work at the *Herald*, but Fran was home and, after hearing Bill Nelson's name, willing to talk.

While the taxi waited, she spoke in her front hall to the men about Tim Feeney's girlfriend, Evie Jeeter. Evie and she had become close friends after meeting at another driver's retirement party. Tim called Evie his wife, Fran confirmed, because they had been living together and he wanted to marry her.

"Tim blows a lot of hot air, but Evie's no dummy," Fran said.

"Then they aren't married," Dan gathered.

"Evie doesn't like his drinking—and worse," Fran put it, "so she refused."

"The drugs, you mean."

She nodded. "Evie can usually handle Tim, but after he got his name in the paper, the drinking got bad, and he went back to the drugs. It didn't surprise me, him getting arrested the other day."

"Are he and Evie still together?"

"Evie's not the kind to put up with that. She left town. She stopped by here to say good-bye. She said she spoke to the police for him, you know, to help him out. But that was the last she was going to do for him."

Cal asked where they could find her.

Fran knew only that she had gone away so as not to be called as a witness at the trial. "She wasn't his wife, you see, so she'd have to testify about his taking drugs and all."

"If she happens to call," Dan said, "tell her we'd like to speak to her."

The taxi driver drove back along Frankford Avenue, under the El. The gloom imposed by the superstructure, a tunnel laid between the walls of retail establishments along either side of the street, matched the men's mood. Cal eyed the meter suspiciously. The city's taxi rates were the highest in the country—and the legitimacy of meter settings often questionable.

"Evie Jeeter has got to be the eyewitness who substantiated the bribe for Huyton," Dan reasoned. "I saw a woman look out the first-floor window of Feeney's house."

Cal stiffened. "You never told me you went to Feeney's place."

"It slipped my mind. It was the day before he was scheduled to testify."

"Jesus, you know better than to question a witness without having someone with you."

"The whole thing lasted ten seconds. I'd spent the night at Mara's—"

"Her apartment's over in the Art Museum area, right?"

"Twenty-second and Green," Dan confirmed. "I grabbed a taxi and was on my way to the office down Green when I happened to see Feeney walk around the corner at Sixteenth. You know the neighborhood there: run-down, drugs, crack. He wouldn't talk to us, remember? But I figured if I surprised him, he might let slip more than he did in that interview in the *Herald*. I jumped out of the taxi and stopped him on the stoop, just as he was about to go into his house."

"Did he say anything?"

"He told me to go to hell. Not much of a conversation. I walked back to the taxi and kept going to the office. It was out of my mind a minute after it happened."

"But don't you see how it looks? That was the same day he deposited the five thousand dollars. We've got to find this Evie Jeeter."

Dan stared at the procession of buildings passing the car window in monotonous review.

"Are you listening?" Cal finally asked. Gaining no reply, he said, "Maybe I'm crazy, but it seems to me this is damned serious. You're on the hot seat here."

"Either way . . ." Dan's voice trailed off.

"Jesus! Huyton isn't joking around. You could end up in prison."

"You're my lawyer. See that I don't."

They rode a while in silence.

Finally Cal said, "You know what you need? Company to take your mind off your troubles. You need to start dating again."

"Come on, Cal. I'm facing a jail sentence for bribing a witness, disbarment, clients deserting me, and you think the solution is I ought to be dating?"

"Not the solution to your problem with Huyton, but all this brooding you've been going through since Mara left. You should be going out, taking your mind off the charges."

"I can see it coming a mile off. Your wife knows somebody."

Cal appeared only slightly abashed at having been so transparent. "Same one I told you about last year, just before you took up with Mara. In my wife's office. She's great-looking. She's Jewish, so you two have that in common. And she just broke up with her boyfriend."

"A new boyfriend? Or the same one she'd just broken up with last year?"

"This might be a good time for both of you."

"There couldn't be a *wronger* time for me, Cal."

"I'm telling you, you need company. She's a terrific lady." Cal's enthusiasm took over. "I'll tell you what, I'll do the worrying for both of us about Huyton and take over more of the scut work. You just promise me you'll call her for a date as soon as we get back to the office."

Dan groaned.

"Just one date," Cal promised. "If you don't like her, that's it."

Resigned, knowing Cal's determination to fix him up in the hope that he would finally marry again and have what Cal called "a normal life," Dan agreed. "And if I don't like her, that's the end of it. You leave me alone."

"Sure." Cal smiled. "But I'm telling you, you're going to be crazy about her."

The day after Peter left her, Susan Boelter canceled all her appointments and did not step out of her house, waiting and hoping for his phone call that would begin the reconciliation and bring him home.

The servants all knew what had happened, of course. Their attempts at kindness only aggravated her despair, making her feel like an object of pity. She tried to busy herself with small tasks, but nothing that would take her outside, where she might miss Peter's phone call.

Susan could not bear her and Karen's eating supper alone in the dining room, so they ate in the breakfast room. Because Peter's late appointments often caused him to miss dinner, Karen did not comment on his absence. Susan asked about her day, her schoolwork, her friends, anything she could think of to keep the conversation going.

At nine-thirty that night, deciding she could no longer hide Peter's departure, Susan went to her daughter's room. Karen was seated at her desk, doing homework. Her stereo was pounding out rock music. Susan had never understood how Karen could concentrate, but the child did well at school, so Susan had given up that particular battle as a meaningless cause.

"I've got to speak to you," Susan began.

"Okay."

Susan could hardly hear her and turned off the music. She sat down on the end of the bed. Since last night she had been pondering how to put this. She felt no more prepared now than she had the moment Peter left.

"Karen, you know that your father was supposed to come back from New York yesterday."

The girl nodded.

"Well, he did."

Karen's face brightened. She stood up, about to run out of the room to greet him.

"He's not here," Susan had to tell her. She went up to her daughter. "He won't be coming back, at least not for a while. He . . . he wasn't happy here, he said. With me, that is. So he moved out."

Devastation slowly marched across the child's face. "You chased him away?"

"No, it wasn't like that. I wanted him to stay."

"Then why did he leave?"

Susan shrugged helplessly. "He decided he would be happier not living with me."

Karen was suddenly crying, all the clouds behind her eyes opening at once. Susan put her arms about her daughter and pulled her tightly against her body. She was crying, too.

"He's gone," Karen cried out. "He's left me."

"He loves you. You know he loves you. He'll want to see you soon. He loves you."

Susan wanted to believe that—and not to hear the voice inside her heart telling her that it was only she herself he did not love.

Susan sat by Karen's bed until her daughter finally fell asleep. She herself slept fitfully that night. She was up and waiting for Karen at breakfast.

Susan tried to make the ordinary conversation she always did as a way to help Karen understand that her life would go on, in many ways unchanged. She also wanted to give her the opportunity to discuss her anguish. But Karen was too upset.

Susan walked her out to the driveway and waited with her for the school bus. Then she returned to the house to wait for Peter to phone her. All her thoughts were in disarray. She acknowledged that she and Peter had had their share of spats, particularly these last few months as he began to drink more under the pressures he said he was feeling at the *Herald*. But never had he walked out or refused to speak to her. Almost as distressing as the act itself was the uncertainty of what it meant, what he intended. If only she could speak to him, she was sure they could iron out their differences and resume their life together.

Finally, at noon, she decided to phone *him*. Even to hear his voice would have been a relief. But he did not take the call or else was out, she could not be sure. She waited at home until about two-thirty, mostly pacing about her bedroom and glancing repeatedly at the clock on the dresser.

Needing to do some errands, she drove into the village, intending to stop first at the bank to get cash. She parked on the street in front of the bank and walked to the automatic teller machine in the vestibule. Inserting her card, she punched in her number twice, but both times the machine read, "No funds available."

Susan went inside the bank to the area set aside for officers' desks. She had always dealt with Mr. Harrington and waited for him to complete a phone call.

"Mrs. Boelter," he greeted her when he hung up, awkwardly offering her the chair beside his desk.

"There seems to be a problem with the cash machine," she told him. "It says I have no money in my checking account, but I'm sure there's over ten thousand dollars in it. Has anyone else had trouble with the machines today?"

"Uh, Mrs. Boelter . . . I was sure your husband would have told you," he went on.

"He hasn't told me anything."

"Oh, I see." He groped for words. "Mrs. Boelter, your husband . . . he came into the bank yesterday morning. He emptied the joint accounts."

"*All* my bank accounts are joint accounts," Susan exclaimed.

Harrington nodded. "He asked us what the balances were and then withdrew everything."

Susan suddenly felt as if Peter had snatched all the organs out of her body as well.

"Mrs. Boelter," Harrington went on in a concerned tone, "we find that this sometimes happens when there's been some . . . some, you know . . . unpleasantness between a husband and wife.''

Susan jumped to her feet and raced down the stairway to the vault. The bank officer there admitted her past the steel-barred door and signed her in. He took her key and his own and opened the locks on her and Peter's safety-deposit box.

Although she carried the metal box into one of the small private chambers, the moment he handed it to her and she could feel how light it was, she knew that Peter had already removed all of her jewelry.

She sat in the tiny closet of a room and stared at the empty box. Everything of value was gone. She was penniless.

No one was minding the desk at the Jewish Y health club, so Cal just descended the stairs into the men's locker room. To one side was a room where the men could work out. Upstairs was more exercise equipment— for women as well as men. This was an old-time gym, unpretentious and down to earth; it lacked the kind of sleekness he himself liked in a club, which he knew was precisely why it appealed to Dan.

He found Dan on his back in the Universal machine room, bench-pressing a stack of brick-shaped weights. Dan's muscles bulged with each effort, deepening the clefts between them. When he sat up, his legs straddling the black padded bench, Cal was seated at an exercise machine across from him.

''Oh, shit, that date!'' Dan remembered. ''It was tonight, and you're pissed.''

''Perceptive guy.''

''God, I'm sorry. I forgot all about it.'' Dan stood up. ''I'll call her right now to apologize.''

''I already did it for you. When she called me, I phoned around and found out you were here. I told her you were home sick and almost delirious with a high fever.''

Dan sank back onto the bench. ''Thanks.''

Cal eyed his friend critically. ''Actually, that isn't so far from the truth.''

Dan lifted the towel draped across his thighs and wiped the sweat from his face. Cal assumed he was doing so to evade a reply.

''You sure haven't been yourself lately,'' Cal reminded him. ''You've been avoiding things. That's not like you.''

''Avoiding what?''

''Apart from this date tonight? The bribery charges.'' Cal pressed the issue. ''Gil Huyton wants your ass, and let me tell you, he isn't avoiding a damned thing.''

Dan slipped on his warm-up jacket, at the same time reflecting on the answer he owed his friend. When he finally replied, despair propelled the words.

"How the hell can I bring myself to participate in a charade played out by a justice system that hounds and demeans me with false charges after all the years I defended it?"

Agitated, he jumped to his feet. "Even at its worst I believed in it. But the truth is: The deck is stacked. If Huyton can ruin me with only an announcement to the press, then the justice system's a fraud."

"You know his tactics."

"I can't bring myself to play his game, Cal. I don't have the heart for it anymore."

"But if you give in, you're lost. We can beat him."

Dan smiled sadly. "When you think you've spent your life honorably defending the law, but everybody's willing to take the word of a lying snake like Feeney against yours, then there's nothing out there worth winning."

Before Cal could reply, Dan was moving at a limping trot out of the health club.

Dan ran mindlessly along the city's streets. The knee hurt, but he kept going, and numbness gradually eradicated the pain. He ran past tall office buildings, concert halls, and boarded-up storefronts. Heading east, he ran past the jewelry district, its traditional integrity tainted now by European newcomers fencing stolen goods, and then the restored, pristine nostalgia of Society Hill's two-hundred-year-old houses and of Independence Hall, its idealism worn now only on patriotic holidays. He ran past Elfreth's Alley, the country's oldest continuously occupied residential street; past Christ Church, where Franklin, Washington, and Adams worshiped; and past men and women stopping passersby for change or already asleep on street vents or in doorways.

He ran for hours, roving in great loops through North Philly and then west and then south again. Paper scraps swirling about his feet, he ran past men sharing liquor in brown bags as they loitered on street corners till early morning because they had no job to wake early for; past burned-out and crumbling buildings; past crack dealers and whores (both tight-hipped males and short-skirted females), mutually dependent, futureless. And he ran past abandoned autos and sleek new ones with suburban license plates slowly cruising for drugs and sex.

Dangerous faces swung around in surprise as he suddenly appeared under the circle cast by a streetlight before disappearing again. Greater imagined terrors—fantastical, invisible, lethal—rolled like sea monsters in the deep darkness beyond them. He ran on, his mind growing incredibly clear.

God, he used to love this city, he remembered. He had felt a part of it and wanted to matter in it. He had believed that defending people and the law was a noble way to spend his life. But he also recalled that that was when people cared about Philadelphia and about America, when they believed that they were an indissoluble part of an idea bigger themselves, that despite their differences, they were united into one people and were willing to sacrifice for that belief. He saw that cohesion and commitment die in the disillusionment of Vietnam, of the Sixties, of Watergate, of drug-induced crime and family breakup, of an economy crushed under mountains of debt left behind by slick or inept politicians unwilling to risk defeat by demanding sacrifice of citizens no longer willing to offer it.

America had fragmented. Values had become relative. Free speech, justice, tolerance, a better life—the common assumptions in which Americans and other civilized peoples once believed—had now become twisted into rationales for self-interested personal moralities that undermined those ideals. Money bought political favors, the tomorrow of ordinary, voiceless citizens mindlessly mortgaged to pay for the orgies of more powerful people today. Like the drug dealers and users, he realized, like the prostitutes and the homeless littered along these streets, he himself had no hope for the future and no notion of where he fit into it.

Amid all the chaos, he persisted in demanding to know, wasn't there a purpose to his life? Wasn't there some greater significance to his consumption of air, food, space, and time than the motions he went through at work? Some faith greater than his despair? Some reason that would make his long, anguished journey toward confrontation with the unknown at death worthwhile?

He was too practical a man to place hope in the unproven promise of heaven. He was not even sure if he believed in God, certainly not in a God so cruel or neglectful as to abandon multitudes of slum dwellers around the world to hopelessness and death and to slaughter six million Jews, a million and a half Armenians, a million Cambodians, and untold natives of Africa and the Americas.

And if no God existed, perhaps no purpose existed for him, either, except to procreate another being who would someday wander as blindly as he. Were his mind, his culture, his yearning for immortality merely inconsequential twitches around a biological urge no more singular than a lizard's? Could that be all?

Hours later, when he was too exhausted to think any longer, he made his way back to the Y to retrieve his street clothes and house keys. The club was closed.

His office building was nearby. He found the night watchman, who let him into his office.

He fell asleep on his sofa.

Dan awoke to find Susan Boelter standing over him and struggled to sit up.

"The front door was unlocked," she said, "so I came in."

He stood up. Pain clubbed at his knee. He clutched the sofa arm to keep from falling.

"You aren't drunk, are you?" she asked.

He shook his head.

"I didn't smell any alcohol," she said. "I recognize the slightest whiff of it now."

He realized that she must have been watching him for a while before he awoke. He tested his knee and, deciding he could walk on it, lumbered to the restroom like a man with one shoe off. The clock in the reception area read six minutes after eight. He splashed cold water on his face, hoping to force alertness back into it.

Susan Boelter was sitting on the leather sofa when he returned. He took the adjacent armchair.

"What can I do for you?" he asked.

"I need to talk to someone. A lawyer. I don't know. You see—" She stopped to take a breath. "—my husband has left me—"

The last sentence caught in her throat, and she halted abruptly, closing her eyes tightly to repress tears.

"I'm sorry to hear that," Dan said, but he did not know whether she heard him.

Women's crying made him uncomfortable. He was about to go out to his secretary's desk for tissues when Susan fished one from her handbag and dabbed at the corners of her eyes.

"Yesterday afternoon," she continued, "I learned that Peter took all the money from our joint bank accounts—"

"Mrs. Boelter—Susan," Dan said, interrupting her. "I'm not a matrimonial lawyer."

And did not want to be. Divorce was all about money and parting and tears and loss, things that evoked too much anguish from him for too little purpose. He dealt with ultimate threats: life and death and freedom. Even more than to matrimonial work and its emotional demands, Dan had an aversion to representing the women of Susan's rarefied class; to his way of thinking, they were seeking handsome rewards for having pursued unproductive, indulged lives; they were decorative at best and obsolete at worst.

"I don't know any matrimonial lawyers," she explained. "I don't even know if I need one. You said you went through a divorce yourself."

"Well, yes," he admitted, "but it's not something I do for a living, or want to."

"Perhaps I'm being overly worried." She forced her body straighter in her seat, trying to subdue her apprehension with will power. "I . . . might just be blowing what happened out of proportion."

Moved by her despair in spite of his preconceptions, he yielded slightly. "If you'd like to tell me about it . . ."

"Thank you."

As she had when he dined at her house, she spoke with candid objectivity, even about her own involvement in events, where it might have been natural to show herself to sympathetic advantage or to elicit his pity.

"The difficulties in our marriage started three years ago. On March thirteenth. That was the day . . . This is all very hard for me to talk about. It's confidential, isn't it?"

"Yes."

She gathered her strength and began again, her voice barely above a whisper. "Peter and I had tried to have a second child for a long time. Three years ago, when I became pregnant, it seemed almost a miracle. And the tests told us it was a boy. Peter wanted a boy so much to carry on his and the family's name. But . . . but something was very wrong with the pregnancy." Her hands gripped each other so tightly that the knuckles showed white. "I miscarried, and the infant was born dead. I nearly died as well. They had to operate." She abbreviated the painful memory. "I'll never be able to have more children. After that, something seemed to go out of Peter's commitment to the marriage.

"His father died that year. Peter was so eager to step into his father's shoes in the family. It gave him a focus and a purpose. But after the baby died, he no longer seemed to care. He became frantic for distractions. I needed him then, but I understood. His loss was different from mine. I had lost a child I didn't know but already loved. Peter had lost his reason for being part of a family, his reason for caring about its destiny."

She wanted Dan to understand. "Sometimes our relationship is wonderful. For long stretches we talk and enjoy doing things together. But there's this dissatisfaction in him, like a dormant virus. All of a sudden, it can flare up and rage out of control." Her expression grew resolute. "I know, though, that when it passes, things will be good between us again."

"Was there some specific incident that preceded his leaving?"

Without going into details, she explained that on Tuesday she and Peter had argued at a board meeting and that Peter had left their home that night and emptied the bank accounts and the safety-deposit box the next day.

"I was sure he'd cool down once a little time passed. If I hire a lawyer, maybe I'm forcing this thing to a stage he never intended. It's such a drastic step. If we could just talk it out . . ."

She looked at Dan full of hope, seeking confirmation of her conjecture. He moved forward to the edge of his seat.

"Susan, I think you ought to understand that emptying bank accounts and safety-deposit boxes is the first thing that divorce lawyers advise their clients to do. The odds are pretty strong that your husband already has a lawyer."

Her face started to crumple, but then she inhaled deeply and her chin jutted forward. "Then I haven't made a mistake coming here. I want you to represent me."

"I can't—" he started to say, but she hurried on, hoping to convince him before he could refuse.

"You're somebody who stands up to Peter. People usually don't, you know. They either want something from him or are afraid of what the *Herald* might do to them. I need a lawyer I can trust to stand up to him."

Dan explained again that he and his firm handled only criminal work, not matrimonial, that he would be doing her a disservice by taking on her case, especially now that he himself was facing a trial.

"Oh, God!" she said glumly. Her skin grew as pale as a skull. "There'll be no one on my side I can trust.

"Well," she finally said, "if it has to be."

She took another deep breath and stood up. At that moment she seemed so tragic and so valiant that Dan put his hand on her arm to halt her.

"Susan, you really need a lawyer who specializes in divorce. I'll be glad to give you the names of some good ones. And if you think it'll help, you can call me whenever you want my advice."

That seemed to hearten her. "Thank you!"

She sat down again, her smile resurrecting color in her face. "Knowing that makes me feel better. You probably think I'm acting somewhat hysterical. Next to your own problems, I imagine mine sound pretty minor."

"I don't want to alarm you, but unless I miss my guess, your problems are just beginning."

7

Peter had already met with the first three lawyers to whom Dan spoke on Susan's behalf, thus precluding all three from representing her, even though Peter might not ultimately choose any of the three as his attorney.

"He's doing it to block you from hiring them," Dan surmised when she returned to his office.

Susan did not think Peter would do such a thing to her.

By afternoon she had settled on an attorney named Harold Ramsay, whom Dan convinced to see her before meeting that afternoon with Peter. Dan kept from her what he could not remedy: that Ramsay had not been on his short A-list. Within days she was served with papers from Peter's lawyer commencing a divorce action.

The weeks that followed were harrowing for Susan. She suddenly felt herself slewed through whirlpools of emotions: by turns bereft, guilty, angry, and needy as she experienced the loss or threatened loss of everything she cherished. And always some part of her believed that eventually she and Peter would reconcile.

She had become used to having money and influence, and to having the systems that structured life's complications operate with effortless deference on her behalf. She was a Boelter, the wife of the *Herald*'s publisher. People were always eager to smooth her way. It was not something she demanded, but something she had unconsciously grown used to. All of that assistance seemed to drop away at once.

Peter had ceased supporting her, and she was suddenly destitute. Checks started to bounce on bank accounts that no longer contained any funds. When she tried to charge several household items at the hardware store, the clerk informed her that her charge account had been closed. So had all her other charge accounts in the village. When she attempted to pay by credit card, she learned that Peter had also canceled those; they had been adjuncts of his own cards. Storekeepers now insisted on cash, which she did not have.

Susan had always been given a substantial allowance for running the household, for her and Karen's clothes, and for pocket money. Large items, like property taxes, Karen's tuition, and the like, had always been paid directly by Peter. Susan learned that he had failed to pay the water bill when she received a letter from the authorities warning that the water would be turned off unless she paid the overdue charges. All she could do was add that urgent need to the inventory of others she was asking her lawyer to obtain the means for her to meet.

To calculate the household and personal support Peter had provided, she scrutinized old bills and her canceled checks going back three years. Both parties would have to file statements detailing their finances. She knew that Peter would try to hide his own situation as much as possible.

Despite her desperate financial situation, Ramsay had strongly cautioned her not to take a paying job. Her case asking that Peter continue to provide funds for her to live on might be undermined if she did. Peter might even have a valid cause for removing her as the full-time, if unsalaried, head of the Boelter Foundation.

She let all of the servants go, except for a part-time stable boy and Jenny, the cook, who had been with her and Peter since their marriage. She and Jenny did all the cleaning now, and on weekends she tried to do as much of the gardening as she could.

Word of her plight traveled quickly within her social circle. She learned just how quickly when Amelia induced her to stop by the Dellwyne Country Club one afternoon to play tennis. Many people she had considered friends treated her with cold abruptness. Clearly, they had chosen to side with Peter, with whom their vested interests lay.

Bewildered, she asked her sister-in-law, "Why do they have to side with anyone?"

"I guess because they're sure Peter would want them to," Amelia answered.

That same logic, Susan knew, prevented Amelia from offering a loan to help Susan out—Peter might consider the loan an unwarranted intrusion into the squabble. But then again, Susan would never have accepted it.

Just as Susan and Amelia were sitting down to lunch in the club dining room, a man entered and walked up to their table.

"Susan Boelter?" he asked in a voice that carried easily around the large room.

"Yes."

Everybody watched the process server hand her a document. For tax purposes, her and Peter's automobiles were owned by the *Herald*. Peter had now ordered that her Jaguar be seized.

He was using every advantage the legal system gave him to tighten a noose of debt around her neck.

Particularly wearing on Susan was her loss of control over her life. From adolescence on, she had achieved whatever she set her mind on, despite having only her own wits and determination in her tool bag. When she married Peter, she knew she was relinquishing some independence in exchanging it for love and for a status as his wife that she believed to be secure and unassailable, with rights and prerogatives. John Boelter's reliance on her advice, which he trusted as much for its impartial honesty as for its astuteness, had given her great, if indirect, influence over the newspaper. He had perpetuated that role for her after his death by naming her to head the Foundation. Although Peter had sometimes resented her friendship with his father, she could not conceive of him wanting her out of his life. Or of herself ever floundering helplessly with no resources of her own, dependent on him for subsistence, fearful about her fate, at his mercy.

An area of great heartache for Susan was the effect the separation was having on Karen and on their relationship. Attempts at conversation quickly and inevitably led to recriminations, as if Karen were seeking reasons to hate her.

One night Karen's school adviser phoned Susan to discuss the deterioration teachers were noting in Karen's course work and behavior. Homework was haphazardly done, her attention was sporadic, and she had become a minor discipline problem, as well. Gingerly, the woman asked if the problem might be caused by something happening at home.

Ordinarily, Susan would have resisted an intrusion into family privacy, but this was not an ordinary time, and Karen's welfare came first. She explained the nature of the strain Karen was under. The woman had suspected as much, observing that the school often saw a behavioral change in children when marital discord was disrupting the home. She would alert the other teachers and the school's guidance counselor, a psychologist. Perhaps Susan could arrange for Karen to meet with the woman for a conversation.

Susan went looking for Karen and found her downstairs at the kitchen table, having tea with Jenny. Both were in bathrobes. The cook, a round, good-tempered woman in her fifties, who had never married, was a loving, uncritical presence in the child's life. "Poor lamb," Jenny had said to Susan when she first learned that the girl's father had left. "She's the one it's going to be hardest on." What did the two talk about during their sometimes late-night conclaves? Susan had no idea.

Both hands around her tea mug, a plate of cookies set between her and Jenny, Karen glanced up as her mother entered. Her smile instantly dissipated.

"Sorry to intrude," Susan told her daughter, "but I've got to talk to you."

Reluctantly, Karen followed her mother upstairs to her room. She took her desk chair, Susan the end of the bed, facing her. Susan informed her about the phone call from school.

Karen became furious. "You actually told Mrs. Henderson that you and Daddy were separated? Oh, God, how could you?"

"It isn't a disgrace—"

"Now every kid in school will know about it."

"I'm sure that's not so. The school's very sensitive to individual problems."

"You don't understand a thing. The teachers will all be extra polite and extra considerate. The kids will know in a second."

"Your teachers are concerned about you."

"It's none of their business!" Karen shot back. She crossed her arms. "I will never, ever forgive you for this."

"Karen, please—"

"I'm not going to school. And I'm certainly not going to reveal all my personal thoughts to some busybody woman I don't know."

"You may like her. She's got a lot of experience advising young people whose parents aren't getting along."

"Daddy would never have done this to me!"

"That's probably true. He would have considered it interference. But ignoring your problems won't make them go away."

"*You're* my problem! If you're so worried about my school work, get out of here so I can do it!"

Nothing Susan could say could induce Karen to resume their conversation.

After several weeks of ignoring her, Peter began seeing Karen on weekends. Her rebelliousness toward Susan quickly grew worse. Rules became sources of irritation. Karen seemed to go out of her way to break them, simply to test the limits of her mother's patience and her own independence.

At supper one night Karen announced that her father had given her permission to have a party that weekend at the house he had rented in Chestnut Hill. She refused to reveal whom she had invited, but Susan was sure she knew. Twice that week a boy driving a red Miata had dropped her off after school. He had to be at least four years older than Karen to have a driver's license. Susan had tried to question her daughter about him, but had gotten no answers.

"You aren't really ready for boys—for friends—who are so much older than you," Susan tried to reason with her.

"You have no right to tell me what to do when I'm with my father."

"There are some things you can't handle yet."

"Like makeup?" Karen's voice was taunting. "Daddy sees nothing wrong with makeup."

Susan's anger flashed. "You're far too young to wear makeup. You will not wear it, do you understand?"

"Daddy thinks I look good in it."

"*I'm* in charge of your upbringing, not your father. You will not wear makeup, and you will not have a party with friends who are inappropriate for you."

"I'll wear whatever I want to wear," Karen declared with arrogant fury that sounded to Susan so much like Peter.

Taken aback, Susan firmly replied, "Young lady, if you insist on using that tone of voice, I may decide that you will not see your father at all this weekend."

Karen's eyes blazed with her agitation. "You're just jealous because Daddy loves me and doesn't love you. He left you because he can't stand you, and neither can I."

Susan slapped her daughter hard across the cheek. They stared at each other for a shocked moment.

"Oh, God," Susan whispered. "I'm sorry."

Karen's hand slowly rose to touch her cheek. She ran from the room.

Only then did Susan notice that the door to the kitchen had swung open. Jenny, the cook, had entered with a tray bearing the main course.

"Please take Karen's dinner to her, Jenny," Susan requested.

Several minutes later Jenny returned with the tray. Karen did not want supper.

Susan was no longer hungry, either. She told Jenny to put dinner in the freezer. She would heat it up some other night. She then went up to her study and, for a long while, stared out the window at the sky growing dim over the garden. Finally she went to Karen's room to apologize again and to talk to her. But the door was locked from within, and Karen refused to answer her requests to open it.

Amelia and Susan's friendship had begun soon after Susan married Peter. Susan had felt enormous compassion for the other woman's loss so early in her married life and her years since as a widow. Amelia had understood the difficulty a wife faced marrying into the Boelter family, and she was drawn to Susan's strength and to what for Amelia would have been her daring frankness.

The women's closeness was enhanced by their both having to deal with their demanding mother-in-law, Amelia to a lesser degree because her parents had been among Margaret's circle of friends. Margaret had always resented Susan's close relationship with Margaret's husband. But her deepest resentment derived from the smart, strong-minded young woman's having married Peter and divided the loyalties of that favorite child, whom she had pampered and indulged and shielded from her husband's dictates.

Susan had rented an old Ford from a local auto-body shop. The morning after the incident with Karen, she drove over to Amelia's house for coffee, as she often did without calling first. Amelia had become her life preserver, the person to whom she was able to pour out her emotional distress and who provided a sympathetic ear.

She needed that sympathy now. "It was awful to slap her, I know. And as soon as I did it, I hated myself. But she provoked me so. It's as if I no longer have any hold over her."

"How is she getting along with Peter?"

"Wonderfully, to hear her tell it. Everything I do is wrong. And he can do absolutely nothing wrong."

"She's angry at you for breaking up the family," Amelia said.

"At me? I've done everything I could to keep us together."

"She'd never blame Peter. Girls all need their fathers at her age. He's gone from the house, and she needs to be sure she isn't losing him. She knows deep down she'll never lose you."

"That makes a lot of sense," Susan acknowledged with some surprise. She cherished Amelia's uncomplicated friendship, but had never considered her a source of wisdom.

"It ought to make sense. It cost me a hundred dollars. I talked it over for you this morning with my therapist."

"You discussed *me* with your therapist?" said Susan in surprise.

"I've been going to her for so long that it's a treat for both of us when we have something new to talk about."

Amelia refilled Susan's coffee cup. "You might consider boarding school. Johnny and I get along much better now."

The cup trembled for an instant in Susan's hands. "I couldn't bear for Karen to be away from me."

Amelia understood. "Just be prepared. She won't give you an easy time of it. She's trying hard to hold on to her father."

"And he's playing the role of loving parent to the hilt."

Amelia chuckled. "With all that attention, she has to be having the time of her life. We both know how charming Peter can be."

"We sure do know that," Susan stated hollowly.

Although Peter had moved away, he had been required to file for divorce in Montgomery County, where Dellwyne was located. Pennsylvania was one of the few states to adopt a no-fault divorce provision while still granting faster divorces if an innocent party could prove the other spouse was legally at fault because of desertion, adultery, cruel and barbarous treatment, bigamy, or other causes. But that was an impossibility here, because Susan was legally blameless. So to gain a no-fault divorce, Peter would have to wait for two years of separation if he could prove the marriage had irretrievably broken down. She hoped that with so much time ahead of him before he could dissolve their marriage, he might come to his senses and return home.

Harold Ramsay, her lawyer, applied to the court for continuation of the support Peter had provided Susan and Karen before the separation, which he had so abruptly and completely cut off.

As he became acquainted with the facts in Susan's case, Ramsay's initial encouragement faded, until his face became as long and lugubrious as some of the nineteenth-century barrister caricatures on his wall. His voice became doleful, as well. Although the law mandated that the property acquired by the couple during their marriage be equitably distributed between them, in Susan's case that marital property would not include either the estate in Dellwyne and its furnishings or Peter's most valuable holding, his stock in the Herald Corporation. Peter had inherited those assets from his father three years before, so they were owned by Peter alone. Any increase in their value would be shared, but the market value of both newspapers and real estate had declined since then. Still, Ramsay believed that Peter's large income would allow Susan to claim ample sums to maintain her lifestyle.

His gloom lifted somewhat when he laid out a strategy that might allow her and Karen to continue to live in the house in Dellwyne. A judge might well conclude that moving the child out of her home would be a terrible psychological blow during an already trying time. "That would prevent your husband from seizing it and would force him to pay all your household expenses. There are many ways to skin a cat, Mrs. Boelter. Things are not nearly so bleak as they may appear on the surface."

Susan's own gloom had not lifted. "Mr. Ramsay, I have no money left. Most of what I got for selling my engagement ring and the few pieces of gold jewelry that were in my dresser drawer went for your retainer."

His face brightened. "Oh, your chances are excellent to get that back when the court rules on my motion that your husband pay your legal fees."

Susan wondered whether Ramsay would be fighting as hard for his other motions as he would for that one.

He suddenly remembered something. "Your husband's lawyer did hold out one hopeful possibility: that his client might consider a reconciliation. But he said you were too stubborn to consider it."

Susan's hope soared. A reconciliation. Peter back with her.

"That's all I've wanted from the beginning," she cried out.

"I'm so pleased. Where are my notes on that?" Ramsay slowly perused the yellow pad he had scribbled on. "Ah, yes, here it is, here it is. He says that his client will be happy to return to you . . ."

"Yes," she whispered.

"All you need do, he says, is agree to the sale of his family's newspaper."

Susan's breath fled with her elation.

Ramsay pressed her for an answer. "Is that something you'd be willing to do, Mrs. Boelter?"

She finally managed to inhale and speak. "That particular point, Mr. Ramsay, is not open for negotiation."

Mason Willoughby, a man in his late sixties, leased half his office space to the Boelter Foundation, kept its books, and dispensed the grant money for it as Susan directed. He had been her father-in-law's accountant, executor of his will, and his trusted friend. He had become her friend, as well.

Susan did not sleep very much that night. The next morning she drove to the office suite they shared. He had suspected that she and Peter were having problems. Now she had to tell him that they had separated.

"Peter said he was tired of being my employee," she explained. "He says he'll come back to me if I agree to his selling the *Herald*."

Mason Willoughby was a man whose tact and formality derived from an earlier, more courteous era. He thought carefully before he took an important action or gave an opinion, disbursing his words as frugally as he did money.

His thumb and forefinger pulled down the corners of his mouth, lengthening the lines carved deeply along the inner flanks of his cheeks. The same two fingers then removed his tortoise-shell glasses, laid them on the blotter, and squared them up within the rectangular space. Finally he spoke.

"I think giving in to Peter would be a mistake."

"Perhaps if I resigned from the Foundation. That would remove the aggravation from our relationship . . ."

"An even bigger mistake—and a failure of your duty."

"There seems to be a difference of opinion as to what my duty is."

"Do you think you're wrong to reject a sale of the *Herald?*"

"No, I don't," she said. "But let's be honest, I'm not one of John Boelter's heirs. It's crazy that I should have a bigger vote than any of them."

"That's exactly the way John wanted it."

"Yes, I know. When he was dying, he made me swear I'd always vote my conscience, no matter what. But I never understood why he picked me."

"He trusted you. He believed you'd never act for your own benefit, but only for the family's. And the city's, too, and the paper's employees'. You were the one person in the family whose integrity and judgement he was sure he could count on. He knew just how important that forty-percent vote might be someday."

"Important enough to ruin my marriage?"

"Do you want my opinion on that, too?"

"Yes."

"Your resignation won't end the strife and induce Peter to return."

"Then what will?"

Mason realigned the already aligned glasses while he decided how to put his feelings into words. "Susan, I view Peter far more critically than you. If this . . . this crisis had not occurred, I would never have said what I'm about to, but you asked my opinion."

"I value it, Mason."

His gaze lifted to hers. "I consider Peter Boelter selfish, immature, and manipulative. He utilizes his charm or whatever else he can muster to get his way. His father had to pay a lot of money and pull a lot of strings to silence potential scandals—"

She interrupted. "That was before we were married."

"I always suspected that Peter married you to get back into his father's good graces."

Susan felt wounded by the harsh evaluation of the man she still loved so dearly, an evaluation that belittled her own worth to him. Her entire being had been focused on the hope of Peter's return.

"He married me because he loved me. There were so many women in his life who were rich and pretty . . ."

"But none that his father admired like you. Your feelings finally caused him to soften toward Peter. . . . And, I suppose, so did Richard's death."

She shook her head. "He understood that Peter was ready to take on responsibility and settle down."

"But he also knew his son. The only thing Peter respects is power. By putting the Foundation in your hands, John gave you power over Peter. He knew that someday it might protect you."

Willoughby ignored the anguish on Susan's face. "If you relinquish that power, any chance you might have to win Peter back will be lost, if that's what you want—or to gain a fair divorce settlement, which might be more sensible."

Susan did not reply, but ruminated as she stared at the elderly accountant.

He interrupted her thoughts. "Susan, if you need any money . . ."

She touched his arm in gratitude. "Thank you, Mason. That's very generous. But I won't borrow anything from anyone. I really just wanted your advice."

"Which wasn't exactly what you wanted to hear, I gather."

"You don't know Peter like I do."

"Perhaps. But please promise me something."

He waited for her to nod. Only then did he go on.

"Promise me that you won't do anything rash—anything that would lower your guard. You might not think I know your husband, but I do—and have since the day he was born. Unless you have something he wants or fears, Peter Boelter will stomp all over you."

8

Early one morning a blond white woman, age twenty-five, was found unconscious in a parking lot at Thirteenth and Locust. Working late in a dress shop, she had been attacked when she went to her car. Brutally beaten, with her underclothes torn away and her skirt pulled up over her head, she was close to death when she was found.

As expected, the motive proved to be rape. Vaginal swabs showed the presence of seminal fluid. As was also true with Cassy Cowell and Jane Hopkins, however, no defense wounds, such as broken nails or scratches, could be found to indicate the victim had fought back and the rapist had not been a secreter, so his blood type could not be determined or matched to those of suspects.

The victim, whose name was being withheld because of the sensitive nature of the crime, proved to be luckier than the first two women, however; she would live. When she finally regained consciousness a day later, she spoke to the two detectives in charge of the investigation, but could add little to what they already knew. She had never seen her attacker. An arm from behind had garroted her. Unable to breathe, she passed out. She remembered briefly waking, but being unable to see. Cloth covered her face, and a man was on top of her, trying to penetrate her sexually. She grabbed at his genitals to push him out of her. A fist hit her face hard, and then some part of him, maybe a forearm, pressed down on her windpipe. That was the last thing she remembered.

The detectives thanked her and withdrew from her room. Even before talking to her, they had been sure that her attacker was the same person who killed Jane Hopkins and Cassy Cowell. All three women had been attacked in a similar manner from behind, only a few blocks from each other. This time, though, the attacker had left a clue: A hospital nurse cleaning up the victim had discovered among her blond pubic hairs a single dark one. That fact was being kept from the public as the police searched for the attacker.

Harry Stallworth had been in charge of the Hopkins and Cowell cases and had testified at Ricardo Montano's preliminary arraignment. In his forties, the stocky man was fighting a bulging waistline and beginning to bald, but wore a full, neat beard and mustache because shaving caused a painful rash. He had risen steadily to the top detective rank. He hoped no one would try to promote him any higher, although he never told that to his wife, who would have liked the increase in pay. He did not want to spend his days behind a desk watching the people under him go out on cases. He loved being a detective.

His partner was a young white woman named Kate Bascombe. She had been moved into Homicide after Cassy Cowell's body was discovered because, being young and pretty like the victim, she could play decoy to help catch the killer. Stallworth had quickly learned that she was a capable detective.

As they walked out to their car parked near the hospital's entrance, they were met by Scott Feller, who was just stepping out of his own car.

"Got anything, guys?" he asked.

Stallworth frowned. The *Daily Mirror* had allotted yesterday's crime a paragraph only on an inside City page. But Feller had recognized the similarity to the earlier crime and, tapping his Police Department sources, had learned that investigators believed they were dealing with the same man. This morning the *Herald*'s front page had proclaimed, "RAPIST-KILLER ATTACKS NEW VICTIM." Feller's story, which had nicknamed the attacker the "Phantom Rapist," had increased the pressure on the police to find the perpetrator.

"Have you talked to Montano yet?" Feller inquired.

"He has an alibi," Stallworth gruffly replied. It wasn't the tightest alibi he had ever heard, but that wasn't any of Feller's business.

Stallworth was not surprised that the reporter addressed no questions to Kate Bascombe. She and Feller had dated for a while, but she broke it off when something she had confided in the repose of her bedroom appeared under his byline. "Fucking user!" she had growled. One thing you had to give Bascombe, Stallworth conceded: She had a way with words.

Feller asked several more questions, receiving no information. Stallworth was about to end the interview and get going, when the reporter asked, "Why wasn't Tim Feeney a suspect in the Cowell killing, at least?"

"For one thing, nobody reported seeing his truck parked near the alley. You've got to figure at least one or two cars would have passed by. A case with that much publicity, the chances are someone would have let us know if they'd seen it."

"A sex act doesn't have to take that long—"

"Harry," Bascombe acidly interjected, "Scott's speaking from experience."

Stallworth ignored her jab and responded to the reporter. "He was only six minutes late getting to the next newsstand. He'd have had to see her on the street, park, drag her half a block down the alley, rape and kill her, and then come back to the truck. With all that, someone would sure as hell have heard something. Even if he'd been a few minutes early when he parked there, I figure he couldn't have had the time."

"He didn't need to show off his technique," Feller replied. "All he had to do was cover her mouth while he pulled her back into the alley, hold her down, ejaculate, and dump her body."

"Sounds like your kind of evening," Bascombe remarked.

Stallworth continued, "I just don't see someone on the job jumping out of a truck for a quick rape. No stalking, no time to build up the inner excitement, to threaten her."

"But it *is* possible," Feller continued. "Feeney could have been thinking about it for hours, just looking for a victim who was alone and vulnerable."

"You two should double-date," Bascombe observed.

Stallworth remained dubious about Feller's reasoning. "If the three crimes *were* committed by the same man—I said 'if,' now; I'm not saying that they were—but *if* they were, that leaves Feeney out of it. He's been in prison for weeks."

Feller shook his head. "Yesterday a judge forced Huyton to release him on bail on the drug charge."

"Shit!"

No one had informed the detectives. Stallworth broke off the conversation and slid behind the wheel of his blue Ford.

"One more thing," Feller pointed out, leaning into the open car door. "Feeney's black Irish. Dark hair, like Montano. Like that hair they just found on the parking-lot victim."

Doubly irritated now, Stallworth slammed the car door shut and rolled down the window. "You print one word about that hair or any other clue we haven't publicly reported, and I'll arrest *you* for the fucking crimes!"

He hit the gas pedal and roared away.

"Wouldn't that be nice," Bascombe remarked when they were into the flow of traffic.

"He knows more than he should about the case. All kidding aside, Kate, is he the rapist type?"

She snapped her safety belt into place. "They all are."

The partners let the silence drift on. Stallworth wanted to reflect on the conversation with Scott Feller and the troubling notion that Tim Feeney could no longer be eliminated as the rapist-killer. He had suspected that Feeney might have ID'ed Montano to divert suspicion from himself, but Huyton had been so pleased to have an eyewitness lock up their case that he rammed Montano's arrest through while leaving the responsibility with the police force. The DA had gone to his political ally, the mayor, and goaded him into chewing out the police commissioner for dragging his feet when "they already have the killer in custody." Stallworth had indeed taken Montano in for questioning, but as he grew increasingly doubtful that he possessed sufficient evidence to make an arrest, the police commissioner phoned him personally, bypassing several levels of command, and ordered him to arrest Montano for the crime.

Stallworth had heard in confidence from a friend up at headquarters that after the charges against Montano were dismissed, Huyton blamed the case's failure to stick in court, which made him personally look bad, on sloppy police work. The mayor then blasted the police commissioner for the error, while warning him not to mention a word about the dispute and to collar the rapist fast—whoever the son of a bitch was—with charges that would stand up.

Questioning Feeney now about the attacks, Stallworth reasoned, could be a fast route back to pounding a beat. The DA was building an important case against Dan Lazar for bribing Feeney and would not feel very charitable toward a cop who suddenly made Feeney a suspect.

The phone's ring jarred Dan awake. He groped for the receiver and opened one eye enough to glance at the clock radio. Four thirty-seven.

"Hello."

"Hi."

"Jamie?" He sat up and turned on the bed lamp.

"Yeah, Dad, it's me."

"Are you all right? It's one-thirty out there."

"I guess so."

Dan always phoned his son in California before the boy's ten P.M. bedtime. "Are you okay? Is something wrong?"

"It's Mom and that dork Ronald."

"Ronald?" Dan was still trying to shake the fog out of his brain. "Is he the one you said had the car dealership?"

"Two. Fords and Toyotas. He took me to the back where they work on them. That part's pretty cool."

"Then what's bothering you? Why are you up at one-thirty?"

Dan had given up cigarettes seven years before. But it was at odd moments like these that he missed them. A cigarette would somehow formalize his waking state and dress the act of speaking to his son at this strange hour with the trappings of normality.

"Ronald's sleeping over tonight. They don't think I know. They waited till I was in bed, but I could hear them coming up the stairs and giggling a lot. You know how Mom gets when she's all giggly?"

"Yes." At least he and his son shared an unfavorable opinion of her giggling state.

"Well, I'm sure they're in there doing it. I mean that's why she had to be getting giggly, right?"

Dan felt a pang at not having known that his son even knew what "it" was and that adults did "it" for fun. During their brief visits or their phone conversations, discussing "it" had never seemed appropriate. His son was growing up in great leaps he could only guess at when they were apart or glimpse during odd moments like this one.

But how did he himself feel about Hannah's making love to another man? Throughout their contentious marriage and often more contentious separation, in which Jamie's welfare became the shuttlecock endlessly batted back and forth, the thought that she might take a lover had never crossed his mind. That was not Hannah; she was a nesting creature who had mistakenly built her nest with the wrong mate in the wrong place.

A small pang of jealousy squeezed his heart. The Surfing Rabbi's daughter had a body bred to adorn California beaches and out of place in adult clothing. He remembered long legs that drew him inside her like narrowing stockyard fences, but little about her performance as a lover, whether she was sensuous or perfunctory or ardent. He supposed she was none of those things because he could not remember. Yet he felt conflicted by this news of her sexual activity. She had once been his, and somehow, among his instincts, she still was. Now she had escaped the last of his proprietary assumptions.

"Your mom's an adult, Jamie. She has a right to have a boyfriend."

Dan supposed that was true, but not in her own house and when Jamie was there. Dan determined to have it out with her on the phone in the morning.

The resentment in the boy's voice crested. "He keeps wanting to

'shoot hoops' with me. That's what he calls it, like I'm going to think
he's a regular guy if he says, 'Let's shoot some hoops.' I mean, Dad,
that's something I do with you.''

Oh, God! Dan thought. He's as terrified as I am that someone will take
my place.

Dan forced himself to say, "Just because you do it with him doesn't
mean we can't do it when we're together.''

"Mom keeps telling me to be nice to him. If she loves him so much,
let her go 'shoot some hoops' with him. I mean, Dad . . . I really think
she's serious about this guy!''

Now Dan fully, finally understood the boy's concern. Hannah, the
nester, had found someone to share her nest. Jamie did not know where
that left Dan—or him.

"Jamie, I'm your father. I'll always be your father. Nothing your mom
does is going to change the way she and I feel about you.''

"I miss you a lot, Dad.''

"I miss you, too, Jamie.''

"It would really be great if you were here.''

"I'll come out soon. I promise. We had a great time skiing over New
Year's, didn't we? But I just can't right now. I've got stuff here that's too
important.'' He tried to chuckle. "Cal will have my head if I don't stick
around.''

"Say hello to him for me, Dad.''

"I will, Jamie.''

"Oh, Dad, one thing. Nobody calls me Jamie anymore. Could you call
me Jim or James?''

Dan could barely speak. "Sure, no problem,'' he finally managed to
say. "You'd better get to bed. You've got school tomorrow.''

"Right, Dad.''

As they exchanged good-byes, Dan thought the boy sounded reassured after voicing his fears. He himself felt bleak. Nothing was more important to him than his son, but his fucking ex-wife was trying to lock
him out of the boy's life in favor of this character she had scrounged
up, this . . . car dealer!

Sleep would be impossible now. He decided to go running along the
river and maybe afterward to the health club for a workout. He stood up
and winced as pain sliced through his knee. He started to jog in place,
hoping stoicism would discipline the pain to recede. But it grew worse,
and he remembered that the orthopedist had scheduled him for an MRI at
eight forty-five.

He reached for the book he had been reading the night before, but then
withdrew his hand and went, instead, to the front door to see whether the

newspaper had yet been delivered. The book would be too depressing right now. It had been tracing the wanderings of Spain's Jews across Christian Europe as they sought sanctuary after the Expulsion. Long excluded from France, Italy, and England, they were victims of universal hatred, belonging nowhere, having only each other, refugees in a menacing world who vainly awaited the coming of a messianic age for their salvation.

More and more, Dan himself had been feeling like that.

Later that morning he directed the taxi taking him from the hospital to his office to stop alongside City Hall long enough for him to pick up something to eat at Rooney's snack bar.

The ex-cop folded his arms and glared at Dan. "I see where your boy Montano was out on the town last night. Raped some woman in a parking lot. Make you feel good?"

"What are you talking about?"

Rooney shoved a copy of the *Herald* at Dan. "Has to be Montano."

"Give me a break. Without knowing where Montano was last night, you're ready to hang him and ask questions afterward."

"Shit, Dan, we can't let the guy keep running wild and attacking women like this. I figure your best bet is to cop a murder three on the homicide, and the DA drops the rapes."

"Rooney, you want to prosecute people by ESP, or do you want to sell me a Three Musketeers and a package of cheese crackers?"

"All that fat and sugar, not to mention the—"

Rooney's wife grabbed Dan's money and handed him a paper bag containing the candy and crackers. She glared at her husband.

"Sometimes I want to put another bullet in there!"

Cal was waiting when Dan hobbled into the office.

"How did the MRI go?" Cal asked.

"Did you know they lock you into a metal tube for three-quarters of an hour?" Dan grumbled. "A tube! Scary as hell. You think they're either going to shoot you out the end like a torpedo or seal it up and bury you like toxic waste."

"They going to operate?"

"The orthopedist will let me know tomorrow after he gets the tests."

"Montano tried to reach you," Cal informed his partner. "I took the call. He says the police have really been hassling him. He's not running any girls on the street anymore, but Stallworth somehow found out where he'd moved to and stopped by to question him about this new rape case."

"Did you tell him to say we represent him and the cops have to speak to us?"

"I told him," Cal said. "He swears he didn't do it."

"We both know what that's worth."

"The problem is he hasn't got the best alibi for that night. His new apartment is only a few blocks from the parking lot on Locust where they found the woman."

Dan glanced down at a pink phone message he had picked up at Mary Alice's desk. "That may be why Mara phoned me."

"You sound disappointed. Did you really think she'd want to kiss and make up?"

Dan shrugged noncommittally.

Cal shook his head. "One thing you can be sure of with that woman: Whatever she's doing now and whoever she's doing it with, she sure isn't looking back."

Mary Alice made an appointment for Dan to see Mara the next morning.

At her insistence, Susan's lawyer had moved for the Montgomery County court to order that Peter attend marriage counseling sessions. Although Peter was still withholding money from her, and his lawyer was successfully delaying the support hearing she had anticipated would alleviate her financial distress, she was desperately hoping that talking out their disagreements with the help of a professional might bring Peter and her back together.

Because of the court order, Peter showed up. Struck anew by his looks, Susan remembered her pride and jealousy when women's eyes followed him across a room. The coolest women seemed to melt when he chatted with them, in part, she guessed, because a large component of his appeal was a youthful audacity that could verge on insolence. Simultaneously charming and insolent, that was Peter.

His gaze fell on her as he took a seat. She smiled instinctively, wondering whether that was the right thing to do.

He tipped his head and smiled back. "How are you? You're looking a little thin."

What should she answer? she asked herself. That she was eating less to save money or that she had no appetite and sometimes could not even hold anything down? Both were true.

"You're looking well," she replied. That, too, was true.

Peter said nothing more until the therapist asked him to recount his list of marital grievances. He named several, but was unwilling to discuss ways to resolve them and repair the marriage.

At the end of the session Susan asked Peter directly to provide her with the support payments he had been withholding, if not for her sake, at least for Karen's.

"That's for the court to decide," he replied coldly. "And so is this."

He drew an envelope from his pocket and, handing it to her, strode from the room.

Inside were legal papers. As she unfolded the document, her gaze fell on a phrase that burned out her eyes like cobra venom: "the best interests of the child would be served if she lived with her father."

Instantly, Susan understood. Peter was now seeking custody of Karen.

A meeting at the Foundation with an arts group had been scheduled for the end of the day, but Susan was too distraught and phoned to cancel.

Desolate, she drove home slowly. Everything was being snatched from her. Peter was trying to force her out of the house and into poverty, leaving her with nothing. Having already seen much of Karen's security chopped away, Susan considered it essential that the child not be uprooted. The frightening thought struck her that a judge might use that very same reasoning to restore Peter's house to him and grant him custody.

My God, how could Peter say Karen would be better off with him? Susan had been almost totally responsible for Karen's upbringing, often having to coax Peter to take part. Although an occasionally affectionate father, proud of Karen's beauty and cleverness, he was far more frequently a careless one, negligent about her welfare and about the pyschological bruises his word or act might inflict. Now he was seeking to take Karen from her. She guessed he must have decided that if the cost of gaining his objectives in the divorce was living with his daughter for a while, well, it was a big house.

Susan began to shake with fear. She managed to pull to the shoulder of the expressway and thrust the gearshift into park. Tears were streaming down her face, and she was shaking so hard that she hugged the steering wheel for stability. The horn's blare sounded like a keening in her brain. She had always been so strong; no setback could intimidate her. Her strength, her single-mindedness, had gotten her everything in life she had grown up wanting. But now, for the first time, she was terrified, not only because she lacked money again, but because of Karen. She feared for her daughter under the care of so heedless a parent as Peter, and she feared for her own loneliness if she were to lose her.

Nearly twenty minutes went by before she was able to resume the drive home.

*　　*　　*

At the sound of footsteps on the stairway, Karen came out of her room and followed her mother into the bathroom, where Susan had gone to wash her face. She waited until her mother had finished drying off.

"Daddy just called me. He says he wants me to live here with him."

Susan felt a cold wind race through her veins. "How do you feel about it?"

Karen allowed what might have been spite to peek out from behind her smile. "Daddy and I wouldn't have to wait till weekends to do things together. Oh, he's coming to the Devon to watch me ride. It might get a little hairy if you came, too."

Susan loved to watch Karen ride. The child was gifted on a horse. The Devon Horse Show was the premier equestrian event of the year, as well as the most socially prestigious. Peter wanted his friends to see him there with his daughter—and without Susan.

"He says you'll have to sell the horses," Karen added.

"Not Prince," Susan assured her. Karen's horse meant too much to her, Susan knew, and she was too good a rider. Other sacrifices would be made, but not that one.

"He also says you'll probably have to fire Jenny."

"Probably. We haven't got very much money."

"Daddy doesn't want your money problems to hurt me. He says it will be terrific to live with me."

Susan kept her voice calm. "Honey, I know this may be difficult for you to accept, but he's using your feelings for him to get at me. If you live here with him, he saves a lot of money that would go to support us here together. He knows how much you love him and how afraid you are to lose him."

"He loves me!" she replied in staunch defense.

"Did he ever pay this much attention to you before?"

"He couldn't because you always interfered. He told me that."

Susan took her daughter's hands. "I'm sure in his way he does love you. But right now he's using your feelings for him."

"He told me you'd say that," Karen retorted fiercely. "He told me you'd say he was doing it for the money. But he loves me. He's the one who wants me to be happy."

Karen yanked her hands away and rushed out of the bathroom.

The two ate dinner in near silence. At first Susan tried to make conversation, but receiving only grunted replies, she soon gave up the effort and lapsed into disheartened thought about her worries again.

After dinner she went to tell Jenny that she could afford to keep her on for only two more weeks. She hoped Jenny could find work soon.

"Mr. Boelter already called to tell me that he'd like me to come work for him," Jenny informed her.

"Oh!" Susan could only reply. "That's good. You'll still see Karen."

"That's what Mr. Boelter said."

Peter, ordinarily so negligent about others' feelings, had already thought of that, as well. Susan felt like a chess piece being systematically surrounded.

"Isn't George now working for him, too?"

"Yes, weekdays, like I'd be. It will be nice not to have to make acquaintances all over again."

"Well, then, things have worked out well for you."

Jenny's face displayed her concern. "Mrs. Boelter, how are you going to take care of this big house by yourself?"

"I'll cook for myself and close off most of the rooms. I thought maybe I'd board some horses for other people, to help pay for the stable boy."

"It's such a shame this whole thing, Mrs. Boelter."

"Thank you, Jenny."

Back up in her study, Susan could barely think. Peter was simultaneously seeking to take the child and convincing her to come. And Karen was listening to him, believing him. Susan's fear of losing her daughter began to overwhelm her.

She started to lift the receiver to talk to Amelia and then remembered that her sister-in-law had said she would be out tonight. Distraught, she paced her bedroom until well after midnight.

Susan woke early after patches of fretful sleep and saw Karen off on the school bus. She then drove over to Amelia's house for one of their breakfast talks.

She stepped onto the concrete driveway near the kitchen and noticed a dark-blue Mercedes roadster parked almost out of sight behind a shed. Recognizing it, she raced into the house through the kitchen door, past the maid preparing breakfast, and up the stairs. She burst into the master bedroom.

"You fucking bastard!" Susan screamed.

Amelia and Peter, naked, were jolted awake. Peter sat up. Amelia grabbed for the blanket to cover herself.

"You're bastards! Both of you!"

Susan flung herself at Amelia, who was nearest to her, pummeling her frightened sister-in-law and screaming obscenities at her.

Peter jumped from the bed and pulled Susan off of Amelia. He flung her up against the wall.

"Get hold of yourself and act like a lady."

"How could you do this to me?" she yelled at him. "How could both of you do this to me?"

"With great pleasure," he answered. "You didn't expect me to give up sex just because I couldn't bear to have it with you, did you?"

She fought to strike him, but he held her wrists too firmly.

"Anything to get you what you want!" she screamed. "You fucking . . . fucking . . ." Her words were drowned in sobs.

She ripped her hands free and rushed to the door.

The maid had not been quick enough to stop Susan downstairs, but now she was standing in the doorway. Susan ran by her and out of the house.

Never in her life had Susan acted so irrationally, so emotionally, but never in her life had her deepest emotions been so provoked. She felt utterly betrayed.

9

Dan's copy of the *Herald* was open to the Sports pages. Two other lawyers, older men, who had already finished breakfast and were on their way out of Hi, Johnny's, had stopped at his booth to chat with him. Both were paunchy and had shoulders bent into roundness by decades of slogging to make a living from other people's tragedies.

"The Seventy-sixers, Charlie?" Dan teased. "You took the Seventy-sixers and got only three points against the Bulls. In Chicago?"

The short man in a gray suit nodded back glumly.

Dan shook his head in mock despair. "If the City Welfare people booked your bets, they'd have the money to end homelessness."

The man was eager to change the subject. "How's your problem with the DA going, Dan? That's more important."

"The only way I could lose, Charlie, is if you bet on me."

The other men broke into laughter as they continued toward the front of the restaurant. Dan wished that he felt as confident as he sounded.

Dan noticed a tall, blond, very well dressed woman standing just inside the entrance looking around for someone. The woman, he realized, was Susan Boelter.

She caught sight of him at the same moment, smiled slightly with relief, and headed toward his booth. She had to be greatly concerned about something to seek him out here instead of phoning for an appointment, yet her expression appeared serene and her confident carriage unburdened by the merest apprehension. Breeding, again, he decided. You can't beat good breeding for looking good under pressure.

He greeted her, rising out of his seat.

"Your office told me I'd probably find you here," she began.

He motioned toward the unoccupied side of the banquette, and she slipped into it.

"You said if I needed someone to talk to . . ." The words trailed into silence. Then she quickly added, "If it's an imposition or you're busy, please tell me and—"

He discerned a faint quiver of her bottom lip she could not control and said, "I meant it."

"Peter seems to be getting his way in everything."

She suddenly bent her head, struggling to contain herself. Half a minute passed before, once more in command of her emotions, she began to recount the events of the last eighteen hours. She spoke simply and clearly, with no self-bias or plea for sympathy. Again that candor, he noted. Emotion halted her only twice, the first time when she mentioned that Peter was seeking custody of their daughter and the second when she reported having just come from finding him with Amelia.

"You actually walked in on them naked in bed?" Dan sought to confirm.

"I'm afraid I lost control of myself. I hit her and tried to hit him."

"Real punches?"

"As hard as I could. At that moment, if I could have killed them both—" She took a deep breath.

"You surprise me," he said with a laugh.

"It's not funny."

"The idea of you losing control, as you put it, seems as likely to me as you mud wrestling."

Susan's mouth clenched, and she started to slide out of the booth. Dan's hand stopped her.

"I'm sorry. I didn't mean to insult you. Actually, it was a compliment."

"My reaction in that bedroom was unforgivable. But I'm glad I saw them and could stop fooling myself."

Dan thought he should advise her. "It might help in court. You no longer have to go the no-fault route, if it's not to your advantage. His adultery makes you the injured party. That might translate into a larger award."

"I wasn't thinking that. I just want what I'm rightly entitled to. I thought marriage was a partnership, I really did. We each did our part and should share equally."

"That's a lot of money for a judge to take away from a very influential man."

"Ramsay says that, too." She paused. "Every time I think things can't get worse, they do. Now I might lose my daughter. In the legal papers Peter claims I'm an unfit mother. God!"

Susan dipped her head, fighting back tears. After several seconds she looked up again at Dan. "You know the worst thing about this custody fight he's started for Karen? In my heart, I'm sure he really doesn't want her."

"And what about Amelia, did Peter want *her*?"

Susan scrutinized Dan's face to be certain she wasn't being ridiculed. "I . . . I don't think so. But don't ask me, I'm the wife."

"Why would he sleep with her then?"

"He needs her vote to sell the *Herald*."

Susan explained John Boelter's reasons for making her sole trustee of the Foundation and her suspicion that Peter was now working to convince the other shareholders in his family to vote for a sale of the *Herald*, thus overcoming her opposition.

"Amelia's brain follows her heart—and parts south," Susan observed. "He's already got her vote."

"That's what you were all doing that day I ran into you at the *Herald*, deciding whether to sell the paper?"

She revealed Peter's secret negotiations with Oren Lawlor, that the *Herald*'s price was depressed because of the recession, and that Lawlor intended to close down the paper in favor of the *Daily Mirror*.

"For the time being, I'm standing in Peter's way." Bitterness slid back into her tone. "Someone recently told me that the only way to protect myself from him is to fight the sale. He said that if Peter doesn't need someone, if he senses powerlessness, he'll destroy that person without a second thought."

"And not selling the *Herald*, is that important to you?"

She gestured toward the open newspaper. "Do you ever read the *Mirror*?"

"The *Mirror*'s a rag."

"Then you know why I can't let him sell the *Herald*."

Dan had something else to say, but the young woman who owned the restaurant, noticing that a waitress had not come by the table, hurried over to take the order. He folded up the newspaper.

"Hi, Johnny," Dan greeted her, and introduced her to Susan, who decided on the sourdough walnut raisin roll and coffee.

Dan grimaced and ordered his usual chocolate doughnut and coffee.

"There really is a Johnny," Susan said.

"There *was*. Two owners ago. The baker ran off with his wife. She was big as a house, but both guys were crazy about her. Johnny was inconsolable. He used to stand around staring at the cash register, where she used to sit. Finally he sold the place."

"And you all called the next owner Johnny, too, because that was the name over the door."

"Right. So, she's the third Johnny."

Susan laughed. "What's her real name?"

"Never asked. Would ruin the mystique."

"And I'll bet that chocolate doughnut is the same thing you ordered back then."

Dan, agreeing, laughed, too. "Coffee wasn't as good, though."

Susan sat back, still smiling. "Less than an hour ago I never thought I'd laugh again. You were the right person to come to."

"Made me feel better, too."

Susan's expression clouded. "I forgot. I was so wrapped up in my own problems, I forgot about yours."

"Hey, I'm fine, not a care in the world. Good food. Good company."

She was studying him. "You're worried."

Dan was about to fashion another denial when she stopped him. "Please. At least be as forthright with me as I've been with you."

Johnny appeared with the breakfast order, giving Dan time to consider Susan's request.

"I'm not exactly *worried*," Dan finally admitted, when they were alone. "But I don't know if I can find a word for it. If I could, maybe I could cure it."

They ate in silence until Susan put down her coffee cup and said, "What should I do, Dan . . . about Peter and the divorce? How do I fight him?"

"You said he wants your vote to sell the *Herald*. Well, to get what you want from him, you might have to agree to it. That seems to be your only bargaining chip."

"Never," she said, shaking her head. "Never."

"If it was Karen or the *Herald*, which would you choose to keep?"

"What a callous way to put it!"

"That's what it may come down to. Love versus duty, which one?"

Susan refused to consider the question.

The district attorney's office was across from Penn Square and City Hall. Walking toward it along Arch Street, Dan felt the ache in his knee. He had just been to the orthopedist. The MRI had revealed a torn cartilege. An operation would be needed to repair it. The doctor had also found arthritis corroding the knee joint, but could do nothing about that. He had cautioned Dan against jogging, which would speed up the disease's ravages. Dan suddenly felt much older.

He climbed stiff-legged up the front steps of the handsomely renovated brick office building. Although a brass plate indicated that it contained the district attorney's office, far more boldly and prominently placed in the pediment above the front doors was the name of its previous occupant: "YMCA."

"Mara Szarek," he told the detective at the long, high desk in the lobby.

He signed in and waited while the detective, a younger man he did not recognize, phoned upstairs for confirmation. The lobby's rich paneling gleamed softly under the indirect lighting. A dark-red carpet enhanced the understated opulence. The contrast from the department's former cramped and run-down premises still startled him.

The weather had turned unexpectedly hot and caught him off guard. He had dressed in a wool suit, which now stuck to his shirt and his legs. Occasional rivulets of sweat trickled down his ribs. Adding to his discomfort, the air-conditioning seemed to be out of order, making the building's interior even warmer than the outdoors.

Dan pressed seven as the elevator doors closed. He exited onto a vestibule open to the skylighted atrium and walked through glass doors into the building itself. He sought Mara's office along the sterile white corridors faintly highlighted with beige door bucks and blue colonial trim on the woodwork. The premises would be relatively empty until the courts adjourned for lunch and the lawyers and detectives rushed back to make phone calls and consult with each other. At two o'clock, when the courts reconvened, this floor would empty again.

"You holding up okay, Dan?" a hoarse voice called out.

The speaker was Eddie Grecco, the detective who arrested Dan on behalf of the DA.

"Yeah, I'm fine," Dan answered. "Just here for a conference."

"Who with?"

"Szarek. I'm looking for her conference room."

Grecco furtively glanced around to make certain no one was paying undue attention to them, then spoke with exaggerated casualness. "Let me show you where it is."

He slipped into the room behind Dan and shut the door.

"Dan, I'm real sorry I had to take you in."

"I told you that day, Eddie, couldn't be helped."

"Well, the whole thing stinks. I just wanted you to know that. They're having trouble with the charges themselves."

"What have you heard?"

"You know who Evie Jeeter is?"

"Feeney's girlfriend."

"Right. They located her in a motel in Bucks County, and she agreed to come back for questioning. She broke up with Feeney, and now she's changed her story because she's got no reason to protect the guy anymore."

"What's she saying?"

"She says she looked out of their place on Sixteenth that morning and saw you with Feeney, but never saw any money change hands. The first time she saw the cash was when he came inside and pulled the roll out of his pocket. They've had her here all morning, but can't get her to tie you directly to the cash."

"Thanks, Eddie. How's Huyton treating you?"

"The guy doesn't trust cops. He knows I'm an old-timer here and in line for a promotion, and he's just waiting for me to fuck up." Grecco glanced up at the clock. "Hang in there."

A moment later he was gone like a passing shadow, and Dan slipped into one of the contemporary black leather chairs to await Mara and Gil Huyton.

Minutes passed slowly by. Dan glanced frequently at the large round clock. He remembered clocks like this in school that stretched time into endless, ticking monotony. His mind would quickly wander from a tedious lecture to the opportunities a waiting world held out like a fistful of Atlantic City sightseeing brochures. As he got older, he realized that the opportunities were far fewer than he had fantasized, that if you weren't born rich, you had to fight for every one. Otherwise, you got nothing. So, you worked your way through Temple University because you couldn't afford Penn or Princeton and you delivered pizzas in Margate if you wanted a summer at the Jersey Shore. And it also meant you fought for bigger things: You marched in civil rights rallies and led your college cronies in sit-ins. But it meant, too, that when your country asked you to fight, you owed it that duty, and you enlisted in the Marines, even though you knew it meant you'd go to Vietnam.

Dan decided that after fifteen minutes of being kept waiting, he would make a show of his aggravation and stalk out. Just as the clock ticked the quarter hour, the door opened and Mara entered. Despite the heat, she looked cool, dry, and chic.

Instead of taking a chair, she sat on the edge of the table facing him. Her voice was tender with concern.

"How are you doing, Dan? I hope the bribery charges haven't gotten you down."

"Hey, every morning I wake up and feel good all over just knowing that I'm Gil Huyton's very own personal accused."

"Wait till I tell you what I've gotten him to agree to in your case."

"The death penalty, with time off for good behavior?"

"He's willing to drop the criminal charges."

Dan's eyebrow lifted cynically. "I take it you located Evie Jeeter, and she wouldn't lie about seeing me take money from her boyfriend."

"Yes," Mara replied, momentarily thrown off stride.

"So, Huyton has no choice; he *has* to drop the charges."

"He isn't ready to go that far. He thinks there's still enough to have you disbarred by the Disciplinary Board."

Dan displayed his anger. "Lawyers who steal from their clients get disbarred! Not lawyers who do their jobs by trying to find out what the testimony will be against their client!"

Mara leaned forward excitedly. "That's it exactly. Montano."

As she gripped the table edge for balance, her arms pressed against the sides of her breasts, deepening the crevice visible just above the open collar. The well-remembered perfume was dizzying.

She's absolutely irresistible, Dan thought. All of her. Her rolls of dark hair, the startling blue eyes framed by the long lashes, that seductive mouth, the smoky, sensual accent. She's the least reliable woman I've ever known, and yet I still want her desperately. Like a fly who yearns to be eaten alive by the spider who ignored him.

"Exactly what *about* Montano?" he asked.

"I understand he didn't go back to Colombia."

"No."

"This must be very difficult for him, still living in a city where people believe he may be a rapist and even a killer, and he can't prove that he's not."

"The man's a pimp and a lowlife, Mara. Why all the compassion?"

"The police will always be after him," she went on earnestly, "always be snooping around his life, always be suspecting him. He'll only be free of that if he can prove he's innocent."

"How?"

"By ending once and for all the suspicion that he's guilty." Her manner turned confidential. "And I'm sure we can do that for him. It's not common knowledge, but we found one of the perpetrator's hairs on the woman in the parking lot. Testing it against a hair from Montano's head could prove he wasn't guilty."

You're sure he's guilty, Dan told himself, and who knows? You may be right. A match of his hair to the one you found would be like loafing his fingerprint on a murder weapon. There's no way I can let you get within a city block of Ricardo Montano's hair.

Dan smiled sweetly. "Sorry, lady, no dice. You don't have strong enough probable cause to suspect him, so you can't get a court order forcing him to turn over hair samples. I'm sure as hell not going to have him do it voluntarily."

Mara's face did not betray her disappointment. "I'm only thinking of his welfare."

"So am I. I'd rather not do your detective work for you."

Her expression became apologetic. "I'm ready to go into court for the order."

"And you know I'll be able to stop you."

Mara slid off the table, her expression sad. "Dan, sometimes you're your own worst enemy." She sounded genuinely concerned. "Gil's meeting with the First Assistant DA now. I'm going to have to get him."

When she reappeared with Huyton, he was jacketless. His sleeves were rolled up, his tie knotted tight.

"Mara tells me you won't agree to have your client submit a hair sample."

Dan nodded, appreciating that whatever else he might be, Gil Huyton was not a hypocrite who wasted time in counterfeit salutations. "Have you gotten a hair sample from Tim Feeney yet? He's as likely a suspect in these rape-murders as Montano."

The query's implications were obvious. If Feeney was the criminal, then his claim that Dan bribed him to recant his identification of Montano had been a lie; he would have been naming Montano in order to shift his own guilt.

"I'll make you an offer, Lazar. I'll get Feeney to agree to give a hair sample if you get Montano to do the same. You do that—play fair with me like that—and I'll withdraw the disbarment charges we filed against you with the Disciplinary Board."

"How do you know Feeney will go along?"

"If he doesn't, I'll know he's guilty and nail him to the wall. I want to catch this rapist before he strikes again, whether it's Montano or Feeney."

Dan leaned back in the chair, considering the offer. *Oh, Lord, it's tempting,* he thought. *I'd be out of this mess clean as a whistle, reputation intact. My life would go on as before.*

But they've got nothing on Montano now and no probable cause to suspect him. They're just fishing. If he is *guilty, I'd be selling him down the river, offering him up to the prosecution like a pig for a barbecue.*

Then I really would deserve to go before the Disciplinary Board for disbarment.

Dan stood up. "I wish I could take the deal, I really do. But I think you know that I can't."

Huyton was surprised. "You're going to cover up for a creep like Montano?"

"Dan, you can't do this to yourself!" Mara cried out, trying to reason with him. "You could be disbarred!"

"I can't help that. I guess I'll just have to see you in court."

In the lobby, as Dan was signing out, his eye caught Evie Jeeter's name higher up the page. She had come in several hours before Dan and not yet signed out. He reasoned that Huyton had kept her in one of the offices until he knew whether Dan would accept his offer. Dan decided to stick around on the steps outside and wait for her.

Twenty minutes later a woman emerged from the building. He thought he remembered seeing her face in the first-floor window of Feeney's house. She was wire-thin with dry yellow hair and worried eyes.

"Ms. Jeeter?" he asked. "I'm Dan Lazar."

"I recognize you."

"I want to thank you for telling the truth to the DA."

"No need for thanks. I won't lie for Tim anymore. I used to. You know, call in to where he was working and say he was sick when the truth was he was too drunk or drugged out to go to work. He never appreciated it or the kind of home I tried to make for us. So no more lying."

"Do you know where he might have gotten the five thousand dollars from?"

"He wouldn't tell me."

"Any guesses?"

"Well, I always thought he was reselling drugs at work, but I couldn't be sure. Look, I don't really think I should be discussing this."

"Just one more question: Do you know why he told the DA that I bribed him?"

"Mr. Lazar, you ever play Monopoly when you were a kid?"

"Sure."

"Well, Tim calls you his get-out-of-jail-free card."

Dan spent the rest of the afternoon holed up with Cal and Rick, trying to lay out their defense strategy in the disciplinary proceedings he was facing. Rather than drag the matter out, Dan had insisted that Cal arrange with the Board's chief disciplinary counsel for an immediate hearing.

"Unfortunately," Cal pointed out, "Huyton did his homework when he filed the charges. Half the lawyers on the Disciplinary Board seem to hate your guts.''

"Come on," Dan argued, "like who?"

"Remember Judge Finegold."

"He *is* an ignoramus. He had no right to hold me in contempt for telling the truth."

"He's retired now from the bench and sitting on the Disciplinary Board."

Rick recalled, "Ken Bosco doesn't like you very much."

"Judge Bosco's son?"

Cal nodded. "You want me to remind you what you called him? It made all the papers."

"Okay, that's two," Dan conceded.

"It's not just that you have some enemies on the Board, Dan. Sometimes in a disciplinary proceeding it's not even whether you're innocent that matters. You have to *look* innocent. Anything less, and they can say you failed to act in accordance with the highest ethical standards."

Dan threw up his hands. "I'll be damned before I lower myself to the level of the Boscos and Finegolds."

Cal was worried. Dan's considerable pride might impede his defense. "I'll fight like a demon for you, Dan, you know that," Cal asserted, "but you've got to help me."

"If they can't see the charges are phony and contrived, then there's nothing more I can do. Whatever happens, happens."

Next morning, almost before he had a chance to second-guess himself, Dan picked up the telephone and called Susan Boelter.

"How about going out to dinner with me tonight?"

She thought a long while.

"Look, this is just dinner," he added.

"I'd love to," she said, then had an additional thought. "Could I ask a favor?"

"Sure." Several possible requests flashed through Dan's mind.

"Could we take your motorcycle?"

10

She figures as long as she's slumming for the evening, she might as well do it up royally, Dan grumbled as he swung the blue Harley up into the twists of Albemarle Road, tilting over and back like a slaloming water-skier.

Phoning her was really a stupid idea, he berated himself. All right, I was in the mood for company and enjoy talking to her, but an odd couple like us stuck together for an entire evening could be deadly. What will we talk about? I mean she's a goddamn *Winstead!* It sounds like some kind of formal title, like duchess or archangel. Miles Standish and the first Winstead over here probably spent their nights at the Plymouth Colony playing gin rummy together. Or maybe they got together for some racy Bible study.

Dan pictured the Puritans imposing a PG-17 rating on the Bible's erotic sections, caning children found secretly peeking at the Begats. Coming of age in those days probably meant being allowed to read about David and Bathsheba and being let in on the secret that Hester Prynne hadn't won her scarlet A for varsity aerobics.

By the time he braked the Harley in Susan's driveway and slid off, his amused bemusement had managed to subdue much of the fine rage into which he had worked himself. Nonetheless he was still ambivalent about the evening, and the heat wave had begun to bake him again.

The front door was open. No one was in sight. He wandered through several of the large downstairs public rooms. The emptiness of the vast house seemed eerie to him, like an end-of-the-world movie where the semi-star walks alone through a city devoid of another living being. Noticing wide French doors open to the garden, he stepped out onto a brick patio. Before him, flower beds and hedges curled about each other in an ornate minuet that advanced to dusk-shrouded trees in the distance.

He heard a snipping noise and followed the sound around one corner of the building. Susan, in a black silk pants suit, was crouched before a bed of purple hyacinths. She looked up.

"I was sure I had a few minutes left."

"I'm a little early."

"Cutting these is good therapy. I keep imagining that each one is Peter's throat." She dropped her gaze for an instant. "I've been full of the most incredible anger. I feel like I've been such a fool."

She stripped off her work gloves, placing them and the shears into her gardening basket beside purple flowers she had clipped, and stood up.

"This garden has been here in some form for over two hundred years," she said. "It's all going to run wild pretty soon. Still, one has to try to hold back chaos somehow."

"With only your trusty gardening shears."

She ignored the sarcasm in his voice. "Do you mind coming into the kitchen with me for a moment? I want to put these into something."

She led him back through the French doors. In the long hallway that ran the length of the house, she picked up a crystal vase containing wilted white hyacinths.

The kitchen was huge and had two pantries recessed into alcoves. Stainless steel appliances gleamed softly on one side. On the other, in front of windows that looked out onto another part of the garden, were a large wooden table and chairs. Dan took a seat.

"You seem to be the only one around."

"The only employee left is Jenny, our cook," Susan explained, dropping the dying flowers into the garbage container, "and she'll be here only a little while longer. But Karen is spending the weekend with Peter, so I gave Jenny off until Monday."

"Are you still worried about Karen?"

Susan emptied the discolored water into the sink and refilled the vase with fresh water.

"She seems to have had a wonderful time with Peter at a rock concert last night," Susan said, forcing cheerfulness into her voice. "Can you imagine Peter at a rock concert? People there probably didn't know what to make of him."

"They probably thought he was a narc. A narcotics agent," Dan explained.

"I understand the slang," she said with a laugh as she arranged the purple hyacinths in the vase. "I'm not that sheltered. Would you like a drink before we go? You can choose just about any room. Peter had a bar installed in most of them."

"Thanks, but I've already been through the museum," Dan groused, "and I'm not much of a drinker, especially when I'm driving. Some of that tap water will be fine."

Susan went for glasses. "I don't drink at all, but it seems to be the main social activity of our crowd. A lot of them are uncomfortable speaking." She chuckled at the thought. "They get more interesting after a few drinks."

"Like Midge?"

"Poor Midge. He's not very comfortable with people socially unless he's had something to drink. He doesn't handle it well."

Susan placed a glass of water in front of Dan and took the seat across from him. "Peter tells me my not drinking comes from self-righteousness, that I want to feel superior to him. That's not true. I don't like to drink because I don't like losing control. His whole personality changes when he drinks. I can't talk to him. That frightens me."

"You don't seem easily frightened, certainly not of your husband. If anything, I got the feeling he might be intimidated by *you*."

"By me?" Susan scoffed. "When?"

"When he mentioned how you impressed his father. It seemed to me he was sarcastic about all your good qualities because they intimidated him—*you* intimidated him. That may be why he's trying so hard to cut you out of his life."

She eyed Dan shrewdly. "And you seem angry at me."

"Let's face it, you're crying poverty and trying to hammer your husband for heavy bucks, and you're a Winstead."

"What do you think being a Winstead means in my case? Regattas at Newport? Garden parties for the DAR?"

"Something like that."

"And, of course, trust funds to buy the silver spoon that will feed me from cradle to grave. Never a worry in the world, except whether to wear white after Labor Day and would it be tacky to buy a Rolls."

"Something like that."

"For us, actually, it was nothing like that. I grew up in a small town near Boston in a big old house that had been in the family for generations and always seemed to need repairs we couldn't afford. My brother went to Choate and Harvard. By the time I came along, what little money my parents may have once had for my education was gone. Neither of them had a paying job."

"How did they make ends meet?"

Susan reflected for a moment on what she could gauge of Dan's discretion and empathy. She had already told him so much, and he had listened sympathetically. She decided he could be trusted with her recollections of her family.

"When I was about twelve or so, I came home from school and saw bulldozers knocking down trees in the woods behind our house. I ran to alert my mother. She told me that part of our property had been sold to a housing developer. It turned out that whenever economic catastrophe threatened, my parents would sell off another piece of the land our house was on and live on the proceeds until they ran out. Five acres here. Ten acres there. Our assets were continuously shrinking, and there wasn't much left."

"Sounds like Chekhov's rural aristocracy."

"What came to mind at the time was the Cheshire cat in *Alice in Wonderland*. Someday soon, I thought, everything but our smile will be gone. My mother told me to look on the bright side: I'd have a whole lot of new friends close by."

"She sounds like a practical woman. Making the best of a difficult situation."

Susan chuckled dryly. "She wasn't the least bit practical—not what one usually thinks of as practical, anyway—and barely acknowledged the existence of our new neighbors. She—both my parents—seemed almost oblivious of everyday reality. She prepared me for a perfectly ordered, secure world of privilege that no longer existed for us. Other girls wore jeans to school. Jeans were for farmers or hoodlums, she told me, for the ill-bred. I had to wear dresses."

"What did she think of the boys you dated?"

"I didn't date. None of the boys in town were 'appropriate.' A crushing word. I couldn't go to dances or parties unless she knew the boys' families, but of course, she didn't know any of the families in town—and wouldn't have approved of them if she had. She prepared me for coming out parties in Boston I couldn't afford to attend or give, for picnics and tea dances no one held anymore, for polite courting as extinct as the dinosaur."

"You make her sound a little dizzy."

"Not dizzy, far from it. In many ways she was a remarkable woman. She spent her time gardening and reading Keats and Shelley and Jane Austen, abhorring almost anything from our own era. Yet she attended every rally to end the Vietnam War—the newspapers were always putting her photo in the papers—but she never noticed that my shoes were coming apart."

"I don't picture a woman like that getting caught up in the peace movement."

"The war was very simple in her mind: One didn't attack less-fortunate people for trying to be free. Supporting a war like that would be immoral."

"I found out the hard way she was right."

"About those kinds of things, she usually was. Acting properly was essential to her. It was the only thing she paid attention to in me. Not just good manners—that was automatic—but one's moral duty."

"Impressive."

"And cold. She insisted on telling you exactly what she thought—no matter how hurtful. Principles were what she had in place of love."

Susan's expression lightened. "When I was young, I had a very poor friend down the road named Sarah. She had this wonderful, loving family. There seemed to be children and pets everywhere. Her mother was a large, bosomy woman who hugged us all impartially and talked to me as freely as to her own children. That's how I knew what I was missing out on. Once, when my parents forgot my birthday, she baked a cake and made me a new dress. I used to dream Sarah's mother would adopt me."

"Sarah would probably have given anything to be born with the Winstead name."

A flicker of resentment lit Susan's eyes. "The only legacy my parents and grandparents didn't squander. It was a constant reminder of what I no longer had."

Susan stared into her glass of water as if it were a crystal conjuring up the past. "I went back out that day to watch the bulldozers eat up our land. This enormous yellow one kept smashing things down closer and closer until it seemed inevitable that it would soon roll over me and our house. But I refused to give ground. I stood in its path, daring it to attack me. . . . I was so incredibly angry."

"About what?"

"Everything. All the things I was being denied—parents I could talk to, who paid attention to me, the college education I might not get but my brother had taken for granted, the dances and parties my Boston cousins went to, a new coat because the other was in tatters and two or three sizes small on me, school books I didn't have to borrow from friends with the excuse that mine had gotten lost."

Susan halted, allowing the head of steam she had built up to vent itself. "I could go on and on. My family had once been rich. Everyone thought we still were. We had owned companies and houses and land—the *Herald* was only a part of what we once owned. And yet, despite having almost nothing left by the time I was born, I was still 'upper-class' and burdened by the obligations that entailed. Everybody expected things of a Winstead, including my very honorable and very oblivious mother and father.''

"You blame them for a lot.''

"Blame wasn't the issue then, and it isn't now. As that bulldozer rolled toward me, I realized my parents were helpless curios. They were incapable of protecting me or of giving me anything, even love. Especially love. At that moment I knew that if I was to make something of my life and not end up an ineffectual curiosity from another age, like they were, the only person I could depend on was me.''

"So the bulldozer stopped.''

Susan laughed. "Just long enough for me to scurry out of the way. But I vowed that I wouldn't let myself fade away like my parents or my grandparents or the other Winsteads who had wasted their lives and everything we once had. I would reclaim everything I rightly should have had. And not just material things. I was entitled to love and emotional fulfillment—everyone is. And to a position in life that was more than just a name. . . .''

Dan scoffed, "How about little incidentals like the *Herald* or this estate you're living on?''

"Of course I wanted to live well and to have some effect on an important newspaper—I was set on becoming a journalist,'' she replied frankly. "But what I wanted most was regaining the love and affection and family feeling that seemed to have slipped away from us.''

She smiled, her voice quickening. "Until my parents sold it, we had a big painting of one of the earlier Winstead families over our mantel: a prosperous, protective father sitting on a sofa beside a loving mother . . . surrounded by four happy children, one of them my great-grandfather. I used to stare at it longingly for hours. I had a right to a family like that . . . to a life like that. But I knew I had to work for it.''

She spoke with such fervor about values close to his own heart that Dan found his skepticism slipping away.

"Within days,'' she remembered, "I found an after-school job. A year later I won a full scholarship to a good girls' school. And then another to Bryn Mawr. That's how I came to Philadelphia.''

"Your folks must be proud of you.''

"They're both dead now. But they probably didn't give what I did a second thought; they expected it of me. Praise was rare in my family. My mother was sure it made children conceited or, as she used to put it, 'big-headed.' '' Susan smiled sadly. "I used to picture a little girl my age floating over the countryside with a head the size of a blimp because her parents praised her a lot.''

At the core of Susan's being, Dan perceived, was neither upper-class hauteur nor reserve, but a Yankee compulsion for honesty that goaded her to reveal herself. Like Dan himself, Susan had not been born rich, but had been determined to get what she wanted and to where she wanted to be. And like him, she refused to lie to herself or others, because the truth about who she was and where she had come from was all that she had to guide her on her voyage.

"You haven't told me about your father," Dan said.

"He was sweet and kind and bewildered most of the time; his mind was adrift somewhere before the turn of the century. He was a historian—or at least would have been if he had taught somewhere or had published more than one little book."

"Your father was R. A. Winstead?" Dan's tone conveyed his awe.

"You've heard of him?"

"Industrialism and the American Spirit."

She clapped her hands with delight. "Yes. That was it."

"He changed the way we view American history. A couple of books have just come out based on his theories."

"Really?" Susan was astonished. "His historian friends used to tell me his work was important, but I was sure they just wanted me to think well of my vague, forgetful father."

"He was important, all right."

"Thank you," she said, and lightly touched Dan's arm.

Dan had grown introspective. "To change the way we see the world. To leave behind a legacy like that . . ."

The atmosphere had grown somber. Susan stood up. "How about my motorcycle ride?"

"Sure."

In the driveway he handed her a helmet.

"Why the fascination with my bike?" he asked.

"A girl I stayed friendly with in town after I went away to school had a boyfriend with a motorcycle. He was tough-looking and wore black leather, and I was sure she was doing the most forbidden things with him. I envied her like mad. Privately, of course."

"Don't tell me the Sexual Revolution passed you by."

"I didn't even have a proper date until I was in college. Even after I was away from home, and my mother couldn't supervise me, I was either working or studying all the time. Very dutiful child."

Dan mounted the motorcycle. Her face vibrant with anticipation, Susan put on her helmet. Visor up, she stared at the bike, her expression slowly eroding.

"You all right?" he asked.

"I think this may have been a mistake." Her voice was strained.

"I can call for a taxi."

"It's not the motorcycle." Her voice fell. "I'm not used to the idea of going out with a man who isn't my husband."

"Let's forget it then. We had a good conversation. I met R. A. Winstead's daughter. A short evening, but interesting."

The rims of her lower lids began to redden, but she shook her head resolutely. "No, I've got to get used to the idea that . . . that Peter and I won't get back together. Do you really mind very much having dinner with me?"

He laughed. "It beats fish sticks with Mrs. Paul."

He flipped down his black visor. She did the same with hers and mounted behind him. He jumped on the starter pedal and slowly rolled down the driveway. As they headed out of the property and picked up speed, her arms reached around his waist.

"That must be what it's like to be a ninja," she said excitedly when Dan turned off the engine in the restaurant's parking lot. "Fast, dangerous, invisible in the night."

Although he considered the dinner perfectly innocent, to minimize the chance that Susan would be recognized, Dan had chosen an Italian restaurant outside the city that was not too well known.

She stepped off the bike. The restaurant's name spilled red and blue neon light over her.

"Women all feel so vulnerable. I think we'd all love to possess that kind of secret ninja power to give us confidence."

"You always look confident."

Her glance conveyed surprise at such an improbable deduction.

Just inside the entrance Dan gave his name to a man standing at the reservation desk.

A voice boomed out. "His money's no good here, Angelo. He's my guest."

Carlo Paoluzzi was sitting in a large semicircular booth beside a good-looking young woman with masses of red hair who was wearing a low-cut blue dress. He motioned to Dan to join him while sliding to one side to make room in the booth. The Mafia don's driver and another man were seated at a nearby table that commanded a view of the dining room.

Dan started to introduce Paoluzzi to Susan, but she said, "I recognize Mr. Paoluzzi."

"Carlo, this is Susan Boelter."

Paoluzzi looked quizzically at Dan. "The newspaper guy's wife? Ooh, not bad, counselor."

"She's kind of a client, Carlo."

"What does 'kind of' mean?" Paoluzzi turned to Susan. "I hope you don't mind my asking a few questions. The counselor here is pretty good about keeping his personal life to himself. I see him with a beautiful lady, I get curious."

"Carlo," Dan said, "Susan and I had planned a private dinner."

"Privacy can come later," Paoluzzi said with a wink at Susan.

She smiled. "I think Mr. Paoluzzi's company would be fun."

Dan shrugged and stepped aside, so she could slip into the booth before him. Far from being scandalized or fearful, she appeared to be fascinated.

Paoluzzi, introduced his date as "Rita, a great little mambo dancer," and then turned to the owner.

"Angelo, I want to make sure my friend gets the best meal of his life. Bring us some antipasto to start and the spiedini. The veal chop Milanese. That fettucini you make I love so much. Hey, you know, everything the best."

"Leave it to me, Carlo," the owner said, pleased at being able to accommodate his powerful customer.

"So, counselor?" Paoluzzi inquired again as he poured red wine into the newcomers' glasses.

"Susan and her husband are getting a divorce. I'm advising her."

"On a Friday night," Paoluzzi observed with a grin. "You're one hell of a dedicated lawyer." He turned to Susan. "You know, the counselor and I go back a long way."

"Carlo and I grew up in the same part of town."

"Toughest Jew I ever met," Paoluzzi remarked by way of concurrence.

"We were just kids, Carlo," Dan said, trying to end the story.

Paoluzzi ignored him. "We're maybe fourteen, fifteen. I'm hanging out on the corner with a bunch of the guys when he comes by. I wasn't much for school, but I recognize him from there, and I tell him this is our block, and he's got to fork over a quarter to go by or else go back where he came from. Like a toll. Now, you gotta remember, there's five of us, and he says, 'This way's closer to my job. I'm going through.' We start for him, and he moves in front of Joey DiAngelo—a big kid, who could hold his own—and pops him one and Joey goes down. I mean, out! He takes a fast shot at another guy and backs the guy up. But it's four or five to one, like I said, and we're all around him. We beat the hell out of him and take all the money he's got. I figure he learned his lesson."

A grin broke over Paoluzzi's face as he anticipated the rest of the story. "The next day, it's the weekend, and we're all outside. This time maybe ten of us. And who comes walking down the street? Danny here, his face all swollen and beat up, like he just went ten rounds. I say, 'You going to work?' He says, 'No, just making sure I can when I need to.' ''

Paoluzzi laughed heartily. ''I mean, what the hell can you say? I realize this guy's got the kind of balls he wouldn't a stopped coming unless we'd a killed him.''

''What happened then?'' Susan asked.

''I bought him a beer. You gotta admire a guy like that, know what I mean? And you know what he says when I hand him the beer?'' The grin wide now, Paoluzzi dropped his hand onto Dan's arm. ''He says, 'You still owe me two bucks.' ''

Susan turned to Dan, who looked uncomfortable.

Dan said, ''This place is outside your usual stomping grounds, isn't it, Carlo?''

Paoluzzi nodded. ''The feds could tape me at the other place because I wasn't getting around enough. People knew where to expect me. That isn't smart in my line of work.''

Susan spoke up. ''I've never before met anyone in your line of work. May I ask you something?''

''Between us?''

''Yes.''

''Go ahead.''

''I've always wondered: Do the other guys elect you to be their boss, you know, like Indians elect their chief?''

Paoluzzi roared with laughter. ''It's the kind of election where the other candidates kinda drop out along the way.''

To Dan's amazement, the publisher's wife and the mob boss, intrigued by each other, seemed to cement an instant friendship, with Paoluzzi discreetly explaining the ins and outs of his profession and Susan reciprocating with the customs and mores of Old Philadelphia's select few. Dan noted the concern gathering on the brow of mambo-dancing Rita. She recognized her man's signs of sexual interest: the body turned directly to Susan, the provocative intonation in his speech, the occasional wink to punctuate a comment. Dan recognized his own stirrings of jealousy and began to take a greater part in the conversation.

Afterward, outside in the parking lot, Susan accepted the helmet Dan handed her without looking at it. She was thinking about something.

''Carlo and I understand each other, Dan. We both come from a dying class with a dying code of honor all its own. The rules are different for us.''

Her beauty, sad now and pale white beneath the moon, suddenly overwhelmed him.

''Do you find him attractive?''

"Maybe. In a brutal way. You feel how potent and how dangerous he is, and the fear can arouse you. You mistake it for desire."

"You didn't feel even a *little* desire for him?" he asked, stepping closer to her. Dan's whole being vibrated with desire for her.

Susan felt her own feelings stirring. New and confusing, she tried to sort them out as they bumped against the bruises caused by Peter's rejection and her urge to retaliate and her need to revive. She resisted giving Dan a polite, evasive reply.

"Not for him, no."

"You're married," he reminded her.

"I thought I was. . . . But I was the only one who did."

"I want to make love to you, Susan."

Her gaze hung in the grasp of his. "That doesn't seem wrong to me anymore."

He abruptly stepped back, shaking his head. "It's much too soon for you, and it's too risky for you legally."

She took a deep breath. "You're right, of course."

If her eyes had dropped, even for an uncertain instant, then he might have kept to his resolve and curbed his rashness, but her eyes stayed on his and, in them, he glimpsed a hunger as great as his own.

He pulled her to him and kissed her, the wordless decision made.

Susan nestled against Dan's back all the way into the city. Her body felt rigid to him, expectant.

He kissed and embraced her again in his bedroom. With deliberate care, he unfastened the buttons down her back and slipped his hands beneath the material and against her skin. She felt a little awkward, even timid, he thought, as if she remembered the moves, but was not quite comfortable making them.

"Let me," he said softly and, unbuttoning the sleeves, as well, lifted the black blouse off her. A moment later he had undone her slacks and slipped off her underthings. She sat self-consciously on the edge of the wide bed while he removed his own clothes. The murky light from the front hall washed through the half-open door and across her like the foam edge of a wave.

"You keep staring at me," she said.

"You're lovely. Your body is beautiful. I couldn't tell underneath your clothing."

"It's strange to hear a man talk to me like that."

"Does it bother you?"

"No."

Dan plucked a condom from the night-table drawer.

"Thank you," she said. "I wouldn't have thought to—"

He kissed her in midsentence to dissolve her embarrassment and drew her down to the quilt.

He bent to her throat and brushed his lips against the elegant curve. Her eyes closed for a moment as she tried to savor the feeling, then opened.

"Are you all right?" he asked.

She gazed a long while at his face. "You have nice eyes. They make me feel safe."

That assurance unlocked her passion. His hand slipped to her breast, cupping it for a moment then slowly strumming the nipple as it tightened. Her breasts arched harder into him. She shivered as his fingers floated down between her legs.

She kissed him fiercely, and her hips began to move in rhythm to his hand.

"Don't stop, please."

Her entire being seemed poised on the tip of his finger.

"Now," she said finally. "Now."

He lifted himself over her, seeking the opening with his hardness. When at last he thrust into her, she was ravenous for him.

Much later, as they lay facing each other, Dan saw the glitter of a tear on her cheek.

"Sorry?"

"Oh, no." She paused to examine her inner dissension. "It's just . . . it never occurred to me that I'd ever make love to anyone but Peter."

"Or that you might enjoy it?"

"Yes, that, too. The world is suddenly very new to me."

11

Susan and Dan met several more times in the weeks that followed, always at his apartment and always when Karen was spending the night at her father's or sleeping over at a friend's. They ceased to chance dining out, which made additional sense while Dan was recuperating from the surgery on his knee. Usually he ordered Chinese food delivered. Once when he bought steaks to broil, she confessed to eating almost no red meat. He put the steaks into the freezer and called up the Chinese restaurant once again. While he and Susan waited for delivery, he played slow ballads for her on the piano.

During those suppers, they allowed themselves to linger in unhurried conversation, certain that the night would bring release from sexual hungers and, with it, transient relief from private rages and from concerns stoppered up since their last tryst. She was fascinated by Dan's upbringing. Growing up amid a city's rush and turmoil and imminent violence seemed as exotic to her as her youth in a small semirural community seemed to him. He admitted that one of the reasons he had taken this apartment was because it was built near Dock Street, where as a boy, he used to help truckers unload produce. In payment, they would let him take home apples, peaches, lettuces, tomatoes, eggplants, carrots, melons.

"We were poor," he reminisced, "but we always had fresh fruit and vegetables on the table."

Despite their dissimilar backgrounds, recent events had given them much in common: Both faced crucial legal onslaughts that aroused dire fears—in Dan, of disgrace and isolation, of a life adrift without even the pretense of purpose; in Susan, of losing everything that was precious to her. Both dreaded separation from a child who was their heart's ultimate joy. And both had suffered a lover's abrupt rejection.

The more time Dan spent with Susan, the more he came to trust and admire her candor. Where his facade, open and gregarious, was a screen around an inner being he guarded from prying eyes, she said what she thought and what she felt, but invariably with a graciousness that stripped off the thorns.

He was taken, too, by her beauty, which like her personality, was straightforward, clean-lined, unstudied. For all his previous misgivings about her upper-echelon status, he felt comfortable with her, in part, he decided, because their friendship had formed at a time when she was wounded and alone, when she had temporarily become what he had visualized himself all his life as being, an outsider menaced by an insider, by someone possessing the capacity to bend justice to his will. Dan could provide Susan with a lawyer's advice tempered by a lifetime's wariness.

She provided him with what? he wondered for a while. Sex, certainly—a prodigious, fiery urgency he had never expected lurked within her. But also something just as gratifying and as necessary, he eventually realized. Mara's departure had gouged tire tracks of mistrust across his heart, the scars of caring too much for a woman. He assumed that Susan, lovely, effortlessly regal of manner, earthily carnal as a lover—my God, the lust she evoked in him—considered him an acceptably attractive man. That was enough, although he sometimes wondered whether she thought she was settling for second best, was stuck with another woman's discard. At times the sex they shared was for both of them, he sensed, as much an act of therapy as of passion.

He felt no long-term obligation to her and believed she felt none toward him, that even if their differences had not been too great to be bridged, she was still too unsettled to risk the emotional intimacy of love. He refused to consider whether he harbored any deeper feelings for her, sure that would be futile. Despite the pleasure she obviously derived from their lovemaking, Dan suspected that Peter still owned her devotion. Not only was he apprehensive about her eventual rebuff, but right now even a single additional complexity in his life would be one too many.

Dan's hearing before the Disciplinary Board was a strange, predictable exercise held in the posh surroundings of a rented public room at the Ritz-Carlton Hotel. Although he had characterized Gil Huyton as the villain who was misusing the facts and the players to encircle him and bring him down, in actuality, the Philadelphia DA had simply filed the charges with the commonwealth's Office of the Disciplinary Counsel. That agency swiftly investigated and determined on its own to press the matter.

However, testimony at its hearing left the crucial moment outside Tim Feeney's house on Sixteenth Street so ambiguous as to invite damaging interpretations. Feeney was better prepared as a witness and more respectful of the forum than he had been at the Montano trial. He appeared sure of every word when questioned by the chief disciplinary counsel and unshakable under Cal's searing cross-examination. Asserting that he took Dan's money because he was a drug addict who would have said or done anything to feed his habit, he now claimed that counseling and his time in jail had gotten him off drugs; that he repented having perjured himself for drug money; and that he hoped to start a fresh life, free of cocaine. Telling the truth now about Dan's bribery, he maintained, was the first step.

With her former boyfriend staring at her, Evie Jeeter grew nervous and seemed less credible than he about her version of the incident. Tim had been late arriving home from work that morning, she said. She heard voices just outside the front door and looked out a window. He was in conversation with a man, whom she later learned was Dan Lazar. She saw no money change hands, but did see a lot of cash a moment later, when Tim came into the house. He used it all up and more on drugs.

In contrast, Dan was surly and occasionally irate when Cal put him on the stand to refute the bribery charges. At one point he called it "a demeaning charade" and contended that he should not even have to defend himself against such patently false and flimsy evidence. On cross, his exchanges with the Board's counsel became so acrimonious that he twice had to be warned to restrain himself.

Swayed by the unfavorable appearance of his brief street encounter with Feeney, exasperated by his quarrelsome testimony, a majority of the Board found against him. Although nothing could be proven with certainty, something very wrong appeared to have occurred.

Disbarment would have been too heavy a punishment for that uneasy perception, so they made Dan an offer to settle the charges. If he would agree to wind up his work for present clients in the next two months and then submit to a six-month suspension from the practice of law, they would recommend reinstatement afterward and agree to seal the papers and keep the deliberations confidential. Otherwise, they would recommend disbarment. The offer was intended to be, in effect, an insulting slap on Dan's wrist.

Cal was adamant that Dan should decline the offer and fight the decision in state supreme court. "There's a chance we can convince the

judges. The evidence against you isn't conclusive. The record shows that
Feeney has been an unreliable witness in the past. We should fight for a
clear acquittal.''

"That's a long shot," Dan replied. "The court rarely reverses the Disciplinary Board, and all the negative comments about me would be printed
up for every lawyer and reporter to read. Let's stick to the offer. I lose
whether I take it or leave it. But if I let them disbar me, I lose a lot more.''

Cal argued to no avail, insisting that if this had happened only a few
years earlier, Dan would have fought to wipe this slur from his professional integrity.

Dan did not disagree. The hearing had been the final arson that burned
him out. The slow strangulation of his ideals over the years had left him
disillusioned and vacant. Always lurking in the back of his thoughts now
was Mara's rebuke that he had become a mindless hired gun, obsessed
with winning and not with justice. The significance that he once believed
underlay his life had eroded, and he had collapsed into the void.

"I'll take the deal, Cal. They're doing me a favor. They're giving me
time off to think about things.''

"What things?''

"My life. Where it's going.''

Cal's own priorities had always been simple and clear; one worked to
earn a good livelihood and to be respected. "What about the cases you're
handling?''

"I'm onto something in the Paoluzzi case that might just end it. If it
pans out, I'd be just as glad to start the suspension after that. You and
Rick can handle anything else I've got.''

"Then what do you do?''

"Go away for a while, spend time in California with Jamie. Just think
about doing something else with the rest of my life.''

"Will you be back?''

"I don't know. Maybe I'll move there to be close to him. Or maybe
take a job playing piano in some Colorado ski town or, who knows, drive
a semi or run away and join the circus. Whatever is out there, it has to be
better than this chickenshit.''

Susan's financial difficulties deepened. Nearly everything she personally owned, including her filly, had long since been sold off. She was
buying gasoline now in two- and three-dollar increments. She rented stall
space to a couple of weekend riders and arranged to sell flowers from her
garden to a local florist. That allowed her to clear perhaps seventy dollars
in a good week. Karen happened to mention the arrangements to her
father, and his lawyer immediately demanded that Susan cease and desist

selling Peter's property. She had to stop. Ramsay, her lawyer, remained adamant that her case would be hurt if she took even a part-time job.

A few days later Susan and the Boelter Foundation were served with a summons and complaint from Peter requesting that the Foundation sell its block of stock in the Herald Corporation, its only major asset, back to the corporation. He was claiming that the IRS would penalize the Foundation if it failed to diversify its stock portfolio. What remained unstated in Peter's papers was his intention to resell that block, along with the rest of the Herald Corporation's stock, to Oren Lawlor.

That same day Ramsay phoned to let her know that her motion for spousal support had finally been set down for a hearing at the Montgomery County courthouse at the end of the week. But the rest of her lawyer's news was more worrisome. A single judge, Arthur Bowman, heard all the Montgomery County matrimonial matters, and he had decided, because the issues were entangled, to consolidate her request for support, Peter's for custody, and the actual divorce action into a single case, which he would now hear.

The week was an anxious one for Susan. She met with Ramsay much of Tuesday and Wednesday to go over her testimony and reread the court papers. Despite his chronic inclination to pessimism and the setbacks so far, she began to realize that Ramsay was a tenacious and effective advocate where the law allowed him to be.

He had had Karen interviewed by a child psychiatrist who specialized in divorce and similar childhood traumas. The woman was prepared to testify that Susan was an excellent mother and role model for the child, and that rebellion was normal at Karen's age, as was her desperate eagerness to please a father she feared might be leaving her.

The accountants and appraisers Ramsay had retained to audit Peter's records and the Herald Corporation's books, which were accessible to Susan because of the Foundation's stock ownership, had uncovered proof that when all the extras paid for by the company were included, Peter's true income was much larger than he had disclosed.

"We probably won't get what we're asking," Ramsay cautioned her, "but your husband will probably have to pay a lot more than he wants to. I expect we'll meet somewhere in the middle." The lawyer wanted to be straightforward with her. "But even the amount the judge decides to award you personally will probably depend a great deal on which way he jumps on the custody issue."

"Do you really think he'd take a child away from her mother?"

"The courts typically award custody to the wife, Mrs. Boelter," Ramsay said reassuringly. "Don't worry."

Susan stared at him with astonishment. "Don't worry? I don't know where the money will come from to buy food this week. I owe thousands of dollars in unpaid bills, not counting your bill for another three thousand dollars that you keep telling me the court will someday make Peter pay . . . and there's Karen's school bus bill and . . ."

She sought to control the fear rising to her throat. "And now she may even be taken away from me. How dare you tell me not to worry!"

Chest out like a pigeon, beaming, waving jauntily at people who recognized him, Carlo Paoluzzi and two associates on trial with him strutted out of the U.S. Courthouse on Market to cross the plaza to his car waiting on Sixth. A barrier of reporters and TV crews stopped him for an interview.

"Hey, come on up here, counselor!" Paoluzzi called out to Dan, who had purposely hung back, and then confided to the cameras, "The mouthpiece was a killer in there."

Dan cringed. The crime boss loved to sound like the media's idea of a mobster, using an outdated movie vocabulary he never used in private. Dan reluctantly made his way to the microphones.

A reporter asked him, "Could you tell us why the judge threw out the government's case?"

"We were able to prove that the FBI obtained a warrant to install a listening device *after* they began to eavesdrop, not *before*."

Scribbling as he spoke, Scott Feller quickly got to the heart of the matter. "In effect, they lied to the judge."

"Let's say their eagerness got in the way of their scruples. By illegally monitoring Mr. Paoluzzi's conversations, they violated his constitutional right to be free from unreasonable search and seizure. So the judge suppressed the tape recordings as evidence."

Paoluzzi crowed, "It was brilliant the way he found out how the feds tried to screw me."

The TV reporter spoke again. "Mr. Lazar, you've listened to the tapes. Did Carlo admit to murder and extortion on them like the prosecution claimed?"

"Hey," Paoluzzi interjected with a happy laugh, "I'm just an ordinary citizen the government's been picking on." He pointed diagonally across the street. "See that over there? That's the Liberty Bell. Thank God for American justice."

The Liberty Bell! Dan marveled. How the hell did Carlo Paoluzzi even know what the Liberty Bell was, much less where the thing was? Dan realized he would miss the continual, if potentially lethal, element of surprise that Carlo Paoluzzi added to his life.

The group moved past the reporters and into the waiting limousine. Dan was last.

Just as he slid into the backseat, the same TV reporter leaned in to ask him, "Is it true you were recently suspended from practicing law?"

Angry and ashamed, Dan slammed the car door closed. Without a good visual and no sound bite, he knew, the television station was unlikely to use the material on its news program.

Fucking Huyton! he fumed to himself. The Disciplinary Board had agreed that the settlement he had made to accept suspension would be kept utterly confidential. The leak had made Dan even more eager to get out of Philadelphia and maybe this profession.

He halted the limousine after a block, across from Independence Hall, and prepared to step out.

Paoluzzi magnanimously offered, "I hope you put yourself down for a big fee on this one."

"I'll send the bill over by messenger this afternoon. I'd like you to pay it right away. I'm taking a long trip."

"You want it in small bills, counselor?"

Paoluzzi and his associates thought that was very funny.

Karen was in her school's version of the *The Mikado* on Thursday night. One of the Three Little Girls from School, she had worked happily with her mother to sew the costume. Susan's pleasure at the joint activity curdled when Ramsay insisted she add it to her affidavit to indicate how good a mother she was.

Liquor on his breath, Peter arrived during the operetta's last act, just in time to greet his daughter when the curtain fell. Karen barely took notice of her mother's presence, hanging on Peter's skimpy praise for her singing in a trio he had arrived too late to hear.

"I'll pick you up early Saturday morning," he told his daughter as he quickly took his leave. "I'm playing in the club golf championship. You can walk the round with me. We'll spend the rest of the day by my pool. Susan, pick her up around five-thirty or so." He leaned over to kiss his daughter, a habit that had commenced only after he sought legal custody. "I've got a terrific present for you."

Through the open auditorium doors, Susan thought she glimpsed Amelia under the interior light of the Mercedes as Peter opened the door and slid behind the steering wheel.

"This car is really awful," Karen complained when she and Susan were driving out of the school parking lot. "The kids notice things like that."

"Tell them I had a head-on collision with poverty. And I wasn't covered by insurance."

Karen kept silent for a while. Susan thought she might still be reflecting on the car's embarrassing condition, but then her daughter said, "Mom, do you ever think about the baby who died?"

"Yes."

"I think about him a lot. We never got to know him, but I think about him a lot."

Susan slowed to a stop at the red light in the center of Dellwyne. She turned to Karen and gripped her hand. "Me, too."

"I feel kind of like I got away with something, and he got caught for it."

"You had nothing to do with it. Something went wrong inside me."

"I know, but I still sometimes wonder why it went wrong for him and not for me."

Susan leaned forward and kissed her daughter tenderly on the forehead. "I'm just very grateful that it didn't. I don't know what I'd do without you."

"I love you, too, Mom."

A car horn sounded from the rear. Susan straightened up and accelerated through the intersection.

They had just turned into their driveway when Karen suddenly exclaimed, "Wasn't Dad really great to come see me?"

"He's the best," Susan replied sarcastically. "Generous, too."

Karen's head swiveled around. Her mother rarely criticized her father to her face.

"The divorce trial thing starts tomorrow," Karen remembered.

Susan nodded.

"You don't really want a divorce, do you?"

"I didn't at the beginning. Your father was the one who pressed for it. But I do now."

Out of the corner of her eye Susan could see Karen shaking her head. Who would not want someone as wonderful as her father?

12

"Mrs. Boelter," Harold Ramsay said, beginning his direct examination of Susan, "please state your full name, address, and occupation."

To build his case for her to receive substantial support payments, Ramsay had already put two financial experts on the stand who testified about the extent of Peter's income and resources. Judge Bowman had indicated that the motion for support and, thus, the economic issues would be considered first, then Peter's motion for custody, and finally, if appropriate, the question of divorce.

In answer to her lawyer's questions, Susan described the family's expenses and lifestyle at length and what she knew of Peter's finances. She grew emotional as she maintained that the marriage had been a happy one for many years. She loved her husband and had been shocked and dismayed when Peter announced that he was leaving her. She ascribed his anger to her refusal to vote his way as a director of the newspaper's holding company.

An impassive presence on the bench, Judge Bowman had a square countenance that appeared to Susan to be as inexpressive as granite. With every answer she gave, she wondered what his reaction might be. Suddenly she found out. He interrupted her lawyer's questioning to question her himself.

"Times have changed, Mrs. Boelter. We have an equal rights amendment in Pennsylvania. An able-bodied woman capable of earning a living on her own must do so. She can't count on being supported by her husband forever. You were a newspaper reporter and editor, I believe.''

"I want to work, Your Honor, but I haven't been in the job market for fourteen years. My husband insisted I quit working when we were married.''

The judge lifted a set of papers, already marked at the point he wanted to consult. ''His lawyer claims you quit your job right after the wedding in order to force his client to provide all your living expenses.''

"That just isn't true. I gave up my career to help him build his. It's what he wanted. Isn't marriage supposed to be a partnership? Am I supposed to be penalized for spending the last fourteen years caring for my husband and our home and our daughter?''

''Now that you're separated, Mrs. Boelter, different rules apply. What's to prevent you from getting a reporter's job?''

"Right now, given my daughter's present state, I believe it's very important that I be home for her all day this summer and, starting in the fall, after school. But, Your Honor, even if I can find a job that would allow that, there are only two newspapers in this city. One won't hire me because it's run by my husband, which is presumably why the other one won't hire me, either.''

''And so you'd rather live off your husband's earnings and be a parasite.'' Frowning, he gestured to Ramsay to resume his examination.

Susan had expected a slashing cross-examination, but Peter's lawyer, a short, nattily dressed man, interrogated her on only a few minor points and then, excusing her, gathered his papers to put on his own case. Instead of calling Peter as his first witness, however, he put a man named Arthur Newell on the stand.

''Mr. Newell, please state your profession.''

"I'm a private detective. Mr. Boelter hired my firm to look into his wife's behavior.''

''What did that entail?''

"Trailing her mostly, to see whether she was having an affair with anybody.''

''And what did you learn?''

"The first night I follow her—bingo!''

Susan turned rigid.

''Objection!'' Ramsay cried out, caught off guard by the revelation. ''Your Honor, we're supposed to be dealing with economic issues in this part of the trial. Mrs. Boelter's private life after her husband deserted her is irrelevant to this case.''

''That's just not so, Your Honor,'' opposing counsel rejoined. ''Her sexual behavior is relevant up until the moment of divorce. We can prove that she had both the inclination and the opportunity to commit adultery.

Her private life is especially relevant here because an adulterous wife forfeits her right to support.''

Judge Bowman's eyebrow lifted slightly. "So far, gentlemen, we haven't heard anything very private. Mr. Ramsay, you're overruled.''

"The night I'm hired," the private detective continued, "I observe the subject leaving her house on Albemarle Street—that's in Dellwyne—on the back of a motorcycle with a man I later identify as Daniel Lazar.''

Peter's attorney took care to point out to the judge, "Mr. Lazar is a well-known lawyer, but does not represent her in this matrimonial action.''

In colorful language, the ex-cop then resumed his testimony by describing how he then trailed Susan and Dan, first to their dinner at the Italian restaurant and then to Dan's apartment house.

"I park in the basement garage near them and then follow them to the elevator and get into it, so I don't lose them. I make out like I'm not paying attention to them, like I live there. You know, I take out my house keys. I pull out some letters, like I'm looking at my mail. Let me tell you, judge, the way they was staring at each other they wouldn't have noticed me if I was wearing pink ballet clothes and riding a giraffe.''

Ramsay was on his feet again. "I object. This is garbage.''

"Overruled.''

"Well, they get off together at his floor," Newell continued. "So I ride the elevator one floor higher, then back down to his floor and catch a glimpse of them just as they're going into his apartment. He's got his arm around her, and she's giving him big eyes, like he's just discovered a cure for cancer or something. I snap a fast photo and spend the night in the stairwell with the door open a crack to give me a view of his door. The two of them were shacked up all night and didn't leave till next morning.''

Susan leaped to her feet. "That happened after I caught my husband in bed with another woman!''

The judge banged down his gavel. "Mrs. Boelter, sit down! Anything you wish to say can be said through your attorney.''

He gestured for the private detective to go on.

Newell himself or one of his colleagues seemed to have followed Susan every night she had been with Dan. He ended his testimony by submitting a gallery of photographs of the couple, which were entered into evidence.

Ramsay's cross-examination tried to establish that except for a well-lighted kiss in the Italian restaurant's parking lot before she went to Dan's apartment, Susan had never been seen doing anything in public that would place her character in a bad light, and that she had simply begun a relationship with a man after her husband abandoned her.

In rebuttal Peter's lawyer brought out that the detective had no way of knowing precisely when Susan's relationship with Dan started. "For all you know, it might have begun before the date your services were retained."

"Sure," Newell answered cheerfully.

Peter's counsel immediately turned to the judge. "Your Honor, this proof of Mrs. Boelter's flagrant sexual misconduct makes her demand for support laughable. We request that her application for support be dismissed."

Ramsay jumped to his feet. "Peter Boelter is no innocent babe here. He's a philanderer trying to misuse the judicial process!"

Peter's lawyer pointed an accusing finger at Susan. "Your Honor, we move to modify our divorce complaint to include a demand for a fault divorce based on Mrs. Boelter's flagrant adultery."

"If my client did have an affair, such conduct was certainly mutual and, therefore, is not to be held against her in this action. This whole thing is just a tactic for Peter Boelter to keep withholding money that's due his wife, so she'll be forced to give up her rights."

Bowman chose to ignore the issue for the moment. "We've got a lot more testimony to hear, both on support and then on custody, before I consider dismissing any charges."

Susan had reddened with embarrassment as her secrets were publicly divulged by the private detective. Now they were being turned into weapons that threatened her financial security. Peter's lawyer's next declaration, though, struck at her heart.

"Your Honor, it's plain that Mrs. Boelter's sexual escapades make her an unfit role model for a daughter who's at a particularly impressionable age. My client is greatly concerned that his daughter's psychological well-being is in constant danger as long as a woman of such easy, sleazy morals is the custodial parent."

Ramsay placed a bracing hand on Susan's and whispered, "We'll get our chance."

Peter was next on the stand. He began by attesting to his having been married to Susan for nearly fifteen years and separated from her for several months.

"I left because I believed she was being unfaithful to me," he said with an air of melancholy.

Incredulous, Susan furiously scribbled a note to the contrary to her lawyer.

"My suspicions began," Peter continued, "when she invited this Lazar fellow to our house for dinner. And on my birthday!" he added, shaking his head at her perfidy.

Peter finally renounced his wife, he claimed, because "her affair with

Lazar was destroying me . . . that and the way she was neglecting our daughter.'' In point of fact, he stated, he had had to forbid the child from attending a party where drinking ''and who knew what else'' would be taking place. He professed to having seen Karen every weekend for months and gave the impression of being a profoundly wronged husband and a devoted father.

Over two hours of cross-examination, Ramsay forced Peter to contradict himself on several points and to admit that his income was greater than previously claimed. The questioning then turned to the incident in Amelia's bedroom. Aware that it had been witnessed by Amelia's maid, Peter admitted that his wife had found him naked in bed with his sister-in-law before the date that the detective had seen her going into Dan Lazar's apartment. He laid the blame for his own infidelity on her violent and wanton nature.

''The woman drove me to it,'' he insisted. ''After months of enduring her tawdry affair with Lazar, I certainly had good cause.''

Ramsay pointedly asked, ''Wouldn't you say that after she found you and her sister-in-law, her dearest friend, in bed together, *she* became the one who had good cause?''

Susan quickly glanced over to assess Judge Bowman's reaction and thought she detected a fleeting male smirk that derided as hair-splitting the time distinction that had devastated her. No matter what the date, it seemed to say, she was fucking around.

Peter's next answer seemed to enforce the locker room ambience. ''A woman—a man's wife—is expected to have more dignity than that. She was out of control in that bedroom, dangerous—exactly the sort of behavior I fear my daughter being exposed to.''

As Peter's cross-examination concluded, his lawyer immediately announced, ''Your Honor, I believe it's now appropriate to call Ms. Jenny Fanning to the stand.''

Jenny, the cook, entered and walked up to the front of the courtroom. She was nervous and wearing one of her two churchgoing dresses.

The early questioning dealt with brief spats she had witnessed between husband and wife, most significantly the dispute at the breakfast table just before Peter's trip to New York. The door to the breakfast room had been ajar, and Jenny had overheard Peter forbidding Karen to attend the party and then Susan contradicting the way he had handled it. Jenny's recollection made Peter sound like the compassionate, thoughtful parent and Susan as having criticized him without justification.

The lawyer's last questions penetrated to the marrow of Susan's character. ''Ms. Fanning . . . Jenny . . . did you ever see Mrs. Boelter strike her daughter?''

"Yes, I did." Her chin lifted resolutely. "I saw her strike the child very hard. In the face."

"Did she say anything?"

"She threatened to forbid Karen from visiting her father."

"What was your reaction?"

"I was horrified."

Ramsay's cross-examination elicited that Susan was generally a good and caring mother. However, Jenny insisted on repeating at the end of it, "But hitting that sweet child. That was unforgivable!"

Bowman announced that the adjournment for lunch would be brief. He wanted to move through the rest of the testimony as quickly as possible.

Unable to eat before she returned to the stand for purposes of rebuttal, Susan spent the short break pacing across the plaza outside the courthouse considering what she would say.

Only moments after she returned to the courtroom, the tipstaff announced the judge's entrance, and the trial resumed.

Upon returning to the stand, Susan averred that she had been a faithful wife throughout their marriage, but that she felt her loyalty had been cruelly repudiated by the sight of her husband in bed with her best friend and sister-in-law. Ramsay took her through many questions to display her compassion and her fitness as a parent.

When Ramsay shifted to matters raised by Jenny Fanning, Susan confessed to having struck Karen and to remorse at having lost her temper.

"What was the argument about?"

"Peter was allowing our daughter to do things that were inappropriate for someone so young. I felt all the attention he was giving her and the laxity of his discipline were attempts to gain her favor in this divorce."

"Isn't it true," Ramsay asked, "that your daughter taunted you that night until you were provoked to the limits of any reasonable person's temper?"

"Yes, but I wish with all my heart I hadn't lost my temper, that I could take back what I did."

The cross-examination was grueling, with Peter's lawyer boring into every incident Susan had discussed, every motive she had asserted. The clock was close to striking five when the cross finally ended and Judge Bowman spoke up.

"We've heard all kinds of allegations today. I'm convinced that both parties are equally guilty of sexual misconduct and that neither can be permitted to gain an advantage as a result."

Susan caught Ramsay's pleased glance that her infidelity had not been held against her.

Bowman continued, "A major issue in this litigation—and several times today testimony has touched on it—is who'll have primary physical custody of the couple's daughter. Therefore, I'm scheduling the full custody hearing for first thing Monday morning."

He frowned in reflection for a moment. "I'm sure both parties will produce testimony from expert witnesses—psychiatrists, psychologists—to support their own arguments for custody. But it seems to me that a thirteen-year-old girl is old enough to know which parent she'd be happier with. Mrs. Boelter, please bring in your daughter first thing Monday morning. I want to talk to her privately in my chambers. Till then, the father's current visitation rights will continue."

He banged down the gavel.

For several seconds Susan did not move, trying to come to grips with the devastating news that the issue of custody would be left up to Karen. Was there any doubt whom the rebellious, father-worshiping thirteen-year-old would pick?

In the corridor outside the courtroom, Susan charged up to Peter and his lawyer.

"You've been almost derelict as a parent. Now, just to win a good financial arrangement, you want to take Karen away from me."

Peter shrugged, palms blamelessly out. "As the judge said, that's up to Karen."

"She's still a child. She can't possibly know what's best for her."

"You treat every little problem like a psychological crisis. At her age I went away to boarding school."

"Oh, God, you're planning to get custody and then get rid of her. She needs us now. How can you do this to her?" Tears of anger and anxiety filled Susan's eyes. "Who'll look after her and guide her? You certainly won't. Even if she stays, you'll be out until all hours at business meetings—or what you used to tell me were business meetings."

Peter was losing interest.

Susan's heart was breaking; Karen meant everything to her. "All right. If you want me to agree to a sale of the *Herald* in order to keep my daughter, I will."

Peter laughed. "Your timing is lousy. This morning my mother finally agreed to vote her shares with me. Midge will be no problem. I don't need your vote."

Susan felt a surge of relief. "Then you won't want custody of Karen anymore."

Flames leaped deep within Peter's gaze. "More than ever. And I'm going to force you out of the Foundation, too. I've beaten you at every turn. You're as good as finished. I'm going to make sure you have nothing—*nothing*—left to threaten me with."

"This is just a game to you!" Susan realized with a shock. "Like golf or billiards. The money is meaningless, you have so much. This whole thing was just to dominate me, to prove you could win. That terrible masculine compulsion."

"As American as apple pie," Peter agreed with an easy smile, and then walked off toward the elevators. "Like they say, it's everything."

At bottom, beneath the obscuring film of charm, Susan knew that she had finally glimpsed the viciousness that composed his character. What a horrendous, destructive father he would be to his daughter!

She screamed after him, "Karen will never be safe with you! I can't let you have her!"

Both lawyers had to restrain her.

"How can you let him do this to a child?" she rebuked Peter's lawyer.

"That's how I make my living," the man replied, as if the question had been a stupid one, and hurried after his client.

Susan suddenly noticed the tipstaff, who had stepped into the corridor and had been watching her.

"Will he tell the judge?" she asked Ramsay when they were alone.

"Probably," the lawyer acknowledged.

"I'm going to lose her, Harold. I haven't got a chance."

Normally Karen was responsible for mucking out her pony's stall. But she stayed in school that afternoon preparing for the second and last performance of *The Mikado,* so Susan went to the barn and, with a pitchfork, heaved the old straw and the manure into a burlap sack and began to pitch a thick layer of fresh straw onto the stall floor. Emotion overcame her, and she had to stop for a moment; even this onerous task for her daughter was precious because Karen was soon to be snatched from her.

Whenever Karen appeared on stage that night, Susan's eyes filled with tears. Her daughter was so beautiful in the kimono and high, black Japanese wig. How much she would miss her! Even the unremarkable joy she derived each day just from glancing at her once in a while would soon be denied her. So little time, she kept thinking. So little time.

She had baked chocolate-frosted brownies as a surprise for Karen when they returned home. They would sit together at the kitchen table, drinking milk and eating brownies, and she would explain about Monday and court. But after the play concluded, and the cast and crew came out to greet relatives and friends, Karen asked if she could spend the night at her girlfriend's house.

"I'd hoped we could talk tonight," Susan said. "Just the two of us."

"We can talk in the morning when you drive me to the country club. It's still on with Dad tomorrow, isn't it?"

"Yes."

Karen appeared relieved. "Great. Thanks for coming, Mom."

She kissed her mother on the cheek—they were nearly the same height now—and then turned to locate her girlfriend and the girlfriend's parents. Suddenly she turned back.

"Oh, I almost forgot. How did it go in court today?"

"We'll talk about it in the morning," Susan told her.

"Great."

Susan watched her daughter chattering with friends for a while and then rushed into the night. She sat unmoving in her car for several minutes. She felt like a prisoner counting down the hours to her execution.

Finally she turned the ignition key and experienced a rush of gratitude when the old engine sprang into full-throated life, not balking as it had that morning. Only after she found herself on the highway into the city did she realize that she had to inform Dan that his name had come up in court today. She owed it to him to let him know. But it was also an excuse for seeing him, she realized. She could not bear to be alone, and needed to talk about her predicament to someone who cared about her and would enclose her within his sympathy. He was the only real friend she had.

She parked on the street across from his apartment house and walked to a pay phone on the corner. After several rings, when she was about to give up, he answered.

"Hello," he said.

"I'd like to come up."

"I have company."

"Oh. It didn't occur to me."

She awaited his reply for what seemed like a long while and then said, "I'm sorry I bothered you."

"Give me fifteen minutes."

"You're sure it's all right. If I'm imposing . . ."

"Stop being so courteous. Fifteen minutes."

She returned to her car and watched the building's entrance. After ten minutes a young blond woman in a short skirt emerged, and the doorman flagged down a taxi for her. Dan had once taken Susan to a nearby piano bar. Was this the young waitress she had met there whom he had once dated? She could not tell. Two other people emerged a minute later.

Perhaps *they* were his company. When fifteen minutes had passed, she went up to his apartment.

He opened the door immediately, dressed in an open white shirt and black slacks.

"I'm sorry if I interrupted something," she said.

"Just finishing up a meeting."

"With that blond woman?"

"A meeting."

"I should never have barged in on you . . ."

He reached out and drew her into the apartment, holding her tightly against him, sensing that she wanted to cry. She felt relieved and foolish as she did. He lifted her chin and kissed the wet tracks down her cheeks and then pressed his mouth against hers.

He drew her down onto the hall carpet. They made love feverishly. When she came, she cried out terrible screams of rapture and loss.

In bed she lay on her side supported by an elbow, her free hand lightly, possessively, stroking the contours of his chest.

"There's something you should know," she began with quiet apology. "Peter has had detectives following me. I don't think he's using them anymore. I didn't see anyone follow me up here, but I can't be sure."

"That came out in court today?"

"Yes. Will it cause you problems?"

"It doesn't matter one way or the other. I'm leaving next week."

"Oh, God, you too."

She fell back and stared up at the ceiling. "I'm going to lose her, Dan."

"You're sure?"

"The judge is going to ask her on Monday who she wants to live with. It's no contest. I don't know how I can bear it."

"You've told me yourself, this is a stage she's going through. A year or two from now she'll change her mind. You can go back into court."

Susan's voice was angry with her bitterness. "As long as Peter is alive, he'll never let me have her back. He wants to crush me and leave me with nothing."

She sat up, her gaze unfocused. "How do I stop him from taking my daughter and destroying her life and mine? That's all I've thought about all day. How? I'll do anything."

She grabbed Dan's arm and stared wildly at him. "You're a lawyer, tell me some way to stop him!"

Dan glimpsed a fury within her that startled him.

"Now, *you're* leaving, too," she remembered. "Will it be for long?"

"Yes," he said, not certain what his answer would be until the words were out of his mouth.

"When will you be back?"

"I don't know."

She left the bed and quickly dressed. She halted at the bedroom door.

"Are you going to stop me?"

"No."

Her shoulders slumped. "Two ruined people, and we haven't even got each other."

Karen was already waiting when Susan picked her up the next morning at her friend's house to drive her to the country club. Susan had been up for hours, consumed by worry over how best to explain the upcoming court hearing to her daughter and to blunt the manipulation Peter was bound to apply all day.

As she usually did, she finally spoke directly.

"We have to talk about the divorce trial. The judge has to decide whether you're to live with your father or with me. He wants you to come to his office Monday morning. He wants to ask you which of us you'd rather live with."

Susan glanced over at Karen, anxious about the response. The girl continued to peer silently ahead through the windshield, so Susan went on.

"You and I sometimes fight over decisions I don't think you're old enough to make for yourself—"

"Because you're just too strict," Karen retorted sharply. "You think you have to boss every minute of my life."

"I try to do what I think a parent is supposed to—teach you and protect you from mistakes until you're mature enough to avoid them on your own."

"I'm thirteen."

Susan anxiously delved for an answer. Ads, movies, records all purveyed to young people the myth that the teen years were a time of instinctive wisdom hampered by parental interference. How to persuade Karen—so self-confident—of her own immaturity, of her need for guidance, of Peter's certain neglect.

"If you were a mother," Susan finally settled on, "would you think it best for your thirteen-year-old daughter to live with you or with her father?"

"I wouldn't be divorced!"

"Sometimes things don't work out as you'd hoped they would."

"A father can be just as good a parent as a mother!" Karen snapped.

"I want you to know that I love you, and I'll always love you. I hope very much that you'll choose to live with me."

"Daddy said I'll have to move out of our house if I do."

"The lawyer isn't sure. He's hoping that if you stay with me, we'll have the house till you're an adult."

Susan wanted to say so much more, in the hope of hitting upon a phrase, a reason, that would convince her daughter. But every thought that came to her sounded like either an attempt to impose guilt or begging. Karen would scorn such pleas. Like her father, she despised weakness.

Peter's Mercedes roadster was already parked in the country club parking lot. He was probably on the practice tee, tuning up for the match.

"I'll pick you up between five and five-thirty," Susan said.

"Right."

Karen leaned over and kissed Susan on the cheek. Susan impulsively hugged her.

Karen searched her mother's face for a moment and then slipped out of the car and up the walk to the large brick clubhouse.

Susan stared after her, hoping her daughter would turn around for a last glance, but Karen continued into the building.

Susan had never felt more disheartened or desperate. She tried to lose herself in cleaning the house and tending the garden, but her anguish continued to obsess her, and each minute of the day passed like a year.

Finally, at five, she left for Peter's house to pick up Karen. He had taken a house in Chestnut Hill, long an exclusive reserve just within Philadelphia's city limits. Although no longer restricted to the white Protestant upper class, Chestnut Hill still contained a mix of opulent estates and large, expensive houses on suburblike blocks.

Susan and Karen then drove back across the river to Dellwyne, stopping at the supermarket before returning home.

Less than three hours later, wearing a long-sleeved white blouse and black skirt, Susan answered her door and was met by a Philadelphia policeman, cap in hand. He was in his thirties with a blond crew cut, and he wore a distraught expression. His squad car was parked in the driveway.

"Mrs. Boelter?" the police officer murmured.

"Yes. Is something wrong?"

"I'm Officer Blaney. I've got some bad news, I'm afraid. May I come in?"

She led him back a few steps into the front hall and turned to face him. He carefully placed his cap on the hall table, taking all the time he could to delay having to relate his news.

"Mrs. Boelter," he finally said, "your husband is dead."

"Oh, no!" She clutched at the table and stared unfocused at the police officer for several seconds. "He can't be!"

"I saw him myself."

She collapsed slowly into a chair. "How did it happen? Where?"

"In his house. Your sister-in-law found his body and ran next door for help. She phoned nine-one-one—it must have been around six-thirty. I drove right over there. It's only a few minutes away—I work out of the Gypsy Lane station. I found your husband lying at the bottom of the cellar stairs. In a swimsuit. There was a strong smell of liquor. He wasn't breathing."

"Some kind of accident?"

"That's not my judgement to make, ma'am. The Mobile Crime Unit is already over there, and the medical examiner's office will do an autopsy. But if you're asking my opinion, it looks like he was drunk and tripped going down the steps."

Susan continued to stare at the policeman.

"Are you all right, Mrs. Boelter?"

She nodded, and then stood up. "I have to break the news to my daughter."

"Do you want me to come with you?"

"It would be better if I did it myself. Do you mind letting yourself out?"

"Sure," he replied, but concerned about her, watched her slow, painful shuffle down the hall.

After a few steps she stopped, her feet seemingly incapable of slogging any farther through her grief. Peter had acted detestably to her, but she had loved him for fifteen years and wanted to believe that for nearly all that time he had loved her, as well. Far deeper than hers, she knew, would be Karen's grief. The child had loved him blindly and unreservedly.

"Are you okay?" the police officer called out.

"Yes," she answered without turning back.

She began to move down the hall again, her pace quickening a bit with every step, her stride lengthening. There was a bright side to what had happened: At the instant of Peter's death she had suddenly become a very wealthy widow. In fact, she was now in full control of the *Herald*.

13

Dan tried to sleep on the plane to California but, apprehensive, could not. He had not laid eyes on his son since January, when they had separated at the Aspen airport, he flying east and the boy west. Now, for the first time, he would be visiting Jamie in California. Jim, he thought. I've got to remember he wants me to call him Jim. Dan was placing so much significance in their reunion.

He had no regrets, however, about leaving Philadelphia, even though weeks remained before his suspension was scheduled to go into effect. Any that might have lingered when he let Susan walk out of his apartment only a few days ago were firmly put to rest yesterday when she had invited him to her house for lunch to say good-bye properly. Before then, Dan had discounted the depth of his own relationship with her because he suspected that they had been drawn together only by their adversity. Now they did not even have that in common.

For a few minutes after sitting down to the salad she had prepared, they had talked about how unexpected and tragic Peter's death had been and how devastating—for her and especially for Karen, who was now riding in the woods. Although Susan had appeared to be agitated by the death of someone she had loved and lived with for so long, who had fathered her child, she did not pretend that she would miss the man who had tried to destroy her life in divorce court.

When Dan spoke about his imminent trip, she had tried to appear attentive, listening out of well-mannered obligation, but her mind had been elsewhere, evidently engaged by a hundred new blessings and challenges. Death was a magic wand that had turned her from a scullery maid into a princess. Under a will he had not yet bothered to revise, Peter had left all of his stock in the Herald Corporation to Susan and Karen equally. Susan received everything else, including the house. The will also named her as executor and trustee in charge of Karen's stock. Peter's shares, added to the Foundation's, gave her control of fifty-five percent of the Herald Corporation stock, more than a majority. His death had been a twist of fate that had rescued and utterly resuscitated her life.

Susan had long pondered what she saw as the *Herald*'s problems, but had been rebuffed by Peter when she raised them and suggested solutions. But she would become publisher now, and she revealed to Dan some of her plans to overhaul the *Herald*.

Dan had sensed an eager, vibrant energy beneath her sorrow that he supposed Peter had dampened over the years and that had been allowed to find expression only at the Foundation. He supposed, too, that only her ingrained graciousness had precipitated this luncheon invitation. One wrote thank-you notes for gifts, one phoned one's hostess to express appreciation for a previous night's dinner party, and even if one was in mourning and busy with more pressing matters, one treated a departing lover to a final luncheon.

Because of her preoccupation with her concerns, he had understood her coolness, her distance. But that distance had made his leaving much easier—and inevitable. While silently saying good-bye, Dan had tried to memorize the perfect planes of her face, the classic Anglo-Saxon nose, the thoughtful hazel eyes, to sear the image of another Susan into his memory, the woman who had screamed in rapture on his hall carpet only days ago.

Dan caught sight of Hannah waiting for him at the plane's gate, and then he recognized Jamie standing beside her, as tall now as she. The appealing brown Edwardian mop had been sheared short, making his suddenly visible ears appear too large, his neck scrawny, and his nose elongated and prominent. Scarecrow limbs emerged from T-shirt and shorts. Jamie looked almost like a stranger.

Dan's first impression of Hannah was that she appeared to be less frantic, less resentful than he recalled, although from their phone conversations he knew how difficult she still could be. The sandy hair was now worn long, its frizziness tamed by a ponytail, and her clothing more tailored than the assertive haphazardness she had assumed in the East. The Surfing Rabbi's daughter was now dressing like an adult.

She had hated being his wife, in great part, it occurred to him now, because she had not yet won credentials of her own. Either the years had mellowed her or, more likely, gaining her graduate degree in psychology and beginning to work as a therapist had finally defused her habitual defensiveness. It seemed to him that all the wives—or ex-wives—that he knew who were at loose ends became therapists, as if drowning in their own problems gave them the expertise to advise others. Instead of turning out the scientists and engineers it needed to compete globally, America was turning out therapists to ease its distress over its decline.

Frequently glancing up happily at his father, Jamie held his parents' hands as the three proceeded to Baggage Claim. At the line in front of the Avis counter, Hannah bribed Jamie with change to buy a soft drink. As soon as he was gone, she turned to Dan.

"I'm not pleased you're here, Dan. I want you to know that."

"There was no way I was going to miss my son's graduation."

"Did he tell you that he still owes twenty-two math assignments?"

"Twenty-two?"

"Actually twenty, but two are redos. They'll graduate him into junior high even if the papers aren't in, but they shouldn't, and I haven't told him that they will. It's important he realize that he can't always get away with things. But with you here, math is the last thing on his mind."

"How did he end up that far behind?"

"You're implying it's my fault."

"I'm not implying anything, Hannah."

"Not in those words, but you are. I know you."

Dan was already worn out by the conversation. "How could the school let him get away with it until the very last minute?"

"He has your magnetism without that surliness when you're angry. People want to help him. He trades on it." She paused. "His math isn't the only problem. I'm concerned about how your being here will affect Jim and me."

"It's not exactly news that you'd like me out of your life, except for my monthly checks."

"The minute Jim heard you were coming, he became unbearable to Ron."

"That's the auto dealer."

"My fiancé. Ron's a good man, and he'll make a good stepfather to Jim. Same religion. Same values. But your visit has revived all Jim's fantasies of you and me getting back together. He's been doing everything he can to break up my relationship with Ron."

"That's *your* problem. I've got enough of my own."

"Dan, the boy needs a man to emulate who's there all the time."

"You were the one who decided to move to California."

She curbed the retort about to fire from her. "We aren't even out of the airport, and already we're fighting. I honestly didn't want that to happen. Yes, I did move here. And no, there isn't any way you can be a father figure to him day in and day out from the other side of the country."

Her voice cracked, her emotions getting the better of her. "Jim needs a stable home with a full-time family. Ron would give him that. I love Ron and know that he loves me. But the way Jim is acting toward him, I'm afraid he'll just decide to walk away."

"I'm thinking of moving out here permanently."

She stared at Dan with dismay. "I think it would be terrible right now for Jim."

"And for you."

"And for me."

"Now, that's more like the Hannah I know and adore."

"Where to?" Dan asked after he and Jamie had checked his suitcase at the Beverly Hilton and were back in the rented car. "I hear Universal City's fun."

"I've been there five times."

"Well, then, what *don't* you do all the time?"

Jamie broke into a smile. "I want to play basketball with you and eat in a deli."

"You said Ron plays 'hoops' with you."

Jamie eyed his father sharply. "Yeah, but I mostly let him take me to ball games, you know, when he wants to show Mom how nice he can be to me. But now that you're here, I don't have to do any of that with him."

Dan bought an outdoor basketball, and they drove to a school playground. The courts were empty. They played one-on-one, with Dan trying to ignore the ache in his knee. He pushed himself to play well and scored the last four baskets. Jamie seemed thrilled. Dan could not tell whether that was out of reassurance that his father was still the man he looked up to or because Ron could not have played as well. Dan would have settled for either.

They played horse for another hour, competing at shooting baskets. By then, it was late enough to drive to Fairfax Avenue to find a good kosher delicatessen. Afterward Dan drove Jamie home.

Hannah had taken a large apartment in Santa Monica. On the kitchen counter was a note for her son: "Either ten math assignments are completed tonight—*neatly*—or *no* Little League tomorrow."

"Stay a while, Dad," Jamie urged. "Mom and Ron won't be home till late. Want to play something?"

"You've got homework."

"You just arrived. Why don't we get it out of the way together and then have a real father-son talk?"

Dan shook his head. "I deal with better con men than you every day of the week, kid. No TV, and no help with your homework."

"Will you take me to Little League in the morning?"

"Try and keep me away."

They hugged. Dan held his son tightly for a moment, adjusting his memory to the boy's new dimensions.

Dan drove back slowly to his hotel, feeling like a turtle locked away in his car. He tried not to get lost among the proliferation of roads criss-crossing the endless landscape that clumped into enough occasional simulations of urban life to call itself a city and finally, at the sea, simply ran out of room.

One reason he had come out was to determine whether he'd want to resettle here. Despite the pollution and last month's riots in the ghetto, there had to be something to the place. Millions of people lived here, with thousands more moving in each year. He would try to keep an open mind. After all, he had managed to track down a decent corned beef sandwich.

In the fourth inning Jamie hit a long triple into the gap in left center and scored on an infield out. As he slapped his teammates' hands on the way back to the dugout, he flashed a smile at Dan and then a second one at a large red-headed man with a mustache sitting alone at the top of the bleacher-style seats. Dan climbed up to join the other man, who looked to be in his late forties.

"Ron?"

The man stuck out a large hand for Dan to shake. "Dan, right? I recognize you from the photo in Jim's room."

Dan shook the hand and sat down beside him.

"The boy's pretty good," Ron commented.

"You've seen some of his games?"

"All of them. A few of the practices."

"You play any ball yourself?"

"Some, in high school. Stuck to football in college. It paid the expenses."

They were silent until a batter hit a hard shot to Jamie's right at shortstop. Jamie backhanded it and made the long throw to first.

"Nice play," Ron said.

"Does Hannah ever come to watch?"

"Usually. She just didn't want to step on your toes today."

"She seemed pretty tough about his doing his homework before he played."

"She's too tough sometimes. She doesn't really understand boys. But she's right that he's got to know there are limits, that he's got responsibilities to meet. He can't think he'll always be able to slide by." Ron caught himself. "Sorry. I didn't mean to sound off like that. You're his father."

"You have any kids of your own?"

"Wasn't married long enough the first time. And back then I guess I was too involved in building up my business."

"Cars, Jim says."

"He told you?" Ron sounded pleased.

After the game Dan invited Ron to join them for lunch.

The other man grew embarrassed. "I'm in the way. Got things to do."

He hastily shook Dan's hand. "Maybe I'll see you around."

After Ron left, Dan remarked, "I like him."

Jamie did not seem to know whether agreement or disagreement was called for.

"He's all right," the boy finally volunteered.

"And he likes you. I'm glad about that."

Jamie appeared to relax.

Dan realized that he had already accustomed himself to the possibility of an arrangement he had subconsciously come out here to oppose: expanding their family by adding one more father.

Dan spent the time when Jamie was in school mostly driving around to get a feel of the city. He had several lawyer friends in Los Angeles and had lunch with one who imparted a sense of what practicing law might be like here. Not much different from anywhere else, especially criminal law, he was told. The big fees come from drug dealers who can pay top dollar.

Hannah had bought Jamie a dark suit for graduation. When he consulted Dan on the tie, both agreed that it was "dead." They went to Nordstrom's and picked out a livelier one, then caught an early movie.

At a pizzeria afterward, Dan suggested they go away together for a week or two. "How about camping? You say you like that."

Jamie began to laugh.

"What's so funny?" Dan asked.

"You and camping? Come on."

"We could rent one of those VRs."

"RVs."

"You know what I mean."

"I have a Little League game on Saturday—I can't disappear on the team."

"I forgot about Little League. Maybe we could go to Disneyland afterward. We'll talk about it."

Susan had scheduled a meeting that morning with the managing editor, Leo Kucaba. She intended to settle once and for all the issue of who was running the *Herald*.

Several days before, she had sketched out for him her ideas for revamping the newspaper to make it more stimulating and readable and, thus, more valuable to advertisers. For years, newspapers all over the country had been steadily losing readers to television and to indifference, and the *Herald* was no exception. She wanted to reverse that erosion. She told Kucaba to put teams to work designing a new front page the eye would find easier to follow and new local sections for particular suburbs. She wanted sports given more prominence and wider coverage—market studies had determined that the competing *Mirror*'s good Sports section was the main reason men bought it. And she proposed several new weekly sections. One would induce younger adults to start buying the newspaper. Others—called Real Estate, Autos, Science, and Style— would attract advertising from home sellers, car dealers, computer stores, and furniture and housewares vendors.

But Peter's death had convinced Kucaba that he was now indispensable and had free rein to run the paper as he wished. He had simply ignored Susan's directive, considering her changes backhanded criticisms of his management. After three decades in the business, he wasn't about to be told how to run a newspaper by some society matron.

Scott Feller was waiting for an elevator in the lobby of the Herald Building when she arrived. She had a question for him.

"I've been telling Leo Kucaba that we need more investigative journalism from you. Has he said anything?"

"You've got to be kidding. For months I've been asking for more time to do investigative pieces. He keeps turning me down. I got so frustrated a while ago when he told me not to follow up on a tip that I insisted he discuss it with your husband. Same result."

"What was the tip?"

Feller related to her the rumor that the police hierarchy and the DA's office were fighting about botched cases.

"Leo's right about using staff time effectively," she said, "but that's exactly the sort of story we should be looking into. Do it. I'll see that your workload is lightened.''

Feller's excitement was obvious. ''Do you want to tell Leo, or should I?''

''Oh, I will.''

An hour later a shocked Leo Kucaba was negotiating his severance package in Midge Boelter's office, and Susan was outlining her new policies to the editors gathered in the newsroom's conference room for the morning rundown of that day's stories. Now occupying what had been Kucaba's chair was Fred Moore, the deputy managing editor, whom Susan had respected since the days when both were neophyte reporters. She knew he was as eager as she to refashion the stodgy *Herald* into a newspaper for the next century.

Her next announcement disconcerted the solid circle of white males almost as much. She told them that she was not about to expand staff during these hard times, but any hiring or promotions that *were* approved would favor capable women and minority candidates, who had been discriminated against up until then.

At the end, she informed the group that she was meeting that day with the unions to see if a new contract could be worked out. ''Unless we can control costs, there won't be a paper or jobs for either side to bargain about. But some of the union leaders have privately indicated they're ready to be reasonable.''

She stood up, about to leave in order to let Fred Moore exercise his new authority.

''The *Herald* has been a great and profitable newspaper in the past. I intend it to be again. Anyone who doesn't share that vision or isn't up to the challenge or who disagrees with our new directions can join Leo Kucaba in early retirement. The rest of us are taking the *Herald* full speed ahead.''

Jamie's graduation was held outdoors, with students, teachers, and guests on folding chairs set up as an amphitheater on the athletic field. Too late, Dan remembered he had no camera. Ron, laden with both a Nikon 35mm and a Sony camcorder, assured Dan he'd make copies of everything for him.

Soon after they returned to Hannah's apartment for a small luncheon in Jamie's honor, the phone rang.

''A long-distance operator for you, Dan,'' Hannah informed him.

Dan took the call in the bedroom, sitting on the side of the bed.

''Hello.''

"Mr. Daniel Lazar?" the operator asked.

"Yes."

"Go ahead, please."

"Dan?" The voice was Susan's. "I got Hannah's phone number from information. I'm sorry to bother you . . ."

"What's wrong?"

"Gil Huyton just left here. He came by as a courtesy because we're old friends; he wanted me to be prepared."

"Did he say what for?"

"Not in so many words, but we both knew what he meant."

"What was that?"

"In the next day or so he's probably going to arrest me for Peter's murder."

14

Jamie entered the bedroom just as Dan was saying into the receiver, "You know I've been suspended, Susan. They may not let me take your case."

"I need you, Dan."

Jamie's face grew worried. Dan patted the bed. His son sat down beside him.

"Tell me one thing," Dan asked Susan, "and I've got to have the truth. Did you do it?"

"I didn't, Dan. I swear it."

"I'll get back to you."

"You've got to help me, Dan."

Dan said good-bye and replaced the receiver on its cradle. He stared at the floor in deep contemplation.

Jamie eventually spoke up. "Are you going back to Philadelphia?"

"Yes."

"But you said you'd live out here for a while, maybe even move out here."

"An emergency has come up."

"That woman on the phone, that Susan, you're going back for her?"

Dan put his arm around his son. "You know how you told me we couldn't go away together right now because your baseball team's relying on you to be there Saturday? Well, this woman is about to be charged with murder, and she's relying on me to help her."

"She probably did it."

"She says she didn't. She may be telling the truth."

"*I* need you, too, Dad."

"You'll always have me; that won't disappear just because I have to go back to help a friend. We'll talk on the phone most nights, like we do now, and we'll see each other during vacations. Your mom is right about one thing, though."

"About what?"

"You need something I can't give you: being part of a full-time family that eats dinner together and checks whether you did your homework and sees you off on the school bus every morning."

"You could live here, with Mom and me."

Dan eyed his son with comic skepticism.

"Okay," the boy conceded, "I know, it's not realistic. Mom tells me that all the time."

"Hey, you're not losing me because she's found Ron. I'll bet even Ron loves you. You're getting the best deal going."

Dan kept to himself that L.A. had proven to be alien country to him. He had spent more time inside a car the last few days than he usually did in a month and, instead of finding a purpose out here that made his life worth living, had spent most of his time waiting around to be Jamie's father. L.A., he realized now, was probably the last place he could ever fit in.

He had something to clear up and forced himself to go on. "You heard me say on the phone that I've been suspended from practicing law."

"Yes," Jamie admitted reluctantly, his voice strained with pain.

"Do you think I could really be guilty of doing something that bad?"

"No."

"Well, I didn't, but there was no way to prove it. This woman may be facing false charges, too. That's why I have to go back. Do you understand?"

Jamie nodded. "We'll spend time together at the beach house this summer, right?"

"Sure."

"And we'll still go skiing in the winter?"

"Anywhere you want. Name it."

"There'll be another Winter Olympics in a couple of years."

"Tall order, but if that's what you want . . ."

Jamie shook his head and wrapped a hug around his father. "Just testing."

*   *   *

Dan had phoned Susan from the L.A. airport last night to inform her that he would be arriving in the morning and would take a taxi right to her house. Her understanding, she told him, was that the influential women in Peter's family were putting pressure on Gil Huyton to charge her with murder. The Huytons, the Boelters, and Amelia's family had been close friends for decades. Amelia and Margaret, now beset by sorrow, were convinced that Peter's death had occurred too fortuitously for Susan's benefit, that about to lose everything in divorce court, she had killed him as a matter of her own survival. It was as if the scandal surrounding John Boelter's original inheritance of the paper had recurred like a family curse—or, worse, like a family technique.

"Thank you for coming back, Dan," Susan said. "It's been a nightmare."

They were seated in the large period drawing room where drinks were served during his first visit. Although Susan was taking her time about rehiring staff, both to hold down expenses and because she felt more comfortable with fewer people, the house was slowly returning to normal. A maid Dan recognized from his initial visit answered the front door. Through the window, he could see a gardener crouched over a flower bed. Susan lifted a cup and saucer to pour coffee for him from a silver coffeepot.

"Milk, not cream, and no sugar?" she remembered.

"Yes."

She handed him his cup and saucer and poured coffee for herself.

A week ago, facing destitution and the loss of her daughter, she looked like the last survivor of an epidemic. Her husband's providential death had brought a reprieve, but the suspicion that she had caused it had yanked her back down into hell again. Yet, no worry was apparent on her face, no anxiety in her voice.

Knock, knock, he silently called out to her. Is there a real person under there? I used to think so. He remembered her rage at Peter the last time they made love—and her passion. Was her upper-class self-control concealing her emotion, he wondered, or was this cool detachment the real essence of Susan Boelter?

"Do they have any evidence that points to you?" Dan asked.

"I was at Peter's house during the time the police think he died. I arrived there to pick up Karen at about a quarter after five or so and left maybe half an hour later." She reflected for a moment. "Actually, ten to six. The police say Amelia found his body in the cellar at six-thirty."

"Half an hour there seems like a long time just to pick Karen up."

"She and Peter were still in back at his pool when I got there. In their bathing suits. We all talked together for a few minutes. Then, while Karen went to get dressed, Peter asked to talk to me alone."

"About what?"

"He was angry. Karen had decided she wanted to live with me. She was going to tell that to the judge on Monday."

Dan was surprised. "You were sure she'd want to live with Peter."

"She was so dazzled by him that I figured . . ." She let the sentence slip into silence. "But spending that day with him, she realized how inconsistent and uncertain her life with him would be. I was thrilled."

"What did Peter want to talk to you about?"

"I thought a settlement offer, so I told Karen to get dressed and wait for me out front in my car. I went into the house with him. Peter had won the club golf championship that morning and had started celebrating right afterward. He was thoroughly drunk by then. As usual when he had been drinking, he became abusive and started an argument. He began to yell at me. I yelled back. We both told each other exactly how we felt."

"Was anybody else in the house?"

"No, the servants were off for the weekend."

"And he was alive when you left?"

"Alive and still drinking."

"That would be at around ten minutes to six?"

"Yes. Peter's house is in Chestnut Hill. Karen and I drove back across the river and then up to Dellwyne. We stopped at the supermarket in the village to buy some things, and then drove home."

Dan stood up. "I'd like to talk to Karen."

"She's out riding in the woods." Susan looked down at her hands gripping each other, allowing Dan finally to glimpse the anxiety her countenance was trained to deny. "I think if we could have the funeral and she could say good-bye to him, it would begin to get a little easier for her."

"You haven't had the funeral?"

"Peter's body hasn't been released yet. They said it would be soon, so I set the funeral for tomorrow morning."

"It might pay to have your own autopsy done first. Let me check into what's happening at the medical examiner's office."

"Thanks. Would you like to have dinner with us tonight? Say, six o'clock? You could talk to Karen then." A reticent smile peeked through the worry on her face. "And to me, as well. I missed you when you were gone."

"You only phoned me when you were in trouble."

"You didn't make yourself easy to find. All the time we were having lunch before you left, I had the feeling you couldn't wait to disappear."

That was probably true, Dan found himself admitting. Perhaps she had good reason for this restraint she was displaying toward him.

"Six o'clock," he confirmed.

Susan offered to drive him to the city—she had a series of meetings at the *Herald* with various union heads to hammer out the last points of the new labor contracts. In return for their considerable concessions, they wanted a written guarantee that the Boelter family would not sell the paper for ten years. They did not know that Susan wanted that as much as they did.

Dan declined the ride. He had a taxi waiting outside.

"I'm grateful to you," she told him as they walked to the front door.

"I'm just going to look into things. I'm not promising I can do much more."

"But you'll investigate."

"Yes. As a friend."

She leaned forward and kissed him briefly on the lips. "Thank you. You're the only person I trust. I hope you believe I could never do such a thing."

Dan did not reply.

Dan's immediate impression when he entered Mara's office was that the pressures of the job were wearing her down. Long an ADA, she should have been hardened to the endless flow of horror and tragedy that moved through a district attorney's office, but she was thinner now and her expression somber.

He declined her offer of coffee. She poured herself the last cup from what must have been a full pot only a few hours earlier; she seemed to be running on caffeine.

"I ran into Cal at City Hall the other day," she began. "He said you'd gone away."

"To see Jamie. I came back early. This morning, as a matter of fact. Susan Boelter was told she may be charged with her husband's murder."

"Are you still sleeping with her?"

"Jesus! How did you know that I was?"

"I've read the transcript of her divorce trial," she added. "The woman was furious at her husband."

Her tone conveyed no undue sexual interest. Sex interested her immensely, he knew, but only when she personally engaged in it. Evoking no guilt and requiring no exclusivity, it was simply a basic urge: You wanted sex from someone, or someone wanted sex from you. It was both a hunger and a medium of exchange.

Dan pointed out, "She may have been angry at him. But I sometimes felt she was also still in love with him. Did you know him?"

"Only slightly. Gil introduced me to them when they showed up at the Montano hearing."

"He was a fascinating man."

"Tell me about him."

"He was amusing, charming, easily bored, and very sure of himself. He could be kind one minute, cruel the next, and you could never be sure which was coming. The only thing you could be certain of when you first met him was that he'd been born rich."

"And you don't think she killed him?"

"That's what I'm trying to find out. Is Huyton pushing you to bring charges?"

"He thinks the evidence against her's conclusive." Mara's mouth tightened into a thin line. "You know Gil—he doesn't believe in accidents. Peter Boelter was his friend. If he's dead, someone had to have caused it. Someone has to pay."

"Sorry you took the job?"

"On the contrary," she said, her voice firmed by her ambition. "Gil will probably run for the Senate in the next election. I think he'll back me as his replacement."

Her face softened into a grin for a moment. "I'm a prosecutor at heart, Dan. You still want to believe there's some good out there. I know there isn't."

"You said Huyton thinks the evidence against Susan is strong. What exactly is it?"

Mara opened a manila file, briefly glancing at the contents while sipping her coffee. She then began to outline the facts, starting with the chief medical examiner's estimation of when Peter died.

"Kieffer fixed the time of death at between five-fifteen and a quarter to six. Not only does Susan Boelter admit to being alone in her husband's house all that time, we have corroboration from the woman who lives next door, a Mrs. Hildreth. She was outside in her garden and had a full view of his house, his front lawn, and the street. She saw no one else enter his house while she was outside, which was till just around six, when her husband arrived from work and she went inside her own."

"What about Amelia Boelter?"

"Nine-one-one logged in her phone call at six thirty-one. If you assume she was in Peter's house for two or three minutes, at most, before she found the body, she didn't arrive earlier than, say, six twenty-five."

Mara scanned the statement Amelia had given to the police. "Peter failed to answer his doorbell, but the door was unlocked, so she went inside. She looked around and called out, but got no response. The cellar door was open, and the light was on. She looked in there and saw Peter Boelter lying at the bottom of the cellar steps. She ran next door to Mrs. Hildreth's for help."

"She didn't go down the steps to check on him?"

"She says no, that she immediately ran next door. They called the police from the Hildreth house. The police made it from the station in a couple of minutes. The ambulance arrived seven minutes later and confirmed that he was already dead."

"But how can you be sure it wasn't an accident? I understand he'd been drinking."

"We're still awaiting some other lab tests, but you're right about the drinking. His blood-alcohol level was high. Point nineteen percent. But that's irrelevant. Peter Boelter was killed by a heavy blunt instrument with a sharp protrusion."

Dan's face revealed his surprise. "I thought he fell down the cellar stairs."

"Someone threw him down there. After he was dead."

"Did you find a murder weapon?"

She shook her head. "Everything else points right at Susan Boelter, though: the time, the motive, the opportunity."

"You sound pretty certain."

"Did you know she physically attacked Amelia Boelter after she came upon the woman in bed with her husband? Fists, nails, cursing. That came out at the divorce trial. Not quite the most ladylike behavior!" Mara hesitated. "I'd like to ask you something, Dan—off the record, just for my own curiosity."

Dan nodded.

"Is she a passionate lover?"

"What?" He was startled and embarrassed by the question.

"Does she really let go and get into it? You used to like that about me."

"What's the point of this?"

"I figure there are passions simmering inside Susan Boelter you don't see on that cool surface of hers."

"And?"

"Susan Boelter was being provoked by every kind of passion that can drive a woman. Love, money, jealousy, revenge." Mara ticked off the items in an angry, abrupt manner, apparently appalled by the waste of a life for such commonplace reasons. "She loved him, but he walked out on her and was sleeping with another woman. She loved her daughter, and he was going to take the daughter away. She loved the newspaper, and he was going to sell it. She had an opulent life, with money to burn, and was about to lose that, too.''

''And you think that in a fit of rage, she picked up something and killed him with it.''

''The anger helped, but I think she planned it,'' Mara reasoned. ''Probably brought the weapon with her. Killing him was the only way to retaliate and to make sure no other woman could have him. It would also stop the paper's sale and allow her to keep her daughter and all his money.''

''She says her daughter had already decided to live with her.''

Mara pulled another interview report from the file. '' The girl told a school friend we interviewed that she wanted to live with her father.''

''She had a change of heart.''

Mara's eyebrows raised. ''Convenient.''

''It sounds like you're going for an arrest.''

''I may have to. The evidence is building up.''

''The first time I met Peter Boelter he joked that he was hoping a juicy crime of passion would electrify the city and boost the *Herald*'s circulation. Ironic, isn't it?''

''It's horrible.''

He stood up. ''I'd like a copy of the police reports and the autopsy report.''

She hesitated.

''You'll have to turn copies of everything over to me if I decide to take the case,'' he reminded her.

''Gil won't like your getting involved. He feels you got off too lightly as it is with that suspension. He'll fight tooth and nail to keep you out.''

''How do *you* feel about it?''

''I think she did it, Dan. I'll even try the case myself if we can be sure we have enough to charge her. I want her to pay for that life she took. But you and I once meant a lot to each other. You shouldn't be the one fighting me in court.''

Dan deliberated briefly. ''The Disciplinary Board gave me a couple of months to finish everything up. I still have time. If I decide to take her case, I'll ask them to push back the suspension.''

''Why should they?''

''How would it look if they tried to prevent someone being tried for murder from picking the lawyer she wants to defend her?''

''There's no way they'll approve of a lawyer who's representing his lover.''

''Nothing in the Canon of Ethics prevents it.''

"But it's frowned on, you know that. And for good reason. They could say you won't be objective, that you obtained the fee by using undue influence—"

He interrupted her. "If I take the case, there's no way I'll take a fee."

Mara gazed reflectively at him for several long seconds and then observed, "Love is really a funny thing."

"I'm not in love with her."

Mara laughed. "Well, you're sure hot for *someone* right now, and I know it isn't me. That bothers me. Isn't that terrible?"

Dan was astonished to realize what Mara had instinctively sensed; he could not even remember how badly he had once missed her.

"Dan Lazar," she said, shaking her head at an irony she considered far more apt than the one he had pointed out. "Trust you to fall for a murderess."

Dan immediately noticed the "WELCOME HOME, DAN" sign that Mary Alice had taped to the front of her desk.

"How did you know I was back?" he asked.

She lifted her head from the phone cradled against her shoulder and her fingers from the computer keyboard. "Louise, in the DA's office. She called to tell me."

"She on with you now?"

Mary Alice shook her head. "Norma, from Mental Health. Dan's back," she said into the mouthpiece, and then looked up at Dan again. "She already heard it from Louise."

Cal's door was open. He had seen Dan enter and had come out to greet him.

"I heard you were back."

"That Louise gets around."

The men went into Cal's office, where Dan closed the door and recounted what had occurred in California.

"Sorry it didn't work out with Jamie the way you were hoping," Cal responded in sympathy.

"Probably better this way."

"You back for good?"

"I don't know. Susan Boelter asked me to come back. She's about to be arrested for her husband's murder."

Cal emitted a soft whistle. "You'll have to petition the Disciplinary Board to push back the suspension." He appraised Dan for a moment. "You involved with her?"

"Why do I have to be involved with her just to help her out?"

Cal waited for an answer.

"Yes," Dan admitted, "I guess I am."

"Shit! Then take my advice and don't represent her."

"Mara says the same thing."

Cal's eyes rolled up. "You mean they already know about you two at the DA's office?"

"Yes."

"They'll cut both of you into little pieces."

"I only agreed to look into it. I'll need an investigator. I'd like to use Rick."

"Sure. He's in his office."

Dan stood up. "I won't take a fee. You ought to know that up front, Cal."

"Another reason not to take the case." Cal confessed, "I was hoping you'd be back fresh after six months, with all the demons exorcised, the midlife crisis or whatever the hell it is behind you, ready to fight the world. But not like this. This will tear you apart."

"You said you wanted me to date again."

His partner refused to return Dan's smile. "Not her. She's from a different world, Dan. She's too rich, and she's in too much trouble. Promise me if she's charged, you won't take the case."

Dan stared at Cal, pondering, then left the room to find Rick and arrange to meet him in the morning.

The Office of the Medical Examiner was housed in a modern brown brick building in West Philly, on University Avenue across from the VA hospital. Dan's few visits there had been unpleasant, but brief. This time promised to be worse: He knew the victim personally. Death was neither a condition nor a concept with which Dan felt comfortable, and which he avoided contemplating if he could.

He had seen death everywhere in Vietnam, but had survived with his sanity intact by treating his tour there as a nightmare interlude from which he would wake upon his return, by forcing himself even then not to think about the villagers accidentally blown apart or about the black-garbed men he had cut down, or about the companions suddenly felled, bloody and open-eyed. Comrades may have thought him callous for refusing to reminisce about buddies suddenly gone from their midst, but even at twenty-two and just out of college, he had been wise enough to understand that acknowledging death's power to plunder life would rob his own, that death itself was the enemy. The Viet Cong, whom he had nothing against, were only its messenger.

The lobby's floor was covered with a blue carpet and its walls with wood paneling. A door in the corner hid a room in which friends and relatives identified corpses on a closed-circuit television monitor. Beside it was the Grief Assistance Room. Two black women sat on a sofa, one whispering encouragement to another, who was crying as she prepared to view a body.

A phone call from the district attorney's office had smoothed the way for Dan to examine Peter's body in person. The receptionist made a phone call and then directed him along the white corridors to the stairs leading down to the morgue in the basement.

Dan stepped out into chaos: a large room heaped with equipment and cartons. Walking toward him was a tall, young black man dressed in an argyle sweater over whites, his shoulders swinging to a silent, inner beat as he blew into a silver clarinet. A moment later Dan realized that the clarinet was a long hero sandwich wrapped in aluminum foil; the man was eating a late lunch and listening to music through small, red earpieces.

"Hey, man," the other said, lowering the sandwich and pointing a friendly finger at Dan, "I recognize you from the news."

They shook hands, Dan squeamishly wondering what that hand had touched before the aluminum foil. The worker introduced himself as Rudy and said he was an autopsy technician. Dan explained that he was there to view Peter Boelter's body.

Rudy thought for a moment. "He's around here somewhere. Everything's still kind of disorganized."

"I noticed."

"We got a lot of new equipment going in, too, but the flood really messed things up."

"Flood?"

"Water main broke. Like Niagara Falls around here." Rudy's face brightened. "I remember, now. Important dude. The flood happened just before he got here. We lost him for two days. Bodies floating, stacked up. Rushing through autopsies fast as you could deal cards. You wouldn't believe it." He laughed. "Great time to get away with murder."

He turned and, chewing once more on the exposed end of his long sandwich and bouncing to his music, happily led the way toward the refrigerator rooms like a pied piper of the netherworld. Taking one last bite, he propped the sandwich, aluminum end down, against the wall and pushed open the metal door.

A cold blast of wind from twin giant blowers near the ceiling rushed out. The unmistakable odor of death assaulted Dan's nostrils. Oh, God, he knew that smell! Nausea tumbled his inner organs. He leaned against the wall to steady himself.

When he looked up, Rudy was standing in the center of the refrigerated room, looking down at a row of bodies wrapped in plastic and lined up like ski bags at Baggage Claim. Placing a finger at one name on a list, Rudy bent down to a bundle and opened the plastic. Suddenly exposed to view was the naked body of an obese woman. She lay supine with her short-cropped head tipped back to exhibit a gaping slash across her throat.

"Damn! Sorry about that," Rudy apologized, still chewing. "No one's where they should be since the flood. We supposed to be getting new computers, but someone hijacked them babies for another department. The CME's down at City Hall right now trying to get them back."

Rudy rewrapped the woman and made a note on the list.

"Doesn't this ever get to you?" Dan asked.

Rudy shook his head. "Not when you come from my neighborhood. Got so if I didn't recognize who was laying on the street when I went to school, I didn't pay it no mind. When you dead, don't matter who you are, man, you just part of the garbage."

Rudy glanced up from the list. "He's in Room One."

Dan followed the technician out and across the corridor into another re-frigerated room. The sight overwhelmed him. Here bodies going to or coming from autopsies lay on gurneys, some covered with sheets, some not.

"He's over here," Rudy called out. He had lifted a sheet to expose a tag attached to a big toe. Dan veered toward him without looking to either side.

Rudy slowly slid down the sheet. Peter Boelter's elegantly handsome profile facing upward emerged first, and then his unclothed body, sur-prisingly well-muscled for a man so thin. His face was paler than in life, gravity having drawn the blood to settle along his underside. Were it not for the incongruous stitching to close the Y-shaped autopsy incision on his chest and abdomen, one might have thought he was asleep. Similar stitching, Dan knew, had closed the scalp after examination of the brain, but that incision was hidden by the dark, longish hair.

"Good-looking guy," Rudy commented offhandedly. "I sewed him up. You knew him?"

Dan nodded and drew the chief medical examiner's autopsy report from his inside jacket pocket. The cause of death had been a crushing blow to the skull. "Blunt trauma," the report stated, but Dan could see no wound. He bent down to look under the head. Obligingly, Rudy lifted it up by the hair. The base of the skull was smashed inward, the skin gashed open to expose bone, blood, and bits of brain tissue.

Dan instinctively closed his eyes and waited to be overtaken by nausea a second time, but realized that with the initial shock having passed, he had ceased to think of the inert form on the slab as Peter Boelter; it once contained him, but lifeless, was Peter no longer. He could now observe it with some detachment.

He peered closely at the wound. It was a deep, horizontal depression across the base of the skull, split open like parted lips to reveal bloody bone and brain. A sharply deeper cut was located in the middle of the wound.

"Whatever hit him was heavy and had a sharp edge," Rudy said. "Leastways that's what Doc thinks."

Dan read from the autopsy report. The medulla had been nearly crushed and the upper cervical cord partially severed.

The chief medical examiner and the staff neuropathologist had concluded that the bruise on the front of the brain was far less extensive than it should have been.

"If he was hit in back of the head," Dan asked Rudy, "why do they expect a wound on the front of the brain?"

"Contra-coup. That's what they call it. Brain's kind of loose in the skull. When someone falls back hard enough to kill them, the brain's thrown forward, like when you're in a car accident, you get thrown forward."

According to the report, the contra-coup bruise's scant size was evidence that Peter was already nearly dead when his head hit the step, his heart barely pumping blood into the bruise; the killing blow had been struck earlier.

Dan moved down to the far end of the gurney, noting abrasions on both sets of knees and shins. He had seen another on the forehead and one on the back of a shoulder when Rudy lifted the head. The report said that the scrapes, too, had occurred once his heart had almost stopped, after the killer tossed the body down the stairs. He asked Rudy how someone could tell that from observing the scrapes.

"Color mostly. They're more yellow and glassy than they should be. Blood almost stopped pumping by then, so you don't get that red-brown blood color in the little cuts."

"They look a little red-brown to me," Dan observed.

"Doc says not enough."

"Any more lab tests come back?"

"The labs even more disorganized than we are right now."

"Did you shoot photos?"

"They should be in the file." Rudy did not sound optimistic that the file would readily come to hand.

Dan handed him a twenty-dollar bill. "Do me a favor? Shoot another roll just to be sure. The brain, too."

A shrewd glint invaded the technician's eyes. "That color film's expensive."

Dan peeled off another twenty. "I'll wait outside for the roll."

He turned back to stare one last time at the somewhat-less-than-complete remains of Peter Boelter, now finally and uncharacteristically at rest. Here was someone whom men envied and women wanted, who had been blessed from birth with wealth, power, good looks, and charm, but who had never seemed content, despite sparing himself nothing. Possessed of a vein of cruelty, he rarely spared others, as well. Until the moment his life ended, it must have been both haunting and wonderful to be Peter Boelter.

Dan phoned Susan from a pay phone, advising her that she ought to allow him to hire someone to perform a second autopsy. "The funeral's already set for tomorrow," she replied.

"Postpone it."

"Is this other autopsy absolutely essential?"

"Well, we have photographs of everything. And they preserve slides here taken from key tissue parts your own expert could look at when the time came. But you never know. Another autopsy might turn up something new."

"It sounds ghoulish, everybody picking over Peter like that." He heard a shiver in her voice. "We've all gone through enough. It's time to put an end to it. Dan, people are already flying in for the funeral. The arrangements have all been made. I'll take my chances."

15

The visit to the morgue had left Dan feeling fragile, a fact he recognized only after he found himself driving timidly along the highway out of the city nearly fifteen miles an hour under the speed limit. The afternoon was warm and cloudless, yet he had instinctively chosen to take his car, not his motorcycle. On any other day he would probably have denied the feeling, with its implication of a weakness of will. But today, forced into deep reflection, he could not.

Peter was maybe, what, a few years younger than he? Without warning, a guy with everything to live for was gone. For himself, too, Dan knew, one misstep on a steep stairway, one break in a blood vessel, one angry client, and it could suddenly be over.

Why had he left his son and returned to this city before he had discovered where it was he wanted to go, before he had glimpsed his life's purpose glittering on some far horizon? Was his guilt about leaving Jamie and the frustration he was feeling to no purpose? There had to be a reason.

The siren call of a woman? Even if, as Mara suspected, he was in love with Susan Boelter, he felt that something else as well had drawn him back. The deep ennui he felt and this almost elemental yearning for meaning had gnawed at him long before he ever met Susan Boelter.

He stepped on the accelerator and flipped on the radio, seeking music that would crowd out the recurrent questions, variations on the larger perplexity that had obsessed him for months.

Susan stood outside the wooden fence that ringed the raked earth enclosure on the far side of the barn and watched Karen put her horse through an equestrian routine. The sun glinted off the colt's mane and the girl's golden hair, tiptoeing chestnut and frozen rider seemingly lost in the dance.

"She spends hours like that," Susan remarked as Dan came up beside her. Karen had won in her class at Devon this year. But she was riding now for consolation, not to train for competition.

"Does she talk about her feelings to you?"

"Mostly she just clings to me. She's so sad all the time. I have to sit by her bed at night until she falls asleep."

"She thought her father walked on water," Dan remembered.

"I just wish it hadn't taken this catastrophe to bring her close to me."

The routine came to its end, and Susan called out that they would be having dinner soon. Without a word Karen guided her horse out of the ring and toward the stable. Susan and Dan walked to the house.

Hoping to gain more insight into the man than Peter had permitted others to see, Dan asked to see Peter's study.

The room was large, with modern furniture. Two small white sofas near the door faced each other across a black lacquered coffee table. At the study's other end was a desk and a tall black desk chair with white armchairs facing it. The walls were a light gray, the carpet salt-and-pepper gray.

One wall contained dark wooden bookcases and cabinets. The center cabinet concealed a bar. Books were lined up on a few of the lower shelves. Dan read some of the titles. They were predictable: nonfiction best-sellers, mostly about business, a large number about the newspaper business. The other shelves were filled with golf trophies and industry awards. The trophies seemed to be arranged chronologically, the earliest for tennis and golf. By Peter's college years they were only for golf. The last in the progression were a row of seven identical abstract sculptures. They were tall and angular. Dan lifted one at random. The gleaming, silvery metal reflected patches of the room.

" '1987 Dellwyne Country Club Golf Championship,' " he read aloud from the inscription on the base.

"Peter won it just about every year that he played," Susan explained. "I'm surprised anyone else bothered to enter. He was that much better than everyone. If he'd been born into a different family, he might have taken a crack at the golf tour, but his father didn't consider it a serious profession."

"Peter wasn't hungry enough to succeed as a pro."

"Probably not. And week after week of tournaments would have bored him. But I wish he'd tried it. He ended up doing what his father wanted and resenting him. I sometimes got the feeling, especially over the last few years, that he was boiling inside. And that he'd been boiling that way all his life, only now he could afford to let people see it."

Dan replaced the heavy trophy carefully. The idea of Peter's submitting to anyone's mandate, even his father's, took some thinking about. He was a headstrong, totally willful man with some of the urges of an unruly child, the kind who could eat one or two favorite candies from the first box and then rip open the next and the next.

"Karen's room is filled with trophies, too," Susan said. "For horsemanship, of course, and swimming. A few for golf. She already shoots in the high eighties. She knew it was something Peter would respect."

Dan turned his attention to the industry awards. The plaque in the place of honor was from the American Newspaper Publishers Association.

"He got that the year after John died. It was really recognition for John and the *Herald,* but Peter was in his glory accepting it."

"He wasn't bothered that he hadn't earned it."

"I think he was."

Dan went to the desk, a glass plank laid atop white cube pedestals with drawers. Behind it and the desk chair was a long, white cabinet. He assumed that a fax and the other office equipment Peter had taken to his new home had once sat there.

"I haven't had the heart yet to move into his office," Susan said. "I feel more comfortable in my little one upstairs."

Dan began to open the desk drawers, studying each item. He was looking for an address book or notes Peter might have left behind when he moved out, something that would point him toward people who might have had a motive for killing Peter. He found nothing of importance. Atop the desk were toys for the distracted executive that were more revealing: a small Slinky, a line of five swinging silver balls, and a wooden contraption with a crank to turn rods that moved perpendicular to each other to no purpose.

Dan stared at the empty desk chair. "Everything's just waiting for him to arrive. There's a space left here where he used to be. I get the feeling that you could pour plaster into this room, and a statue of Peter would form right in the chair."

"That isn't how I think of it. It's like a pharoah's tomb, with all the things he'd want to take into the next life." Her voice was suddenly tinged with bitterness. "Lacking only his concubines."

Without looking at her watch, she announced, "It's time for dinner."

* * *

Dinner was served in the room where Dan had lunched with Susan before his trip to California, a glass-enclosed porch overlooking the garden. Dan gathered that Susan and Karen took all their suppers here now, so as to avoid the dining room, with its heavy furnishings and sharp memories of meals there with Peter. Susan had cooked the dinner herself.

A new attribute had been added to her personality: an air of command. This house and its privileges were hers by right now. Her whim, not Peter's, now ruled its hallways.

"Dan would like to ask you some questions," Susan told Karen after the maid had served the main course and withdrawn. He sensed mother and daughter had already discussed the need to submit to the interview.

"I'm just trying to understand what happened the day your father died," he began, "to help your mother if I can."

Karen nodded.

"You were at the country club with him that morning," he began. "Did anything unusual occur? Maybe someone made a remark to your father that was threatening or out of place."

Karen shook her head.

"What about the people you were with?"

Karen answered haltingly, her voice subdued. "The man he was playing against didn't like Daddy's jokes about being so far ahead, but he laughed at them. They had played matches together lots of times."

"Did you have lunch at the club?"

"Yes."

"Were other people there? Did they say anything?"

"The head of the club made a speech about how they probably shouldn't even bother to hold the tournament anymore, just give Daddy the trophy. He bought everybody drinks. They were having fun."

As Dan had noticed before, the pretty face and body were a young Susan's, just blooming into a woman's.

"Then what happened?" he asked.

"Daddy had a present for me. He remembered my birthday was coming up."

Susan interjected. "More likely, he remembered that you were going to testify in court in two days."

Karen ignored her mother's harsh remark. "He had the present in his car and gave it to me when we drove to his house after lunch. A video camera."

"Did you go directly to his house?" Dan wanted to know. "You didn't stop anywhere?"

"No. We spent the afternoon at his pool."

"Just the two of you? Was anyone else there? Someone who worked there or perhaps just showed up?"

"Just us." She shook her head, a faint smile at the recollection momentarily relieving her gloom. "We swam and talked. I did homework and tried out my camera."

Dan's voice quickened. "Did you tape anything?"

"Mostly Daddy and me at the pool."

"I'd like to see the tape," Dan told Susan. Then he asked, "Karen, had you decided by then which of your parents you were going to tell the judge you wanted to live with?"

"Yes." Her eyes fixed on her plate.

"Would you mind telling me?"

The words took a long while to climb to Karen's lips. "I wanted to live with Mom."

"I understood you told a friend you wanted to live with your father."

"I changed my mind."

"That seems odd. He had just bought you an expensive gift. You were having fun together."

She glanced at her mother contritely. "I used to think he drank only because he was angry at Mom, that he wouldn't when just the two of us were together. I always thought he would stop because he'd be happy. But that day I realized he wouldn't; he'd keep on drinking and become, you know, angry and mean each time, even though he loved me."

"Smart girl."

"I . . . I was afraid he wouldn't take care of me."

"Did you tell him that you had decided to live with your mother?"

"Yes," Karen said, her sorrow and guilt overwhelming her. "He kept after me until I had to."

Susan spoke up. "When I arrived to take her home, they were standing near the pool house. He was yelling at her, threatening her in the most vile way. Her things were in the pool house. I told her to get dressed and wait for me in the car."

"How did Peter take that?"

"I think he realized nothing would change her mind. Karen's like him that way. He seemed to accept it and get hold of himself. He asked me to go into the house with him, so we could talk in private."

"Did you see your father again?" Dan asked Karen.

The child's body began to heave with suppressed sobs. Susan quickly went around the table, and Karen buried her head in her mother's skirt.

To Dan, Susan said softly, "She has this idea that Peter might not have continued drinking that day if she had chosen to live with him, that he was so angry at her, he didn't pay attention to the step and tripped.''

Karen finally gained enough control of herself to ask her mother, ''May I go now?''

''Just a couple of more questions, okay?'' Dan requested apologetically. ''After changing in the pool house, you then went right to the car?''

She nodded.

''How long before your mother came out of the house?''

Karen whispered, ''Maybe fifteen or twenty minutes. They were still yelling at each other when she came out to the car.''

''Thanks. Sorry to have made you bring up all of that. But you might be asked to talk about it again in court.''

Karen peered up anxiously at her mother, who tenderly kissed her head and let her leave the room.

Susan returned to her seat, allowing the silence to settle in before she finally said, ''I can't convince her that choosing to live with me didn't somehow cause his death. She loved him so much, and he was such a bastard.''

Susan rang for the maid and ordered the coffee brought to the family room upstairs, so Dan could watch the videocassette.

The first camera shot was of Peter on the back lawn, the pool and pool house behind him. He was in a bathing suit, blue and brief, revealing his slim, muscular body. Peter was smiling as he announced to the camera that he had just won the golf championship ''for a record seventh time'' and his daughter was ''capturing the glorious day on tape.'' He winked, laughing at the camera in a way that was characteristic of him, and raised his glass. ''I'll drink to that,'' he said.

''He looks so alive,'' Susan said.

''And pretty drunk already,'' Dan observed.

The next shot was a jerky pan that moved from left to right, beginning at high rear hedges separating this house from the one behind it; then lawn and trees; then Peter, glass on a table beside him, reclining on a white chaise with a yellow mattress set on an expanse of flagstone near a white clapboard pool house. Shots of Karen swimming and laughing followed. The angle of the shadows indicated that the tape had been shot in the middle of the afternoon.

Karen then took the camera sightseeing, experimenting with it as she walked about the area and, in a single shot, across the patio and through a door that led into the kitchen.

''This is the kitchen,'' her voice announced.

The tape ended soon after, during the camera's tilt up the legs of the table in the breakfast area, as if Karen had gotten bored with her new toy and had decided to go back into the sun.

"This cassette may be needed if there's a trial," Dan instructed, "to show how much he's been drinking. But don't volunteer it. Happy daughter. Loving father. Luxurious setting. The jury might not believe she changed her mind about living with him."

"Do you believe it?"

"Yes, but then I knew what Peter could be like when he drank."

Susan stood up. "I just want to check on Karen for a second. Then let's go out to the garden. It's a beautiful night."

Dan waited for her at the French doors leading to the rear patio, watching the sky to the west consume the last of the day in a huge bonfire of flaming clouds. Or the wound of a dying man, he thought. This world is dying, its blood is spilling across the universe. It's dying of all the things we do to it and to each other out of greed and our blind need to survive.

Susan emerged from the house, and they walked toward the crimson light.

"So much has happened in less than a week," Susan mused. "And tomorrow he'll be buried."

She put her arm through Dan's and guided him toward a white octagonal gazebo at the nexus of converging paths.

"I notified Gil Huyton personally about the funeral tomorrow," she continued. "I think I embarrassed him. If he does intend to arrest me, I may have bought myself an extra day or two." She laughed. "I also phoned Margaret and Amelia."

"Did they come to the phone?"

Her smile frayed. "No."

They climbed the two steps onto the gazebo. Dan turned beneath the roof's overhang and looked out on the beds of flowers along the paths.

He raised his arms. "I feel like John Philip Sousa about to lead my band in a Sunday afternoon concert."

"My father-in-law actually did put it here for concerts. You can see the space in front for chairs."

Susan sat down at one of the corners of the eight-cornered bench that ringed the inside of the railing. Dan took an adjacent seat. The angle allowed him to face her somewhat. He turned the rest of the way.

"Did you learn anything at the morgue?" she began.

"I'm not a forensic pathologist."

"But you must have gotten a sense of why the medical examiner thinks Peter was murdered."

Dan nodded. "The injury doesn't exactly fit the step they found his head lying on, and the abrasions on his skin occurred after he died." Dan kept to himself the minimal bruising on the brain; for the time being, she did not need to know that what was human and unique about Peter had been removed for study and replaced before burial.

"You mean he thinks Peter was already dead when he fell down the stairs," she said quietly.

"Or nearly dead. His report also questions whether someone tumbling down steps would have hit his head with enough force to inflict such a deep a wound."

"What do you think?"

Dan shrugged. "If you're put on trial, you get your own expert who's willing to refute the findings."

She was insistent. "That's not what I'm asking, Dan. What do *you* think? Do *you* think I killed Peter?"

"I've got a lot more digging to do before I'll know enough to make that kind of judgement."

"No!" she cried out. "Not evidence or judgements! In your heart, Dan, in your most secret heart . . . do you believe I killed my husband?"

"That's not a fair question, Susan. It's not even a relevant question. I'm a lawyer. It doesn't matter what my opinion is. The only thing that matters is what a jury ends up thinking."

The orange flecks in her hazel eyes flared, as if mirroring the red light. "It matters to *me!* I want my lawyer to believe with every fiber of his being that I'm innocent."

She was forcing him to confront an issue he had only half thought through all day. Crickets nagged the long silence until he spoke again.

"Susan," he finally decided, "I can't represent you."

"You can fight the suspension, isn't that what you told me?"

"It's not just the suspension."

"Then why?"

He peered upward into the concavity at the center of the rotunda roof, where the eight beams met at their highest point, as if the reason hung there in that darkness. She was owed the truth, he understood, and not evasion. His gaze lowered.

"I can't represent you because I'm in love with you."

He said it simply, as a fact, seeking no answering vow, no reciprocation. If he had understood his motives better, he might have realized that he actually feared her admitting that his love was reciprocated, with its instant assumption of his responsibility for her welfare and its certainty of his eventual rejection and disappointment. He did not trust love and did not trust women. Love was heat and desire to him, and it always burned itself out, leaving desolation.

He particularly distrusted the love of a woman so different from him. Of all the many women he had dated and slept with, he had taken only

Hannah and Mara seriously, and they were Jewish. If he had been eager to climb socially, Susan's blond WASPness, her new wealth, her patrician birth and social ranking, would have lured him, but he had grown up resenting people like Susan and ridiculing such superficial social striving. He was a dark-eyed, dark-haired Mediterranean, demonstrative and emotional, a tough street brawler from a race reviled over all the earth, especially by people who looked like she did. Each difference separated them further.

And the final distrust, ingrained over the years of criminal defense work, was a client's claim of innocence—*every* client's claim of innocence. How much more wary should he then be of a woman who could seize his heart and confuse his reason.

"I love you, too, Dan." She leaned toward him, the burning eyes consuming him. "Oh, God, I wish we were in some little room locked away alone right now."

"Damn it, I don't want to be in love!" he cried out. "There's no point to it, and no room for it. Loving you complicates my life. It's a mistake for both of us."

He saw hurt in her expression now, but hurried on. "Susan, the lawyer who defends you has got to be logical and objective. He can't have personal feelings that get in the way of his thinking."

"I didn't kill Peter. That's the truth. I want a lawyer who believes that, who cares as much for saving me as he would for saving himself. It can't be just another case to him. My life is at stake."

"Susan, try to understand. A trial isn't about truth, it's about winning. It's a contest to sway a jury, those twelve people. Everybody says they're after the truth, but they're really after something that will *sound* true—whether for yea or nay—to those twelve people. But the actual truth is coincidental. By the end of a trial, if the lawyers on both sides have done a good job, the truth is battered beyond recognition or so disguised in new clothes that no one can really be sure what it is anymore."

"But that has nothing to do with our loving each other."

"Love is about *truth*! It can't survive without truth. We strip ourselves down to who we really are for the people we love—or as close as we can let ourselves come to it—so that we can trust each other. Anything less is a ruse; it's a maneuver, play-acting."

Smiling, she reached out to touch his face.

He tried to ignore her touch. "Susan, that trust is fragile. Subjecting it to the ploys and deceptions that pass for omissions, to all the tactics that go into winning a trial, can end up destroying that love."

"I don't believe it. I refuse to believe it."

"Believe me, every client lies. If not outright lies, then murky areas the client tries to keep that way. During the trial you'll do and say anything to save yourself—it's your sole priority, and that's natural and right. You'll cover things up to me, to the judge, to the jury. Everything you've vowed to me—all that 'truth'—could get shredded into confetti.''

"I'm innocent. I have nothing to fear,'' she said fervently. She was staring into his eyes, measuring his love against hers.

He did not reply.

Her eyes turned bleak. "If you loved me, you'd believe me, you would fight for me.''

When he still did not reply, she stood up to return to the house.

"First Peter abandoned me,'' she said, "now you have, too.''

16

The Dellwyne Episcopal Church, handsome and self-satisfied atop its plush lawn, monitored one end of the affluent village, and the police station the other, God and government keeping the four blocks between them safe for excellent shopping.

This morning, tributaries of dark-suited people converged on the sidewalk in front of the church, eddied a bit there as acquaintances greeted each other and exchanged obligatory expressions of sorrow for Peter Boelter's untimely death, then flowed like a wide river between iron banisters up the steps and through the open doors. Television news crews and newspaper photographers waited, as if inspecting salmon by the side of a slew, to photograph and interview celebrities. And many were here today: a cabinet officer ("The president joins me in offering sincere condolences . . ."); two senators; the governor ("The world has lost a champion of freedom . . ."); four congressional representatives; Philadelphia's mayor; various state, city, and county legislators and judges; one cardinal ("People of all faiths mourn the passing of . . ."); major newspaper figures; and innumerable captains of industry, the two most recognizable of whom touted cars and sausages, respectively, on TV.

The press had descended on the event after "a highly placed prosecution source" generated a front-page story in yesterday's final edition of the *Mirror* by leaking the chief medical examiner's finding that Peter Boelter had been murdered.

Out of respect for the occasion, Dan drove the Mustang out and not the motorcycle. He had promised to explore the facts surrounding Peter's death and, despite the exchange in the gazebo, intended to follow through. He considered the funeral a convenient occasion to identify the cast of characters for Rick, who was waiting for him in the church parking lot.

As the two lawyers walked around to the front of the church, Dan noticed a stocky black man and a younger white woman leaning against a blue car directly across the street. With Rick following, Dan veered over to speak to them.

"How you doing, Harry?"

"Dan," the male detective acknowledged, not hiding his annoyance. "You know my new partner, Kate Bascombe?"

Dan did not, and neither of the others knew Rick Moss. Introductions were made all around. Then Stallworth allowed the reason for his annoyance to surface.

"You really ripped into me on cross at the Montano hearing."

"Come on, Harry, you didn't think you had a strong enough case to try him, did you?"

Stallworth did not reply.

Dan prodded him. "I got the feeling that arresting him wasn't exactly your decision."

"I've had stronger arrests," the detective conceded, recalling that he had been forced to make the arrest before he was satisfied with the quality of the evidence. The inability to tie Montano to the earlier murders or the subsequent parking-lot rape had strengthened his doubts. The blame had been unfairly placed on him when the case fell apart.

"Once Huyton gets an idea in his head . . ." was all the criticism Stallworth was willing to make. Like most police officers, he instinctively disdained defense attorneys for trying to free suspects he had worked hard to apprehend. The DA, however, had become a bigger irritation. "Sorry. I heard about your trouble."

"Damn! For a decision that was supposed to be kept confidential, more people have heard about my decision than *Roe* v. *Wade*." Dan gestured toward the church. "You two on this case?"

Stallworth shook his head, then gestured toward two men standing at the far corner. One, holding a camera with a long lens, was snapping photos of mourners entering the church. "Just giving Corcoran and Parenzi another pair of eyes for a few hours. I got to know a lot of the people at the *Herald* while checking out Feeney for the Cowell case."

"Come up with any new suspects?" Dan inquired.

"Who do you represent?" Stallworth wanted to know.

"Susan Boelter asked me to look into it, to make sure no one jumps to the wrong conclusion."

Bascombe eyed him. "Seems like a nice woman. It's a shame. Sometimes people get carried away."

"You guys think she killed him?" Dan asked, wondering whether Bascombe's glance meant that the police, like Mara, knew about his affair with Susan.

"It sure wasn't the butler. He and everyone else were off for the weekend."

Rick pressed the detectives for information. "Have you found a weapon?"

"Not yet," Stallworth replied.

"Any objection to our going out to Boelter's house afterward and having a look around?" Dan wanted to know. Trying to obtain a court order to search the house while he was supposed to be going on suspension soon would open up a can of worms. "We won't touch anything."

Stallworth had no objection. The various investigators had already examined everything. "Use Corcoran's name. I'll let him know."

"Thanks," Dan said, and prepared to leave. "Don't take any wooden confessions."

"We wouldn't," Bascombe impishly replied.

"Not bad," Rick commented admiringly as he and Dan started back across the street to the church.

Pews had been roped off and seats allocated in a strict hierarchy supervised by Chet Donaldson, the *Herald*'s business head. First row on the left had been set aside for immediate family, second for more distant family. First on the right for high government officials, second for lesser ones. Farther back, close family friends on the left; industrialists, financiers, publishers, and the just plain rich on the right. After them on both sides came executives at the newspaper, other employees, and, finally, other mourners. A special place beside the *Herald*'s executives had been reserved for top union officials, with whom Susan had just concluded contractual negotiations. She wanted rank-and-file workers to see them honored by management.

From his seat in the rearmost pew, Dan could see, just outside the entrance, Gil Huyton vigorously holding forth for the press. At his side was his wife, a quiet, long-faced woman, with large teeth, who had also known the Boelters since childhood. Dan was certain Huyton was the "highly placed prosecution source" who had leaked the medical examiner's report—no subordinate would have dared do so without his approval. How else could he be sure to dominate press coverage at the funeral?

Susan arrived with Karen before the others in the family, both wearing simple black dresses. Dan observed Huyton's discomfort when she briefly stopped to chat with him and his wife on the steps, but then recalled that the DA often looked that way. Susan did not notice Dan watching her as she passed him moving down the center aisle. Her attention was fixed on her daughter's sorrow, but soon broadened to acknowledge dignitaries eager to register their presence and express their condolences.

The other women in the Boelter family arrived soon after. Although obviously grief-stricken, they, too, took care to converse with the most powerful in attendance. The *Herald* was important in this state, but even in their own rights, as major political contributors, so were they. They stopped to speak to Huyton, who was at his aisle seat by then. Nearby, Susan was conversing with John and Marti Rosenthal, industrialist friends from Oregon, whose vast lumber and paper-mill interests supplied the *Herald*'s newsprint. The other Boelter women also stopped briefly to greet the Rosenthals, but did not acknowledge Susan's presence.

Midge was the last of the family to arrive, a woman his own age with him. She wore a diamond ring on her engagement finger. Dan conjectured that the loss of Peter's hegemony might have set free the initiative in Midge to solidify the relationship.

Susan had taken the aisle seat in the front pew, putting Karen between her and the other Boelters. She had picked the speakers to eulogize Peter. The minister was the first. A kindly older man, he displayed tact by not reminding listeners that Peter had been on the verge of divorcing Susan. About to fall back on the cliché "the love he and his wife shared," which he often used on such occasions, he caught himself and sidestepped over to the more general "his loving family."

Karen's head sank onto her mother's shoulder at the minister's first words. Susan kept her arm around her daughter and could often be seen whispering to comfort her.

Amelia, too, was falling apart. Margaret, though, was fixed on the speakers, following every word, seemingly ready to take them to task if they stinted in their praise. At the close of the service, with an intimidating glance, she signaled Amelia and Karen to rise; now that others in the church could view their faces, they were expected to stiffen and show their steel.

Walking out of the church and down the front steps behind the coffin and its pallbearers, the women kept their chins high and their expressions disciplined. Only their red eyes revealed their suffering.

Complying with her mother's gesture, Karen slipped into the rear of the first limousine. Margaret suddenly realized that Susan expected the entire family to ride to the cemetery in the same car.

"I will not ride with the woman who murdered my son!" she hissed, close enough to Susan to be sure others would not overhear.

"The bereaved widow!" Amelia exclaimed in a similar harsh whisper.

"Pretending you still loved him and that he loved you. Everyone knows you hated him, that you killed him!"

Margaret's despair flared out again as rancor. "Your ruthlessness won't do you any good. You'll pay for killing my son!"

Amelia completed her mother-in-law's thought. "Our lawyers assure us a killer can't profit from her crime. We're going to court to bar you from any interest in Peter's will."

The two women stomped away. After a moment of indecision, Midge and his fiancée followed. Susan watched them disappear into the second limousine and then sought out Chet Donaldson, who was standing among the pallbearers. She drew him away from the others.

"Whatever happens, I want you to sign the union contracts on schedule Monday. Then, immediately announce the *Herald*'s restructuring plan and put it into effect."

"Sure. That's what we all agreed to."

"Promise me. Whatever happens."

"Yes, of course."

Assured, she stepped into the first limousine and settled beside her daughter for the short ride to the cemetery.

Peter Boelter's rented house in Chestnut Hill was on Walker Drive, a winding, tree-lined street off Germantown Avenue. A succession of large, handsome houses were set back on lush lawns along either side. Peter's was in a Tudor style: brick below and, commencing at the second story, dark half-timbers splayed on a stucco facade that ended beneath a steep roof with many gables. A young, uniformed policeman stood in a menacing position—legs apart, arms down, hands at either end of a nightstick—rigidly guarding the front door.

Standing on the curb beside Rick, Dan gestured toward the policeman. "Think those guys will ever replace lawn jockeys?"

A woman in jeans who appeared to be in her sixties was kneeling beside a flower bed on the lawn to the left of Peter's property and perhaps fifteen yards from the side of his house. Several flower pots sat on the lawn beside her. She wore oversized yellow gloves and was digging into the earth to open a cavity for one of the plants. Dan assumed she was Ellen Hildreth, the woman who had witnessed much of the coming and going on the day of Peter's death.

She looked up and pushed away a lock of gray-streaked hair with the back of her hand as the two men approached. Gold-rimmed eyeglasses were perched atop a pug nose. When she stood up, the men could see that she was short and thin and her expression amiable. They introduced themselves.

"I've already spoken to the police several times," she advised them.

"We're not with the police," Dan replied. "We're friends of Susan Boelter, Peter's wife. We're trying to find out for her exactly what happened."

Evidently Mrs. Hildreth liked Susan, because she smiled. "She and I chatted a few times when she brought her daughter here. And of course, I saw her here that last day."

"Would you mind telling us what you remember?"

Having already recounted her recollections many times for the authorities and for friends, Ellen Hildreth spoke concisely, limiting herself to the facts. She had not seen Peter and Karen arrive from the country club in the early afternoon. She had come outside to garden much later, at about a quarter past five. ("You don't want to water until late in the day.") She was sure of the time because she had just put a roast into the oven that would be ready at six-fifteen, when she and her husband usually ate. Just as she was coming out of her house, Susan Boelter drove up and parked on the street. The women waved hello to each other as Susan walked up the path to Peter's house.

She herself had gone to the far side of her own lawn for a while. When she returned, she heard some yelling and, a few minutes later, saw Karen leave the house and go to Susan's car. Then, when her gardening took her around to the side of her house, she heard loud arguing, which she was sure came from Peter's kitchen—it faced the side of her house. She couldn't make out much of what was being said. The wife's voice was clearer than the husband's and, at one point, could be heard exclaiming that he would never get custody of the daughter.

"She sounded really angry," Mrs. Hildreth remembered.

"How long did they argue?" Dan wanted to know.

"Quite a while. Then I saw her walk back down the path to the sidewalk."

Rick asked, "You didn't see her come out the door?"

"I was working on the marigolds. You can't see the front door from over there."

Dan walked back toward where she had pointed. The marigolds formed a border between the two side lawns, after which a high hedge separated the properties the rest of the way back. From where he now stood, he could see Peter's kitchen windows, perhaps fifteen feet away, but at too high and oblique an angle to provide a view inside. The house blocked sight of nearly all of Peter's property. Also as Mrs. Hildreth had maintained, Susan could not have been seen walking out the front door; she would have come into view only when she was halfway along the path toward the sidewalk. Hearing anything on the front steps, even a loud argument, would have been difficult.

Dan turned back to catch Rick's eye and indicate he wanted photos taken from here. Before he could ask, Rick patted the camera that hung from his shoulder.

"You're sure of the time she left the house," Rick was asking Mrs. Hildreth as Dan returned.

"Yes, Mrs. Boelter drove away in the car with her daughter at ten minutes to six. I looked at my watch to see whether I ought to go in and check the roast, but decided not to be a worrywart and stayed out in the garden. She's such a nice lady. It's so sad for her losing her husband like that, even if they *were* having some marital problems. And for that pretty daughter of theirs."

Rick inquired, "Did anyone come or go after that?"

"Only Craig, my husband. He arrived home from the office just before six, the way he usually does, and we went inside for a drink."

The men asked a few more questions that elicited no further information. Thanking her, they walked across Peter's lawn toward the entrance. The policeman's hard eyes tracked their approach. Dan waved a friendly hand.

"Detective Corcoran said it would be all right for us to have a look around inside."

After a while the barest flicker of name recognition could be observed behind the stern expression, as if a slow chip inside the young law officer's head had finally processed their request. He released one end of the nightstick and unlocked the front door. Dan decided that with crime so prevalent, perhaps he had too hastily written off police-officer lawn statues. You could sell male and female ones, like Ken and Barbie dressed in blue uniforms or, in integrated neighborhoods, Harry Stallworth and Kate Bascombe.

"You won't touch anything," the patrolman said with the force of a command as the lawyers moved by him and into the house, closing the door behind them.

Over the course of his career, Dan had visited many murder scenes and had never failed to experience a vague disquiet, a creepiness, the feeling that ghosts perhaps were lingering about. That feeling was strong now as he stood beside Rick in the hall that ran down the center of the house.

To break the tension, he asked Rick, "How did you become an investigator?"

Rick was measuring the interior spaces with an instrument the size of a flashlight that bounced sound waves off walls. "My uncle's a bail bondsman in Trenton. He hired me one summer to check out potential clients, track down jumpers, that sort of thing. I had a knack for it. Worked for him and then off and on for a detective agency while going to school.'' He chuckled. ''Long hours, but the money was a lot better than at McDonald's.''

By now Dan, too, was assessing the layout. A large living room was to the right of the hall. The study, which he chose to look at first, was to the left. The room contained an array of business machines: a copier, a fax, and a computer on a sideboard behind a period desk. The telephone was similar to the high-tech model installed at Dan's law offices. Neither the desk nor the sideboard contained any photographs; the shelves held few books. He guessed that Peter had rented the house furnished, intending his stay here to be temporary.

Dan examined the desk drawers for a personal phone book, but if there had been one, the police had taken it.

''Try the speed dialing numbers,'' Rick suggested.

None of the telephone's speed dialing buttons had been programmed.

Finding nothing in the cabinets, they went into the living room. Two sofas, chairs, the usual tables, a bar built in to a wall cabinet, a stone fireplace, undistinguished paintings that probably came with the house. Little of interest here, either.

The men proceeded down the hall. A small dining room was located next on the left. Beyond that was a large, modern kitchen. At the end of it was the breakfast area containing the table Dan had seen in Karen's video and, open to it beyond, what would have been called a family room in a less-palatial neighborhood. The entire space formed an L, at the bottom of which were sliding glass doors that led out to a brick patio and a large rear lawn. The swimming pool and pool house were situated in the center of the lawn. Dan left Rick to his measuring and went outside.

Black cast-iron chairs were arranged on the patio in careful order, as if they had not been used that day. He walked across the grass to the turquoise pool. A plastic raft floated lightly atop the water. Grouped to one side of the flagstone that formed a larger rectangle around the pool were white chaises and armchairs with yellow mattresses and seat pads. A white beach umbrella had been left open above a round table. Nothing was different from the scene in the videocassette, except the emptiness: The man was now dead, and the girl no longer laughing.

Dan went over to the pool house. The building was twenty-or-so feet wide, with dressing rooms for men and women on either side of a bar and serving area. A blue bikini hung from a hook in the changing area of the women's dressing room. Karen's initials were written in indelible ink on the label. A pair of swimming goggles hung from the next hook. A shower was in the rear.

Dan inspected the bar. Seven clean, bevel-sided Baccarat glasses stood upside down on a tray beside eight similarly inverted champagne glasses. The small refrigerator contained only a single, unopened bottle of champagne. Dan recalled that Peter was a scotch drinker, but he could find no scotch bottle.

He returned to the house, but locating no scotch in the living room bar, rejoined Rick in the large kitchen. White wooden cabinets lined the walls and the center island, atop which a Jenn-Air stove had been built. The other appliances were a refrigerator-freezer and, across from it on the wall with the window, an oven and a microwave, a dishwasher beside a double sink, and a clock radio near the window.

"No scotch anywhere," he said. "The guy drank scotch. Damned good scotch."

Rick pointed to the white Formica countertop next to the double sink. On it were two round patches of black fingerprint dust. In the center of each was an empty spot, one octagonal, the other a triangle with rounded points.

"The glass he was drinking from," Dan confirmed, "and the scotch bottle probably. The shape looks right for Glenfiddich. It's what he drank." The police had taken the items as evidence after dusting for fingerprints. "The room looks so neat."

"I guess when you have servants, everything gets put away."

Dan began opening doors. "I guess so. That's another thing. Here was a guy used to being waited on hand and foot by servants, insisted on it. But he had nobody here on weekends."

"The people who worked for him said he liked his privacy. Maybe he wanted a chance to relax alone."

"Boelter didn't strike me as the kind of guy who liked being alone . . . or who'd cook for himself."

"He and the daughter had lunch at the country club that day. He probably had lunch there every weekend and ate out at night."

Dan found the door he was seeking. Steep concrete stairs descended to a darkened basement.

Dan flipped on a light. The chalk outline of a man's body, the limbs flung wide, sprawled at the bottom of the steps like a grisly Keith Haring painting. The head had been drawn around the outer corner of the bottom step.

The two men started down, gripping the single banister bolted to the cellar wall. The room was cold. Halfway down, holding his camera, Rick stumbled and had to catch himself.

The basement, formed out of poured concrete and unfurnished, was empty except for HVAC equipment beside oil and water tanks in the rear and a number of cardboard cartons stacked along the wall opposite the stairs. An air conditioner gave off a steady hum as it cooled the basement. A humidifier removed the dampness. Dan examined the cartons. Seven bore the names of French wineries. Three were labeled "Glenfiddich." One of those was open, with four bottles inside.

The men crouched down beside the chalk-outlined figure. The corner of the bottom step was stained a dark brown.

"I saw the skull wound in the morgue," Dan said. "Looked to me like it matches the corner of the step. Wide, with a deeper cut in the center. There were scrapes on the body, too, as if he fell down the stairs."

"The guy was drunk," Rick theorized, peering up at the steep descent. "He tripped as he started down to get another bottle of scotch, got scraped up as he fell, and then slammed his head against the corner of this bottom step."

"Kieffer says no." Ernest Kieffer was the chief medical examiner. "Not much of a bruise, a contra-coup, he calls it, on the front of the brain. Should have been a bigger bruise."

Rick nodded. He had read the report. "If he was still alive when it happened."

Dan placed his palm on the concrete floor. "Cold. This room's got to be in the forties. I want you to get a thermometer and measure the temperature. The floor, too."

"I also ought to talk to other people in the neighborhood. Maybe they saw or heard something."

"And time the drive from here to the supermarket in Dellwyne."

"I already did. I swung by on the way to the funeral this morning. Fourteen minutes at a pretty good clip."

Dan stood up. "Let's go tell Terminator Two on the stoop outside that you'll be in and out."

Rick's car phone was ringing as they emerged from the house. He ran down the front path to answer it.

"It's the office," he called back, and waited for Dan to join him. His expression was grim. "There's a message for you from Susan Boelter. She was just arrested for her husband's murder."

Susan had been arrested just after the graveside service at a very old Philadelphia cemetery.

Mara had chosen to handle the preliminary arraignment herself. This would be a big case, and she did not want a technicality to cripple it in infancy.

"You didn't waste any time," Dan charged when he and Cal confronted her in the tiny courtroom in the Roundhouse. "The woman just buried her husband."

Mara was unsympathetic, her expression severe. "I can't work up much pity for his killer. I didn't want to wait till she was back outside the city limits. Besides, news of the investigation had leaked out. Two reporters called us this morning asking for confirmation that she was the suspect."

"I wonder where they heard the rumors," Dan said sarcastically.

"You can't represent her, Dan."

"That's why Cal's here."

Mara's stare shifted from one former colleague to the other and then led them over to the clerk. Corcoran and Parenzi were standing by to testify, if needed.

With Cal at her side Susan Boelter pleaded not guilty. Cal argued that she was not a threat to flee the court's jurisdiction and should be released on her own recognizance.

The black judge possessed little sympathy for the Main Liner.

"A rich white woman's no different from any other defendant who's run through here. Make your argument at the preliminary hearing."

That hearing might not be held for another ten days, which Susan would spend in jail.

Cal fixed the judge with a critical gaze. "Is that what you want quoted in the papers . . . in the *Herald*? That you have it in for rich white women? Not five minutes ago I saw you grant bail for a black woman who put her husband in the hospital with stab wounds."

Mara spoke up. "Your Honor, I've been asked by the district attorney to request that in this special case you agree to release the defendant on bail."

The judge considered for moment. "One million dollars bail."

"We'll post a bond," Cal agreed.

As Mara was walking by him, Dan offered his thanks.

"Believe me," she replied, "it wasn't my idea. Gil was as adamant about arresting her as I was. But even when it's murder, he and his kind still offer their own crowd these little courtesies."

Dan drove Susan home. Both were silent until the car was on the highway headed west toward the Main Line.

Susan voiced a question. "Does this mean you'll be my lawyer?"

Dan had been pondering the facts and now began to do so aloud. "A good argument could be made that Peter's death was an accident, but even if it wasn't, that you didn't do it. The biggest problem is that Kieffer, who's CME—"

"What?"

"Chief medical examiner. He fixed the time of death at between five-fifteen and a quarter to six. You were the last person we can definitely establish was with Peter when he was alive—the only person, so far as we know, who was even in the house until Amelia showed up maybe thirty-five minutes after you left."

"Then you don't believe me, either."

"I'm trying to stick to provable facts. Kieffer relied on his investigator's observations to make his finding. The investigator took the temperature of the corpse—"   •

"Don't call Peter that!" she said sharply, interrupting.

"I thought it would be easier—more impersonal."

"It isn't."

"*Peter's* body temperature was taken by the medical examiner's investigator when he arrived at the scene at about seven o'clock. Using that figure, Kieffer did some calculations based on the drop in body heat from 'normal'—to come up with a time of death, which he sets at an hour and a quarter to an hour and three-quarters before that."

"While I was there," she tartly pointed out.

"The CME didn't go over to look at the house himself—his investigators do that for him. He relied on his investigator's report."

She heard the excitement growing in Dan's voice and asked, "What difference would that make?"

"There was a flood at the medical examiner's office that night. Everybody there was pressed into service to move bodies and supplies out of danger. The investigator was probably in a hurry to get back and forgot to take the ambient temperature—air and floor. It wasn't listed in his report."

"Why would that matter?"

"Normally it wouldn't. House temperatures don't vary that much. But that basement is very cold. A dead body in a cold environment, wearing only a bathing suit, lying on concrete, would lose heat much faster than in a normal room or in the sun. Kieffer's calculations never took that into account. A strong argument could be made he fixed the time of death earlier than he should have."

"What does that all mean?"

His gaze shifted from the highway to Susan. "That Peter may have died *after* you left his house."

She grinned excitedly. "I have something to show you. I went looking for it after you left last night."

She opened her handbag and drew from her change purse a small slip of paper. "It's the supermarket receipt. I keep them for the household accounting each month. I stopped at the supermarket for a few things after Karen and I left Peter's that night. The receipt is stamped with the date and the time I paid at the checkout counter." She read the time aloud. "Six-oh-nine P.M."

Elated, Dan slammed the ham of his fist against the steering wheel. "Which places you with absolute certainty some fourteen minutes away from Peter's house in Chestnut Hill at nine minutes after six. You'd had to have been there for a few minutes to shop and go through the checkout. We can eliminate your having killed Peter after that because it would have taken you a couple of minutes to return to your car in the parking lot, stow the groceries in the trunk, and drive back. Amelia was at Peter's by the time you would have arrived back there. So, if we can prove that Peter died after you left his house at around ten minutes to six, you're in the clear."

His lawyer's mind was swiftly touching all the bases. "Would anyone at the supermarket remember seeing you there?"

"I think so. I talked to the assistant manager. And the cashier knows me."

Dan again pounded the steering wheel in jubilation. "It starts with an investigator who's hurried and distracted. The chief medical examiner with other things on his mind then misreads an accident as a murder. A prosecutor who gets the report is compelled to seize a suspect. And, in you, Huyton has the perfect suspect: desperate, apparently vengeful, about to lose everything in a bitter divorce, but standing to gain back everything and more by the victim's death. All the pieces fit. Almost well enough to pass for the truth, if you don't examine them too closely."

Beyond reasonable doubt. That was the criterion. My God, the doubt about her guilt was big enough to drive a dozen juries through side by side. But that was strategy, the means to win, a lawyer's craftsmanship. What mattered to him here, he realized—the single, towering factor— wasn't the adequacy of the defense he could raise, which was usually his only consideration, but whether Susan had actually killed her husband.

But why was he demanding indisputable proof that exonerated her? Why couldn't he believe her simply because he trusted her? Had the years of representing the city's scum—the greedy, the ruthless, the truly evil— made him so distrustful of every soul that brushed up against his that his cynicism and his disillusionment, like crack dealers working in an apartment building, had driven out his ideals and left behind only a vexing, bewildered longing to fill the emptiness with something better?

He swung off the Schuylkill Expressway at City Line and, at the stoplight, turned to stare at Susan, into eyes that stared at his. He pondered her innocence, trying not to confuse it with the love he felt for her or with hope.

Quietly, she asked, "Will you take on my case?"

In that moment the man who fully trusted no one forced himself to make a judgement based solely on faith—on the honesty Susan had always exhibited, and on the belief she had implored him to have in her.

"If the Disciplinary Board will let me," he told her, "I'll represent you."

But how to explain the reason for his decision? How to describe an inner need suddenly swollen to urgent compulsion that he himself was groping to understand?

Almost sheepishly, he finally said, "It seems very important to me that before I finally decide whether to quit this town and maybe even what I've been doing for a living, I defend someone—one person at least—I can truly believe is innocent."

17

Dan's beach house at Barnegat Light on Long Beach Island, off the Jersey Shore, had been built for the pleasure of those inside the house, not to impress those viewing it. Seen from a distance on the narrow road, it might have been a weathered wooden crate washed up on the grass-stubbled dune. From within, though, three sides of floor-to-ceiling windows and glass doors opened onto surrounding decks, erasing the separation from sand and sea. The top floor's glass-walled bedroom and its balcony also faced the ocean.

Susan and Karen had just arrived and were reading the note Dan had left for them taped to the front door when he returned with purchases from the deli. Already in tennis shirt over bathing suit and wearing sandals, he put away the food while they changed in the guest room. The kitchen was at the rear of the open, uncluttered living-dining area that occupied most of the floor. In a black one-piece bathing suit, Susan came up beside him.

"The house is wonderful," she told him. "Thanks for inviting us. Reporters are camped out around the entrance to our place. We had to sneak out the stable road."

She laid a copy of the Sunday *Herald* on the counter. A banner headline read, "HERALD'S PUBLISHER CHARGED WITH KILLING HUSBAND."

"The story doesn't pull any punches," she said proudly. "I insisted on that. I took myself completely out of the loop. Fred Moore has total authority on everything dealing with my case." Her smile widened.

"What do you think of the paper's new look? Honestly, is it more appealing, more readable?"

"Great. Not a chance that anyone within fifty miles of a newsstand will miss the fact that you're up for murder."

Susan chuckled. "When I met you, you were angry at Peter and the *Herald* for abusing their power. You seemed to feel that instead of preserving and protecting the truth, they slanted the facts about you and your client to support their own interests. Now I make sure the newspaper is scrupulously honest, even though it hurts my own interests, and you're disgruntled about it."

"You don't have to commit suicide," he grumbled, and cut short a debate by leading Susan out to the deck.

The wide, white beach was empty. The next houses were several hundred yards to either side. A freighter was slowly zippering the seam between ocean and sky.

"This is so private and peaceful," Susan said enthusiastically.

Dan explained that miles of property here were originally owned by one man. He sold land to a few friends who wanted to build houses and, when he died, donated the rest to the state for a nature reserve.

"Did your wife like the house?" Susan asked.

"Are you trying to know whether to feel uncomfortable because it's really another woman's house?"

"Are you trying not to answer the question? Did she like the house?"

Dan resigned himself to talking about Hannah. "Yes and no. It reminded her of California, where she came from. But this beach was too isolated. Her idea of the beach is Malibu, an urban ghetto with sand. She used to turn on the news here every few hours just to make sure a hurricane wasn't on the way."

Susan laughed. "You're defaming a poor woman who isn't here to defend herself."

"You know any other house with a full carton of hurricane lamps in the basement?"

"Am I very different from her?"

"She was all Eastern European anxiety and self-doubt from head to toe. You're very comfortable with who you are. I guess that comes with your passport when you arrive on the Mayflower."

"I think I'm glad she didn't like the house." Susan grinned, admitting the aptness of his insight about why she had inquired. "But I have trouble fitting my image of you into this place."

Dan explained that when he was a boy, his father used to take him to the crowded public beach in Atlantic City for the day. His father told him there were rich people who actually owned homes on a beach. Dan decided that someday he would make enough money to buy one for himself and his father, so that they would not have to return to the city at the end of the day.

"My father doesn't come out here much, though," he said. "He feels uncomfortable, as if he's accepting charity."

Wearing a long T-shirt over a swimsuit, Karen had stepped shyly onto the deck while Dan was speaking. She was silent and withdrawn, as she had been whenever she was with him.

Dan noticed that all the while, her gaze had been fixed on three small figures sitting atop the ocean about a quarter of a mile down the beach. One finally windmilled in front of a wave and stood up on his surfboard.

"You surf?" Dan asked her.

"Uh-huh." She had learned the sport the previous summer.

Susan restrained herself from reflexively reminding Karen to say "yes." Correcting her daughter's speech was no longer a priority.

Dan offered Karen his son's surfboard.

"I've probably forgotten how," she told him.

"You'll remember in no time."

She moved closer to Susan. "Maybe later."

Dan recalled the confident, bold child who had bounced into her house after a swim meet. With the footings cracked beneath her security, she was fragile now and heavily dependent on her mother.

"Why don't we walk down the beach and check it out?" Susan suggested.

Karen shrugged, which Dan took to mean yes, and scuffed behind the adults to the garage. She helped him lift the red and yellow surfboard off the wall. Each hooking an arm over an end, they walked it down the beach together, Susan alongside.

Dan waved in one of the surfers just completing a ride, a friend of his son, whom he introduced to Karen. The boy invited her to join the group. With a tentative glance back at her mother, she followed him into the ocean. Susan watched her paddle out, reassured by the community's lifeguard atop the white surveillance chair elevated high above the beach.

"She sleeps in my bed with me most nights. She's already lost one parent, and she's terrified she may lose me."

Susan watched Karen become a bobbing figure beyond the wave break.

"If only she were older! Margaret ruined her own children. Now she can't wait to get hold of mine to ruin. I raised Karen to be outspoken and spontaneous and independent. Just the sort of behavior that offends Margaret."

"You and Margaret don't like each other, I gather."

"She's been cold to me since I've known her, but she became positively glacial after I lost the baby. She never offered a word of comfort, as if any sorrow of mine wasn't worth her bother. Or maybe she thought I'd failed Peter because now he'd never have a son. Whatever it was, she avoided me as if I had some sort of infection she might catch.''

The chain of surfers flattened onto their boards and began to paddle hard ahead of a wave. Karen and a tall, gangly boy managed to catch the wave, their boards tilting downhill like runaway sleds. They rode it awhile, and then both cut out and headed out toward the others, chatting as they paddled.

Dan took Susan's hand and started walking back to the house with her. Her eyes were fixed on the footprints they had left like crumbs along their route.

"The only thing that's made the last twenty-four hours bearable is knowing you'll be defending me."

As they climbed the wooden stairs up to Dan's deck, Susan unexpectedly laughed. "Casanova Carlo left a phone message at my office wishing me luck. If I ever need a character witness . . .''

She glanced up at Dan. "You were all set to change your life, and I dragged you back. Sorry you returned?"

Dan's answer was to draw her to him. "The kids usually come in for lunch about one. We have a couple of hours to ourselves. Let's spend it making love."

"Oh, yes! You clever man, having a surfboard and knowing things like lunch times!" She ran her hand down his back, slipping it into his bathing suit. "Driving out here, I thought how much I wanted to make love to you and wondered how we'd be able to."

They coupled on top of Dan's bed, the ocean breeze through the open glass doors lifting some of the heat. He felt a closeness to her that had been absent before he knew he loved her. The last time they had made love, the night before Peter's death, Susan's anger and hurt and need and his knowledge that he was leaving her and Philadelphia had combined into frantic and mutual sexual hunger. Today, perhaps because she was now sure of him, she was languorous and sensual, luxuriating in the sensations she felt and provoked in him. Her climax this time rolled out of her, moaning, like an earthquake, with aftershocks and tremors, and then rolled back in to join his own.

"With Peter gone I no longer feel guilty being with you," she confessed afterward. "I can let myself go. I rarely could with Peter. I always thought he was judging how well I performed for his pleasure."

During their last few months together, when Peter had had too much to drink, a fearsome resentment of her sometimes surfaced. Once, when they argued after a dinner party about his excessive drinking, he became outraged and forced her to her knees. Hands gripping her hair, his hips snapping forward and back, he seemed to take as much pleasure from the sex he exacted from her gagging throat as from the subservience his strength imposed. He ejaculated on her face, as if urinating on an insect. The next day, contrite, blaming the liquor, he abjectly apologized and vowed it would never happen again. Wanting to believe him, she forgave him.

Susan rolled onto her side to face Dan, intent on making him understand how much he meant to her. "What I love most about you, I think . . . that makes you so different from Peter . . . is that you don't have to pretend to be strong. You don't feel threatened by being tender." She ran her finger along his lips. "Do you mind my telling you that?"

"I like hearing it."

Her voice fell quieter. "Once in a while, then, will you tell me that you love me?"

"Yes."

"I used to think Peter loved me, but he never said a word. I was probably lying to myself. Toward the end I seem to have done a lot of that." She gave a rueful smile. "That isn't like my mother's daughter."

"We all lie to ourselves when we want someone to love us."

Am I doing that with you? Dan wondered. Do you truly love me, or are you trying to make sure I stick around to save your life? Those were not questions he could ask without doubting the answers.

"When you and I first met," Susan said, "you sometimes seemed so angry, I was sure you hated me. Did you?"

"I didn't really know you."

"But that's what was so confusing. You *didn't* know me, yet I sensed this anger."

Dan thought for a moment. "You represented something I've always distrusted: power . . . especially upper-class power. Do you know a banker named Robinson?"

"Edgar Robinson?"

"That's his son. One summer, when I was about sixteen, my dad broke his leg, and couldn't work. A friend of his who worked as a waiter at one of the Main Line country clubs got me a job busing tables in the dining room. We really needed the money. But the first weekend on the job, Robinson had me fired. He said I was staring at his daughter."

"Were you?"

"All I wanted to do was pay the rent." Dan's teeth were clenched. "He was a cruel, stupid son of a bitch, but it didn't matter. He happened to be born with money and power, and I happened to be born with shit."

Susan surprised Dan by sitting up and addressing him with some indignation. "I'll bet you'd still be hating *me* if you hadn't learned I grew up poor. I only became a human being to you in my own right out of some kind of reverse snobbism. That's awful."

Dan reflected on the accusation; it troubled him.

"No," he finally decided. "What attracted me was your honesty . . . before you ever told me about your folks. But no matter how I tried to belittle you in my own mind, I couldn't deny that you were absolutely genuine. I'm sorry I wasn't more open-minded. It was unfair. Forgiven?"

"Yes," she said, but still seemed bothered.

He tried to change her mood. "Talking about your folks . . ."

He went to the wall of books that formed an arch around the door leading to the second-floor landing and bathroom. He returned with a worn volume, her father's thin book.

"This is for you."

Thanking him, she ran her hand over it. "I remember his excitement when it arrived from the publisher. He'd been expecting it for days. He never paid attention to mundane things like mail, but he started checking the mailbox each day. That morning, I saw the mailman arrive, and raced upstairs to my father with the package. He unwrapped the string and unfolded the brown paper, and we stared at the three copies the publisher had sent him. He pulled me onto his knee and read the first page aloud. I couldn't understand his excitement about those long, incomprehensible words, but I felt enveloped in love."

She kissed Dan, widening her recollected love to include him, and then stared at him in appraisal.

"You try to make people think you're just some tough-guy lawyer, but you're so much more. You always find a way to surprise me. This house, your playing the piano, your interest in history."

"I majored in history. My dad got me started. That was his field before the war. Once a week we'd go to the public library together, exchange last week's books for this week's."

"What hooked you on history, though?"

"Looking backward lets me get hold of things, understand them. The present's too chaotic. Some of the fascination probably also comes from having so little history of my own."

"What do you mean?"

He asked her, "How far back can you trace your family tree?"

"My father's family to the early fifteen hundreds. My mother's about a hundred years later. I'm sure if I went over to England to look at the records, I could go back further."

"Most Jews probably can't trace back past their grandparents. We were refugees, outcasts. Our history is mostly a succession of massacres . . . or else escapes from massacres: the Roman Rebellion, the Dispersion, the Crusades, the expulsion from Spain, the pogroms, the Holocaust. Even in Israel Jews are still in danger."

"But you once told me your father's family lived in the same place for five hundred years."

"Until World War Two. The Germans who invaded deported the Greek Jews to the death camps, burned all their records, and plowed under their cemeteries. They wanted to wipe away any memory that the Jews there had ever existed. Used the gravestones to build a swimming pool for their soldiers."

"That's awful."

"Whatever history we have is usually collective—as a people, not as individuals. That we're Jews is about the only thing we usually know, so we hang on very tightly to that."

"And I'm a gentile to you," she realized, "a *shiksa*. Isn't that what Jews would call me?"

"Yes."

She stroked his face. "A *shiksa* and maybe soon a convicted murderess. You didn't get a great deal when you fell in love with me, Dan Lazar."

That afternoon, after Karen and the gangly boy went into town for ice cream, Susan and Dan lay on chaises on the deck. She asked him what would happen now that she had been charged with Peter's murder.

"We prepare our case and keep trying to come up with evidence and witnesses to clear you. One help is that the prosecution has to turn over to us whatever documents they've come up with. Understand, a close case usually turns on one or two pivotal points. Maybe getting a certain piece of evidence admitted or whether a jury believes a particular witness's story. It can even turn on a single fact, a single word. We have to dig harder than the prosecution, be better prepared."

Dan asked Susan if she suspected anyone of having a reason to kill Peter. She could think of no one.

"What about Vinnie Briggs?" Dan asked. He remembered Peter's tirade against the union leader at his birthday dinner.

"Briggs gave him a lot of trouble, but he was very cooperative with me about the new contract we just signed. He helped convince the other union leaders."

"Anybody you can think of Peter may have argued with? Someone with a grudge against him—an employee maybe."

"Peter fired someone after an argument," she recalled, "but I can't believe that would be a reason for him to be killed."

"Who?"

"A man named George Jurow, a sales executive. Peter fired him at a meeting in front of a lot of other executives. Angry words were exchanged."

"Do you happen to know where can I find him?"

"At the *Herald*. Everyone said he was excellent, but that Peter had been too impatient for results. I hired him back."

"There may be other people at the *Herald* I should talk with, too. And I also want to speak to Amelia and Margaret."

Susan could see no point in that. "They're the ones telling Gil Huyton that I killed Peter."

"What I want to find out is *why* they're telling him that."

"Everybody loved Peter. Only a monster like Susan could have murdered him." Amelia's clutched handkerchief stanched her tears.

She sat beside Dan in the ornately furbished City Hall chamber that housed the orphan's court. Dan had occasionally chuckled over Pennsylvania's retention of an ancient designation that states less enamored of antique ceremony mostly called probate court. Until recent years, at Christmas, as if out of a Dickens novel, lawyers and court officials would perform as the Orphan's Court Orchestra and the Orphan's Court Glee Club.

Having learned from Susan that Amelia's insecurity made her compulsively early for appointments, Dan was waiting there when she arrived, Rick beside him. Although her mother-in-law would not be coming to watch the hearing, she and Margaret were petitioning both for a halt in the distribution of Peter's estate and for Susan's removal as executor until after the murder trial established Susan's guilt or innocence.

Dan assured Amelia that he had come here solely to talk to her. Seated on his other side, Rick listened, eyes directed elsewhere, as if disinterested in the conversation he was there to overhear.

"Peter was just livid when he heard about you and Susan," Amelia recalled, "but I don't hold it against you. She has this power over men. They find her so sweet and so clever that they just fall all over themselves for her. I told Gil Huyton . . . I told him none of us knows the real Susan. Not even me, and I was her best friend."

"And sleeping with her husband, did you mention that?"

"His life with her was unbearable. Underneath that pretense of goodness, she's a vicious woman. I still have a mark where she scratched my shoulder."

"She says Peter romanced you because he needed your vote to sell the paper."

"Peter loved me!" Amelia hotly replied. "He said he knew it for years. He was too honorable to tell me before he left her."

"Then why did he marry her?"

"Oh, I'm sure he liked her well enough. But his father was the one who wanted him to marry her. He was crazy about her. Well, you can understand it, can't you? She was young and good-looking, and John was dazzled by the fact that she was a Winstead and that some old musty relative of hers was one of the *Herald*'s founders. Having her in the family would cure whatever suspicions there might be about his right to own the paper. And she knew how to play on that. Right from the start. She put it right into her letter when she invited him to speak at her college."

"Did John Boelter show you the letter?"

"He didn't offer, and I wouldn't have dared ask. My father-in-law dominated all of us—the entire family was terrified of him. Susan, though, she had him wrapped around her little finger. I've always been sure as can be that she was sleeping with him."

Shocked, Dan required several seconds to reply. "Couldn't he have simply enjoyed her company?"

"John Boelter wasn't one to spend time with a woman he couldn't get something from. This family hides a lot of secrets."

"You mean about how he inherited the *Herald*?"

"I mean that for twenty years he kept a mistress in the next house down from his and stopped off there every night on the way home. Nobody outside the family ever knew. Poor Margaret!"

Amelia's accusation against Susan sounded to Dan like the unfounded grudge of a woman seeking to salve her grief by blaming someone else; out of anger, she had divulged a family secret about her father-in-law that gave credence to her invention about Susan, using the true to shine up the false.

"I can't believe he would have let his son marry his lover."

"You don't understand the men in this family. It was just like John to arrange for his mistress to join the family, to have her close at hand like that. He would have enjoyed privately knowing that he held something over Peter, that he was besting his son in some way."

This image of John Boelter was not the one Susan had reverently drawn for him. Was hers the accurate one, or was Amelia's? More important, Dan asked himself, which image of *Susan* was true?

Amelia read his thoughts. "You don't believe me, do you?"

"No."

"Men never do where she's concerned. Didn't you think it was a little more than coincidental that she fired Leo Kucaba and replaced him with Fred Moore?"

"Should I have?"

"She dated Moore before her marriage. They continued to see each other. She said they were just friends, but I could never be sure."

I *am* sure! Dan insisted to himself in disagreement. I know Susan. I trust her.

He had deeply deliberated the decision to defend her against murder charges, finally coming down on her side because he believed in her character. He was convinced that their affair would never have begun if her marriage had remained intact.

After letting almost a minute pass, Dan said with concern, "Finding Peter's body must have been horrifying for you."

"Oh, God!" Amelia said, remembering.

"I'd like to understand what happened the afternoon Peter died. Can you talk about it?" Dan did not want to scare her into silence by sounding like Susan's advocate.

"I'll try."

"What time did you get to his house?"

"A few minutes before six-thirty. I live only five minutes from his house, just across the river. I drove over to see him."

"Was he expecting you?"

"No, and I didn't bother to call him first. But I guess you know we were more than friends."

"When had you last seen or spoken to him?"

"The night before. At Chez Henri. In Bryn Mawr. We met there for dinner."

"So, not having seen him since Friday night, you missed him and drove over to his house."

"Yes, exactly. I rang the doorbell. No one came to the door, so I rang again. Still no one answered it. I would have gone away if the lights hadn't been on in the house. So I tried the door. It was unlocked."

"Weren't you concerned that Peter might have had another woman there with him?"

She smiled indulgently. "We loved each other. He wanted to marry me as soon as his divorce came through. I was sure he was out at the pool and didn't hear the doorbell."

"So you went in."

"I called out for Peter, and when no one answered, I went through the house. In the kitchen I noticed the cellar door was open and the light on. An empty liquor bottle was on the counter. It was next to one of the bar glasses I gave him when he moved in. He kept the liquor in the basement. I thought he might have gone down there for another bottle."

"And you went to look."

"Yes." Tears filled her eyes. "Peter . . . Peter was at the bottom. Just lying there. Not moving. Blood . . . around his head."

"Was he on his back?"

"Yes."

"Did you go down the stairs to him?"

She shook her head. "I just started screaming and ran to the nearest house. A woman there helped me call the police."

"Did you notice how Peter was dressed?"

"In a blue bathing suit."

"How long were you at his house all told?"

"A couple of minutes at most."

"You left as soon as you saw his body?"

She vigorously nodded her head, as if to clear it of the memory. "What an awful way to die! How could a woman be so vengeful, so desperate, that she could kill the man she claimed to love?"

Good question, Dan thought.

Amelia engaged his eyes a moment longer than he expected and then asked, "Are you still seeing Susan? Not just as a lawyer, I mean."

"All rise" unexpectedly sounded loudly from the front of the courtroom, saving Dan from having to answer. As he jumped dutifully to his feet, Rick slipped out for a drive to Chez Henri in Bryn Mawr and from there to Chestnut Hill to speak to more of Peter's neighbors. His meeting the day before with Vinnie Briggs had turned up nothing useful, the union leader maintaining that he had been at his office that Saturday until he went to dinner around seven.

Dan was surprised that Amelia had not shunned him. Indeed, she had shown interest in pursuing a personal relationship despite knowing both that he had been Susan's lover and that he had been charged with bribing a witness, a charge he himself felt shamed by. He mentally leafed through possible reasons: her loneliness; an addiction to men attracted to her envied sister-in-law; that his differing background made him an exotic turn-on for her; and finally, the most probable, that his misdeeds were irrelevant to her.

She herself had said that the Boelters were a family that harbored secrets. Having occasionally been retained to dispose discreetly of an awkward DWI arrest, Dan had gained a sense of how members of these wealthy, powerful families guarded their privilege, inconspicuously pulling levers and exchanging favors to bury their potential scandals away from prying eyes. Doubtless many had counted on John Boelter and his sons to exclude such news from the *Herald*. People like the Boelters were brought up to be gods, whom the law of ordinary mortals could rarely reach. Amelia herself had been raised in such a family. The dishonor that attached to Dan's reputation would not deter her—everyone in her crowd concealed some infamy or other and was none the worse for it. As long as Dan could serve some interest, he was acceptable.

And then a question ignited in his brain like a warning flare. Did Susan, too, consider him joined to her in a union, not of souls, but merely of temporary mutual self-interest?

At the end of the orphan's court hearing, the judge ordered Susan removed as executor until her guilt or innocence was decided by the criminal-law process. In the meantime she would remain as acting publisher, her salary providing for her and Karen's upkeep. The Herald Corporation's board of directors, however, would be equalized—three directors picked by each side, so that no major decision could be made solely by either. An impartial chairperson would be named with the final say on major decisions. Both sides quickly agreed on Mason Willoughby, John Boelter's trusted accountant. He would also replace Susan as executor of Peter's estate.

Amelia turned to Dan, her mouth set in an expression of vindictive satisfaction. "We've stopped her. She married Peter for his money, and then she killed him for it. She never loved him."

Her expression softened. "She said she told you once that I might be put off that you were Jewish. I'm not, you know. She just wanted you for herself."

18

All morning Dan pored through statutes and cases and law review articles that Lexis summoned up on his computer screen. He was developing legal arguments for his petition requesting the Disciplinary Board to defer the start of his suspension long enough for him to represent Susan at her trial. Their sexual intimacy presented an additional obstacle to be surmounted.

"Damn that son of a bitch on 'L.A. Law'!" Dan shouted out as he realized that this new article was saying much the same as the last he had read.

Cal had been walking by the open door and, hearing him, leaned in to ask, "What's the problem?"

"That character on 'L.A. Law' who's always getting laid. Because of him, the public thinks we're all sleazy lechers who sleep with our clients."

"Arnie Becker isn't sleeping with this particular client, you are."

"Well, by itself, that won't disqualify me. I just have to show I didn't—" He glanced at the computer screen. "—capitalize on the relationship to coerce her into laying out money to retain me."

"That's only one side of the equation," Cal pointed out. "Maybe you pressured her into having sex with you as the *price* of representing her."

Dan glared at his partner's aspersion. Then, realizing that Cal was simply expressing the claim the commonwealth's lawyers might well make, he acknowledged, "There's always that, too."

Cal was preoccupied by another thought. "Have you considered the possibility—just the possibility—that the medical examiner's report might be right, that she did kill her husband? When the prosecution charges someone as influential as this lady, they usually have strong evidence. Their case sounded damned good at the preliminary hearing."

"We've been over the flaws in the autopsy report. You agreed with me."

"I agreed that we could make a good argument. But you and I both know that it would be defense lawyer's tap dancing. We still don't have conclusive evidence that her husband was alive when she left his house."

"True," Dan reluctantly agreed.

Susan came in at lunchtime to prepare an affidavit to be added to Dan's papers for the Disciplinary Board. Her contention would be that her Sixth Amendment right to be defended by a counsel of her own choosing would be violated if Dan were not permitted to represent her.

He explained, "You'll have to add a statement that I didn't use our private relationship to pressure you into retaining me."

"You mean sex? Of course you did. I was lying there helpless with desire, desperate for your body, when you demanded that I hire you."

"Susan!"

She grew serious. "Is it absolutely necessary that these Board members know about my personal life?"

"In this matter, yes."

"I hate that, letting people pry into my behavior and feelings."

"Because they might see the human being behind the upper-class facade?" Troubled by Amelia's accusations, Dan added, "Or because you're afraid some unsavory secrets might come out about you?"

Her voice softened to just above a whisper. "Because it leaves me with nothing of my own."

Jurow's jacket was draped over an armchair, and his tie was opened at the neck. Inclining toward overweight, he had snub features set on a rounded face. Head of Sales and Marketing, he had the customary salesman's amiableness, but also a decisiveness that must have marked him for early ascent. Dan and Cal had done some digging around before coming to the *Herald* to interview him and others.

"I was angry as hell that day," he told the two lawyers. "I'd been here less than a year, and Boelter was looking to pin all the blame for stagnant revenue on me. The guy was a tyrant with a sort of sadistic side to him. He used to pick out one person at a meeting and make him a scapegoat. Say really vicious things. A lot was wrong with this paper he wasn't willing to change—old format, dull content. Instead, he blasted the people who worked for him. He wanted magic. It doesn't work like that.''

"How *does* it work?" Cal asked.

"You keep trying to create a newspaper that people need, that they have a reason to buy. Marketing tries to communicate that reason to potential readers. If they start buying the paper—and if the economy improves—advertisers follow. Boelter wouldn't even let me readjust ad rates, claiming it would hurt revenues. He wanted fast cures, gimmicks.''

"Like hyping Tim Feeney and the Montano case," Dan observed.

"He went wild with that one. But as soon as Montano was cleared, circulation dropped right back down. He figured that was my fault, too.''

Dan referred to a notepad. "When he fired you, you told him, 'Someone will get you good someday, and I hope it's me.' You said his money and his power couldn't protect him forever. Is that true?''

Startled by the realization of his statement's implication, Jurow quickly replied, "I meant someday he'd lose out in a business sense, not that I'd kill him.''

"Do you remember where you were the afternoon he died?''

Jurow's innate optimism seemed to falter. "It doesn't look good—I mean because I saw Boelter that day. At his golf club. Earl Fuller, who's publisher of the *Mirror*, invited me to play. He was thinking of hiring me, and I really had a shot at the job. I needed it badly because Boelter was refusing to pay me what was owed under my contract.''

Cal spoke up. "I thought some tycoon owned the *Mirror*. Lawlor.''

"Fuller's the publisher. He works for Lawlor. But I was warned that Lawlor had his nose into everything. I was wary about jumping into another no-win situation.''

"And you saw Peter Boelter on the golf course.''

"Actually, in the locker room before I went out to tee off. He'd just won a big match and was in a great mood, a lot of people around him. We had to walk by his locker on the way out. I thought he might not notice me, but he did. He seemed to get a kick out of telling Fuller that he hoped the *Mirror* would hire me because that would give the *Herald* a real boost. 'The guy's a dud,' he told him. 'Talks a good game.' Fuller looked at me the rest of the afternoon like I was a worm.''

Dan asked, "Where did you go after you left the country club?''

"I drove straight home. Took my time. I wanted to calm down before I had to face my wife. She was really counting on my getting the *Mirror* job.''

"So Peter Boelter's death was a real blessing for you.''

Jurow nodded. "A lot of people here went to bat for me with Mrs. Boelter when she took over.''

"What time was it that you left the club?"

"Just before six. People who were there can vouch for the time. The paper said Boelter was killed before then."

"Not necessarily, and the country club is only a short ride to his house."

"Oh, shit!"

Dan had earlier phoned Midge Boelter for an appointment, but the latter had refused to see him, claiming through his secretary that he had no information that could aid in Susan's defense. When Dan and Cal stopped by his office, Midge remained unavailable. Family loyalty had presumably pushed him into his mother and sister-in-law's camp.

The lawyers had arranged to meet with Fred Moore, newly named the managing editor. They returned to the newsroom floor just as the afternoon editors' meeting was breaking up. The conclave had locked in the stories that would run in tomorrow's paper, although later-breaking events could still supersede the decision.

Because Peter had valued obedience above talent, the outspoken Moore had been forced to wait behind the stolid, servile Leo Kucaba for this job and for the opportunity to fashion the *Herald* into a first-class paper. Now that Susan had given him that opportunity, he was a perpetual motion machine.

"I understand you used to replace Kucaba on Saturdays," Dan began when he and Cal were finally alone with Moore in his office.

"Saturdays are usually slower at a newspaper, smaller circulation. We have a separate Sunday operation with a Sunday editor. Leo took weekends off. I was deputy managing editor, so I got Saturdays."

"That means you were in charge the day Peter Boelter died."

"That's right."

"And I hear he phoned you here that afternoon."

Moore grimaced at the recollection. "I guess it was about two-thirty, three o'clock. He ordered me to run a story in the Sports Section about some dinky country club golf match he'd just won. Something about his breaking the legendary somebody-or-other's record for the most years winning the thing. You'd have thought he just won the Masters."

"And you objected to running the story?"

"It made us look like a cheap vanity tabloid. But you didn't object with Peter Boelter. You suggested. Objecting could be hazardous to your career. I suggested. He insisted. We ran the story."

Cal eyed the newspaperman skeptically. "People here say you were furious after you got off the phone with him. You kicked a wastebasket across the newsroom and stormed out."

"Yeah, I lost my temper, all right. He said some insulting things. He made it clear I was a wage slave hired to take orders."

Dan pressed the editor. "I understand you were already angry at him for stealing a Pulitzer you should have had."

Moore's face reddened. "I wrote that welfare series on my own time. Weeks of research."

"But Boelter entered it in the Public Service category, where the prize goes to the newspaper and not the reporter."

"He robbed me blind."

"Why did you stay on?"

"I threatened to resign. I'd built the City Section into a powerhouse for him, and he knew it. He placated me by making me second to Leo and giving me a big raise. It avoided embarrassment for the paper and kept me dangling on a string. It was also a way of worrying Leo. Peter Boelter was really a piece of work." Moore reflected for a moment. "Okay, you want the truth? I hated the bastard."

"Before he married Susan or only afterward?"

Moore glanced sharply at Dan as if about to repudiate the assertion, but then he hesitated, inwardly debating his answer. "That was a long time ago. And I was never in her league. She had her eye on bigger fish."

"Peter Boelter?" asked Cal.

Moore nodded. "The problem was that Peter Boelter inherited the worst of his father's traits, and few of the redeeming ones. Like with that club golf championship story, the little vulgarities kept breaking through. Susan has the brains and breeding the others in that family think they have, but don't. That sure touch. I guess she got what she wanted when she married him, but it was a shame."

"Most people would say she struck gold."

"A lot of what made her special got buried after that. Rich men have this role their wives have to fill. And Peter was a demanding guy."

"I understand that over the years you and Susan kept in contact."

Indignation tinged Moore's tone. "She'd occasionally call me up to comment on stories, maybe stop by for a chat if she was in the building, have lunch once in a while. If you're implying it went further than that, you're dead wrong."

"Maybe. But I get the impression that for a lot of reasons, Peter's death was good news to you."

"What the hell do you mean by that?"

"Well, his dying opened up a lot of doors for you with Susan." Dan paused for a beat before adding, "You're managing editor now. And you said you hated the guy."

Moore was on his feet, belligerent. "You're out of your mind! I was home getting ready for a date when someone at the office phoned with the news that Peter was dead. And if you think Susan killed him or that I'd ever think she'd be interested in me from a personal standpoint, then you're even crazier."

"I'm just asking questions. Aren't you the one who once told me it never hurts to ask?"

"I don't kill people, and it's inconceivable that Susan could. You've been around crooks and thugs too long, Lazar. You don't know women like Susan Boelter. She doesn't have an ounce of guile in her body. She's the finest woman I've ever known."

"Then shouldn't you have reporters out investigating for her?" Cal suggested. "We can use every bit of help to get to the bottom of this thing."

"Susan won't let me," Moore replied with some frustration. "She says she'd be abusing her position because it's not something an ordinary citizen could expect. Sometimes she's too damned virtuous for her own good."

She had become a fantasy creature to Moore, Dan realized, purity and goodness painted on an unearthly scrim. Moore had exaggerated her character until the real woman he yearned for had become a divine virgin, instead of a real woman of flesh and apprehensions and sweaty desires, like the women he dated. Dan could imagine Moore's anger and disillusionment when he eventually learned she was Dan's lover.

Amelia, too, had transformed Susan into a creature constructed out of her own necessity. Lonely, needing to justify loving her best friend's husband, she had metamorphosed Susan into an evil, rutting witch. Both people had made of her, and even of Peter, what their own psyches required. Dan wondered, though, whether he was doing the same thing.

They had described a Susan whom Dan had refused to recognize: not the naive, young college graduate who claimed Peter Boelter swept her off her feet, but a wily woman who may have schemed to capture a prize husband. Did he really know her? he asked himself. Or, like Amelia and Moore, did he let his own needs blind his awareness, allowing her instinctively to project whatever qualities he desired and, so, manipulate his feelings into compliance with her wishes?

Had he ever really known Mara or Hannah? he wondered. Or had he also seen in them only what he hoped for in a woman—until they inevitably disappointed him?

As he rose to leave, Dan asked Moore, "Any idea who might have had a big enough grudge against Peter Boelter to kill him?"

"I'd say just about anybody who knew him."

* * *

The girl in the far court failed to put away the overhead and lost the point and the close match. She and her opponent were walking off the tennis court when Dan stopped her.

"Annabelle Warren?"

"Yes," she answered, trying to place Dan's face. She was small and sturdily built, with her brown hair worn in a single braid. She looked older than her thirteen years.

"I'm Dan Lazar, the lawyer for Karen's mother. Do you mind if I ask you a few questions?"

"Okay."

They sat atop the high stools at the veranda bar overlooking the club's tennis courts. He ordered sodas for them both.

Then he said, "I understand the night before her father died, Karen stayed over at your house."

"After the school play," she concurred.

"And that you two stayed up late talking."

"Yes."

"I also understand that Karen told you which parent she wanted to live with."

Annabelle nodded.

"How did she put it exactly?" he asked.

"She just said it . . . that she wanted to live with her father."

"Do you know why?"

The young girl hesitated. "Maybe Karen doesn't want me telling you these things."

"You told the police, didn't you?"

"Yes, but they didn't want to know *why*."

"I'm trying to save her mother. What you tell me might help."

The girl's fingernail scuffed at the condensation on her glass. "Well," she said, making up her mind, "it was really the usual."

"The usual?"

"Moms always hassle you about rules, and dads are willing to buy you all kinds of things because they need you on their side in court, and you really believe that they love you, and you want to develop this close relationship with them. The usual."

"You sound pretty cynical."

"My mom's been married three times. Twice to my dad. The second time was after the stock market recovered from the last crash."

"Did Karen ask for your advice?"

"She was really set on living with her father. I told her to make sure he wasn't just jerking her chain."

"Do you think it's possible she could have changed her mind after spending the day with him?"

"Her mind was pretty much made up."

"But there's a chance?"

"Sure. We're teenagers."

At Amelia's urging, Margaret had agreed to a brief meeting with Dan. From the country club, he drove to her house in Haverford. Far smaller than the one she had relinquished to Peter and Susan after her husband died, it was no less opulent. The house was built of gray stone like many on the Main Line, its wings creating a formal front courtyard at the end of a tree-lined driveway.

She awaited him in what the butler referred to as the salon. Her back was to the window, his chair placed so that he would have to look into the light.

After answering a few factual questions, she declared, "I've agreed to meet with you, Mr. Lazar, so that you would have no misconception about Susan's character. She's a schemer, Mr. Lazar, what we used to call a gold digger."

"Did you think so at the time Peter married her?"

Her mouth tightened with displeasure, accentuating the age lines at the corners. Even now, the vestiges of her looks—high cheekbones, long neck, large blue eyes—suggested the remarkable beauty that a wealthy social parvenu like John Boelter would have fancied. Her portrait as a young woman held the room's place of honor, which was doubtless why she had placed it in this room where she received visitors. She had probably been in her late twenties when it was painted, a form of record her husband had doubtless ordered so that future generations would admire his choice. The artist could not have liked her much, having taken care not to conceal her haughty self-absorption. Or perhaps, Dan conjectured, not concealing it was exactly the flattery she desired.

"My husband pushed his son into marrying Susan," she said. "Neither Peter nor I had any say in the matter. However, at the time it served its purpose."

"You mean, it won back his father's regard for him."

"My husband, unfortunately, was taken by her. She's the sort of woman that men immediately like and women immediately see through."

"And you saw through her."

"It isn't hard to see through a woman who gains her ends by throwing herself at men. Unfortunately, you seem unable to. Giving you the benefit of the doubt, Mr. Lazar, I'll assume you hadn't yet begun your affair with her when you dined with us. I could sense her interest in you, however. It was only a matter of time."

"And the reason you're so sure she killed your son?"

"Because she had lost any hold she had over him."

"Did you ever discuss with him his intention to divorce her?"

"Yes. I gave him my blessing."

Dan was surprised. "Peter didn't appear to me to be someone who needed his mother's approval to make decisions about his private life."

"He would have wanted it. He and I were extremely close."

Or so you think, Dan decided, remembering the sharp-edged bantering between the two on Peter's birthday. He was about to speak again when Margaret addressed the subject he himself was about to raise.

"I know of no one other than Susan who had reason to kill my son, Mr. Lazar. He certainly wasn't involved with another woman when he left her."

"You're sure of that?"

"My son was loyal to his wife—far too loyal for far too long. In any event, he would have told me."

Sarcastically, Dan observed, "I assume then that he asked your approval when he decided to sleep with your *other* daughter-in-law?"

"No need. I was certain that he would. He wanted her vote to sell the company."

Her iciness sent a shiver down Dan's back.

"One last question, Mrs. Boelter. Just for my own curiosity. If you knew for certain that Susan was innocent, would you still want to see her convicted?"

"Of course."

Dan had parked in a lot and was walking to his office when a black man in a rust-colored suit and no shirt, who was standing near the entrance to the office building, called out.

Dan recognized him. "Staying out of trouble, Willy?"

Willy chuckled. "The day's young."

"What's up?"

"The Man has a message for you."

Dan and Cal had successfully defended Willy and another member of the drug gang to which he belonged. More recently, the lawyers had won a conviction on a simple weapons possession for Nate Jenks, the head of the organization and who was known as "The Man." He had been facing the death penalty or, at least, mandatory life for murder. He had gotten out in less than a year.

"What's up, Willy?"

"The Man says you should know that Tim Feeney's got heavy pockets. He just bought himself a G's worth of coke."

"I wonder where he got the money."

"The Man thought you'd wonder about that. It's the same way every first and third Monday of the month. The Man thinks maybe the DA has him on the payroll."

"Tell the Man thanks for me, Willy."

Willy nodded and, in moments, dissolved into the crowd moving along the sidewalk.

Mary Alice put her caller on hold as she saw Dan enter their offices. "Carmella says the DA was screaming so loud about you, she could hear him through the door."

"Carmella?" Dan idly asked as he leafed through his phone messages.

"Judge Bosco's secretary. His son Ken is on the Disciplinary Board."

Dan instantly gave his secretary his full attention. "What was Huyton there about? Did she say?"

"It was a little retirement party for Judge Bosco in his chambers. Huyton and young Bosco went into a private room. Carmella couldn't hear much, but she got the impression Huyton just about told the son he wouldn't replace his father on the bench if the Board lets you push back the start of your suspension."

Her lips pursed, as close to a smile as she usually came. "Want to hear what Huyton called you?"

"I have a pretty good idea. Mary Alice, let me ask you: Doesn't this Carmella, who told you all this, have any loyalty to the judge?"

"Not since he tried to cop a feel when she was looking for something in a bottom file. The father's a creep, and so's the son."

"How can I be sure you won't tell Carmella and Louise and the rest of your Fifth Column the same kind of stuff about me?"

"Easy. Just keep your hands to yourself."

Dan went into Cal's office.

"I've got an H-bomb for you, Cal."

Cal shrugged, the elegant glen plaid jacket falling back onto his shoulders as lightly as an autumn leaf. "A buck says I've got a bigger bomb for you. What's yours?"

"Remember Tim Feeney's girlfriend testified how he sucked the five thousand up his nose and he was broke? Well, one of Nate Jenks' messenger boys just tipped me off that our unemployed friend is flush with cash to spend on drugs the first and third Monday of every month. Jenks thinks Gil Huyton's been paying him off."

"That would explain a lot."

Dan was skeptical. "It doesn't make sense that Huyton would be bribing Feeney to say that I bribed Feeney."

"Hey, Huyton wouldn't consider his end bribery. He'd consider it paying informant money. He's a maniac where you're concerned. Did Mary Alice tell you what he said to Ken Bosco?"

"I'm an annoyance to him, not an obstacle."

"You're an obstacle, all right. You're out there frustrating him from putting away all the bad guys. In his mind, you're the smart-aleck Jew who's getting paid to ruin the old-fashioned America he believes in and making him look bad. And if he doesn't shine as DA, he can't run for the Senate. The only thing that could make him hate you more was if you were black." Cal smiled broadly. "Fortunately, you've got a black partner."

"I'm going to have Rick put a tail on Feeney next time. If he goes to the DA's office and then makes a big buy, we'll know."

Cal cast a shrewd look at Dan. "Might provide the basis for an appeal."

"It's the first time we've stumbled onto something about this bribery business that maybe begins to make a little sense of it."

"Definitely up there in the hundred-megaton range," Cal admitted, "but I still think my news is bigger. You know how it's been like pulling teeth to get discovery documents out of the DA's office on the Boelter case?"

Dan nodded.

"Well, they just sent this over."

Cal lifted a stapled document from his leather desk pad and handed it to Dan. "The medical examiner just issued a supplemental report. The lab found semen in Peter Boelter's urethra. Boelter ejaculated just before he died."

"Jesus!"

"You know that client of yours who has millions and isn't paying us a dime. I think she has a little explaining to do."

19

"Are you asking me whether I slept with Peter when I saw him that day?"

A conference with Susan and her legal team had already been scheduled that day to discuss the evidence turned up so far and the potential strategy for her defense. Curt in his greeting and grave in his manner, Dan asked her into his own office first. He stood close to her armchair, leaning back against the edge of the desk.

"You've said that you were alone with your husband while Karen waited for you in the car."

"Hello, Susan," she replied with mock brightness. "How are you, Susan? I've missed you, Susan. Gee, Dan, I've missed you, too."

"Something serious has come up. You were alone with your husband in his house after Karen went to the car, right?"

Susan eyed Dan acutely. "You usually call him Peter. Why is he suddenly 'my husband'?"

"We've just received a lab report from the medical examiner. Peter had sex shortly before he died."

"Oh." She considered that revelation, then said, "And you think it was with me?"

"Semen was found in his urethra. It's a question I have to ask."

"Do you really think I'd do something so tawdry?"

"The DA's office will claim you did."

Susan rose and put her arms around Dan's neck. "You and I were

216

together the night before Peter died. The sex was incredible. Do you really think me capable of sleeping with you and then with him the very next day?''

Rather than reply, Dan waited for her answer.

She withdrew her arms. ''Having sex with Peter was the last thing I wanted.''

''The DA could argue that you did it in your desperation to win Peter over, maybe convince him to come back or, at least, to be more accommodating in the divorce action.''

''That wouldn't have swayed Peter. He would have despised my weakness.''

''He had sex with someone, unless he whacked off.''

A look of revulsion flitted across Susan's face. ''And to think I was worried you might think *I* was tawdry.''

A moment passed before she said, ''He wouldn't have 'whacked off,' as you so clinically put it. He wouldn't have chanced being unable to perform at his best later that night. Peter was insecure about his sexual performance. He always felt he had to be ready to prove himself.''

If Susan was right that he would have reserved his orgasms for sexual intercourse, Dan reasoned, then Peter had had sex with someone shortly before he died.

''Let me give you the DA's probable scenario. After Peter induced you to have intercourse with him—or you seduced him—he might have ridiculed you for believing his lie about getting back together. You got angry, grabbed something, and killed him—or pushed him down the stairs when he started down for more scotch.''

Was Susan capable of that? Could she have seduced her husband in the hopes of inducing him to reconcile and then killed him when he refused? Dan recalled that her rage at Peter right after the divorce hearing was nearly uncontainable. Another thought occurred to him.

''If Peter was alive when Amelia arrived, she might have been the one on the receiving end of his affection. And the killer.''

''Dan, this is so sordid.''

''This is the evidence. Either we refute it or we try to understand it. We can't change it.''

''Amelia wasn't with him long enough. She ran next door only two or three minutes after she arrived at his house.''

''So she's said.''

Susan reflected for a moment. ''As long as we're being sordid, you ought to know that it would have been rather messy for Peter and me to have had sex. My period came on that morning. I'm very regular. In fact, if you'll look at that cash register tape from the supermarket, you'll find

I stopped off to buy a box of sanitary napkins and a box of tampons for later in the week.'' Susan's next words were choppy with anger. ''Does that put me in the clear in your eyes?''

''The medical examiner also found what he thinks was a trace of blood on Peter's thigh nowhere near any wound. Not enough to test, though.''

''It wouldn't have mattered. Peter and I are both O positive.''

''They might be able to use DNA techniques to increase the sample and try to match it to yours. But I'll fight them on that.''

Susan's gaze locked with Dan's. ''Because you don't believe I'd pass?''

''Because in your case, I think I can hold them off,'' he replied, leaving unexpressed whether he thought her blood sample might match.

He punched the intercom button on the telephone console to notify Cal and Rick that their meeting with her in the conference room was about to begin.

''As I see it,'' Dan began from the head of the oval table, ''we can assert two possible defenses: The first is that Peter Boelter accidentally fell down the stairs; Kieffer either screwed up his post-mortem examination or is purposely trying to pin it on Susan. Our second defense would be that even if it was homicide, he was killed by someone else. Right now our best suspects are Amelia Boelter and George Jurow.''

Fred Moore had been only a long shot for Dan, and his whereabouts after leaving the *Herald* that day had checked out.

''Scratch Jurow,'' Rick interjected. ''I've spoken to Fuller, his host at the country club. Fuller says he noticed Jurow in his car up ahead as he drove back into the city.''

''So,'' Dan slowly enunciated, ''we're down to Amelia Boelter. I spoke to her yesterday morning. She seems to have bounced back from losing the love of her life with remarkable speed.'' He turned to Rick. ''Have you had time to check out her story?''

''Chez Henri was closed yesterday. They wouldn't let me through the gate at her house.''

Dan glanced inquiringly at Susan. ''Would the people who work for her talk to you?''

Susan shook her head and asked, ''Did any other suspects turn up on the list of phone calls Peter made from his house?''

''We've been asking the DA for the phone log, but they've been holding back a lot of documents. Those they do finally send us come very late.''

''Can't you force them to turn the log over?''

''They don't buy our story that I'm your lawyer. They've even blocked us from subpoenaing documents on our own. When my petition comes up at the Disciplinary Board, they'll probably try to get our entire firm disqualified.''

"I'll enter a formal motion for the log," Cal said. "That will give them a deadline to turn it over."

"Make sure you also renew the demand for everything else," Dan suggested, then he sat back pensively. "Well, until we know more about Amelia, that leaves us with defense number one: that Kieffer screwed up the autopsy. But to prove that, it's essential we find a medical examiner with superior credentials who's willing to dispute Kieffer's findings."

Cal frowned. "I've contacted the top names. None of them wants to be put in the position of refuting him. Turns out that Kieffer is a powerful guy in the AMA and some other medical associations—past president of the pathologists, that sort of thing. He could really hurt their careers."

Susan was staring at Dan. "Maybe they just don't believe that I'm innocent."

"A lot of them don't," Dan evenly replied, understanding that she had been questioning his own belief as well as the pathologists'.

"You're a hard man, Dan. You don't compromise much, and you don't extend trust easily."

Cal and Rick quickly excused themselves, leaving the two others alone.

Dan finally answered, "Trusting people too far is a good way to end up disappointed. My father taught me that when I was very young. Our neighborhood wasn't an easy place to grow up. When you're poor, you've got to watch your back every second; everyone tries to take advantage of you."

"I just felt angry."

Dan assessed her critically. "You were never poor. You just didn't have money."

"What does that mean?"

"You had all the advantages America bows down to, and you knew how to capitalize on them."

Susan stiffened. "I'm listening."

"You were born into America's aristocracy. That kind of social cachet is worth a lot on the open market."

"I have a feeling I'm being insulted, but I don't have the slightest idea why."

"Did John Boelter ever personally offer any other young woman a job at the *Herald*? Or invite another woman for supper with his family?"

"I don't know."

"Did he ever spend hours in long conversations with maybe some brilliant sixty-year-old woman reporter or book-review editor?"

"Not that I know of."

"Funny how your father-in-law was on such personal terms only with a Winstead."

"Your tone is offensive, Dan."

"Amelia thinks you were sleeping with him."

Susan's face turned white. Her mouth compressed into a scowl. "And you believe her?"

"He seemed to be sleeping with everyone else."

"I assure you, if I'd slept with him, he'd never have respected me— and he certainly wouldn't have let me marry his son."

"Amelia says he would have enjoyed the irony."

"Amelia has a twisted perspective on the Boelter men. Did she tell you that her husband was drunk when he crashed his car into a tree at a hundred miles an hour, and so was the naked woman they found on the seat beside him? That was all hushed up. Richard was sanctified as the fine, upstanding son, and Amelia holds her head up high as his beloved widow."

"This family hides a lot of secrets, she said," Dan uttered softly. "By the way, she also thinks you've had a long-standing affair with Fred Moore."

"Amelia has too much time with too little to do. She's always rushing into affairs which she then has to buy herself out of. When she's not in one, she's warping her brain staring at TV soap operas about people who are. She sees sexual conspiracies everywhere. If you see them, too, I can't help it."

"What about Margaret?" Dan acerbically inquired. "Is she making it with the chauffeur?"

"I doubt it," Susan quietly replied. "Margaret is probably frigid."

"You know that?"

"Not for certain, but I inferred from a remark John once made that he had sought other women out of necessity."

"And just what were you and he doing when he made that intimate disclosure?"

"That's insulting."

Dan was on his feet, hands on the table, leaning forward with his face only inches from Susan's, his voice strident with emotion. "Damn it, I've got to make a jury of twelve very ordinary people believe you'd rather have eaten glass than harmed a single hair on your husband's head. Their belief in your goodness is the only thing standing between you and a conviction for murder. They've got to see a woman above reproach, a woman who's absolutely virtuous and trustworthy, a woman who remained faithful to her husband despite every hell he put her through.''

"Tough job," she shot back, "considering they'll know you were my lover.''

"Only *after* your husband left you!" Dan growled. Not just the jury, he himself needed to believe in her. "What the hell were you doing before?''

Susan flinched as if he had struck her. "Will my simply saying I was faithful to Peter convince you? Or are you looking for an excuse not to be convinced?''

"What I'm looking for is the truth.''

"I'm not responsible for the rumors people might spread about me . . . or for being who I am. Am I expected to apologize for that?''

"Of course not.''

"Then stop holding it against me. I always sense some wary, buried, angry part of you expects me to ambush you. Dan, the Inquisition was five hundred years ago.''

"Being wary is how I survive.''

"I'm not your enemy!" she cried out. "I love you.''

She suddenly saw into his heart. "That's it, isn't it? All your life you've defined yourself by all the things about the Establishment that you're not. By loving me, you're afraid you'll betray what you thought made you unique.''

"No," he said quietly. "I'm afraid of how much I want to.''

That night was the anniversary of Dan's mother's death, her *yahrzeit*. Dan joined his father at their synagogue, Mikveh Israel. Founded as a Sephardic congregation in 1740, the synagogue was now housed in a Louis Kahn–designed building it shared with the Museum of American Jewish History on Independence Mall. An early congregant was Haym Salomon, who sacrificed his fortune to finance the American Revolution. Unlike Jacob Lazar, few congregants today were immigrants.

During the memorial service, Dan tried to concentrate on the single, indistinct recollection he had of his mother, lying against her wasted cheek in her bed. But he found his mind wandering to Susan and his ambiguous feelings about her. How could I be in love with someone I can't be sure I trust? he asked himself. He found no answer.

After the service, he and his father walked over to his father's restaurant. A waiter there for many years, Jacob had bought it with Dan's help when the previous owner moved to Florida. He had renamed it Kavala, after the city in which he had been born and grew up. The little restaurant had prospered, attracting Greek and Middle-Eastern expatriates and local residents.

A few young couples were finishing late dinners. Older, shirt-sleeved men were sipping *raqui* or syrupy sweet coffee in tiny cups and playing backgammon, *tavlé,* as they called it. Father and son ate *tarama* salad, *kashkcaval* cheese, olives, and pastries filled with spinach, eggplant, and cheese. All the while, the Elias Ladino Ensemble's lively tape of Turkish Sephardic music played on the audio system. His father had re-created the world of his youth, a world that existed now only in his memory.

Only at the end of the meal did he raise the questions disturbing him. "This woman, this Susan Boelter, the newspapers say she's more than a client to you. Is that true?"

"Yes."

"She isn't Jewish, you know."

"I know that, Pop."

"She's also very rich, this woman?"

"Yes."

"Differences like that, they don't make it easy for two people to be happy together."

Dan did not reply.

Something else was troubling Jacob. "For murder in this state they have the death penalty, right?"

"Probably not for a case like this. Maybe twenty years. Or she could get life without parole."

The older man shook his head. "Danny, you never make it easy for yourself."

The red light on Dan's answering machine was blinking like a Morse code signal when he entered his apartment that night. He hit the messages button.

"Hi, Dad, it's Jim. We're in Las Vegas. I didn't want you to call home and get worried when no one answered. We're here because Mom and Ron decided to get married. They probably asked me to come along so I wouldn't feel left out. I thought you ought to hear it from me, you know, that Mom is remarrying. I guess you don't care anymore, so that's all right, too."

Jamie's voice on the tape fell silent. Dan could hear people murmuring in the background. He assumed his son was phoning from a hotel lobby and charging it to his room or to Dan's credit card. He thought the call was about to end, but Jamie had more to say. The boy, like his grand-father, had read about Dan's relationship with Susan.

"A friend brought me an article from *USA Today* about that woman you went back to defend. They say she's your girlfriend and has a daughter around my age. Is she really? Your girlfriend, I mean. Do you like her daughter?"

More silence followed on the message tape, then Jamie said, "They're waving for me that it's time to go to the wedding. It's at someplace where they marry you fast. I'll call when we get back. Is that okay? I love you."

Click.

Dan played the piano moodily for a couple of hours. But Jamie did not call, and Dan did not know where to reach him. Finally Dan began to phone Las Vegas hotels. As he guessed, to entertain Jamie, Susan and Ron were staying at Circus Circus.

Father and son spoke on the phone for nearly an hour, each believing he was doing so to reassure the other.

Dan recognized the large man with heavy eyebrows and a jagged scar on his forehead, as soon as he entered Hi, Johnny's to pick up a chocolate doughnut and coffee to bring back to his office. The man's name was Tom Karp, and Dan had first met him years earlier, after Karp and several of his companions were badly beaten up while trying to organize opposition to Vinnie Briggs's rule at the pressmen's union. Karp was a leader of the dissident faction.

"How you doing, Tom?" Dan asked.

The latter sidled into the takeout line beside him. "Better since we learned something you might be interested in."

"What's that?"

"Vinnie Briggs lied to your man about being at the union's offices until seven the day Peter Boelter died."

"How do you know?"

"Someone slipped us a photocopy of his secretary's appointment book. It shows he left there just after five. He told her he was going out to see Peter Boelter, and she wrote it down."

Karp handed Dan the photocopied page.

Dan scanned it and then inquired, "Do you know why he was going to see Boelter?"

"He heard a rumor Boelter was planning to sell the *Herald* to Oren Lawlor. Lawlor wanted to combine the two papers and fire the staff. Naturally, that scared Briggs shitless. Having a lot of guys lose their jobs would kill his chances of getting reelected."

The two men had now moved up to the takeout counter, the last two in line. Dan asked whether he could buy Karp something.

"Honey bun and black coffee. Thanks."

Dan gave the order. As they waited for the items to be gathered, he asked, "You wouldn't know who might have more information about all this, would you?"

"Sam Knowland. He's a kind of assistant to Briggs. He says Briggs phoned Boelter and then went out to Boelter's place to have it out with him."

"Why's Knowland willing to talk?"

"Couple of reasons. If Briggs loses the election, he doesn't want to be out of a job . . . ."

Dan pressed him. "What's the other reason?"

After glancing around to be sure he would not be overheard, Karp said, "He thinks Vinnie Briggs maybe murdered Peter Boelter."

Rick first spoke with Sam Knowland, who confirmed what Tom Karp had reported, and then watched from his parked car until Vinnie Briggs arrived at his union's building. He then phoned Dan. Fifteen minutes later the two lawyers were striding into the union's offices.

"I'm sorry," Briggs's secretary protectively responded when they asked to see him. "He's going to be in meetings all day. You can leave a message, and he'll get back to you."

She was a good-looking woman in her thirties with white-blond hair and no wedding ring. Knowing Briggs to be the type who would list merit at the bottom of the requirements for this job, Dan supposed he was sleeping with her—or trying to. Any secretarial ability she might display would be an unexpected bonus.

"Tell him it's about Peter Boelter and if he can't see us, our next stop is the DA."

Moments later a sullen Vinnie Briggs opened his office door to admit the visitors. Unbidden, they found chairs facing his desk. No one else was in his office. He had been reading a newspaper.

"Our *firm* is representing Susan Boelter," Dan said carefully. "You told my colleague Rick here that you were in your office the entire day that Peter Boelter died. That wasn't true, was it?"

Briggs's eyes darted between the men. "Oh, you mean the *end* of the day. Hell, it was a Saturday. I might have left a little earlier than usual that afternoon. Four . . . four-thirty."

"Where did you go when you left?"

Again, Briggs's gaze oscillated between the lawyers. "I think that's my own business."

"Did you speak on the phone to Peter Boelter that day?" Dan inquired.

"Jesus, how can I remember every call I made that day?"

"Would my subpoenaing your records from the phone company refresh your recollection?"

"I spoke to Boelter that afternoon," Briggs grudgingly admitted. "Nothing much. Just touching base on stuff, this and that, labor and management. You know how it is."

"You didn't happen to discuss the fact that he was considering selling the *Herald* to Oren Lawlor."

"How could I know about that?"

"I'm also willing to subpoena every crony you have in this place just in case any of them was in here with you when you made that phone call."

Briggs slowly slumped back into his desk chair. "What do you want to know?"

"When you heard Boelter was negotiating with Oren Lawlor, you became worried, isn't that so?"

"Wouldn't you be? Wipe out half the newspaper jobs in the city. There's a time to play your hand tough and a time to start bailing out the boat, right? I said I'd be willing to meet with him right away to come up with an outline for contract terms for the whole union coalition that would give him a lot of what he was asking for, more than he ever thought he'd get."

"What did he say?"

Briggs's anger flashed. "The son of bitch laughed at me. He told me to go fuck myself with my contract. Then he hung up." Briggs jumped to his feet. "Arrogant bastard!"

He began to pace, the small eyes fixed on the carpet. "I had to go see him and convince him that a deal with us would make more sense than selling to Lawlor."

Dan realized that the unions' fears that the family might sell the paper after Peter's death was why they had rushed to make a generous deal with Susan. Their major proviso had been that the family hang on to the paper for at least ten years.

"So," Dan pressed Briggs, "after Boelter hung up on you, you decided to drive out to his place."

"Well, I started to, but I needed a wage and conditions package he couldn't turn down. While I drove, I kept working it out. When I finally did, I was up around King of Prussia and circled back toward Chestnut Hill."

"What time did you see Boelter?"

"I didn't. There were a lot of police cars parked around the house, so I just kept going."

"What time did you drive past his house?"

"Maybe a little past seven."

Rick spoke up. "You weren't curious why the police were there?"

"I figured something rough must have happened. I wasn't going to hang around and get implicated in something."

Dan rose to leave. "You claim you took two hours to make maybe a twenty-minute trip to Chestnut Hill. Vinnie, I think you may be implicated up to your eyebrows."

20

A few days later, Dan stared out his office window, feet up on his desk, his mind distant, grappling with imponderables. On the desk lay several newspapers from other cities containing stories about the trial. The front-page headline on that morning's *New York Post* proclaimed, "SUSAN'S DISBARRED LOVER MAY DEFEND HER."

Cal stomped into Dan's office. "We still haven't seen more than a trickle of documents from the DA's office." He was irate.

Dan's head turned toward his law partner, but his gaze remained unfocused.

Cal continued, "We gave them until today to turn over copies of the police reports, depositions, phone log, the works. Not a damned thing."

"Would they prove she was innocent, Cal?"

"All I'm interested in is 'not guilty beyond a reasonable doubt.' "

Dan's feet swung down. "That's not good enough. Damn it, Cal, I don't know who she is. She says her husband was alive when she left the house, and not a shred of evidence backs her up. Last night, I ran into someone who went to Haverford and knew her slightly at college. He wasn't sure, but he had this vague recollection that she was one of the great party girls at Bryn Mawr. I mean a top student, editor of the paper, but wild. Does he have her pegged right?"

"It sure doesn't jibe with the impression she gave us of her college years."

"Who the hell is she, really? Is she the gracious lady of high society?

Or is she a desperate adventuress who'd seduce her estranged husband, period and all? To meet her socially, you'd think she was the Virgin Mary. All that virtue, it knocks you off your feet, but is it a front? In bed she's practically a nymphomaniac."

Cal's eyebrows raised. "No wonder you refused a fee."

"I took her case because I believed her. Now I don't know what to believe."

Practical as always, Cal began to analyze the strength of her defense. "We've found some interesting information in the medical literature. And we have other suspects now. That's maybe the strongest thing in her favor. We know Vinnie Briggs tried to cover up about going out to Boelter's place that day. And Amelia Boelter looks a lot more likely than before."

"Why's that?"

"Once in a while, for all our sakes, please go through your in-box," Cal pleaded in mock despair. "Rick tracked down the waiter at the restaurant where she ate with Boelter the night before he died."

"Chez Henri."

Cal nodded. "If you ask me, the place is overrated. I wouldn't give you ten cents for their sauces. Heavy, floury."

"Cal, the waiter!"

"The guy says Amelia waited half an hour for Peter Boelter to show up, and the two of them argued all night. Rick took a statement from him." Cal began rifling through the stack of papers in Dan's in-box. "He says Amelia got loud. Angry as hell. She kept saying she was sure Boelter was seeing another woman. She demanded to know whether he intended to marry her or was he just stringing her along for her vote." Cal found the typed statement and tossed it onto Dan's desk. "The waiter didn't know what the vote was about, but he remembered her saying it a couple of times. When Peter wouldn't answer, she stormed out."

Excited, Dan swung down his feet and leaned forward. "Did she give any names? Of another woman he might be seeing?"

"His wife."

"Shit!"

Dan tried to factor the new data into the complex equation with too many unknowns. Amelia had claimed she and Peter were lovebirds, that his death had harrowed her. Yet, only the night before he died, she walked out on him because she thought he was deceiving her with Susan in order to retain her support for a sale of the paper. Bitter toward *him,* jealous of *her,* Amelia could retaliate against both of them with a murder that cast the blame on Susan. On the other hand, if Amelia was correct in her suspicions that Peter and Susan were still sleeping together, then

Susan had lied—to Dan and to the police. Which of the women had Peter made love to just before he died? Which of them was telling the truth?

"We need more evidence!" Dan exclaimed. "And the DA's sitting on it."

He jumped to his feet and started for the door.

"Where are you going?" Cal asked.

"To see Mara. She's hanging on to everything the prosecution is supposed to turn over to us."

"They only released that lab report so they could leak the findings to the press and make Susan look bad."

"Wherever you look," Dan growled, "they're trying to kill her chances for an effective defense. You know what's bothering me?"

"What?"

"Gil Huyton has known Susan a lot longer than any of us, and he hasn't a doubt in the world that she's guilty."

Scott Feller was leaving the district attorney's office building and Dan just entering when they encountered each other in the wood-paneled lobby.

"I just interviewed Huyton," Feller began. "Among other things, he said he intends to call you as a witness."

Dan was staggered. "What the hell do I know about Boelter's death?"

"Huyton says because you and Susan were having an affair, you may have conspired to kill Boelter."

"That son of a bitch! If I'm a witness, that stops me from acting as her lawyer."

"Do you know anything about a quarrel he's having with the Police Department? *He* says they're botching the investigations. *They* say he's botching the trials. I'm trying to get to the bottom of it. It started the beginning of the year, about the time of the Montano case."

"The only thing I heard was that Harry Stallworth would have liked more time to investigate before pressure was put on him to arrest Montano."

"The polls show a lot of voters think Huyton's doing a poor job."

Dan disagreed. "Whatever else you might say about him, he's trying hard."

"You know what kills him, Dan? That his department's being judged on a few big cases they lost, mostly to you. That's why he's so dead set on convicting Susan Boelter."

Dan's anger was still stoked high as he strode down the white corridor toward Mara's office. He noticed Eddie Grecco in a discussion with an

ADA and slowed to catch the detective's eye. Grecco peered straight through him. Dan was too objectionable a figure around here even to be caught nodding hello to.

Mara's secretary was away from her desk, and he walked straight into Mara's office.

"What's this shit about my being called as a witness?" he demanded of her.

"There's a lot we have to get to the bottom of." She was standing behind her desk, a habit of hers, as she read a document.

"Like what?" he demanded to know, shutting her office door.

"I don't think that's something I need to go into now."

"Was the tactic your idea or Huyton's?"

"It's not a 'tactic,' as you put it, Dan. There are definite concerns here."

"They're an excuse to keep a pile of documents you should have turned over to us weeks ago and to block me from representing Susan Boelter!"

The intercom buzzed, and Mara took the call. She turned away to keep the conversation confidential. Dan stalked to the window and peered out across Arch Street at the open plaza. A man had removed his shirt and was taking the sun.

Dan's head twisted back at the sound of the door opening. Gil Huyton strode into the room in shirtsleeves. Failing to notice Dan at the far end of the room, he rushed up to Mara, who was just hanging up the receiver.

"Darling, we won the Dorsey appeal!" he effused.

He threw his arms around her and kissed her avidly on the mouth.

"Unanimous," he exclaimed. "Let's get together at your place tonight. I can stay over. Edith and the kids are still in the country."

Huyton finally noticed Mara's alarm and that her eyes were focused over his shoulder. He spun around to find Dan Lazar staring at them.

"Jesus!"

Dan was the first to regain self-control. "You have to admire the kind of dedicated DA who takes his work—and his deputy—to bed with him."

"My private life is my own business," Huyton blustered.

"Funny you don't feel the same way about my relationship with Susan Boelter."

"What's that supposed to mean?"

"I ran into Scott Feller downstairs. He's looking into how you run this department. Do you think he'd be interested in knowing that you're engaged in a sexual relationship with the head of your Trial Division?"

"Is this some kind of blackmail?"

"Let's call it narrowing down the Susan Boelter case to the important issues."

Mara exploded. "Susan Boelter is a ruthless, cold-blooded killer who thought she could get away with murder because her crowd gets away with just about anything. If I have my way, she'll get mandatory life."

Dan sensed in Mara's wrath her hunger for status and recognition: Susan Boelter possessed privileges that since setting foot on American soil, Mara had struggled to seize.

"I don't care if she's Jack the Ripper," Dan retorted. "She has a right to counsel."

"Look, Lazar . . . Dan," Huyton said, "my relationship with Mara isn't what you think it is. We're good friends, colleagues, but it doesn't go any further than that. I'm a married man, and I take those vows very seriously."

"You know, Huyton, I'm a gullible kind of guy. I believe anything you tell me about why you're spending the night at her apartment. It's too far to drive so late at night. She has air-conditioning and you don't. Anything."

Dan took a seat and leaned back. "The problem is, I'll bet her doorman isn't as trusting as I am. I'll bet he probably thinks that all the nights you've been up at Mara's apartment have been for sex. The reporters who'll interview him, they'll probably think the same thing. And so will your wife—she didn't look like the understanding type."

"All right," Huyton conceded. "What do you want?"

"Just two things: You drop the phony tactic of calling me as a witness. And you support my petition with the Disciplinary Board for me to represent Susan Boelter at her trial."

Huyton glared in frustration. Dan could imagine his one-track mind shooting off worries like sparks from braking locomotive wheels: Will a deal with Lazar be legal? And if it is and I agree to it, can that two-bit shyster be trusted not to say anything about me and Mara? Afterward, will he try to hold me up for anything else?

For all of Huyton's posturing about morality, Dan supposed that the ethics of this particular arrangement would not figure into his thinking.

Huyton spoke up. "How do I know you won't mention this to anyone?"

"You mean will I keep your relationship with Mara as confidential as you kept my suspension?"

The DA broke forward half a step, his hands clenched into fists.

Mara intervened. "Gil, if Dan gives you his word, he'll keep it."

"All you're doing is allowing Susan Boelter a fair trial," Dan said by way of reassurance. But he could not keep himself from adding, "Or is that the part that bothers you?"

Huyton's reply was less angry than it was pained. "Our own differences aside, Lazar, you've got to know how much it hurts me to prosecute Susan. Whatever her provocation, she can't take another person's life without retribution. And I can't let personal friendship stand in the way of my public duty."

Dan inwardly marveled at how resolute a man's principles could suddenly become when his genitals did not intrude on his reason.

"This isn't some favor you're doing her," Dan contended. "Picking her own lawyer is her constitutional right."

Concession slowly infiltrated Huyton's expression. "Okay. I agree. You can represent her. We have a deal."

"And our side will get all the discovery documents by the end of the day?"

"By morning," Mara said. "I have to pull them together."

"Fine," Dan agreed, and started for the door.

"Dan!" she called out. "I'm sorry you had to find out about Gil and me this way."

Dan's face revealed his disgust. "To think that I actually let you sell me that bullshit about its being *my* fault you were leaving me! The moment you said you had a job here, I should have figured you'd already bought yourself an insurance policy."

His hand gripped the doorknob, but a final thought delayed his departure.

"Huyton, a word of advice. Watch your back."

The next morning three detectives assigned to the district attorney's office arrived at Susan's house with a warrant allowing them to search for a murder weapon. They spent hours going through the house, but found none.

Susan arrived at the *Herald* just in time for a private lunch in her office with Mason Willoughby, whom the orphan's court had appointed to approve matters that went beyond the ordinary course of business. Susan had grown increasingly frustrated as the older man, an accountant by profession and conservative by nature, refused to authorize expenditures for new programs or equipment. Although he could not prevent her from adding to the news hole—two pages more each for the City Section and for the Sports Section, thus challenging the *Mirror*'s strongest appeal—he flatly turned down her request to lower ad rates, which the staggering *Mirror* would have had to match. And he refused even to consider her request for the money to purchase new color presses. She contended they were essential in competing for consumers and advertising against magazines and TV and would sharply cut production costs by reducing the number of pressmen required to print the paper, a right granted by the unions in the new labor contracts.

Instead, Willoughby informed her that he had spoken earlier with Oren Lawlor, who still wanted to buy the *Herald*. Lawlor wanted to meet with her today, before he left town.

"The *Herald*'s not for sale," Susan asserted. She noticed the wisp of anxiety in the old man's eyes. "You've talked to Margaret and Amelia. They want to sell."

He has to be thinking, she surmised, that if I'm convicted, the family will gain ownership of my shares and control of the Foundation's. The *Herald* would then almost certainly be sold, and he might be criticized for approving these expenditures I'm requesting.

Willoughby disclosed, "Midge will agree to sell, too, if they insist."

"You're sure about Midge?"

Willoughby nodded.

Although she expected it, Midge's defection saddened her. They had always defended each other within the family, and they worked closely now at the *Herald*. She had believed that their interests coincided and that he respected her business sense.

"Susan, selling the paper frees them all from any concern about the future. It was different for them when Peter was alive."

"He was a man. I'm only a woman."

"Susan, he was Margaret's son, Midge's brother."

And Amelia's lover, she thought.

"Lawlor's desperate," she contended. "This Dream Dollars game the *Mirror*'s running is just a last-ditch effort to keep it from collapsing." Willoughby's eyes revealed uncertainty about business strategies he could not quite grasp.

"I think you should meet with him," he stubbornly insisted. "At least hear what he has to say."

Susan finally relented. "All right. At my house at four. Having the meeting here or at the *Mirror* would announce to the entire city that we're for sale."

"I'll arrange it."

Susan had scheduled a four-o'clock at Dan's office to go over documents just delivered by the prosecution. As soon as Willoughby left, she phoned Dan and asked him to sit in on the meeting with Lawlor. She needed his moral support.

'Mason used to be on my side, but now he's more of an anchor," she explained.

"Your house at four," Dan swiftly confirmed, and hung up. He did not want to give her time to ask whether he, too, was still securely on her side.

As if to refute the stories about his high-handed egotism, Oren Lawlor was displaying genial helpfulness to Susan as he sat with her, Willoughby, and Dan in her drawing room. He maintained that in her time of crisis, he wanted to lift irksome business responsibilities from her shoulders, even to pay her personally a healthy sum for agreeing to the buy-out. Because of her excellent new union contract, he would even agree that the *Herald* would survive the merger and the *Mirror* be folded into it.

"What about the contract's ten-year restriction on selling the paper?" he was asked. Oh, his lawyers had ways to keep legal ownership with the family while transferring the actual benefits and control to his newspaper chain.

With the look of a vulture trying to hide how badly he needed the meal, Oren Lawlor perched forward to make his offer. It turned out to be ten percent less than the offer he had made to Peter.

"You know how the newspaper industry's problems have deepened," he said.

Susan's manner was cordial and confident. "We find it's already turning around. Perhaps your ad rates are too high. We're planning to cut ours again. The major department stores are thinking of giving us a big ad commitment."

"My offer is very generous, Susan."

Her mouth tightened skeptically. "Is that because with Peter gone, our family has one less mouth to feed?"

Dan was startled by the grimly sardonic rejoinder. He could not detect the slightest flutter of anxiety. Apparently as relaxed as Lawlor, she had a poker player's nerves. Dan asked himself, were those also a murderer's nerves? This woman willing to turn down millions of dollars and gamble her future on her own business skills, was she also capable of staking all on a single push of a tipsy man down steep stairs, a single swing of a heavy object?

Lawlor emitted a long, full belly laugh.

"All right, I'm prepared to go a bit higher. But think it over. I'm the logical buyer. Certainly the highest bidder you'll get."

"If the *Mirror* doesn't collapse first," she replied.

Lawlor stood up to leave.

"My lawyers who've studied the murder charges against you believe the odds are far greater that you'll be convicted well before that. When that happens, I'll pay much less than I'm prepared to pay now—and no extra share for you personally. Think about it.''

The gravity of his tone and the raptor's gleam in his eyes conveyed the warning that he played the game too savagely for a fine lady like Susan to survive.

With Willoughby following, he started out of the room and then noticed Karen approaching. Dressed in brown leather boots and jodhpurs, she had just returned from riding. Susan introduced her.

''A beautiful girl,'' the businessman remarked, and then repeated to Susan, ''Think about it. Think about what's best for her.''

Susan asked Karen to see the visitors out and closed the doors behind them.

''Are you all right?'' Dan asked, observing the strain in her face.

''Damn! I can drive him out of business if Mason will just loosen the purse strings. The *Herald* is worth a lot more than he's offering. But he's counting on the murder charge to make me lose my nerve.''

Dan thought back to the complaisant wife and mother who first proffered him hospitality in this house. There were hints then of steel-belted character beneath the resilient surface, of her refusal to yield on critical issues, despite what was to become unbearable pressure from Peter.

Now there was also pressure on her from the DA, from Lawlor, from the other Boelters. Months of it had taken their toll. Her mouth seemed stretched into a tighter line, her cheeks more drawn, her brow more lined, her eyes set more deeply into their hollows than when he first met her.

She exhaled a long sigh and lowered herself into an armchair.

''Life is never easy, is it, Dan? Just a short time ago I was worried about losing custody of my daughter and a monthly check from Peter. Now it's my life.'' Her voice caught.

She turned her head away. She was crying.

Unmoved by the sight, Dan found himself trying to decide whether she had allowed her self-control to slip because the tense meeting had ended or because she was attempting to recement his loyalty.

He bent to his briefcase and drew out the documents Mara had sent over. He wanted Susan to check for errors in the statements given by police officers and witnesses. Did she recognize any of the witnesses? What about the phone log? It listed calls made from Peter's house during the first week of June, up until his death. Rick Moss had used a reverse phone book to match numbers to owners and addresses. Each owner's name had been written beside the appropriate phone number, date, and time.

Dan left Susan in the drawing room and went seeking Karen's company. He found her in the circular driveway in front of the house, gaping at his motorcycle.

"Like it? It goes back a ways. They don't make them like this anymore."

"Mom said you took her out on a Harley, but I didn't believe her. I mean, we're talking about Mom."

"Want a ride?"

The thirteen-year-old hesitated as he handed her his helmet. Then, as if gathering all her courage, she put on the helmet and swung onto the seat. Dan kicked down on the starter, squeezed the clutch lever with his left hand, slipped into gear, and turned the throttle with his right.

Karen directed them along a route out the rear gate that opened onto woodland horse trails and eventually looped back to the driveway. A small skid turned the machine to the curb near the steps of the portico entrance.

"That was *so* cool!" Karen exclaimed, flipping up the helmet's visor.

Dan dismounted and sat down on the portico step. Karen slid up to his seat on the bike.

"Would you teach me how to ride it?" she asked.

"If your mom gives you permission. But only on the property until you're old enough for a license."

She nodded. Her hands circled the thick rubber handgrips. "Grandmother—you know, Mom's mom—she's dead now, but she once told me that Mom had a boyfriend when she was a teenager, who used to pick her up for dates on a motorbike. Grandmother called him a 'hood.' She hated him."

"Your mom told me her *girlfriend* was the one who dated the guy with the bike."

"Mom laughed when I asked her about it, and she changed the subject, so I figured it really *was* true. She doesn't do that with me anymore— change the subject."

"You two still getting along well?"

Karen nodded. "It was tough when I was in the middle between her and Dad."

"You miss him?"

"Sometimes." She abruptly released the handgrips. "I don't really want to learn how to ride it."

"Karen, I'm not trying to be your dad. I'm just a friend. It's okay to have friends."

She appraised Dan for several seconds. "I guess if you want to teach me, it's all right." She grasped the handgrips again.

The front door swung open. Susan stepped out of the house. She was alarmed to see Karen on the motorcycle.

"Dan took me for a ride," Karen said, dismounting and setting the helmet on the seat. "That was okay, wasn't it?"

"It's dangerous," Susan snapped. "Dan, you know better than to subject my daughter to those sorts of risks."

He eyed her evenly. "Your mother once told her you used to date a real bad dude with a motorcycle."

"A girlfriend's date once gave me a lift home. That's all. My mother enjoyed thinking the worst of me."

She moved a strand of Karen's hair back into place. "What time are Amy and her folks coming to pick you up?"

"Six. They're taking us for pizza before the movie." Karen's voice rose at the end of the sentence, as if asking for permission.

"You'd better shower and dress."

Karen shyly smiled a good-bye at Dan and went inside.

"Find anything in the documents?" he asked, getting to his feet.

"They were all photocopies."

He nodded. "The DA keeps the originals and sends us photocopies. We copied them over for you to look at."

"The phone log, too."

"Right. The prosecution subpoenaed it from the phone company and copied it for us. What matters is the people Peter called. Anyone out of the ordinary?"

"No." Her agitation broke through again. "It's just that the prosecutors seem to have all the initiative on their side. I'm just supposed to sit still and wait for whatever they want to do to me. They went through the house today like locusts."

"Did they find anything?"

Susan glared at Dan incredulously. "Of course they didn't find anything."

"Are you all right?"

"No, I'm not all right." She let her anger emerge. "How could I be? I'm about to be tried for murder. And I've got a lawyer who isn't sure I'm innocent. Things like that tend to get under one's skin."

"I haven't said that."

"Doubt is written all over your face. You have that telltale 'Is she telling the truth?' look. You keep thinking maybe I killed Peter and I've been lying to cover it up. That's right, isn't it?"

Dan did not reply.

Her eyes glistening wetly with the same angry distress she had displayed in the drawing room, Susan tilted her head to one side, evaluating him. ''Since you put so much stock in honesty, be honest with me, Dan. Aren't you worried that you might be fucking a cold-blooded killer?''

When he still did not reply, she spun away and charged into the house, slamming the door behind her.

21

Dan drove his motorcycle aimlessly for a while, then found himself on a road that ran through Peter's neighborhood. He turned onto Walker Drive and slowed as he passed the house.

A yellow vinyl tape still blocked access to the locked front door. Keeping people out and keeping secrets in, Dan thought. Will what happened here that night ever be known? Will the bricks ever give up this last Boelter family secret? Dan chuckled at how much Peter would have loved the mystery and fuss his death had caused, especially if it had been an accident all along.

No sign of forced entry had been found. Someone Peter had angered had crushed his skull, or else in a drunken fall, Peter had killed himself. The attribute in him that had provoked either his homicide or his careless self-destruction had been a lifetime forming. Dan realized that he did not have the vaguest idea what it might be.

What a strange man he was! Dan thought. Dan sensed that Peter's character—why and how he had lived as he had—was the key to why and how he had died as he had. To defend Susan to the fullest, Dan decided, he must comprehend Peter Boelter.

Dan wheeled around and headed back across the bridge to the Main Line. Amelia's address, he recalled, was only a few minutes away. She had spoken openly to him before. She might do so again.

The maid asked him to wait at the front door. Amelia soon appeared. She had been riding her exercise bike and was dressed in shorts and a halter. She had good legs, he noted. Rich women always had good legs.

"On your way to see Susan?" she asked.

He shook his head. "She and I had some differences. I'd like to talk to you."

"Come in," Amelia said happily. "We can chat in the library."

As she stepped back to let Dan enter, he noticed a thin pink line on her forearm.

"You cut yourself?" he asked.

"A few weeks ago."

"How did it happen?"

"Silly, really. I stumbled in the greenhouse. A pot broke."

He thought she had hesitated before coming up with an answer, but he could not be sure. "Would that have been in early June?"

"Around then. It looks worse than it was. I'm so glad you dropped by. It's almost dinnertime. I hope you'll join me."

"Yes, thank you."

His answer evoked a smile of pleasure. "One more night of TV, and I'll turn into one of those great lumpy women with thick ankles and straggly hair."

"Are you going away this summer?"

"Our place in Maine. When Johnny finishes summer school. I really didn't want to be up there alone. Margaret's decided to go to Europe this year instead—too many memories in Maine of her boys growing up, I imagine. Midge and his fiancée are staying around the city until the end of August."

"Beautiful house," Dan commented.

Although dark and ponderous on the outside, the large stone mansion was indeed beautiful within, much like Susan's in the ceremonial interior filled with period decor and large paintings. A wide staircase led up from the foyer to the second floor. Dan could imagine Amelia, in a striking gown, descending in a grand entrance to one of her parties. He did not privately condemn her for the superficiality of a life built on social events and on her image at them. They relieved a loneliness with which he himself was too well acquainted. He felt a pang of guilt that he was playing on that loneliness and on the attraction she felt for him to induce her to talk to him.

"I'm hoping you can tell me more about Peter. I can't get a handle on him. Do you know anything about the boys' childhood?"

"Only a little. My husband didn't talk much about it. Except once, after a really uncomfortable anniversary party for his parents. He said his and his brothers' childhood was the battlefield his parents waged their marriage on.''

"That must have been difficult on the boys.''

"When they were very young, they had a governess they liked. That helped. A woman they called Nanny Gilda.''

"Is she still alive?''

"She's in a nursing home. Margaret says the woman is senile. But Midge says he visited her for her eightieth birthday last year, and she's fine.''

Entering the mahogany-paneled room, Amelia rang a bell. "Maureen can bring us drinks. I'll just get into something a little more presentable.''

A moment later a young, light-haired woman in a maid's uniform arrived. Amelia told her to bring them a cold shaker of martinis and hurried upstairs to change.

Dan scanned the books on the low shelves. All were hardcovers, mostly popular fiction. One shelf contained psychological self-help books aimed at women, with the word "love" predominating in their titles.

Maureen returned with a tray containing two tall glasses, a pitcher of martinis, small dishes containing green olives and pearl onions, and a plate holding a round cheese encircled by crackers.

Dan smiled at her. "Have you worked for Mrs. Boelter very long?''

"Almost three years now.'' Her cadence sang in an Irish lilt.

Dan remembered having heard her name before. "Maureen, you were here the morning Susan Boelter unexpectedly showed up.''

Blushing, Maureen nodded faintly.

"Were you also here the night Peter Boelter died?''

"I was at the movies.'' She seemed pleased that his inquiry had switched from the embarrassing clash in the bedroom. "Just before going out that night, Mrs. Boelter gave me the evening off.''

"Before she went to Mr. Boelter's house, you mean?''

"Yes.''

Maureen began to pour Dan a martini.

"What time did she leave here?'' he asked.

"Around six o'clock.''

"Are you sure?'' Dan tried to strain the excitement from his tone.

"My boyfriend drove right over to pick me up when he heard I'd been given the night off. We were in a rush to get to the movie theater in Ardmore by six-fifteen. We left here just as Mrs. Boelter was leaving for Mr. Boelter's house.''

Dan suddenly noticed a blur of color to one side. He glanced toward it. Amelia was standing in the doorway, horror on her face.

"Get out of here!" she screamed at him. "Get out of here right now!"

"I'm sorry," he said quietly.

"All along you were a spy for Susan, just pretending you wanted to see me. A dirty, sneaking spy!"

He could detect her mind searching for the most terrible indictment of him she could make.

"I trusted you!" she finally cried.

Seeking to leave tormenting thoughts in his dust, Dan raced the motorcycle flat out as it climbed into Fairmount Park and careened around curves, so perfectly balanced on the knife's edge of terror between life and death that every neuron in his brain had to concentrate on survival. He remembered a hilltop with a wide clearing from which one could view the veins of expressway and street and river that connected the park to the rest of the city sprawling to the east. High above the strivings and confusion, with the buildings tiny and the people negligible, perhaps the thoughts that would catch up with him—his doubts about Susan's behavior, his distaste for having used Amelia's attraction to him to gain information—would not seem so demoralizing.

He slowed to stop on a knoll at the top of the hill, but he did not turn off the engine. Reflecting for only an instant, he started the bike rolling forward and then dismounted, running alongside to keep it steady and pointing it down the incline toward the edge of the clearing. He twisted up the throttle. The bike picked up speed across the grass tromped down by visitors until he was running full out to keep up with it and, finally, had to release the handlebar.

The blue machine roared past him, headed toward the rise at the rim of the cliff. It hit the little bump and flew into the sky, seeming for a moment as if it might merge into its quintessence above. Slowly, though, like a falcon with wings folded to dive at a prey, it arced downward, and then started to tumble end over end in a free fall until it hit a rocky outcropping and rebounded outward, forming a smaller arc this time. Hitting once more, it swung sideways and began to spin as if on a lathe as it bounced down the slope and tore a scar through bushes and earth before it disappeared into a grove of trees.

He loved life, he had realized, not danger. He loved it more than his work, as much as the truth that gave it structure and almost as much as his son, who gave it perpetuity. He possessed too rich a life and cared about too many people to continue doing something so foolishly dangerous as high-speed biking. Death, when it finally came, would have to struggle for him, to pull each clawing fingernail off the doorway he would be clutching at.

Dan had expected a ball of flame from a ruptured gas tank that would engulf the machine in a pyrotechnic, orgasmic annihilation, but there was none, merely the anticlimax of unremarkable silence. He would have to content himself with the slow glory of sunset. He sat on the precipice and watched the sky dim from vermilion to black and the lights in the scenery below slowly form a still-lake mimicry of the universe above. Susan's house somewhere in the far distance behind him, Amelia's, nearer, deep within woods, and Peter's across the river were all enclosed by darkness now.

Amelia had been delighted by his unexpected arrival and ingenuously welcomed him, relying on his honor to wall himself off from Susan's interests when he was with her. Nonetheless, when he saw a scratch on her arm that might have come from a fight with Peter and had an opportunity to interview her maid, he had bored in as he was legally obligated to do for his client. An attorney who failed to pursue evidence that might aid a client would be grossly negligent. And despite being overjoyed to learn that Amelia had arrived at Peter's house some twenty-five minutes earlier than she had claimed—evidence that might go a long way to clear Susan—he still felt a residue of remorse at the way he had obtained it.

Would he have pursued the evidence for Susan even if he weren't her lawyer? he asked himself. The answer, he knew, was yes. He loved her and would do anything to protect her. But his earlier certainties about her character had corroded into ambiguities. Was she truly the person he loved, or was she some counterfeit whose ambition had fashioned her into the image of an admirable woman she reckoned he would love?

Susan said Peter was alive when she left him, but had presented proof only that she had departed at around ten minutes to six. Both the cash register receipt and eyewitnesses corroborated her presence in the super-market a quarter of an hour later; the assistant manager and a cashier both told Dan's associate, Rick, that after reading about Peter's death in the newspaper the next day, they had remembered Susan's visit.

Amelia said she found Peter dead at a little before six-thirty. But she had actually left her house for the five-minute trip some twenty-five minutes earlier. That would have given her and Peter time for quick lovemaking before an argument drove her to kill him or he stumbled down the stairs. In either case, in her panic, she might have made up a story of arriving late, so as not to be accused of the killing. A struggle might have caused the scratch on her arm that left a smear of blood on his thigh. Or the blood could have come from Susan, who was having her period. Amelia had argued with Peter the previous night, just as Susan had in court the previous day.

Was Amelia the liar, or was Susan? Did one of them kill Peter? And if so, which one?

A single immutable fact was what Dan needed in order to point one way or another, toward Susan or away from her. Toward guilt or innocence. He had to know if he was defending and in love with and, as she had angrily put it, fucking a killer.

After he had brooded for a long while, he noticed some of the lights below going out. He stood up and began to walk across the clearing toward the descending road. Once out of the park, he would have to convince a passing driver to give him a lift.

Suddenly he halted in midstride, remembering that he had promised to teach Karen to ride the motorcycle.

"Guilt!" he shouted aloud, and kicked at the dirt. "On top of everything else, guilt! If it isn't one kind, it's another. Perfect!"

He shambled forward.

"And craziness, too!" he muttered, laughing. He kicked at a pebble and sent it skittering ahead of him. "I've *got* to be going out of my mind! First I trash a fifteen-thousand-dollar bike, and now I'm talking to myself."

Dan was back in Chestnut Hill the next morning. Willoughby, as executor of Peter's estate, had decided he had an obligation to rerent Peter's house for the duration of the lease. The district attorney's office had agreed that he could, and Peter's maid was coming in to give it a good cleaning before it went on the market. Dan wanted another look before then.

He parked in the driveway. The yellow tape had been removed, and the front door was slightly ajar. Inside, music had replaced the disturbing silence that had confronted Dan during his previous visit. He followed the sound to the kitchen. A middle-aged woman, hands on her thighs, bent at the waist, was staring into the cabinet beneath the sink. The radio on the windowsill was playing soft rock.

The woman glanced over at him, but then back into the cabinet. "The police took away everything. I can't find my sponges and rubber gloves, my wash rags." She straightened up. "How do you people expect me to clean up?"

"I'm not with the police. My name's Dan Lazar. I'm Susan Boelter's lawyer."

"I'm Brenda," she said, with an intonation that indicated she had been told to expect him.

"You haven't been back here since Mr. Boelter died?"

She shook her head, still upset that the interim had seen the disappearance of her implements.

Dan asked about a matter he and Rick had discussed when they had first visited. "Why is it nobody worked here on weekends or nights? Not you, not the butler or the cook. All week a staff of three for a household containing a single man. And then, on the weekend, no one. Mr. Boelter didn't seem like a man who did much for himself around a house."

Her severe expression softened into a grin at the thought of her employer's pitching in with the cleaning and cooking. "He sure wasn't the neatest man in the world. I'd come back Monday morning and find the house a mess."

"What about the bedroom?" Dan recalled a king-size bed.

"That's no business of mine!" she replied with some asperity.

"Both sides of the bed were usually messed up when you came in to clean Mondays, is that it?"

She wrestled with her conscience. "Are you sure you have to know? The man's dead and gone and entitled to his privacy."

"I have to know," he assured her.

"Well," she reluctantly said, "as a matter of fact, yes, both sides."

"Did you ever see a woman here?"

"Mrs. Boelter, that's his sister-in-law. She came by once in a while. I stayed late one time when George was out sick and served them dinner."

"Next morning, how was the bedroom?"

Brenda appeared pained. "Mrs. Boelter's a nice woman. She sometimes has me help her maid with the spring cleaning. She recommended me for this job."

"You might have to answer these questions in court."

The woman's gaze dropped. "She sometimes stayed over."

"Have you been upstairs yet?"

"I was going to. Mr. Willoughby told me to put on fresh sheets and straighten up."

"Just let me take a quick look around up there first, all right?"

Brenda stared at him strangely. "You sure this stuff isn't just so you can gossip it around. You're not from one of those nosy TV shows are you?"

"No. Have you been down to the cellar?"

"Not yet," she answered with a shiver, and went to the broom closet, where after some delving in the back, she located a worn-out sponge and some rags. They would have to do. She poured a strong cleaning liquid into the pail, which she lifted into the sink to fill up.

Dan surveyed the kitchen, but nothing caught his eye. He opened the cellar door and squatted down to examine the edge of the floor that formed the top of the stairs. An aluminum strip finished off and held down the vinyl tile flooring. A man whose balance had been lessened by alcohol could certainly have caught his foot on the strip and stumbled forward. Dan inspected the first step. The riser appeared to be at least an inch higher than the ones below it. He would check to make sure Rick had measured it.

He flipped on the lights and slowly descended, looking for anything he might have missed. Nothing appeared different. The room, still cold, was empty except for the wine and liquor cases. He stared at the blood-stained corner of the bottom step, still encircled by the chalk outline of Peter's head, and tried to decipher its secret. The concrete edge was sharp and clean. It could have cracked open a skull and knifed inward. The problem was to find a respected forensic pathologist who agreed.

There were so many possibilities as to the cause. What if Susan actually *had* been involved? In what way? The worst would be that counting on Peter's drunken unsteadiness and slow reactions, she had pushed him head-long down the stairs. The least would be that she inadvertently stumbled against him, causing him to lose his balance. Between an active murder and a pure accident lay yet a third possibility: the negligent, but unplanned, action the law called "manslaughter," homicide that lacked the intent to kill. All three could have been precipitated by a push from Susan, but her intent for each would have been different. How to determine that intent? Dan pondered. How to know the nature of a possibly unconscious urge her conscious mind might have rejected? How to assign blame?

After a few minutes, when no answers came to him, Dan went back upstairs. Brenda was vigorously scrubbing the floor, singing along with the radio.

On the second floor he checked the master bedroom. The blanket on one side of the bed was drawn down, and the sheet unmussed. The sheets and pillowcase on the other side were unwrinkled. No sign that anyone had engaged in quick, feverish copulation.

This house! This silent, inscrutable, infuriating house! he growled to himself. If at that instant lifting it off its foundations and shaking it would have caused all of its secrets to come tumbling out, he was sure he would somehow have found the strength.

Back in his car he momentarily considered driving to the base of the cliff in Fairmount Park to assess the damage to his motorcycle and whether it could be repaired. Virtuously, he rejected the idea.

Almost unconsciously, however, he found himself driving back to the office by way of Rising Sun Avenue and slowing as he passed the Harley dealership. Maybe a good used one, he thought. Just to keep at the beach for going to the deli. If he was careful when he biked and kept to the speed limit, maybe he would be technically within the bounds of his new resolution of responsibility. Instantly, repugnance welled up at this backsliding that would ruin one of the great spontaneous statements of his life.

He forced himself instead to muse on the irony of the street name where America's motorcycle was taking its stand in Philadelphia.

Dan slipped into the morgue's basement through the loading dock and located Rudy, the autopsy technician he had befriended, who was wheeling a sheet-covered gurney.

"Need some information," Dan said.

They briefly conversed.

"But remember, man," Rudy warned, as he turned to continue on his way, "you didn't hear it from me."

At the far end of an open area, Dan poked his head into the autopsy room and shouted Dr. Armbruster's name over the loud, grinding buzz. The noise stopped. Two men in white at the head of an operating table turned toward him. One held a portable electric saw in one hand and the top of a skull in the other. On the table lay a naked male corpse with the brain exposed.

To ward off his revulsion at the sight, Dan joked to himself: What a great horror flick this would make! *Chainsaw Morgue Surgeon.* The idea could make him millions.

"Could I see you for a moment?" Dan asked.

Armbruster nodded, told the man holding the saw that he would be right back, and followed Dan into the corridor.

Ronald Armbruster, the deputy medical examiner, was a tall, very thin man in his mid-to-late forties with ascetic features hidden poorly by a sandy-colored mustache, thinning hair, and thick aviator-design glasses.

As Armbruster approached, his face clouded. He had testified in one of Dan's cases. "You're not allowed down here."

"I want to talk to you about the Peter Boelter case," Dan replied.

"What about it?"

"A little bird told me you're not one of the chief's great admirers." Dan sought some reaction on Armbruster's face, but the other man was obviously not a great one for animation. "I have a theory that Kieffer's autopsy on Peter Boelter may not have been the most thorough in history, that he may have rushed it."

"It wouldn't be the first time."

Dan was startled by the reply. "Does that mean Kieffer isn't as diligent as he should be?"

Armbruster looked around. "Come by my house tonight, about eight. We can talk then."

"I'd like to bring my investigator who's working on the case."

"Just you."

Armbruster quickly gave Dan his address and ducked back into the autopsy room.

All day Dan had put off phoning Susan to confirm their tentative dinner date at his house tomorrow night. He still had not done so when he left early for the health club.

He worked out with a frenzy derived from his frustration at battling perplexity with so little progress, grabbed a quick supper at the nearest coffee shop, and arrived at eight o'clock at the address Ronald Armbruster had given him. It turned out to be a luxury single-family development near Media that announced itself by means of a wooden sign exhibiting the raised words "Grouse Run" and a cutout of a bird that Dan assumed was the said grouse. Three house designs recurred with differing details and greenery along winding roads carefully laid out to give the effect of an older area. Sprinklers showered many of the front lawns.

Armbruster's house appeared to be one of the newest, near a cul-de-sac containing several unsold lots the builder would have to hang on to until the long housing slump had finally passed. It also seemed out of character. Dan's quick impression of Armbruster had led him to expect a different dwelling, the sort of older white Victorian with columned porches and scrolling under the eaves that proliferated near the University of Pennsylvania.

The reason for the housing choice became clear when an auburn-haired woman in her late twenties, at least fifteen years younger than the doctor, answered Dan's ring. From her nervousness, Dan surmised that her husband had confided to her the purpose of this visit. Tight-lipped, she led Dan back to the den, where Armbruster was waiting, and then closed the door to give the men privacy, as if doing so could wall off her well-ordered life from the unforeseeable fallout of her husband's rashness.

"A drink, Mr. Lazar?" the pathologist asked as a formality of hospitality, not actually expecting Dan to accept.

"No, thanks."

Both men took seats in armchairs on opposite sides of a low wooden table with three lines of medical journals laid out on it, each going back exactly six issues.

Armbruster drew down the ends of his pallid mustache in thought. "You asked about Kieffer's performance." He spoke slowly, with long pauses, like an old daisy-wheel printer waiting to receive the next sentence from the computer. "Understand that he's rather new at the job, so there've only been a few months to evaluate him."

"I understand the new mayor appointed him."

"Technically, we're a division of the Health Department, which chose a board to evaluate him."

"But there wasn't any doubt that the mayor wanted him and that he was going to be appointed, I gather."

Armbruster nodded. "True."

"To a job you thought you should have gotten."

"The mayor owed him a favor—and, I suppose, wanted the kind of political person who could lobby the City Council for new equipment we badly needed. You know how broke the city is. The department needed a new gas chromotographer and mass spectrometer for toxicology testing. Our records still aren't computerized. We don't have enough gurneys for all the bodies. Believe me, that's been taking a lot of Kieffer's time. As soon as I saw that politics would be involved in the decision . . ."

"You withdrew your name."

"I'm a forensic pathologist, Mr. Lazar. My work is not with the living, but with the dead. I've devoted my entire life to ascertaining a single fact, over and over."

"The cause of death."

"Precisely. It takes highly specialized training to discern whether someone died as a result of natural or external causes—say, of homicide. Ernest Kieffer, you have to understand, is a different sort of pathologist, one who's spent his life examining the blood and tissues of living people to determine whether a disease exists."

"And he isn't really a qualified forensic pathologist, is that it?"

"Technically, he is. He'd done a bit of forensic work in the army and decided, in fifty-six, when certification for forensic pathologists was just instituted, to gain the certification, just in case. Soon afterward, though, a hospital job came along in a discipline that was more lucrative and more suited to his training, and he left forensic pathology."

Dan understood. "So you're saying that Dr. Kieffer isn't aware of the advances in your field since then."

Armbruster's expression hardened. "He makes some attempts to get up to speed, but he's misguided as to the extent and accuracy of his knowledge."

"And he was performing autopsies, which he wasn't well qualified to do."

"Do you know Kieffer?"

"No."

"Well, he's not the type to take advice. Thinks he knows it all. Not that the rest of us has time to assist on his autopsies."

"And it was incredibly hectic the weekend Peter Boelter died."

Armbruster nodded. "The Boelter case made all the headlines, but a lot of cases came in that weekend. In the midst of everything, a water main broke and flooded us. Absolute chaos. We were trying to stop the flooding and move the bodies to safety while autopsies were piling up unperformed. A long time went by before Kieffer could squeeze in the Boelter autopsy."

"Very late at night, I understand from the report. Couldn't somebody else have done it?"

"He was the one expected to perform the autopsy on an important figure like Peter Boelter. He's the chief."

"And he botched it."

Armbruster hesitated for a long while and then said, "His conclusions are, let's say, debatable."

Dan pressed him. "Will you testify that he made the wrong findings in the case?"

"Oh, no, I couldn't. He's my superior. Professional loyalty and all that."

Dan became irritated. "You'd rather I ruined his reputation on the stand while you stood safely on the sideline, ready to replace him." Because it just may be, Dan thought, that Dr. Ernest Kieffer is nowhere near so inept at his job as you want me to believe.

"I take exception to your characterization of my motives, Mr. Lazar."

"Then what *is* it you're trying to do? A woman may be unjustly convicted if Kieffer came to the wrong conclusions. Either you're willing to testify to that or you're not."

"I thought to offer you some background here."

"Dr. Armbruster, I'm not a reporter. I can't refute Kieffer's findings with unattributed statements from anonymous sources. I need a face on that stand and hard evidence, details of when and how he messed up."

Armbruster formed a steeple with opposed fingertips, the ends of the forefingers touching his lips. Finally he said, "Then I can't help you."

Dan rose to his feet.

"Thanks for nothing, doctor."

Armbruster's hands flattened into a simulation of prayer. "I'm sorry you don't understand the position you put me in."

"Will you at least testify about how hectic things were back then and that the investigator customarily takes the air and ground temperatures at a death scene? Simple facts, that would be all."

Armbruster thought a long time. "I will . . . if I'm subpoenaed. I'd have to then, wouldn't I? Then no one could say that I gave the information willingly."

"Heaven forfend, doctor."

"There's one thing you ought to ask Kieffer about, one thing out of the ordinary about his fixing the time of death." Armbruster told Dan what that was.

"Oh, I will, doctor. Be assured that I will."

Dan saw himself out. Just before he closed the front door, he heard Armbruster's wife scurrying from the kitchen to the den to learn from her husband what had happened.

Driving back into the city afterward, Dan had to keep the car air conditioner on high because of the heat wave. He stopped at Border's, a capacious bookstore on Walnut with a small café on the second floor. As if becalmed in doldrums, he read until it was too late to phone Susan.

Only then did he go home with a bag full of books and, instead, call his son in California, where it was three hours earlier. His depression was not eased by learning that Jamie had switched allegiance from the Phillies to the Dodgers.

Just after ten o'clock the next morning, Rick Moss unexpectedly appeared in the open doorway to Dan's office. He wore a wide, exultant smile.

"I found him!" he cried out in a near shout.

"Who?"

"Ben Ralston. The man who makes our case. I found him."

Rick dove into a chair opposite Dan. "Some mornings, some afternoons, early, late, weekends—whenever I've had the time—I've been going back out to Chestnut Hill, from house to house, looking for someone who might have gone by Peter Boelter's place that Saturday afternoon."

"And this Ben Ralston says he did."

"Better than that!" Rick plumped the heels of both fists on the desk in front of him. "Ralston is a department store executive who buys ad space in the *Herald* and knew Peter and Susan socially. His house is only a few blocks from Peter's. He's in his convertible coming back from playing golf that afternoon—nice day, top down—and takes a shortcut past Peter's house. He hears shouting and slows down to look around. What does he see? Susan Boelter on the front step shouting at her husband through the open door."

"Jesus! Just like Karen said. Corroboration."

"She's shouting out how he'll never get custody of their daughter because the daughter wants to live with her. Ralston's sure he heard her say that. He couldn't hear what Boelter was saying, but he could definitely hear him yelling from inside the house. Finally, she slams the door and walks toward her car."

Dan, too, was now leaning forward with excitement, forearms on the desk. "Bless you, Ben Ralston."

"You know what that means?" Rick said.

Dan grasped Rick's fists with conspiratorial delight.

"It means," Dan said, "we have an independent eyewitness that Peter Boelter was alive and well when Susan left the house. It means she couldn't have killed him. She's innocent, and we have the proof. My God, just like she said, she's innocent."

Rick's smile flashed again. "He's promised us a sworn statement. I'm going right over there to get it."

"Great job. Great."

Dan phoned Susan's office.

"I'm calling to make sure you know what time to come to my house tonight for the celebration," he said when she came on the line. He related what Rick had told him.

"Will Gil drop the charges now?" she asked excitedly.

"I doubt it. He's got a lot of evidence on his side, and he's gone too far with the case to drop it now. He'd look foolish. Mara will probably attack Ralston's credibility on cross, take the tack that he was mistaken as to the time, the facts, whatever. But Ralston is a disinterested third party, and if he's as solid as Rick seems to think he is, the jury might very well believe him."

Dan hesitated, but felt he had to say more after their recent quarrel. His voice turned quiet with contrition. "I'm sorry if I doubted you."

"I didn't know what to do, how to convince you."

One more thing left to say, always the hardest thing for him to say. "And if it's still important to you, I want you to know I love you."

A long silence followed. Dan thought she might have hung up, but she was only thinking.

"It's important, all right," she finally said. "I'll be at your place at six-thirty, okay?"

"Okay." Dan was about to say good-bye when she spoke again.

"Do we have to eat first?"

22

By August, the month before the trial was scheduled to begin, news media from around the country were flocking to Philadelphia. The public was fascinated by the sensational Peter Boelter murder case. The gossip and tabloid press even flirted with the speculation that Susan's adulterous liaison with Dan may have been the motive that spurred her to kill her husband.

She was being charged with murder in the first degree—homicide with malice aforethought and specific intent to kill. Conviction would result in a life sentence with no chance of parole. The jury could find guilt on a lesser count—the prosecution had included the entire range.

Dan and Susan diligently avoided contact with the press by using rear exits, basement corridors, underground garage routes, and hidden access roads. So as not to inflame their already glaring notoriety, they avoided being seen together at all in public. That made their relationship trying and limiting. From its start, Dan had been foreclosed from showing and sharing with her much of the Philadelphia he loved and to which she had never been exposed—his heart's collection of the city's treasures: the remarkable array of jazz clubs burgeoning around town, events at Penn's Landing, cheesesteaks late at night at Pat's, the market at Reading Terminal, out-of-the-way restaurants, ethnic food stores, and innumerable idiosyncratic shops and people. She yearned to take him to places like the ballet and Philadanco and the opera and concerts and art shows and all the eccentric museums adorning the city like jewels. He had the feeling she was getting to know only half of him and he half of her.

Even so, he was happier than he could ever remember being with a woman and allowed himself to believe that Susan was happy, as well, and that she needed him for that happiness. His life developed a stable, almost domestic routine. At Susan's urging, he took greater care about the food he ate, avoiding fats and fried foods, cutting down on coffee, eating more vegetables and little red meat. He agreed to see her doctor for his first medical checkup in years and, when the doctor turned out to be a woman, bravely stuck it out in silent embarrassment. Susan could barely keep a straight face as she asked how his hernia and prostate tests had gone.

He and Susan and usually Karen often had dinner together. On weekends the three drove out in the Mustang to his beach house, which the press had failed to discover. A few times they drove back across the causeway to the mainland and north along the Jersey Shore for a quiet dinner at the Old Mill Inn in Spring Lake Heights. The owner, Dan's longtime friend, slipped them in to a table where they would not be noticed. The seclusion and the reliance of the three on each other to safeguard their privacy enhanced their intimacy and their affection. It was almost as if Dan had a family again.

Two major concerns disturbed his tranquillity. Primary and utmost, of course, was the possibility that Susan might be convicted. He no longer doubted her innocence. But anything could go wrong. Some new piece of evidence, a recanting witness, a stubbornly unconvinced juror, a blunder in his strategy, could cost her her freedom. He and the others in the small law firm were devoting the preponderance of their time to the case. They kept trying to eliminate the unexpected, the variables, as much as possible.

Dan personally interviewed all the potential witnesses and exhaustively prepared them for the rigors of testifying. They had to be able to relate the facts of their testimony effectively, despite the presence of judge, jury, and spectators, and not be rattled by the prosecution's grilling on cross-examination. Legal points that might come up either in pretrial motions or during the actual course of the trial—usually about evidence the defense team would want to include or exclude—were researched and set down in briefs, ready to be submitted if necessary. The three lawyers continued to phone colleagues and acquaintances and to scan directories, texts, and bibliographies in the search for credible medical witnesses to support the theory that Peter had died accidentally—or at least that valid medical evidence did not necessarily implicate Susan.

To enhance Susan's chances at trial, Dan insisted on hiring a jury consultant, Ida Lawrence, with whom he had worked in the past. Her job was to analyze the potential jurors and determine the characteristics of those predisposed toward Susan and those against. She was now in the process of surveying several hundred people, whose answers she would correlate with such personal information as their age, sex, educational level, and ethnic background. On the basis of the survey's results, she would create a list of questions for Dan to ask during the jury selection process. The case had received so much publicity that everyone surveyed had either read about it or seen a mention of it on television. Nearly all had an opinion.

"There's a huge vagueness factor operating here," Ida Lawrence asserted at a meeting with Dan and Cal. The vestiges of a small-town Southwestern upbringing still hung on her accent. "What actually happened that day is so vague that people can read all their own prejudices into it. If they don't trust women, they think she killed her husband for the money. If they harbor resentment against Peter or the Boelters in general—and there's a lot of that, stemming back to his father, who wasn't shy, either, about throwing his weight around this town—they're more likely to think the trial is an establishment power play against her. You want as many of those people on your jury as you can get."

She paused for a moment, trying to decide how to phrase her next remark to Dan. "There's an X factor, too. A lot of people, mostly the older, more religious ones, strongly disapprove on principle of a married woman who has an affair. They think that if her morals are that low, maybe she's capable of murder. When you add in that the affair was with her lawyer, the man who's standing in front of them, vouching for her innocence, well, that's a lot for them to swallow."

Dan added dourly, "And they might even get the idea that I'm out there to cover up for her."

Ida Lawrence nodded. "They watch too many courtroom shows on TV. Our job is to weed those people out. Even so, you'll still have to meet the issue head-on in your opening."

"I intend to. You have any thoughts, Cal?"

"Our client might not be paying us a fee in the case," Cal grumbled, "but she'd damned well better be paying these expenses."

The jury consultant's investigations would last six weeks and cost a hundred fifty thousand dollars.

Dan sensed a deeper misgiving in his partner's words and skeptical glance. Cal was evaluating Dan's objectivity, monitoring him for signs that his feelings for Susan were biasing his judgement and hurting her defense.

Dan's second major concern, and it nagged at the fringes of his consciousness whenever he found himself enjoying the quasi–family life Karen's presence provided, was about his son, who was scheduled to arrive here at the end of the month. How would Jamie react to spending

Labor Day weekend with Susan and Karen, as part of Dan's expanded clan?

Susan had never met Gilda Bechmann, the governess employed by the Boelters when their sons were young. But she, too, had heard from Margaret that the woman was in a nursing home and senile.

On the contrary, Dan found the former governess lucid and healthy and living in a small apartment in a complex for the elderly about an hour outside the city. "The last thing Margaret Boelter wants is for me to tell what I know about her. She sends me a check for a thousand dollars every Christmas. She thinks she's buying my silence."

"Is she?" Dan asked.

"No, it's just that no one's ever asked before."

They were sitting on a parklike lawn outside the apartment complex. Gilda Bechmann used a cane, but seemed capable of walking without it, if need be. She was tall and sat stiffly erect, with all the discipline of her German-American forebears. Dan quickly realized that Margaret had been right to be worried about Gilda Bechmann. Hired by the Boelters soon after Peter was born, the intelligent, meticulous woman had seen and heard and concluded a good deal during her years as governess to the family.

Gilda's recollection of Margaret was of a vain, cold, manipulative woman, who was awed by her husband's forceful personality, contemptuous of his lack of breeding, and hurt by his indifference to her. Gilda gathered that in the early years, Margaret tried to sustain her husband's interest, but could not. He quickly tired of her company and the social activities that preoccupied her.

He had not even needed his wife for sex; the household employees soon sensed that his former relationships had continued after his marriage. However, because his wife had fulfilled her end of the unspoken bargain to give him respectability and sons, he provided her, in return, with a luxurious lifestyle.

Richard, older than Peter by three years and Midge by four, was a bold, independent child, totally self-sufficient and already in a nursery school. He spent a good deal of his free time with his father, who was delighted with an heir who replicated so much of himself and ensured the carrying forward of the dynasty he envisioned.

Margaret was too fearful of her husband to challenge him openly. Instead, having understood that her eldest child was already lost to her, she made her second son the prize she would wrest from her husband's grasp.

Peter was a pretty child, with her own family's looks. Margaret worked to alienate him from his father. Alternatively affectionate and spiteful, she gained his childish adoration while moodily, perhaps unintentionally, persecuting him with frequent, arbitrary rejection.

Richard, even when quite young, was not scared of his father's temper and managed to elicit his father's admiration for his tenacity. Peter was far more sensitive. Partly because of his mother's influence, he lived in terror of his distant, disapproving father's severity, which served only to aggravate their relationship. Gilda could sense the anguish in the child, who yearned for his parents' love and approval. When they ignored or tormented him, he would react with brutal fury toward those around him unable to fight back: toys, servants, his younger brother. Richard either cuffed him or, even more hurtful, like his parents, ignored him.

Midge had none of Richard's dashing verve or Peter's clever charm and seemed doomed to be either neglected by both parents or abused by them for the mistakes generated by his slow clumsiness. Exasperated by his younger sons, John Boelter tried to beat some manhood into them, which only increased their enmity.

Gilda maintained that she tried to bring stability to the children's turbulent world, but found it difficult. Ultimately, she was not their parent and was not entirely comfortable with the embraces they sought. But she tried to be fair with them and to protect the weaker from the stronger. She tried especially to make up to Midge for the attention he received from no one else. That was why, she said, proudly, he still sometimes visited her.

"Why did you leave the Boelters?" asked Dan.

Gilda was silent, deliberating her answer. Then, eyes lifting, she decided, "Someone should know the truth about what happened that day."

Richard was in school the day she took the younger boys on a hike in the woods. When a thunderstorm unexpectedly hit, Gilda convinced a farmer to drive the drenched group back to their house. Midge had found a young bird washed out of its nest. As Gilda put away their overthings, the boys raced upstairs to their mother's quarters to show it to her. Only when Gilda heard their voices moving toward the far end of the house did she realize where they had gone. She rushed upstairs to stop them, but was too late. They burst into their mother's room, Gilda futilely just behind them.

"Margaret was lying naked on her bed." Although repelled by the memory, Gilda remained precise about the details. "Another woman, a friend of hers, was also naked and was kissing her between her open legs. Midge, the poor child, had run to show her the little bird. She jumped off the bed, yelling at him for coming in without permission. When Midge tried to show her the bird, she pulled it from his hand and flung it to the floor and started hitting him savagely. Peter jumped in front of Midge to take the blows for him. I was almost as astonished at that as by what I'd just seen—up until then the boys had not been close. I apologized to Margaret and pulled Midge and Peter out of there, but of course, it was too late.''

"She fired you?''

"Yes, and immediately drove me herself to the train station. She didn't want to take the chance on my telling anyone else in the house what I had seen, particularly her husband, when he got home that night. At the station she gave me a check for a thousand dollars, which she called severance pay, and promised to send me a thousand dollars every Christmas.''

"Warning you never to tell anyone what had happened.''

Gilda nodded. "But if I thought my telling would have helped the boys, I would have.'' She shrugged. "I was just an employee.''

Driving back to the city, Dan tried to fit what he had just heard into everything else he had learned about Peter Boelter and the mystery that enshrouded his death, but he could not.

Early on the third Monday morning in August, Dan and Rick relieved the team of private detectives they had hired to watch Tim Feeney's house. They parked Rick's Sentra on Sixteenth, near the house, and waited.

At around half past seven, Feeney stepped out onto his front steps.

"He looks like shit,'' Rick observed.

Unshaven and bleary-eyed, the former newspaper truckdriver looked as if he had been up all night. He made a halfhearted stab at shoving his shirttail inside his pants, then fished keys from a pocket as he walked to a beat-up red Chevy at the curb.

The lawyers slid down in their seats below window level, but Feeney did not bother to check for surveillance. After a few seconds Rick pulled out of their parking space to follow. In the side mirror he noticed a blue Ford pull out a block behind them and informed Dan. Turning, Dan could make out the two people in the blue car.

"It's Stallworth and his partner,'' Dan said. "The blond.''

"Kate Bascombe.''

"You've got a good memory.''

"Ran into her at a bar a couple of weeks ago. We had a drink together.''

"You sound interested.''

"Maybe one of these days. Right now, it's still winding down with a girl I met in law school.''

"*Woman,* Rick.''

"Jesus, give me a break. Next thing you know we'll have to say 'feminine person' because 'woman' has the word 'man' in it. Even 'female' has 'male' in it. Anyway, Bascombe's still hung up on Scott Feller . . . the reporter.''

"I know him.''

"They went together for a while. Now he's started paying attention to her again. She knows he's a bastard, and it's only because he's working on some story about the Police Department, but . . .''

"I thought I was the only one who had a complicated love life. Did she say anything to you about Feeney?''

"No. I mean we were just flirting over a drink.''

Dan glanced to the rear again. "Well, she and Stallworth are also interested in our friend Feeney. We look like a parade.''

Feeney parked at a meter, and Rick immediately pulled to the curb. As they passed, the detectives acknowledged their presence with a nod and continued on by Feeney's Chevy, pulling into the first parking spot they could find far enough down the block not to arouse Feeney's suspicion.

Feeney dug through his pants pockets for a coin to put into the meter. Either he could find none or he realized that he still had some time before metering commenced. Dan and Rick were sure they would have to tail him on foot now, with Dan in the rear and the experienced Rick doing the more difficult job of staying ahead of him.

Feeney walked across the street to a small park, but he did not enter. Instead, he leaned against the railing surrounding it and waited. The occupants of the two cars flanking his slunk down in their seats and waited as well.

For the next two hours Feeney paced impatiently as he scanned the traffic moving by him. Once, he glanced at his watch and raced across the street. Dan prepared for action. But Feeney simply deposited a coin in the meter and returned to his lookout post at the edge of the park.

Finally, as the time neared ten o'clock and the person he was awaiting had still not arrived, Feeney kicked angrily at a piece of paper blowing across the pavement and shuffled dejectedly back across the street. He started toward a pay phone, then suddenly wary, he changed his mind, perhaps recognizing that his contact might have had good reason to stay away.

About to get into his car, he stopped to regard the stores along the street. His eye fell on a deli. He dug around in his pocket, stared at the change in his open hand, then shoved it back into his pocket, obviously not enough even for a roll and coffee. His hand hammered the roof of the Chevy in frustration. Then he got in and drove back home.

The two cars behind him did not follow when he turned on Sixteenth to park near his house. Instead, they halted, and their passengers got out of their cars to confer.

"Who tipped you off?" Harry Stallworth asked.

"A drug dealer he was buying from," Dan said. "You?"

"A runner for a shylock he gets into between payoffs."

"It sounds like he's got an expensive nose."

"Sounds like until this morning he could afford it."

"Any idea who was paying him off?"

Stallworth appraised Dan for a long moment. "*You* were watching him."

"Jesus, Harry, you sound like Huyton. You think I was about to bribe him and held off when I saw your car?"

"I guess not," the broad-chested detective conceded. "It doesn't make sense that you'd be paying off a guy who already testified against you with a bunch of horseshit."

"I'm glad somebody in law enforcement has some sense. I figure the DA's office might be paying him off for testifying against me."

"That's what we're figuring, too," Bascombe conceded. "We never had enough to tie Montano to the Cassy Cowell murder, and even less to Jane Hopkins or the rape in the parking lot."

Stallworth allowed his anger to surface. "That son of a bitch Huyton has a case blow up in his face, and it's our fault. Then the Phantom Rapist makes himself scarce, and Huyton badmouths us to the press, like we're not trying to catch the guy. All along he's protecting the lowlife critter who's the best rape suspect we've got."

"Feeney," Dan agreed, "who got a sweet-deal dismissal on the drug bust after he testified against me at the Disciplinary Board."

Stallworth sought Dan's gaze to reach an accord. "The police commissioner would rather Huyton didn't know we're tailing Feeney. It's touchy enough between the two of them as it is."

"Huyton and I don't exactly share confidences."

Stallworth's nod sealed the understanding. "Dan, we're sure we're dealing with one guy in all three crimes. Same MO. Feeney has no rape record, but he doesn't like women much, according to the ex-girlfriend."

Bascombe noted, " We figured with his girlfriend gone and no job, Feeney might start to get a little antsy at night, so we've had a tail on him. But maybe the nose candy is keeping him happy. Or soft."

Rick laughed. She smiled at him.

"I'd love to tap Feeney's phone," Stallworth said, "but the DA's the one who has to request court authorization to make the tap."

"If you come up with anything on Feeney," Dan asked, "could you let me know?"

"Sure," Stallworth agreed.

Rick said to Bascombe, "I'll give you a call one of these days."

"In about a month or so, okay?" she replied. Kate Bascombe was a pragmatic young woman. She had a pretty good idea of just how much longer she could count on Scott Feller's continued interest. Next month was when his series was due to hit the paper.

That night Stallworth and Bascombe were woken by a police dispatcher and summoned from their homes to the parking lot at Thirteenth and Locust. The dead body of Tara Martin (née Gertrude Kunkel), the blowsy blond prostitute for whom Ricardo Montano had pimped, had been found less than twenty feet from where the previous parking-lot victim had been found. She had been wearing a black miniskirt and a skimpy white halter top. The top had been stuffed in her mouth, suffocating her. But this time the woman's nails showed evidence of a fight to protect herself. She seemed to have encountered her attacker face-to-face on the sidewalk, and he had dragged her into the lot, behind some parked cars, where he had raped and beaten her. Probably because she could identify him, he also appeared to have manually strangled her—the autopsy would later reveal a crushed hyoid bone.

There had been no eyewitnesses to the killing. But at about five in the morning, the black prostitute who had made up the other half of Montano's scant stable at the time of his preliminary hearing rushed into her local police station and asked for protection. She had just heard about the killing and was frightened. The two detectives drove over to question her.

She informed them that she had run into Tara early in the evening. Tara had been apprehensive because of a quarrel with Montano at a local bar a few hours before. He had tried to induce Tara to work for him again. She had refused, saying she was doing better on her own. He became furious. The bartender had threatened to call the cops, and Montano had left, but he said he'd find her and "convince her." The black prostitute was frightened because Montano had also phoned *her* the day before, saying he wanted to meet her for a talk.

Montano had moved since the preliminary hearing, and it took Stallworth and Bascombe several hours to locate his new address. They rushed over to pick him up for questioning, but missed him by about fifteen minutes. A neighbor had seen him leaving the building with a suitcase.

At about that time, Montano was at a Camden gas station having his car's tank filled and talking to Dan on the pay phone.

"When I heard on the radio about Tara, I figured the cops'd pin it on me. I got out fast."

"They called here. They want to question you."

"Shit!"

"You don't have to answer their questions. I'll be with you and make sure. Can you tell me what happened after you left Tara in the bar?''

"I hit a few more places. You know, to cool off. I mean, what kind of loyalty's she got? I keep out of trouble for a few months, like you told me. But I'm almost broke. I tell her I got to start making a living again. The cunt tells me to get lost.''

"Did you see her after that?''

"No," Montano replied belligerently. "I went home early.''

"I don't suppose anybody can back up your story?'' Dan did not trust the tone that dared the listener to disbelieve him.

"No.''

Whatever Ricardo Montano was doing last night, Dan was pretty sure it was illegal and not being done at home. Montano could have gotten high on something, gone over to where he knew Tara worked the street, and taken out his anger on her. Dan had always considered Montano to be a dangerous, volatile, unpredictable bombshell. A little coked up, he was capable of anything.

Dan offered, "Let me try to make a deal with the police for you to turn yourself—''

Montano interrupted him. "I'm not turning myself in.''

"You're in a lot more danger out on the street. The police are likely to shoot a rapist-killer first and not worry about his rights until afterward.''

That was only part of Dan's worry. The odds that Montano was the Phantom Rapist had suddenly shot up. He might be a lethal threat to any woman he met.

"No," Montano decided. "Nobody's going to believe I didn't kill her. But I tell you this, the cunt deserved whatever she got.''

Damn! Dan inwardly cursed. Mara and just about everybody else had begged him not to try so hard to get the charges dismissed in the Cassy Cowell murder case. Had he doomed a second woman and nearly killed a third?

"Look, Ricardo, I got you off once, I can do it again if you're telling the truth.''

"I'm getting out of town. That much I made up my mind about.''

"If you disappear, the cops will be sure you did it.''

"They'll think I did it anyway. Fucking Tara!''

Dan could not tell whether the pimp's anger gushed out of him because of inner pressure from a deviant rage that had driven him to kill her or from regret at losing her as a source of income.

"Ricardo, let me give it a try with the cops. Call me back in fifteen minutes.''

Montano thought about that for a moment. "No. I'm safer this way.''

"Ricardo—''

Dan heard a click at the other end of the wire.

Oh, Lord, Dan castigated himself, what the hell have I done?

Morning newspapers reported that Ricardo Montano was being sought for questioning and that the police had alerted other jurisdictions to be on the lookout for him.

23

As the month waned, Susan spent less and less time at the *Herald* and the Foundation, and more time with Karen. Behind the high walls around their estate, mother and daughter rode their horses and played tennis and swam laps together and lay for hours by the pool, reading or listening to music on the radio, each periodically switching to the other's favorite stations. Their earlier squabbles seemed as forgotten as pre–recorded history.

At Dan's beach house they were just as loath to be parted. When Karen surfed, Susan usually took a towel to that stretch of beach, hungry for every moment of observing her and, despite the presence of a lifeguard, concerned for her safety in a perilous world. Sometimes she would anxiously discharge fusillades of advice at her daughter, who might soon be motherless, and at other times bundle denial around the child that a conviction was even a remote prospect, as if superstitious that merely mentioning a guilty verdict might bring bad luck.

Dan bought Karen her own surfboard and did not raise again the idea of teaching her to ride a motorcycle. Susan did not need the added apprehension; and some mornings the aches in his knees, not just the repaired one, were forcing him to consider that he might have disposed of his motorcycle not because he was growing up, but because he was growing too old to skid around corners on a couple of wheels with nothing but faith between him and the road.

Very late at night, after Karen was asleep, the two adults would often make love atop a blanket spread on the high dune grasses. Even as Susan became overcome by paroxysms of ultimate sensation, some small part of her mind still seemed to be standing guard beside her daughter's bed, listening for the next breath and tormented with anxiety because soon no one might be there to listen.

Occasionally arguments would ignite between Susan and Dan that ranged in intensity from petulance to rage. At first, making up, they ascribed the outbursts to worry over the upcoming trial. But they gradually began to perceive that the clashes emanated from a deeper cause: innate anger in both of them that could be ignited and justified by the slightest of provocations. They were angry at their former lovers, at themselves, and at forces that seemed everywhere to be menacing them.

Susan habitually suppressed her anger—it was neither ladylike nor socially beneficial. But at moments of extreme strain, it could erupt out of her. She had grown up angry at her parents' inertia, at inheriting the qualifications of privilege and few of its rewards, and at the dependency on men expected of her as a woman. In later years she smothered her self-rebuke at having surrendered her hard-won independence beneath the secondhand security and influence conferred by a wealthy husband whom she loved. Now, possessed of immense power, she inwardly railed at being thwarted in its exercise and worried about the jeopardy into which a far greater power, the government, had placed her.

When Mara left him, Dan suppressed nearly all his feelings. He had known she was ambitious, but always half-imagined that imprisoned within her was a wildly romantic heart he had liberated. The rage he still felt at learning that her departure had been a cynical career move caused him to realize that he had been angry all his life.

He had always both envied and scorned the accommodation that Cal's blackness had made with prejudice—buying comfort with financial success while ignoring slights as the price for it. The son of a man who had been promised acceptance by this country, Dan desired more than that. He craved what others were least willing to grant him, while hanging on to what they expected him to relinquish: He wanted utter acceptance on every level of society, while he maintained the separateness of his identity. He wanted to be a gadfly to the smug tyranny of those in authority, and for them to be grateful for the anguish. And he wanted unqualified love from people he loved, but the freedom to choose when and how he would be responsible for them.

Hannah had detected in him what he had not. Whenever he gained something he desired and failed to obtain the contrary, the conflicting desire would always incite his dissatisfaction. Wisely, she had rejected a husband who did not want to be one. Only now did he finally understand that being a lone wolf meant having to endure loneliness.

That last truth struck him late on an August night soon after the Disciplinary Board formally granted his request to defer his suspension until after Susan's trial. He and Susan lay naked under a warming moon, cradled by the high grass that walled the edges of their blanket. They had just made love, and he realized that despite the danger that he might soon lose her, he was more content than he had ever been.

With Mara, he had known the agitation of infatuation, but never the pleasure of love's certainties. Beneath a timeless universe, where he had just experienced a mortal's brief ecstasy, it came to him that contentment depended on tolerating the nature of such contradictions, that they were intrinsic to the paradox that finite beings were blessed and damned with infinite thoughts. To be happy, he realized, he must abide the disparities wrestling irreconcilably within his own nature. He finally came to the determination that for the sake of a joy that would banish loneliness, he would be willing to do that.

It was not enough simply to love Susan. He must acknowledge that to afford himself such happiness, to be able to draw upon it like a self-replenishing bank account, he must want that happiness more than he wanted isolation. Love of another person could bridge the many conflicts within him. Love of his son, who returned his love without reservation; love of his father, despite reservations; and now love of Susan and what he loved in her—the honesty at the core of her character, her good sense, her humor, her beauty, and her love for him.

"I want to marry you, Susan," he said, rolling onto his elbow and staring down at her eyes, dark and mysterious in the night. "I love you, and I want to marry you."

"I want that, too," she said, reaching up to touch his cheek, a silhouette against the light-flecked sky. "It's been a long time since I've been with a truly good man. It makes me feel good myself. When all this is over, Dan, ask me again to marry you. I'll say yes."

Mara's phone call reached Dan at his office two days later. Her voice vibrated with strangled outrage at being superseded.

"I'm calling to officially inform you that Philadelphia District Attorney Gilbert R. Huyton has decided to try the Susan Boelter case himself. I'll be assisting."

Her rancor was understandable. Winning a conviction in the nationally prominent case could make her reputation as a prosecutor and put her at the top of the list of candidates to replace Huyton when he ran for higher office.

Heatedly, she explained. "He claims he has to do it, that he has to show the public he's too honorable to be swayed by his friendship with Susan Boelter. Damn it! This was my case by right. He gave me his word. I should have realized that he'd step in. He just couldn't resist the publicity.''

"Mara, since when did I become your confidant?''

But he knew that Mara had no other confidant. She was not one to cultivate women friends. She lived totally in the world of men, men who were competitors or lovers and sometimes both. Because she could not vent her rage at Gil, she was venting it at Dan.

An instant later she added, "You and I are meeting with the judge for a pretrial conference on Friday.'' And then hung up.

If he were defending anyone but Susan, Dan would have been glad to prove his mettle in a *mano a mano* against Gil Huyton. For the heavyweight championship. Winner take all. Dan had a string of injustices to retaliate for: the bribery arrest that irreparably tarnished his reputation, the disbarment proceeding, and the added dishonor of having word of his suspension leaked to every jurist and lawyer in the city.

But Dan was not looking forward to this particular title fight. Susan's jeopardy made the stakes too high.

One afternoon, as Dan was working his way through a pile of depressing, if scholarly, forensic pathology papers that might touch upon Susan's defense (while he tried to avoid glimpsing the photos of corpses, if he could), he came upon a footnote that suddenly blazed at him in neon. The author was citing the recent research of a highly regarded Canadian medical examiner for the proposition that the decline in a corpse's body temperature was a thoroughly unreliable guide to time of death.

Four phone calls later, Dan had located the man, spoken to him, received his impressive bio by fax, and made an appointment to meet with him the next morning in Toronto.

Upon entering the man's office at the medical school, Dan greeted him with the words, "You don't know what a relief it is to meet you, Dr. Mallory.''

The forensic pathologist unfolded his long frame from his chair and extended a hand. "I've read the autopsy report you faxed me. I can see why.''

Alan Mallory was in his early fifties, with once light-brown hair turning silver. He had the strong, good-looking features and easy smile more often found in marketing executives than in surgeons of the dead.

They chatted for a few minutes about Dan's flight and then about Mallory's extensive experience as a medical examiner in several Canadian cities and now as a consultant, researcher, and professor teaching the topic, but both men were eager to bring the conversation around to the purpose of the meeting.

"That footnote I read," Dan said, "you said on the phone that it was based on a conversation you had with the man who wrote that paper."

"A former student. Nearly all my research is finished, but I have a few more months of work ahead of me before I'm ready to write up my conclusions for publication."

"Could you lay those conclusions out for me in your own words . . . so a layman can understand them?"

Dan was interested not only in what Mallory would say, but in how he would sound to the jurors. Would he use technical terms that bewildered them? Or be so arrogant about his expertise that they would respond by punishing the defendant?

Mallory explained, "There are so many variables affecting the temperature of a dead body that it's impossible to use any rule of thumb, any simple formula, to calculate the body heat lost over time. That's the long and short of it."

"Could you expand on that for me?"

Mallory's manner was friendly, his tone conversational. "For one thing, some people have higher natural body temperatures and some have lower. And even those vary during the course of a day and, of course, if a person is ill. For another thing, the conditions of the environment in which the body was found affect its temperature. In a very hot room, the body might not cool at all. And in a cold one, like the one in your case, it would lose body heat faster than the so-called formula anticipated. And because it was lying on concrete rather than a mattress. Thin individuals cool faster than fat ones, naked ones faster than clothed ones. All the factors present here."

Dan was delighted with what he was hearing. He sensed that a jury, which naturally shrank from the kind of testimony an ME gave, would react favorably to Mallory.

"To complicate matters more," Mallory continued, "it even seems to be the general rule that rectal temperatures rise a bit for a short while just after death, not decline. In other words, a medical examiner who uses unequivocal formulas to declare that body temperature always drops, say, one degree an hour after death is being dangerously simplistic. The victim in your case could very well have died later than the medical examiner figured."

Choosing words he might use at trial, Dan asked, "After examining the photos I sent you, have you formed an opinion to a reasonable degree of medical certainty as to the cause of death?"

"As far as I could tell, Kieffer's evidence for his theory that the victim was killed by a blunt instrument, rather than the cellar step, is inconclusive. And there are some other findings that bother me."

"Doctor, would you be willing to fly down to testify at the trial? We'll pay your fee and expenses, of course. You'd probably be needed about the middle of next month."

"Glad to. It'd be a miscarriage of justice for anyone to be convicted on the basis of such inconclusive evidence."

Dan sat back, smiling. He had learned over the years that there usually came a time when every good defense suddenly solidified for him and became almost a tangible structure with all the parts perfectly in place, like an architect's model. You could hold it up to a jury, turn it around, show off all its rooms and doors and passageways, and they all connected, everything made sense. The prosecution would have built its own logical model, too, but that was of a different structure. Like an archaeologist, your job was to convince a jury that yours was the closest to what had once actually existed.

That time had come. He finally felt confident that he could present a construct of the events of that fateful Saturday in early June solid enough to withstand scrutiny by a jury. The foundation was down, the studs and beams and joists were in place, and the walls and roof were going up. The integrity of its form would not disintegrate under a stormy attack.

He had found his expert witness.

During his first few days in the city, Jamie spent most of the time with his grandfather or seeing old friends who were not away for the summer. Jacob then left for his annual vacation in the Poconos, and Dan and Jamie left for the beach house.

The first thing Jamie noticed as they drove into the garage was the second surfboard on the wall.

"You surfing now?" he asked his father, instinctively knowing the board's owner, but wanting his father's confirmation.

"It's Karen's."

"Nice board. Is she good?"

"For East Coast waves."

"It's a whole different scene out there," Jamie agreed with some vehemence.

"Come on inside. You'll be staying in the second bedroom till the weekend."

Hoisting his shoulder bag, Jamie glanced at his father. The "second bedroom" had always been called his room. At least his father had not called it the "guest room."

"That when Karen and her mother are coming out?" Jamie asked.

"Yes. Then you can bunk with me."

Dan mentioned Susan and Karen again the evening before they were scheduled to arrive. He and Jamie were reclining on chaises on the deck, backs to the sea, watching the sunset.

"I hope you like them," Dan said.

"How old is she?"

"A year or so older than you. She'll be fourteen soon."

"I don't have to be her friend, do I?"

"No. I hope you will be, but that's up to you."

"You know what I don't like," Jamie blurted out. "That she hasn't got a father of her own."

"It's got to be rough on her."

"I guess," Jamie replied less stridently.

"You worried that she's here all year, and you're not?"

Dan took his son's silence for confirmation. He reached out and gripped the boy's hand. "Nothing will ever change between you and me, Jamie."

The boy grinned, satisfied, but said only, "Jim, not Jamie, Dad. They'll think I'm a kid."

Susan handed Jamie a present when she and Karen arrived, a Walkman to play audiocassettes. Jamie knew she was trying to buy his initial goodwill, but the gift was too exciting for him to keep up his guard.

"I didn't know if you had any tapes," Karen said, "so I brought some of mine."

She was eyeing him as warily as he eyed her. He had grown rapidly this year, but she was still taller.

"Anybody hungry?" Dan asked.

"I want to take a swim first," Karen said.

"I swam already," Jamie declared.

The two kept their distance until early afternoon.

"Anybody want to try the waves?" Dan suggested, noticing the surf had grown higher.

During the long silence the two young people cast sidelong glances at each other.

"It doesn't get much better than that out here," Dan pointed out.

The ocean's lure was too great.

"I don't mind," Jamie said.

"Okay," Karen agreed.

From the deck, the parents watched them start to talk halfway along the beach to the surfing spot. They did not return for several hours. By then they were chattering like next-door neighbors.

"How did it go?" Dan asked his son later.

"It didn't suck," Jamie admitted.

After dinner the four played board games. The children insisted on pairing off as a team against the parents. Afterward they stayed up late talking.

The next day they went surfing together again. Susan commented to Dan that Karen was more animated than she had been in months. "She's always wanted a brother or sister. She's never liked being an only child."

After supper that night Karen and Jamie jointly approached their parents.

"We've been thinking," Karen began.

"Yeah," Jamie added, understanding the need to display unanimity in the proposal, "we've been thinking about something."

He turned back to Karen, looking to her to explain.

"Jim and I think it would be all right if you two stayed together in the same room at night, we mean if you wanted to. We don't mind rooming together."

"You two discussed this?" Dan sputtered.

"Uh-huh," Jamie said, taking the lead because it was *his* parent asking the question. "It seems to us it would be a lot more natural for you."

"Natural," Dan repeated. He mastered his embarrassment enough to glance at Susan. "What do you think?"

"Sounds good to me."

"Okay," Dan said, turning back to the young people, "if that's what you want."

"Come on, Dad. Get real."

The weekend was the happiest of Dan's life.

Early Monday evening, Labor Day, he drove his son to the airport. Jury selection in Susan's trial was scheduled to begin the next morning.

24

"I want you to meet a friend of mine," Dan called out to Susan as she entered the corner entrance of City Hall. "Matt Rooney. Susan Boelter."

The snack bar operator reached over the high display case that masked half his face to shake Susan's hand. Several flashes went off. Dan had arranged for press photographers to encounter her on her walk alone across the plaza and follow her inside. He wanted the public—and potential jurors—who saw her photo in the paper to empathize with her as an ordinary, down-to-earth, good-natured woman, unprotected and in peril.

Rooney's wife, Millie, stuck her head out from behind the coffee machine she had been filling.

"Make sure you tell them where we're located!" she urged the photographers. Most food sellers would have ensured the journalists' goodwill by offering a free cruller or bagel. Millie sought their compliance with a glare.

Dan introduced the two women. Susan ordered an oat bran muffin and a light coffee.

"You read the *Herald,*" Susan noted, glimpsing a folded copy behind the Rooneys.

"I used to buy the *Mirror,* too," the ex-cop said, "but lately I find there's all I need to know about the crime situation and the Phillies in the *Herald.*"

Susan beamed at the success of her new policies. "Glad you like what we're doing."

Rooney reached under the counter. "Dan, I stocked chocolate doughnuts for you this morning."

Susan laughed. "Don't encourage him in those horrible eating habits."

"This is the first time he's gotten them in for me in years," Dan noted. "You worried, Rooney?"

"Tough judge. Pro-prosecution, and he owes Huyton."

Dan could not disagree. Hector Vellarde had been a top ADA through several administrations. In order to bring in his own lieutenant and not offend the Hispanic vote, Gil Huyton had expedited a golden parachute for Vellarde soon after winning office, arranging for him to replace a judge forced to retire because of illness. In two years, if Vellarde did not offend the party, he would doubtless run for his own full term.

"Thought you might be too busy to stop by this morning," Rooney said.

Dan smiled. "Why would I risk bad luck by starting a case without stopping at my favorite snack bar?"

Millie's icy expression melted slightly at the compliment. As she placed covers on the filled coffee containers, she cautioned him, "A lot more press people waiting upstairs for you, Dan. I hear they've packed the corridor."

"Millie, I've got a good-looking, likable client. I'm delighted to have the press to speak to her."

"Smart," Rooney observed with a grin. "You might not let her get on the stand, but she gets her story out anyway. With no cross-examination."

"Rooney, you should have been a lawyer."

"Did you hear that, Millie?" Rooney cackled. "Dan says I should have been a lawyer."

Millie's mouth formed into what on another person might have become a smile. "There'll be no living with him now, Dan."

Dan led Susan through the glass doors to the elevators. As they stepped off onto their floor, a phalanx of reporters and TV crews and equipment awaited them. Bright lights followed them as if they were nightclub performers. Every few steps, the couple stopped to answer questions, politely declining those that were too personal, turning away to other journalists if the questioning persisted. Those reporters would very quickly learn to restrain themselves if they hoped to get a sound bite.

Dan had emphasized to Susan that this was her opportunity to convey her story unconstrained by courtroom rules to the twelve jurors plus four alternates who would be chosen from the hundreds of people now waiting to be questioned in the jury pool. Soon enough, he knew, these corridors would become a sound-bite battlefield with Gil Huyton.

*   *   *

Judge Hector Vellarde was a serious, almost severe man not given to
genial conversation. Dan knew him well, at least professionally. They
had been in the same law school class. A fierce prosecutor, he had been
aggressive if he had the evidence and slow to plea bargain. The word now
going around the courthouse was that he was exhibiting that same au-
thoritarian bent as a judge, tending to rule against defendants and to
impose heavy sentences.

Dan had opposed him several times in court. They had never social-
ized, nor was there reason to from Dan's standpoint; he could not recall
ever seeing Vellarde relaxed. If Vellarde had a sense of humor, he kept
that as well hidden as his thoughts.

As he stood for Vellarde's entrance into the courtroom, Dan wondered
if the jurist would try to curry favor with the politically powerful DA by
subtly favoring the prosecution. Or might he try to demonstrate his tough-
ness to voters by seeing to it that the jury brought back a guilty verdict?
Dan needed a risk taker presiding over the case, someone flexible and so
sure of his legal knowledge that he would allow Dan some scope to probe
testimony and develop alternate theories and suspects. His hope was that
Vellarde had confronted so much unfairness while climbing out of the
ghetto that he would tend to be an impartial referee, but Dan guessed
Huyton was a lot happier with Vellarde than he was himself.

At a pretrial conference in chambers, Vellarde had asked Huyton if he
planned to bring up Dan and Susan's love affair during the trial. Huyton
conceded that he might, "for the limited purpose of establishing that she
no longer felt bound to her husband."

"Jesus, that doesn't mean she'd kill him!" Dan had rejoined, recognizing that Huyton's justification was only a pretext for admitting the
inflammatory subject into evidence.

Vellarde had agreed. "Keep it out, Mr. Huyton, unless you can demonstrate to my satisfaction at sidebar that their affair provided her with
some sort of motive for the killing."

"It can't be a motive," Dan argued, "if I wasn't charged with being
an accessory."

Before Dan could savor the small victory, Vellarde had turned on him.
"Mr. Lazar, make no mistake: If it was up to me, there's no way I'd let
you represent a defendant with whom you're having an intimate relationship. It puts in doubt your credibility as a disinterested advocate on her
behalf. You're not doing her a favor by representing her."

After the conference Huyton had taken Dan aside and handed him an
envelope.

"I want you to know I wouldn't have used these in any event."

Inside, Dan found black-and-white prints, along with their negatives, secretly taken with a night-spying camera. The photos showed Susan and him standing naked together on the bedroom balcony of the beach house. One showed them embracing.

Dan angrily thrust the envelope into his briefcase, not mollified in the slightest by Huyton voluntary handing the provocative photographs over to him. He was certain the action had been motivated by neither propriety nor friendship with Susan, but by the worry that Dan would divulge Huyton's affair with Mara if the photographs were used.

Sexual intrigue had complicated this case at every turn, confusing the basic issue: A man had died, which was just about the only fact everyone would agree on. How had it happened? The prosecution would insist it was homicide. Dan would argue that it was an accident—or, in the alternative, that his client was no more logical a homicide suspect than one or two other people.

Dan glanced over at Susan: pretty, upright in her seat, trying to hide her worry behind a look of composure. It seemed inconceivable that a woman so forthright could be guilty of the cold-blooded murder with which she had been charged. Sensing his glance, she returned it, seeking more to reassure him than to be reassured, he thought. Don't worry, she appeared to be saying, I have confidence in you. You'll make everyone see that I'm really innocent. You'll make everything turn out all right.

Dan turned away to break the spell. He needed to think logically, dispassionately; to concentrate all of his faculties on the witnesses, the testimony, the facts, the jury; to use all of his skill to navigate through the trial's shoals and storms to safety.

Day after day the defense and prosecution teams trooped to the courthouse to question potential jurors in the process known as the *voir dire*. The prosecution sought jurors whom Huyton privately called the "faithful," those instinctively favoring authority. The defense sought those who were better educated and more independent in their thinking.

Ida Lawrence sat silently at the defense table, noting each juror's answers and comparing them to the profiles she had formulated. Despite all her research, Dan was often left with only his intuition into a juror's heart: Did the doctor in the striped tie look too comfortable in the jury box? Dan feared that he did. Wasn't the pretty young secretary who kept glancing over at Huyton after answering Dan's questions likely to vote with the prosecution? Wasn't the copy machine repairman who slouched a little in his chair and fiddled with the papers he held, who answered softly and with few gestures and kept his legs folded under him, demonstrating a submissiveness that would cave in to pro-prosecution jurors? Would the city bus driver be more likely to support the city government that employed him or a woman harried by a rich, high-handed husband? Would an older black woman, who ran a small social-service agency working with deprived families, approve of Susan's work with the Foundation in minority neighborhoods, or might she be concealing a grudge against privileged white women dabbling in do-good projects?

With Ida Lawrence's blessing, Dan rejected the first three. When the bus driver admitted that his brother had recently been stabbed by a girlfriend, the judge rejected him for cause, saving Dan from having to use up one of his peremptory challenges.

Dan badly wanted the social worker on the jury. A college graduate, she managed an organization that dealt compassionately with a spectrum of human problems, often had to fight city bureaucracy to obtain funding, and was a mother who might be concerned about Karen's fate if Susan went to prison. Huyton expended one of his peremptory challenges to exclude her.

The process continued for nearly two weeks; the case had received so much press that Vellarde was granting the lawyers far more time and leeway to exclude than a harried court system could usually abide.

Except for a polite greeting when Dan introduced each potential juror to her, Susan sat in stoic silence. Only once did she reveal her thoughts about the jury selection process. They were back in his office after a day of interviewing a succession of unacceptable jury candidates, most of them ill informed, many poor and either excessively passive or openly hostile.

"I was called twice for jury duty," Susan recalled. "The first time Peter was worried that no matter which way I voted, it would reflect badly on the *Herald*. But the next time I didn't tell him I'd been called and went down. They selected me for the pool in a bank robbery case. The defense lawyer looked at the form with my name and my background and asked if I'd read anything about the case. It seemed to me that everyone in the city had to have read about it. It was front-page news. Police had surrounded the bank, and the people inside were held hostage for hours. Of course I said I'd read about it."

"And of course he immediately rejected you," Dan surmised.

She nodded.

"I once told you," he patiently explained, "the point of your trial won't be to get at the truth, but to convince twelve people that you aren't guilty of the charges. Whatever it takes to do that is what I have to do."

Susan was appalled. "What kind of justice is it that depends on the least-aware people in our society deciding your fate?"

She paused, then almost frightened, added, "Do you really think those people you've been questioning are really a jury of my peers?"

*   *   *

As the jury box filled, Dan began to work more intensively on an outline of his opening statement, dropping index cards into a manila folder marked "opening statement" that he kept in the briefcase he carried to the court each day. In it also was every relevant document, carefully indexed and cross-indexed for fast retrieval. As transcriptions of each day's testimony were delivered during the trial, the material would expand into the "litigation bags" Cal or Rick would help him carry.

The opening was his sales pitch, his opportunity to testify in the case. Dan believed that with witnesses' testimony coming at the jurors in disconnected, often disputed chunks, the purpose of an opening statement was to leave in their minds a coherent narrative into which they could fit the facts as they heard them—*his* version of the events. Knowing that they would distrust any statement he had to read and would instinctively reject flamboyant or bombastic advocacy, he intended to speak directly to them, make eye contact with each, and sound as sincere about Susan's innocence as he actually felt. He had to make them trust him, to make them believe he was speaking from the heart, that he was telling them the truth.

"Sounding sincere is an art," he half-joked to Susan when he and Cal were having lunch with her at Hi, Johnny's. "You know what trial lawyers call the kind of dark-blue suit I'm wearing? 'Sincere blue.' "

"Your sincerity is one of the reasons I chose you as my lawyer," Susan said. "I'd buy a used car from you."

That afternoon the last alternate juror was added to a jury that was as close to fair as Dan could have hoped, better educated than most, and less disposed to take the government's word at face value. Testimony would begin the next day.

Susan was in a hurry to get home to Karen, who had grown withdrawn and fearful again as the trial process began. Dan said that he would phone that night to reassure them both.

He and Cal were walking beneath an archway out of City Hall when a small man slipped from behind one of the red stone columns and fell into step with them.

"What's up, Eddie?" Dan asked, recognizing Eddie Grecco, the police detective assigned to the district attorney's office.

Grecco spoke without turning toward them, his gaze straight ahead. "They had me background-check witnesses, Dan. Take some advice. Don't use Ralston."

Dan stopped in his tracks to confront the detective. "What's wrong with Ralston?"

"Convicted felon."

"Oh, shit!" Cal exclaimed an instant before Dan could. "Our star witness!"

"What was he convicted of?" Dan asked, as he resumed the slow walk.

"Larceny and perjury," Grecco said.

At the sidewalk the detective veered away. Dan turned to Cal.

"Rick was supposed to check everyone out."

"My fault," Cal admitted. "He had so much work, I thought we could save him some by eliminating the solid citizens."

Dan kicked at the base of the building. "Larceny *and* perjury. There goes our airtight ailibi. Damn!"

Dan shoved a quarter into a pay phone and dialed Ben Ralston at the department store where Ralston worked. He hung up a few minutes later with the story. A decade earlier Ralston was head of a small retail chain that was going under. After he testified under oath to a grand jury that he hadn't diverted any money to his own purposes, it came out that he took eighty thousand dollars the company was contractually obligated to pay him the following year. He figured it wasn't stealing—the money was owed to him. The jury saw it differently: He was convicted of grand larceny and perjury.

"He got off with probation," Dan concluded. "But he's finished as a witness."

Perjury was, by far, the more damaging charge. Ralston was a convicted liar, whose claim of seeing Susan quarreling with Peter as she left his house was worthless—or, worse, maybe even hazardous to her case. Huyton would contend that a proven perjurer had so little respect for the truth that Susan could have induced him to lie on the stand, maybe in return for a discount on his advertising.

"Damn! Damn! Damn!" Dan raged. "Back to square one."

He had always been as straightforward with Susan as she was with him. Tonight he would have to inform her that her case had suddenly become shaky. It now rode solely on the expectation that Alan Mallory, their expert in forensic pathology, would wipe the courtroom floor with the city's chief medical examiner.

"A crime of passion turned to poison, that's what we have here, ladies and gentlemen of the jury," Gil Huyton said as he began his opening statement. "Fatal passion."

Hands gripping the yellow pad with his notes, face pressed forward pugnaciously toward the jurors, he gave an appearance of being the classic district attorney: aggressive, unyielding, righteous. Wanting to win over the jurors, he had already thanked them for giving up their time to serve, "essential in a democracy," and for their patience and attention during the long jury selection process, when the need to pick an impartial jury may have caused them to be asked about personal or private matters.

Mara sat rigidly in her chair at the prosecution table, her face an expressionless mask. From the very start this had been her case. She had based her case on the belief that this was a crime of passion turned monstrous, turned poisonous. With little change, Gil Huyton had appropriated that theme from her, as well as all her strategy and preparation, all the memoranda of law she had written, all the outlines and evaluations, the lists of questions for every witness. He had simply stepped into the footprints where her shoes should have been. In one way, she knew, his unquestioning reliance on her work had been a very fortunate show of confidence, but still, weeks after his decision to lead the prosecution, her resentment had not lessened.

After he finished speaking, she would congratulate him, and later, when they were alone, she would praise him again, always keeping paramount her larger priorities: first, to maintain his favor, so that he would support her as his replacement when he moved on to statewide office and, second, to convict Susan Boelter.

Dan listened intently, only rarely jotting down a note. Mostly, he was listening for the hint of an unexpected tactic in the prosecution's game plan. Huyton's strength lay not in cunning surprises and flawlessly concealed traps; rather, he was superb at relentlessly, even tediously erecting a case brick by brick, until it was so solid that the defense was inescapably imprisoned. It was the least-spectacular sort of criminal advocacy, but the most effective.

His voice imbued with the fervor of his belief in Susan's guilt, Gil Huyton outlined his case for the jury.

"The evidence will show that divorce threatened Susan Boelter with the loss of her finances, her home, her influence at the *Herald,* and, most important, her young daughter, Karen. She was desperate, with no place to turn. Finally, only a couple of days before the custody hearing that could collapse her entire world around her, Susan Boelter took the only action that would allow her to hang on to those things she so passionately wanted: She murdered her husband.

"Her passion, you will hear, was at the root of everything: Witnesses will tell you about her passion for money, her passion for the estate from which she was about to be evicted, her passion for the prestige and power of the great newspaper her husband controlled, and her passion for the daughter who was about to discard her. You'll see proof of her passion everywhere, passion that mixed and boiled and turned lethal, passion that drove her to kill the man she had once claimed to love, the husband who was about to abandon her and leave her with nothing.''

Every eye in the courtroom had shifted from Huyton to Susan. She sat erect, reddening, waiting for the long wave of attention to sweep over and past her. It only did when Huyton finally spoke again.

''The name of the case is the *Commonwealth* versus *Susan Boelter*. That means I'm here on your behalf to bring to justice a woman accused of cold-blooded, premeditated murder. Not even the powerful woman who runs the city's largest newspaper is above the law.''

Huyton was no longer looking down at the pages before him. He had memorized every word, and the speech was flowing out of him. ''The city's eminent chief medical examiner, who examined the body of the deceased, will testify before you that Peter Boelter was murdered with a blunt instrument, some sort of club with a sharp edge, and his body was then moved to the basement. Defense counsel will probably try to confuse you with the fact that that weapon has not been found. It's a big world, and weapons are easy to hide. But we don't need the actual weapon, because we have conclusive evidence of its existence, the wound it made. The chief medical examiner will prove that to you.

''And there isn't any doubt in that eminent medical authority's mind as to the time of the murder—he has fixed it between five-fifteen and five forty-five in the afternoon. Just as there isn't any doubt about the only person who was in the house with Peter Boelter during that half-hour period. Susan Boelter herself will testify that during that entire time she was there alone with the victim. And a next-door neighbor will confirm it.''

Methodically, Gil Huyton outlined the evidence that he would present to convince them to convict Susan. As Dan had predicted, no surprises, but rather, an orderly construction of an escapeproof penitentiary around the defendant. Huyton's thumbnail sketch of the evidence he would present was coming to a close when he said something that startled Dan.

''Ladies and gentlemen of the jury, during the course of this trial you're going to learn that Susan Boelter was a woman who seduced her hostile husband just before she killed him. She was able to beguile him with sex despite his having left her months earlier. During the divorce proceedings, he instigated against her, he denounced her brazen sexual misconduct. With Mr. Lazar here—''

''Objection!'' Dan cried out. ''May we approach, Your Honor?''

Vellarde nodded.

Dan argued, ''This is clearly intended to remind the jurors about my relationship with the defendant, an area of questioning you've ruled out of bounds. It's pure prejudice.''

"If you had let me finish," Huyton countered, "you'd have heard me say only that 'with Mr. Lazar here, speaking on the defendant's behalf, he would argue to the contrary, but that the jurors had to weigh the facts for themselves.' "

"These people all read about the case or heard about it on TV before the trial began. How can they possibly disregard such inflammatory innuendo? You used the words 'brazen sexual misconduct' and then immediately connected them to my name. Judge, I'd like you to consider a mistrial."

Vellarde pointed his gavel at Dan. "It took us two weeks to pick a jury, Mr. Lazar. We aren't subjecting ourselves to that process again before the trial has barely gotten under way."

The jurist fixed on the jury. "I'm sure you all appreciate that opening statements are not evidence. They're merely intended to lay out for you the progression of logic inherent in the evidence each side intends to present. You're to give Mr. Lazar's words the same weight that you give the prosecutor's. Both are here to present their cases for your ultimate determination." He gestured toward Dan, as if to say, That's as much as I'm prepared to give. "Mr. Huyton?"

A few more sentences and Huyton had concluded his opening statement. He was pleased. He had taken a calculated risk at the end, and it had paid off handsomely. Still incensed that his adversary had bulldozed himself into the case as his paramour's counsel, which he believed to be a blatant impropriety, he wanted to get the jury wondering what Lazar's motive might be.

Walking toward the jury to make his own opening statement, Dan thought he saw a faint, mocking smile on Huyton's lips as the two men passed. And something else, something in the lift of the man's chin: a sanctimonious pride in his own moral superiority. Unlike Dan, he himself had not lusted after a married woman, a woman contemplating murder. Although an adulterer, he had remained pure.

A strange man, Dan thought. All hypocritical honor and righteous zeal. He could forgive lust in himself, but not in others. He could extend a personal kindness by returning scandalous photos, but in the name of duty be pitiless in official matters.

Dan's gaze swept on to the jury. They knew the background of the trial's principals and had understood Huyton's veiled comment perfectly. Their eyes were wide and their faces shiny now with the prurient expectation that they were about to hear intimate details of Dan's relationship with Susan. By insinuation, Huyton had just made the defendant's private love affair with her lawyer the focus of this public trial.

25

Dan waited for his thoughts to form. Ignoring Huyton's slur would only let it remain on the jurors' minds, distracting their attention from his own remarks. He could not avoid addressing it.

"Mr. Huyton has talked about the defendant's appeal and the defendant's character. Well, I want you to know that Susan Boelter's appeal *stems* from her character, a character I value so highly that when she asked me to be her defense counsel, I accepted. Susan Boelter is a fine, trustworthy, caring woman. I would hope that if your wife or husband or very dear friend were facing a false charge of murder, you'd do no less for them than I'm doing for her."

Sensing that he had defused as well as he could the land mines Huyton had planted, Dan began his opening statement.

"Susan Boelter isn't on trial for her personal behavior or her private relationships. She's on trial for an act the prosecution wants you to believe she committed, the act of killing her husband. But the evidence they rely on to prove she caused his death is purely circumstantial. That means they have no hard evidence. No eyewitness to the killing. Not even a weapon. Just the city medical examiner's opinion. What the prosecution claims to be evidence is as full of holes as a spaghetti strainer."

Dan was being careful not to enhance the impression of either Huyton's or Kieffer's authority by using their titles—never "the district attorney," always "Mr. Huyton"; never "the chief medical examiner," always "the city medical examiner," as if the position were a mundane civil-service clerkship.

"Mr. Huyton has told you it doesn't matter that police detectives looked high and low and could find no weapon. Well, you and I know it matters very much. You can't make up a weapon just because having one would fit your accusations. A woman's freedom is at stake. The reason the police could find no weapon is simply because there *was* no weapon. Peter Boelter died in an accident, an accident he caused himself.

"He was drunk—there's no dispute about that. The alcohol level in his blood was ninety percent above the legal limit for sobriety. If the police found you driving with only one-tenth of a percent of alcohol in your blood, they'd haul you off the road and into jail. You'd be a real threat to have a car accident. Imagine then how drunk Peter Boelter must have been if he had nearly twice that much alcohol in him. Imagine how much more likely he was to have an accident. It would be no surprise if a man that drunk tripped down a flight of concrete steps and killed himself."

Dan leaned back against the edge of the prosecution's table, a technique he believed conveyed to the jury that the district attorney's space and, by logical extension, his charges were not sacrosanct. He settled an earnest gaze first on one juror and then on the next.

"Susan Boelter had just left Peter Boelter's house to drive their daughter home. He was all alone in the kitchen. He had finished his drink and needed a fresh bottle of scotch, which was kept in the basement. He started down for it, but he was too drunk. At the top of the stairs he tripped—probably on the aluminum strip at the edge there that you'll see in the photos—and he tumbled down, smashing the back of his head on the bottom step. Not murder, not some sinister act caused by some evil woman, but just a very tragic accident caused by the victim's own unfortunate drinking habit, by Peter Boelter himself."

Dan's sad tone seemed to convey his sorrow at the self-destructiveness of human frailty.

"Mr. Huyton has told you that it's the city medical examiner's opinion that Peter Boelter died between five-fifteen and five forty-five in the evening. Well, we're going to let you hear directly from a forensic pathologist who's one of the world's leading scientific authorities on time of death. Remember that term, *forensic pathology,* the science of recognizing and interpreting diseases and injuries to the human body. Very simply, this world-recognized expert will tell you that from a scientific point of view, the formula the city medical examiner used to determine the time of Peter Boelter's death is absolute and utter nonsense. The man could just as reliably have flipped a coin to come up with it."

Dan placed his hands conversationally on the railing in front of the jury box. "In other words, it's just as likely that Peter Boelter died *after* the time everyone agrees Susan Boelter left the house as before it. He could even have died during the time that her sister-in-law, Amelia Boelter, who claimed to have found the body, was in the house alone with him."

Dan paused a moment to allow the existence of another suspect to sink in. Then he added, "If by some chance you decide Peter Boelter's death wasn't an accident, then you'll see for yourself that Amelia Boelter is just as likely as the defendant to have killed him."

His voice was low now, confiding in them. "It isn't up to Susan Boelter to explain how her husband died or even to prove her innocence. The prosecution has to prove she's guilty—and do it beyond any reasonable doubt you may have. But you're going to have massive doubts here about her guilt—massive doubts that Peter Boelter was even murdered."

His voice rose with fervor. "More important, though, than any presumption is the truth itself. You'll have to find Susan Boelter not guilty because that's the truth . . . and by the time this trial is over, you'll know it. The evidence will clearly and unavoidably show that she had nothing to do with her husband's death. It will show—and you will have to find—that she is *not guilty.*"

His emotion reverberating in every word, every gesture, Dan slowly and deliberately uttered his final thought. "Men and women of the jury, you are Susan Boelter's only hope to establish her innocence, her only hope to prevent a ghastly miscarriage of justice."

His opening statement had taken less than five minutes.

The first witness for the prosecution was the dispatcher to whom Amelia's 911 call had been routed. A tape of that phone call was played on a cassette player set up on the clerk's table. The voices were clear.

A woman's voice cried out. "He's dead! He isn't moving. He's dead!"

She sounded frightened and confused. Under the dispatcher's prodding, she gave the address and identified herself as Amelia Boelter and the victim as Peter Boelter. The man testified that during the course of her call, he contacted an ambulance by radio. An officer in a police squad car heard the message and alerted the dispatcher that he was also on his way to the scene. Amelia's call had been logged in at 6:31 P.M.

Dan had no questions.

Huyton then asked to place several Philadelphia-area telephone directories into evidence to establish the addresses of the various phones. Dan stipulated that they could be.

Next came the ambulance driver and then the Philadelphia police officer, Paul Blaney, who arrived first at the scene and later broke the news of Peter's death to Susan. He wore his uniform on the stand. Dan had some questions for him.

"Officer Blaney, the basement in which you found the deceased, was it colder than the rest of the house?"

"Yes," the man answered, surprised by the question.

"How cold would you say it was?"

"Objection," Huyton declared. "The officer is not an expert on climatic conditions."

"Your Honor," Dan countered, "this isn't the sort of question that requires extensive university training. We all know when it's cold and when it's hot. We put on a coat or take it off."

The spectators laughed.

Vellarde nodded. "Agreed, counsel. Overruled. Please answer the question, officer."

"It was pretty cold."

"Cold enough to need a jacket?"

"Definitely."

"And the outside temperature was warm?"

"It was a hot night."

"You mentioned that the deceased was wearing only that bathing suit you identified a moment ago, is that right?"

"Yes."

"You said he was lying on the basement floor. Let me be clear about this: His entire back and the backs of his legs were resting on concrete?"

"Yes."

"And the concrete was also cold?"

"It must have been."

"Just one more question, officer. You've testified that when you heard the dispatcher's call to the hospital for an ambulance, you had just left the police station at Gypsy Lane and that it took you four or five minutes to get to the scene. Is that correct?"

"Yes, sir."

"You later drove over to Susan Boelter's house to inform her of her husband's death."

"Yes."

"How long did the trip take from her husband's house to the supermarket in Dellwyne, which I believe is two blocks past the main intersection there?"

"Not long. I made good time. I'd say fifteen minutes at the most, a minute or two either way."

"Thank you, officer. No further questions."

* * *

Over the next several days Huyton slowly worked his way through various police and official investigators who had been called to the scene.

A technician with the police Mobile Crime Unit testified that he found an empty scotch bottle and an empty glass on the kitchen counter. Lab tests established that the liquid at the bottom of each was scotch whiskey. Only the deceased's fingerprints had been found on them. His prints were elsewhere in the kitchen and on the knob and lintel of the door leading down to the cellar. Brenda, the cleaning lady, had left fingerprints all over the kitchen, as had Jenny and George, the other household employees. A smudged palm print on the counter was not clear and could not be identified.

On cross, Dan established that the basement contained cases of wine and scotch, the only place in the house where scotch was found.

"Three cases of it." The witness chuckled. "Expensive brand."

"Was the air-conditioning unit on in the basement?"

"Yes."

"In the rest of the house?"

"No, it wasn't."

"Then it was colder down there than in the rest of the house?" Dan asked.

"Yes, it was."

"Much colder?"

"Yes."

"Thank you."

The investigator for the Philadelphia medical examiner's office was asked about the position and condition of the body when he arrived.

"Several witnesses have testified that the basement was very cold. Did you note that in your report?"

"No, I didn't," the technician replied with obvious chagrin.

"But you agree it was cold down there."

"As I recall, yes."

"Did you measure the air or floor temperature?"

"No, I didn't. I should have, but a pipe had broken at the morgue, and I had to get back fast. I guess I just forgot."

Joe Corcoran, who had been one of the investigating detectives, was called to the stand. He looked to be in his mid-thirties and was built like a football lineman, with a broad, fleshy face and wiry hair that had darkened from red to brown. A seasoned detective whom Dan had questioned before, Corcoran reported that he and his partner, Parenzi, had arrived at Peter's house shortly after the Mobile Crime Unit and what he had seen there. Huyton then led him through the facts surrounding Susan's arrest at the cemetery, including the reading of her rights and taking her back to the Roundhouse for slating. He then turned the witness over to Dan for cross-examination.

Under Dan's questioning, Corcoran acknowledged that the only scotch in Peter Boelter's house at the time of his death was in the basement, but when Dan asked whether Peter might have gone to the cellar for more scotch, Vellarde ruled that the answer would require speculation by the witness and was out of order.

Dan had made his point and shifted to another matter. "Detective Corcoran, did you or your partner or anyone else in the department to your knowledge find a weapon?"

"No, we didn't."

"Was there any evidence in the house to make you believe that a weapon existed?"

"No."

"When you searched the defendant's house, did you find a weapon?"

"No."

"Thank you, detective. That will be all."

Karen was tense as she took the stand to testify about the events on the day of her father's death. She sat stiffly, chewing unconsciously at her lower lip, hands clenched unnaturally beside her. Her white summer dress, with its flower pattern, hung awkwardly, twisted to the side. The fact that she was young, poised between childhood and womanhood, and that she was pretty and blond-haired lent added poignancy to her ordeal.

Gil Huyton had known Karen all her life. He began gently. "Karen, I know this will be difficult for you. I'll try to keep it brief."

With a few questions Huyton caused her to sketch the day's chronology: the morning golf match and then lunch at the country club and the afternoon spent beside the pool. She had read and swum, listened to music, did homework, and talked some with her father.

"Did your father mention that you would be asked to appear in two days at a custody hearing?"

"Yes," she whispered.

"Did he tell you the purpose for your appearance at that hearing?"

"Yes."

"And what was that?"

"To tell the judge which parent I wanted to live with."

"Did your father ask you if you'd made up your mind yet on that point?"

Her answer was slower in coming. "Yes."

"Karen, please tell the jury what you told him."

She was silent for several long seconds, then said, "I told him I wanted to live with my mother."

"But didn't you tell a friend just the day before that you had chosen your father?"

"I changed my mind."

"Karen, you know why we're in court today—your mother is on trial for murder—"

Dan was on his feet. "Sidebar, Your Honor."

As Huyton joined him for the private bench conference, Dan said, "My instincts tell me that Mr. Huyton is about to impeach his own witness."

"That's exactly what I intend to do," Huyton conceded. He had made a calculated decision that if he put Karen on the stand, he could undermine the alibi she would attempt to provide for her mother by confronting her with her own prior inconsistent statement.

Vellarde asked, "What do you have in mind, Mr. Huyton?"

"Less than twenty-four hours before the victim's death, this witness told her girlfriend that she intended to live with her father. Her bias in favor of her mother is self-evident. The girl's giving her mother an alibi. If she says she told her parents she'd be asking the judge in the custody case to let her live with her mother, then her mother had very little reason for killing her father. I have to impeach her statement."

Vellarde nodded. "I'll permit it."

Huyton immediately turned back to Karen.

"You don't want your mother to be convicted of murder, do you, Karen?"

"No, I don't want that to happen."

"And if you thought you might prevent that from happening, you might even tell a little lie, isn't that so?"

Karen looked across the open floor to her mother, uncertain how to respond to the question.

"I might, but I'm not lying now," she finally said.

"Karen, who is Annabelle Warren?"

"My friend."

"Is she someone you confide in? To whom you tell your innermost secrets?"

"Yes."

"Didn't you tell her the night before that you'd made your mind up to live with your father?"

"Yes, I said it, but—"

"Were you lying then?"

"No."

"Then are you lying now when you tell us you said to your father the very next day that you wanted to live with your mother?"

"No."

Huyton cast a knowing glance toward the jury.

During the next few minutes he elicited from her that her father spoke once or twice on the phone that afternoon, but that no one visited the house until her mother arrived to pick her up at around a quarter after five.

Huyton's tone grew more urgent. "What happened then?"

The girl's focus went blank, her voice lost all inflection. As she spoke, she seemed in terror of being overwhelmed by the memory. "They argued. About me and the divorce."

"Can you recall what was said?"

"Dad was angry," Karen answered. "He said he would get custody of me no matter what and make sure Mom got nothing, no money or anything. Mom told me to change in the pool house from my swimsuit into my street clothes and go out to the car to wait for her while she and Dad talked."

"How long did you wait for her in the car?"

"About twenty minutes."

"You said your father was angry. Was your mother angry, too, or was she acting flirtatious?"

Dan instantly interrupted. "Objection as to form, Your Honor. It's a double question and it's leading. Moreover, it's prejudicial."

Vellarde leaned toward Karen. "Do you know what a flirtatious tone sounds like?"

"Yes," she told him.

"The jury will be excused for five minutes," Vellarde announced.

"What's the purpose of the question, Mr. Huyton?" Vellarde asked when the last juror had passed through the rear door and into the jury room.

"Your Honor, the autopsy revealed that Peter Boelter had had sex shortly before he died. The defendant was a cunning woman facing poverty, down to her last gambit, her own body, willing to do anything to save herself. I'm trying to show her state of mind when she sent her daughter out of the house. She was acting flirtatious in order to seduce her husband and make him more accommodating in the divorce action, perhaps even enough to reconcile with her."

"That's preposterous!" Dan rejoined. "There's no way he'd have believed her flip-flop toward him. Or that she'd have done such a thing with her daughter waiting outside. Or that—"

Huyton interrupted. "Mr. Lazar may have personal reasons for not having me bring out the sort of scheme being plotted here—"

Dan grabbed Huyton's shoulder and yanked him around, so that they faced each other. "Are you implying that Susan and I plotted to kill her husband?"

"Gentlemen!" Vellarde barked. "That's enough!"

Vellarde regarded Dan sourly, his mouth drawn. Dan could imagine the contempt with which the jurist regarded the allegedly scheming adulteress and her brawling attorney-lover.

Reporters nearest the railing had overheard the dispute and were scribbling in their notebooks. Any curious juror who ignored the judge's instructions against reading a newspaper or watching the news on TV tonight would learn exactly what had been said while he or she was out of the courtroom.

"Your Honor," Dan declared, "the question is intended to prejudice the jury against the defendant. It calls for a conclusion by the witness—and about a matter no thirteen-year-old could possibly evaluate."

"Children know a lot more than they used to," Huyton contended.

Dan was adamant. "Just asking the question prejudices the jury."

Vellarde shook his head. "The question's a valid one, and the child understands it. She's perfectly qualified to express an opinion as to whether her mother was angry at her father or trying to be nice to him, even flirtatious. Overruled."

As Huyton thanked Vellarde for the ruling, Dan spun away and stomped back to his seat.

When the jury had filed back in, Huyton had the court stenographer reread the question to Karen.

"She wasn't flirting," Karen answered.

"Would you tell us if she was?"

"Yes," she said, but more hesitantly.

Huyton was standing at the prosecution table, looking down at his list of questions.

"Karen, has your mother ever hit you?"

Karen's stricken eyes sought her mother's. She mumbled an answer that the judge gently asked her to repeat more loudly.

She turned to him. "Yes."

"Did she say why she was hitting you?" Huyton asked.

"She was angry about my visits with Daddy," Karen explained. Her gaze jerked back toward her mother, this time with contrition.

"Did your mother appear to you to be very angry when she struck you?"

"Yes."

"Had you expected her to hit you?"

"She just exploded."

Mara whispered something to Huyton, who nodded and then spoke to Karen.

"When your mother told you to dress and go out to the car so she and your father could talk, was she as angry as when she hit you in the face?"

"Oh, no."

"But you've said that she suddenly exploded and hit you, that when she was angry, you couldn't predict what she could do, isn't that so?"

"Yes."

"So, Karen, would I be correct in characterizing your mother's behavior as sometimes unpredictable and violent?"

Karen remained silent, staring at the defendant's table.

"Young lady," Vellarde said, leaning toward her, "you have to answer the question."

Karen's head lifted. "My mother's a wonderful person. She wouldn't hurt my father."

"Commendable," Huyton said, half-facing the jury. No one could mistake that the compliment was not for Susan, but for how bravely Karen was lying to protect her.

"No more questions," he said.

Dan rose to cross-examine.

"Karen, do you love your mother?"

"Yes." She managed the rudiments of a brief smile at him.

"Did you love your father?"

"Yes."

"Would you lie to protect the memory of your father?"

"No."

"Or the safety of your mother?"

"No."

"When she came out to join you in the car, did she act in an unusual manner?"

"No."

"Was she in a rush to leave?"

"No."

"Did she carry a blunt instrument?"

"No."

"Were her clothes in disarray—messed up?"

"No."

"Did she have any blood on her?"

"No."

Dan paused for a moment to indicate one final line of questioning, moving close to the child.

"Karen, was your father drinking that afternoon?"

She nodded ambivalently. Her contrition had flooded back, but now it related to the father whose privacy she was about to betray.

"Out loud," the judge reminded her.

"Yes."

"What was it he was drinking?"

"Scotch," she said. "What he always drank."

"Did he seem drunk to you?"

"Yes."

"Objection," Huyton called out. "This child isn't competent to judge an adult's degree of inebriation."

Vellarde thought for a moment. "Overruled. As you yourself pointed out, Mr. Huyton, children know a good deal more nowadays. Too much."

Dan repeated the question, pleased at this win after the string of defeats.

"He was drunk," Karen answered.

"Could you describe his actions in more detail?"

"He wasn't . . . the way he usually was. He wasn't steady. And he was angry and sloppy and sometimes not making sense."

"Can you remember anything in particular that he said that didn't make sense?"

She shook her head, eyes down.

"Please think back to what was in your mind that day," Dan gently pressed her. "The reason that you decided to live with your mother and not your father, was it because of how drunk you saw him that day?"

"Yes," she mumbled.

"And the reason you made that decision, was it because you were afraid that he wouldn't make a suitable parent?"

She lifted her eyes, tears filling the lids.

"Yes," she said.

"No more questions."

Huyton stood up for redirect. "But you'd seen him drunk before, hadn't you, Karen?"

"Yes."

"Very drunk?"

"Yes."

"I have no further questions."

26

The prosecution's strategy seemed to be to put witnesses on the stand who would paint Susan as untrustworthy in every regard: mercenary, deceitful, lecherous behind her husband's back, a vindictive, physically dangerous woman, whose curdled passion drove her to kill.

The housekeeper, Jenny Fanning, related incidents that showed how avidly her employer cherished the estate in Dellwyne and how desperately she had worked to keep it up after the separation. Then, as Jenny had done in her deposition for the custody hearing, she described the incident in which Susan angrily struck Karen.

Next on the stand was Karen's schoolmate Annabelle Warren, who revealed Karen's admission to her that she wanted to live with her father. "She told me her mother was impossible."

Peter's divorce lawyer followed. At the pretrial conference Dan had fought to exclude the man's recollection of Susan's statements outside the matrimonial court, but Vellarde had ruled that he would allow the jury to hear them for the purpose of indicating her state of mind the day before Peter's death.

After laying the proper foundation with early questions, Huyton said, "You've told us that Susan Boelter was in a highly agitated, distraught state at the adjournment of the matrimonial hearing."

"Yes, she was," the lawyer confirmed.

"You've also told us that she confronted her husband outside the courtroom. Would you say that she was exceptionally angry?"

"Definitely."

"Had anything occurred to cause that exceptional anger?"

"Well, this was a Friday, and the judge intended to discuss with the girl on Monday which parent she wanted to live with. Mr. Boelter insisted that he wanted custody and that his wife wouldn't get a penny from him in the divorce action. He also said he intended to force her off the family foundation she headed. He told her she was 'as good as finished.' He used those words."

"How did Mrs. Boelter react?"

"She became enraged. She yelled at him—I mean everyone out there could hear her."

"Can you recall what she said?"

"She said, 'Karen will never be safe with you! I can't let you have her!' "

The courtroom's spectators gasped.

" 'Karen will never be safe with you! I can't let you have her!' " Huyton slowly repeated, facing the jury now. "You're sure of that?"

"Yes. I wrote it down in my notes right afterward. I intended to use the statement against her on Monday at the custody hearing."

"Was that said in a threatening manner?"

"She seemed to me to have lost all self-control."

"Thank you. No further questions."

Huyton and Mara exchanged a satisfied look as he returned to his seat. Dan stood up.

"Mr. Osborne," Dan began, "you've had a lot of experience as a divorce lawyer, haven't you?"

"Twenty-one years."

"You must have heard a lot of angry threats between parties to divorces and custody fights in that time, isn't that so?"

"Yes."

"Have any of those parties ever killed their mates as a result of those angry threats?"

"No."

"Thank you. No further questions."

Ellen Hildreth, the next-door neighbor, was the first witness in the afternoon and provided no surprises. She recounted that she came out of her house to work on her plants at the side of her front yard at a quarter past five, just as Susan was arriving. For a while she was at the far side of the lawn and then came back to the side near Peter's house. A little while later Karen left the house and waited in her mother's car parked at the curb. That was soon followed by the sound of the couple yelling in

Peter's kitchen. Mrs. Hildreth could not make out much that was being said, but it seemed to be about Karen.

On a sketch of the adjoining properties, she pointed out how her side lawn faced Peter's kitchen, which was too high and angled away to see inside of. Nor could she see his front door or his backyard from there.

She then related that at about ten to six, she observed Susan on the front path, walking away from the house toward her car. Mother and daughter then drove away.

At around six, his usual time, Mr. Hildreth returned home from work. He and his wife went into their house. She heard and saw nothing that happened next door after that. Half an hour later, Amelia Boelter burst into the Hildreth house shouting that Peter Boelter was dead. Ellen Hildreth dialed 911 for her, handed her the phone, and kept her company until the police and ambulance arrived.

On cross, Dan established that Susan gave Mrs. Hildreth a pleasant greeting when she drove up to Peter's house. Nothing angry or furtive about her. She did not appear to be a woman intent on violence. Although visible only from the back when she was leaving, Susan appeared normal to Mrs. Hildreth.

Meticulous, Huyton followed with an expert witness on acoustics who gave his opinion that raised voices in the kitchen would have carried well enough through the open window for someone standing at the marigold bed, like Mrs. Hildreth, to have made out that the couple was arguing.

A professional surveyor then confirmed Mrs. Hildreth's statements about what she could and could not see from her marigold bed.

"It's getting late," Vellarde noted when the surveyor stepped down. Addressing the prosecutor, he said, "You can put your next witness on first thing in the morning. Do you know yet who it will be?"

Huyton conferred with Mara for several seconds while they perused the witness list.

"Yes, Your Honor. Amelia Boelter."

"Amelia always had a flair for the dramatic," Susan whispered to Dan with a smile as her sister-in-law walked to the stand. Amelia had dressed in a black silk suit and a small, black pillbox hat. She wanted no one to mistake the extent of her mourning for the deceased.

Amelia's initial testimony established that Susan was poor when she married Peter and relished her new affluence. Amelia described several occasions that gave her reason to believe that Susan had married Peter for his money. She then elaborated on Susan's "passion" for the *Herald*.

"She would have done anything to hang on to the paper. She almost went crazy when Peter talked about selling it."

Finally Huyton's inquiries moved on to two incidents that bore directly on the case: Amelia's discovery of Peter's body and the fight in her bedroom after Susan discovered her and Peter in bed together.

"Do you have to go into that?" Amelia asked in an embarrassed tone when Huyton moved to the latter topic.

"I do, yes."

Amelia turned to the judge, who nodded. Composing herself, she lifted her head high, as if to indicate that her breeding and her love for Peter would repel any humiliation.

After establishing that Peter was separated from Susan at the time, Huyton moved Amelia quickly through the bedroom incident, concentrating on Susan's tirade and physical attack.

"I was really afraid for my life," Amelia declared. "She was berserk with jealousy because Peter wanted me and not her."

Dan's objection to her conclusion about Susan's motive was upheld, but too late. The jury had already heard the damaging answer.

At the conclusion of her direct testimony, Amelia stood up to leave the witness box, but Vellarde stopped her.

"I just told whatever I know, judge," she explained.

"Mr. Lazar has the right to cross-examine you."

She glanced over at Dan with deep distrust, which she quickly replaced with visible resolve. She took her seat.

"Mrs. Boelter," Dan began, "you and the defendant were sisters-in-law. More than that, you were best friends. Isn't that so?"

"At one time."

"From the time she and her husband married," Dan firmly insisted, "and up until the moment, some fifteen years later, when she caught you in bed with her husband, isn't that correct?"

"Well, yes," said Amelia hesitantly, vaguely sensing where the questioning was going.

"She confided in you, told you everything. She was very unhappy, wasn't she?"

"Yes."

"As a matter of fact, her heart was breaking after her husband left her and told her he wanted a divorce, isn't that true?"

"I guess you could say that."

"Did you ever confess to her during the time that she was confiding all of her marital troubles to you that you were secretly seeing her husband?"

Amelia's mouth angrily compressed, and her nostrils flared. "I didn't consider it any of her business."

"This was her *husband*, Mrs. Boelter," Dan replied with astonishment, carefully screening sarcasm from his tone, so as not to shift sympathy from his client to the witness. "She was telling you how grief-stricken she was that he had left her, and yet you did not consider your sleeping with him any of her business?"

"Peter assured me that his life with her was over, that he loved me."

"And did he ask you for anything during that time?"

"I—" She was confused by the question.

Dan elaborated. "Did he ask you to support his plan to sell the *Herald*?"

"Oh, that, yes."

"Before your affair with him began, did you vote for the sale?"

"No."

"Only after he slept with you?"

Huyton spoke out. "I object, Your Honor. Irrelevant."

Dan turned to the DA. "I don't understand, Mr. Huyton. She's already testified that the defendant found her in bed with the defendant's husband. I'm sure the jury doesn't think they were there for a game of bridge. Her love affair and the subsequent change in her vote goes to the issue of whether she had become biased against the defendant. My intent is also to show that Peter Boelter was an exploitive man who played on this woman's emotions to obtain sex from her and her vote as a director of the family's corporation."

"Objection overruled," Vellarde decided. "Please answer the question."

"Peter loved me," Amelia declared. "And I loved him."

"Let's get into that. You said several times in your testimony that you and Peter were in love. And that you planned to marry."

"Yes, we did. As soon as his divorce from Susan came through."

Dan stepped closer, his tone sadly empathetic now. "That isn't really true, is it, Mrs. Boelter? Peter Boelter had no intention of marrying you, and he made that clear to you the night before he died. Isn't that so?"

Amelia said nothing.

"Isn't that so?" Dan insisted. "Didn't you and he have a dinner together Friday night at a restaurant where you put that very question to him?"

When she seemed intent on remaining silent, he pressed her. "Didn't you suspect that he was seeing someone else, perhaps even his wife?"

After waiting a moment, he asked, "Didn't you want a firm answer once and for all that he intended to marry you?"

Amelia remained silent.

Dan was only a foot from her now. "I remind you, Mrs. Boelter, you're under oath."

"The waiter!" she suddenly remembered with a shock.

Her manner, resistant and lofty, dwindled into despair. Words tumbled out of her. "I did have the feeling Peter was seeing Susan again . . . and

that he was using me to get my vote. I told him so. He denied it. I wanted
him to prove that he loved me by publicly announcing that we would get
married.''

"Did he agree to that?''

"No. And the way he was acting, I wouldn't have believed him anyway. I left.''

Dan strode toward the jurors, as if in thought. When he was at the side
of the jury box, he turned back accusingly to Amelia.

"You've been holding something else back, too, haven't you, Mrs.
Boelter. The night you claim to have discovered Peter Boelter's body,
you didn't really start out from your house for that five-minute drive to his
house at twenty-five minutes past six, did you?''

"No.''

"It was more like six o'clock.''

"Yes.'' Her alibi had collapsed in her library, when her maid inadvertently revealed the truth to Dan.

She had kept the truth from the prosecutors, and they were startled.

"So you really arrived at Peter Boelter's house at five minutes after six
or thereabout?'' Dan said.

"Yes.''

"Why did you lie about the time, Mrs. Boelter?''

"I was afraid that if I told the truth, people might think I killed him.''
She spoke so quietly that spectators in the rear of the courtroom were
murmuring inquiries to neighbors about what she had just said.

"In other words, you were afraid the authorities might charge you with
his murder because you were alone with Peter Boelter for twenty-five or
twenty-six minutes before you rushed next door at six thirty-one, isn't
that correct?''

"No!'' she pleaded, her voice begging to be believed. "That isn't what
happened. I did go over there at the time you said, a little after six. Peter's
car was sitting in the garage, so I rang the doorbell. But no one answered.
I rang again, and then I heard the phone ring inside the house. Only one
ring, so I thought someone must be home and had picked it up . . .'' Her
voice diminished into silence.

"You thought he might be with another woman, and that was why he
hadn't come to the door, was that it?''

She momentarily hung her head with chagrin. "I did begin to think
that, so I finally decided to leave. The phone rang again while I was
walking back to my car, and again someone inside picked it up after only
one ring, so I knew someone was in there. I drove around for a while and
then decided that even if he *was* seeing Susan again, I wasn't just going

to give him up to her. I was going to fight for him. So I went back to his house.''

"What time was that?''

"A few minutes before six-thirty. I rang the doorbell again. Peter's car was still there, but nobody answered. I tried the door, and it was open.''

"And you went in.''

"Yes. There was no one upstairs in the bedroom.''

"That was the first place you looked?''

"Yes.'' Abashed, she let her eyes fall to her hands. "So I went back downstairs to find him. The cellar door was open, and the light was on. I went over to look and saw him lying at the bottom of the stairs. It was horrible. I ran next door.''

"To call for help?''

"Yes.''

"Why didn't you just pick up the phone in the kitchen? There were extensions all over that house.''

"I didn't want to touch anything. You know, for the police.''

"Very collected under such trying circumstances. And yet you sounded frantic on the tape.'' Dan had moved to the rear of the jury box, so Amelia was facing the jurors; they could observe the slightest twitch or halt in her manner. "Peter's neighbor, Ellen Hildreth, testified that the first thing you said to her was that Peter Boelter was dead. Those were also your first words when you called nine-one-one.''

"Yes.''

"You never went down to the bottom of the stairs yourself to check more closely?''

"No, I didn't.''

"Then how could you be sure he was dead?''

"He . . . he just looked dead,'' Amelia replied weakly.

"Couldn't he have been unconscious or shaken up or injured?''

"He looked *dead*.''

"How many other dead men had you seen before then, Mrs. Boelter?''

After a long pause she softly admitted, "None.''

Dan stared at the floor, as if reviewing all she had said, and then looked up at her again.

"One thing isn't clear to me. At dinner the night before, you were so angry at Peter Boelter that you walked out. And yet the very next night, you went to his house. Why?''

"I was going crazy,'' she said, her mouth quivering, near tears. "I hoped we could make up. Whatever he wanted, I was willing to give in. You have to believe me.''

"I do. I believe that's exactly what happened. You went to see him at six o'clock, and you gave in. You let him make love to you. And then, afterward, when you asked him again to marry you, he still refused. You suspected he wanted to go back to his wife and became so angry and jealous that you grabbed a heavy object and hit him with it as hard as you could. Isn't that what really happened during those mysterious twenty-five minutes, Mrs. Boelter?"

"Your Honor!" Huyton cried out in objection. "The witness is not on trial here."

Vellarde disagreed. "The question's a proper one, given the witness's earlier false statement to the police. Overruled."

"In your rage, in your jealousy," Dan continued, "didn't you push him down the stairs or pick up something and bludgeon him to death?"

"No."

"Didn't you kill Peter Boelter because he told you that he would never marry you?"

"No." She was weeping now, the sobs making it difficult for her to be understood. "I loved him. I loved him so."

"I'm sure you did."

Dan directed the final words to the jury, his cross-examination ended. "But we'll never really know what happened during those twenty-five minutes, will we?"

After much urging from Susan, Dan finally arranged for her and Karen to meet his father. He decided on dinner at the latter's restaurant, Kavala, hoping the older man would feel more amiable toward Susan in the place where he was used to extending his hospitality. However, the atmosphere was strained. Jacob eyed his son's socialite Christian lover, an accused murderess, with great suspicion. He warmed for a moment and only toward Karen when he mentioned having heard from Jamie on the phone that his grandson and Karen telephoned each other almost nightly.

"We're friends," Karen said, a small smile breaking through for an instant.

Suddenly, a vanload of TV newspeople who had learned of the group's presence tried to enter the restaurant with a video camera. Jacob rushed to bar the door.

"Out of here!" the old guerrilla fighter warned menacingly. "I've killed better men with my bare hands."

Dan went up to speak to them, while Susan and Karen slipped out the back and went home.

Later that night Dan phoned Jamie and praised his son's sensitivity to

Karen's sorrow; the girl had been going through a hard time since her father died, and Dan was proud that Jamie was helping her work through her grief. He kept to himself his private pleasure that the children's closeness boded well for the future he was considering.

It was eleven by then, and lying on his bed, he turned on the TV news. The first story dealt with Susan's trial. A shot of Dan being interviewed in the courthouse corridor during the lunch break flashed on the screen. Testy that all the reporters' questions had concerned intimate matters between him and Susan, he had snarled that the case wasn't about juicy tidbits for gossip tabloids, but about an innocent woman fighting for her freedom against false charges.

A shot of Kavala's exterior followed. Then his father's face appeared on the screen.

"Out of here!" the rich Mediterranean accent rang out. "I've killed better men with my bare hands."

The news producer might have intended the juxtaposition of the son's and father's bellicose quotes to be humorous or even an indication of barbaric family inclinations, but the effect was far different. The viewer was, instead, brought up short by Jacob's fiery nobility, by the unfamiliar sight of a man of undeniable, elemental principle facing down a shallow-witted attacker in defense of his son's woman.

"You show 'em, Dad," Dan cheered. "You show 'em what we're made of." He even allowed himself to believe that his own remark in the City Hall corridor had contained some small aspiration to nobility.

For an instant Dan felt eternal and indomitable. He felt as if his existence stretched back a million generations to the beginning of human time; to his first incarnations as Adam and Noah and Abraham, as Eve and Rachel and Sarah and as the original Daniel, who had emerged unscathed from a lion's den; to lives that were punctuated, but never ended, by death. He was part of an unbroken progression that would flow forward through his son and his grandchildren and their children for a hundred million generations more. He knew with absolute certainty that all who had gone before lived forever within him. And he, like they, would live forever within those who followed—each a tiny, indestructible, indispensable contribution to the whole.

Dan had belittled to Susan the importance of truth at a criminal trial, as if it was as much a technique as a goal. But truth was indeed what this trial was all about, and a guiltless woman's liberty. Provoked by the press, he had declared that he was championing here the basic democratic rights of fair trial and presumption of innocence. Watching himself say those things on TV had embarrassed him; he suspected that he sounded like some self-appointed street-corner prophet, his phrases clanging with pompous self-importance. But it came to him now that he needn't have felt foolish.

Everything in his life—his maverick defiance and stubbornness; his outsider's religion that emphasized law and moral behavior; even his occasionally embarrassing idealism that this ordeal had forced to the surface—had prepared him for and led him to this moment, this purpose, this single combat to win justice, this quest for truth. If he did nothing more in his life, he decided, his was already a life well spent.

Being a rebel was itself his purpose for existence, his tiny place in the universe; it was the end for which he had always shortsightedly thought his dissidence to be only the means. His struggles to enforce, to guarantee, people's rights were more than simply self-protection for himself against the threat of some future massacre or expulsion. They ultimately safeguarded what he *valued* in life for himself and others: freedom of choice and of thought and of speech—the essence of America safeguarded by its Bill of Rights, basic human rights that people the world over were striving to secure.

Dissent, he realized, was both the vessel and the destination of his life's voyage.

He turned out the light and lay back.

In the moments before he fell asleep, his thoughts returned to Susan's defense. On Monday, Ernest Kieffer, the city's chief medical examiner, would be taking the stand. Logic dictated that he testify at the start of the prosecution's case, but he had been saved for last. They wanted his testimony to stick in the jurors' minds. Because he had established a time and cause of Peter Boelter's death that ensnared Susan, he was the heart of their case. Her fate depended on Kieffer's testimony.

And depended, too, Dan remembered just before falling asleep, on his own counterattack.

27

The law allows experts with scientific, technical, or other specialized knowledge to testify about matters jurors could not be expected to know about on their own. The person's credentials must convincingly establish his or her expertise because such a witness could easily sway a jury, which has no such knowledge.

Well over six feet tall, heavyset, with large straight features, thick gray-black eyebrows and hair that matched his gray double-breasted suit, Ernest Kieffer made an impressive figure on the stand and looked younger than his seventy years. Dan had observed him personally chatting with Huyton and reporters before the court session began. The man was a born politician.

In answer to Huyton's initial question about his credentials, he began, "I'm a member and past president of the American College of Pathologists and also a member of the American College of *Forensic* Pathologists. I've served as head of the Department of Pathology at the Hospital of the University of Pennsylvania. Until recently I also served as professor of pathology at the University of Pennsylvania Medical School." He continued for several minutes to name the committees on which he had served for several national medical societies and the articles and treatises he had written.

"When did you become Philadelphia's chief medical examiner?" Huyton asked.

"At the beginning of the year. I was appointed by the mayor soon after he was elected. I'd always been interested in public service, and agreed.''

Kieffer exuded a self-possession that indicated vast knowledge worn with amiable humility. Dan could see that the jury was buying him.

Vellarde turned to Dan when Huyton had finished eliciting Kieffer's background. ''Do you accept Dr. Kieffer's qualifications to testify as an expert witness?''

''No, I don't,'' Dan declared, getting to his feet.

An audible reaction rose from the crowd. The battle had been joined early.

''Dr. Kieffer,'' Dan asked, ''forensic pathology is a subspecialty of pathology, is it not?''

''Yes.''

''And you say you're a certified forensic pathologist, isn't that so?''

''Both a pathologist *and* a forensic pathologist,'' Kieffer answered, a bit of condescension showing through the humility.

''When were you certified as a forensic pathologist?''

''Oh, in the mid-fifties sometime.''

''And isn't it true that from that time until the beginning of this year, you occupied no position in which you actually practiced forensic pathology?''

''I kept my hand in, kept up to date.''

''Isn't it correct to say that there have been a good many advances in the field of forensic pathology during that period?''

''Certainly. And, as I said, I've kept up.''

''Let me repeat what I asked a moment ago: Were you employed as a forensic pathologist in any capacity during those three and a half decades?''

''No . . . no, I was not.''

''Did you teach forensic pathology?''

''No.''

''Did any of your writing that you mentioned earlier relate to the subject of forensic pathology?''

''No.''

''Isn't it true that your specialty during that period was not forensic pathology, but hematology, the study of the blood, which is a different subspecialty of pathology?''

Huyton was on his feet. ''May I remind the court that the witness has been certified by the American College of Forensic Pathologists and is a member in good standing.''

''Certified nearly forty years ago and didn't practice it until a few months ago,'' Dan emphasized, and could not resist adding, ''the only medical field where the patients can't sue him for malpractice.''

Dan was rewarded by a chuckle from the jury.

Huyton was not laughing. "Dr. Kieffer's distinguished credentials and his appointment as the city's chief medical examiner make him eminently qualified to testify."

"There's that word 'eminent' again," Dan observed. "No one's disputing that he knows what he's doing in his own field, but that's hematology, not forensic pathology."

The annoyance in Huyton's voice reflected his concern that the dispute was dragging on to the point that the jury would start to lose respect for his key witness. "Dr. Kieffer performed the autopsy, Your Honor. He prepared the autopsy report."

Dan smiled apologetically. "He just wasn't qualified to do those things. He's not an expert."

"Your Honor!" Huyton implored.

"May I ask another question?" Dan asked Vellarde, who nodded.

Dan shifted his attention back to Kieffer. "Your friendship with the mayor goes back a long way, I believe."

"We grew up in the same neighborhood. His brother and I were in the same high school class. I'm a good deal older than he is."

"I have here a newspaper article that states you either contributed or loaned a total of fifteen thousand dollars to the mayor's campaign fund. Is that figure correct?"

Kieffer looked insulted. "That had nothing to do with my appointment. I was a well-regarded physician, teacher, and hospital administrator . . . a national figure in medicine, if I do say so myself. The mayor was concerned that prospects were dismal for the City Council to authorize expensive new equipment urgently needed by the medical examiner's office. He felt my presence as chief could sway the Council. I'd raised money in several election campaigns and knew many of the Council members. I'm proud to say that we've now gotten all the equipment we needed."

"And so, the fact that you weren't up to date in forensic pathology and that you were being forced to leave the medical school and hospital because of your age, those were secondary reasons for wanting the job?"

Kieffer's face grew red. "I'm as vigorous as I ever was. I resigned from the hospital and the medical school only because the mayor urged me to come on board."

Dan sneaked a glance at the jury. Had he scratched up Kieffer's facade sufficiently for them to evaluate Kieffer's testimony with some skepticism? Would they no longer just swallow whole whatever the man claimed was scientifically true? Dan held little hope that an acting judge whose future candidacy required party support would disqualify the mayor's buddy.

Vellarde instantly proved him right. He ruled, "Although Dr. Kieffer's certification and his current position qualify him as an expert, he actually performed the autopsy and issued the autopsy report, so he'll also be testifying as a direct witness here. Your objection to the witness is denied, Mr. Lazar."

The district attorney had tried to add to Kieffer's stature in the jury's eyes by qualifying him as an expert and had managed to get him bloodied a bit in the process. Dan watched Huyton straighten his stance with relief and flash the jury an ironic glance intended to convince them that Dan's gripes about this esteemed witness had been out of line.

Turning the page on his legal pad, Huyton systematically began to walk Ernest Kieffer through the autopsy findings.

Kieffer began by stating that Peter Boelter had been struck in the back of the skull with a sharp-edged blunt instrument and then thrown down the stairs. He gave his opinion that impact on the bottom step alone could not have caused the victim's extensive injuries, specifically a crushed medulla and a nearly severed spinal column. Death from such a fall would have produced a greater bruise or contra-coup on the front of the brain. The wound would have matched more precisely the corner of the step on which he was found. And there would have been more blood in the scrapes on the shins, shoulder, and forehead if they had occurred before the killing blow was struck.

When Huyton asked how Kieffer had established the time of death at between five-fifteen and five forty-five P.M., the latter repeated his formula for the loss of body heat over time. And then he stated his other findings: blood-alcohol level of nineteen-hundredths of a percent, evidence of recent sexual activity, and a trace of what might be blood on the victim's thigh.

"Your witness, Mr. Lazar," Huyton said as his direct questioning concluded.

Dan had a narrow line to walk: Discredit Kieffer without appearing to be an ogre in the jury's eyes. Make them wonder about all the disputed points in the man's testimony. The ultimate denunciation would come when he put Mallory on the stand to refute Kieffer's major findings.

He started slowly, first reconfirming that no murder weapon had been found and no blood stains discovered anywhere in the house except for the cellar. He then got Kieffer to admit that a person with that much alcohol in his bloodstream could easily trip on the aluminum strip along the edge of the top step and fall down the rest of the stairs.

Dan placed a color photo of the bottom step on the easel.

"Several police officers have testified that they found the victim lying with his head on the corner of that step. Isn't it true that the triangle formed by the corner of the step fit the depression in the victim's skull?''

"Only to the layman's eye."

"Brain tissue and blood matching the defendant's blood type were found on the step, as well, isn't that true?''

"Yes. But that's also consistent with the victim's head being placed on the corner of the step after he was dead, even perhaps pressed down onto it so as to increase the depth of the wound and deposit tissue on it.''

Harboring little hope of tripping Kieffer up during the early phase of his cross, Dan wished only to raise questions about the key findings. His objective was to ready the jury to accept the contradictory testimony of the defense's expert witness, Alan Mallory, when Dan put him on the stand.

Dan read excerpts from a treatise by well-known medical examiners that stated a fall from only six feet could generate sixty pounds of force, enough to crush a skull hitting concrete, and that even microscopic examination of the laceration at the center of the wound would not rule out a fall as the cause of death. On several of the postmortem photos, he was able to point out dark lines in the skin scrapes and what might have been a contra-coup bruise on the front of Peter's brain, possible signs that Peter Boelter was alive as he fell, that his heart was beating and sending blood to those injuries before his head hit the bottom step.

"His heart may have been beating slightly when he fell," Kieffer countered, "but he was nearly dead by that time and probably comatose. The killer might even have thought him dead when the body was dumped down the stairs.''

Dan elected not to belabor the point. Time enough after Mallory had supported his view on the stand. With an amicable smile, he moved on.

"Peter Boelter died on Saturday, June sixth. That was a hectic weekend for your office, I understand. A lot of other cases were coming in, and new equipment was being installed. That night things got worse: A water main burst and flooded the building. Bodies had to be quickly moved. Records were misplaced—you still hadn't started to computerize your department's records; that started later in the summer. Autopsies were delayed. You yourself had to be in a dozen places at once. A very hectic time.''

"Yes, it was.''

"Didn't a few days go by in all that confusion when the press was asking questions about Peter Boelter's death, but his body was misplaced, so someone finally had to go from body to body and find the right toe tag?''

"Not to my knowledge, no. As soon as I could get to his autopsy, I did it.''

"Your report mentions that you began Peter Boelter's autopsy at just about midnight. You finished at a quarter to one. Is that correct?''

Kieffer smiled. "As you said, it was a busy time for us.''

"That's rather quick for an autopsy, isn't it?"

Kieffer's smile evaporated. "If you're suggesting that I gave short shrift to it, I can assure you I didn't."

"Doctor, your calendar for the following day shows an early-morning meeting at the mayor's office a few hours later—at seven in the morning. Am I not right in assuming that when you had a few spare minutes late at night, you slipped in the Boelter autopsy and got it over with quickly so as to manage a few hours of sleep before your appointment at City Hall?"

Kieffer was angry. "I take my responsibilities very seriously, Mr. . . ."

"Lazar, doctor. Daniel Lazar," Dan said affably, but his mind was reading the other man's.

You probably didn't give this appearance much thought until the last day or so. Just go in and repeat your findings. After all, you're the expert. But now I've got you worried. I've disparaged your credentials, and I'm attacking your credibility. You may end up fatally wounded, professionally crippled. You've gone a long way over the years by knowing how to be liked. You can't understand why I'd attack such a likable guy.

Dan was peering at his notes, as if paying no attention to an answer he had accurately expected to be self-serving. "Doctor, your autopsy report states that Peter Boelter died between a quarter after five and a quarter to six in the afternoon. How did you come up with that particular period as the time during which Peter Boelter died?"

Kieffer repeated his formula about the body temperature dropping a set amount each hour. He quickly added that his investigator had informed him verbally that "the air and floor were a little cold, so I took that into account."

The investigator had obviously alerted Kieffer to his failure to measure the ambient temperature. Dan had a hunch, though, that he could still get some mileage out of the slipup before springing his trap. "Dr. Kieffer, the basement was more than just a *little* cold. Peter Boelter kept it cold enough with air-conditioning to use as a wine cellar. And the floor was concrete—very cold concrete. Shouldn't you at least have stated those factors in your report—even included the exact figures—if you truly did take them into account?"

Kieffer became combative. "I'm sure I took them into account."

Sarcasm edged into Dan's voice; here he had to draw blood. "This so-called formula you used, would it surprise you to learn that *modern* forensic pathologists reject it as inaccurate and scientifically invalid?"

Kieffer became irate. He thrust his index finger at Dan. "I'm a scientist, Mr. Lazar. My findings were based on accurate scientific knowledge.

No matter what sort of slippery questioning you use to try to confuse the jury, there's absolutely no doubt that Peter Boelter died between five-fifteen and a quarter to six. None whatsoever.''

Judge Vellarde had been leaning back in the high black chair. Now, after glancing at the wall clock, he bent forward.

"We're close to the lunch break, Mr. Lazar.''

"Just one or two more questions, and I'll be finished with the witness, Your Honor.''

Vellarde leaned back again.

Dan had gradually moved closer to Kieffer. Now he was standing directly in front of him.

"Isn't it true that your original autopsy report did not include a time of death?''

Kieffer hesitated. "What are you getting at?''

"Your original report, the one you dictated to your secretary after performing the autopsy, isn't it true that it didn't contain a time of death—and that you didn't add that section until later that day?''

"I can't recall.''

"Let me refresh your recollection.'' Dan handed him the initial draft report that had been among the papers he had had copied from the case file when he was at the medical examiner's office.

"Do you recognize it?''

"Yes,'' Kieffer reluctantly conceded, not yet sure where the questioning was leading.

"Does it contain any mention about the time of death?''

"No, it doesn't.''

"Isn't it true that you added that time-of-death paragraph only after you received a phone call from someone at the district attorney's office?''

For an instant Kieffer seemed to slip into suspended animation; his muscles had lost all their power to move. Eventually he managed to answer, "I often speak to people at the DA's office.''

Dan's voice grew harshly accusatory with the information Armbruster had confidentially imparted. "We aren't talking about just *anybody* at the DA's office, Dr. Kieffer. We're talking about someone important there . . . someone who told you that they'd consider it a great favor if your report fixed the time of the victim's death as the exact same time that their suspect, Susan Boelter, was alone with the victim!''

Kieffer drew himself up with dignity. "Perhaps you're used to dealing with liars, Mr. Lazar. But I don't falsify my findings, and I resent the accusation that I do. Peter Boelter died during that half hour. No earlier and no later. And some time before he died, he had sex.''

"And you're sure about that?''

"Absolutely."

"I'm sure you are," Dan said, displaying a derisive expression the jury, too, could see.

"No doubt about it. Sperm found in his urethra," Kieffer persisted. He directed an explanation to the jurors. "That's the tube in the penis through which sperm travels. Some is always left after intercourse."

"Doctor," Dan said, turning on him, "perhaps it wasn't known back when you were certified, but isn't it now fully established that the presence of sperm in a dead man's urethra is a misleading piece of evidence to establish proof of sexual relations?"

"Certainly not," Kieffer replied, but tentatively now. "There's always sperm present after ejaculation."

Dan's voice became a hammer. "But isn't it, in fact, well established that in some cases *rigor mortis* can harden the male sex glands, the seminal vesicles, and cause sperm to be ejaculated well *after* death?"

"Mr. Lazar—" Kieffer shot back. He had recovered his tenacity. "—I don't live in your kind of legal fantasy land, with these tricky hypotheticals and possibles. I'm a professional who knows his business. I'll stake my reputation on my findings."

"You already have, doctor."

"Huyton will try to shore up the weak parts of Kieffer's testimony this afternoon," Dan explained to Susan as she and the three lawyers on the defense team waited in the law firm's conference room for lunch to be delivered. "But all in all, I like the way it went. I think the jury's got to have a doubt or two about Kieffer's reliability. Mallory can deliver the knockout blow."

They were discussing the order of proof they intended to present for the defense.

"We ought to put Mallory on the stand very early in our direct," Cal suggested, "so he can refute Kieffer right away. Everything afterward will just bolster our case."

Dan agreed. "The prosecution should finish up today. We'll probably start our case in the morning, and we ought to be able to put Mallory on by the end of the week."

Rick stood up. "I'd better let him know it's getting close."

"Tell him we'll call him the day before we need him down here, so we can review his testimony with him."

Mary Alice walked into the conference room with a brown bag containing the lunches. Dan's was in a clear, plastic container.

"What is this stuff?" he asked in bewilderment.

"Vegetable salad," Mary Alice informed him.

"I ordered an egg salad sandwich, heavy on the mayo, and fries."

"Rooney's right. The way you eat is going to kill you. From now on, only healthy lunches. And no more sending out for ice cream at four."

"What did Cal get?"

"Turkey sandwich."

"Great. I'll have the same."

Susan reminded him, "We're eating meat tonight. You and I agreed that all that protein once a day is enough."

"Who writes these rules?" Dan threw up his arms.

"You've told me how pleased you are to be eating sensibly."

"But not breakfast and lunch. In my own office. You two and a guy selling candy bars, this is a conspiracy."

"It was my idea," Mary Alice firmly advised him. "Letting you kill yourself wouldn't be Christian."

Dan was now beside himself. "Letting a Jew eat what he enjoys isn't Christian? When did you become so religious?"

"Always have been. You just never asked."

"All along that was God you were speaking to on the phone?"

"Dan, what's your cholesterol level?" Susan asked.

"What difference does it make?"

"You said the doctor gave you a whole list of foods to eliminate from your diet."

"Enough!" Dan grumbled, extending his palm to halt her. "I'll eat this fodder for you. But I warn you, another lunch like this, and I start rooting for the prosecution."

In the afternoon session Huyton went a long way toward rehabilitating Kieffer as a witness. To Dan's regret, the chief medical examiner came off sounding like a man of stature, who had been harried by a shifty defense lawyer trying to confuse the issues and obscure the facts.

Gil Huyton pursued that same line in front of the cameras after resting his case. Dan reminded the reporters that the defendant's proof had yet to be presented.

The next morning Susan arrived early at the law firm and went straight to Dan's office. On top of notes he was reviewing about that day's witnesses, she dropped a copy of the *Herald*, folded to display the top of the front page. The banner headline read: "DA'S FEUD WITH POLICE CHIEF HAMPERING CITY'S CRIME FIGHT." Scott Feller had written the story, the first of a three-part series.

Susan wore a sly smile. "Nice coincidence, the story's timing, don't you think?"

"All we need is for the jurors to think you're using your newspaper to bully Huyton."

Her smile widened. "Jurors aren't allowed to read the paper."

"Believe that, and I've got house lots I'll sell you under Chesapeake Bay."

"Gil comes off looking like a combination fanatic and publicity hound—the Ayatollah Huyton. Turns out that right from the start, he tried to take over control of the whole law-enforcement apparatus. Pushed for his own man to get named police commissioner, but the mayor was new, too, and he didn't want to alienate black voters by firing a black police commissioner who'd taken office only a few months before he did. So, instead, Huyton acted as if the police were his errand boys. They'd like to lynch him. Now the mayor's trying to negotiate a peace pact."

"I thought you were reluctant to use the *Herald* to help your case."

"I can't hold back on publishing the news just because the coincidence is helpful, can I?"

Dan plumbed Susan's words and facial expression for frankness. Finally, he put the newspaper to one side. "I've got to prepare for today's witnesses."

She handed him the newspaper again. "You ought to prepare yourself for Huyton. I guarantee you he's going to be clawing at your throat."

Susan had accurately foreseen Gil Huyton's outrage. He and Dan spent the first fifteen minutes of the court day in Vellarde's chambers furiously arguing whether the *Herald*'s story was a deliberate attempt to influence Susan's case by maligning the district attorney's office in general and Huyton's credibility in particular.

Dan fought him for the high road. "I'm surprised to hear you suggest that the *Herald* should have censored a story just to make you look good. Would you have held off on a prosecution to make the *Herald* look good?"

"We're talking here about a bald-faced attempt to undermine the authority of the legally elected official who's trying that newspaper's publisher."

"What we're talking about is censorship. You're certainly quick to talk to the press when you think it will help you. My client refuses to allow the government to trample on her newspaper's First Amendment press freedoms."

Hands on hips, Huyton barked, "Absolute tommyrot!"

Dan burst into laughter and peered at his opponent with admiration. "Only old money could say 'absolute tommyrot' and feel comfortable doing it."

To Vellarde the matter was inconsequential. "I'll warn the jury again not to read the paper or listen to the news."

"Fat chance it'll help!" Dan muttered.

"What was that, Mr. Lazar?"

"Great, judge, just great."

As the jurors filed into the courtroom for the start of the defense's case, Dan watched for a glint of expectation in their eyes, always a sign to him that their minds were not yet made up. He saw it now in some, missed it in others. One of the latter, an unemployed plumbing supplies salesman, whom Ida Lawrence had been iffy about but Dan had opted to accept, began glancing impatiently at his wristwatch only seconds after taking his seat. Waiting to phone about a job interview? Boredom? Already decided?

Dan made a mental note to concentrate on the man for a day or two. And on the insurance company clerk, a woman who had nodded approvingly once or twice at Kieffer's answers.

Dan called as his first witness the assistant manager of the Dellwyne Supermarket. The man described Susan's visit that Saturday evening and identified the cash register receipt that proved she had purchased several items at 6:09 P.M. He was followed by the cashier who remembered checking out Susan's purchases and that Susan, although in a hurry, seemed to be pleasant and calm and chatted with her.

Huyton and Mara chose to pass up cross-examination. They were not disputing that Susan left Peter's house at ten minutes to six. If they were to convict her of murdering her husband, they would have to prove that the crime had occurred before that time.

Next to be called was Anton Desmarais, the waiter who served Peter and Amelia at Chez Henri the night before Peter's death. One of Dan's main victories at the pretrial conference had been Vellarde's ruling that the waiter could testify as to what he overheard. Although it was far less crucial after Amelia's reluctant admissions, Dan wanted her motives and the discrepancy from her statement to the police emphasized again to the jury.

Desmarais was a talkative, likable Frenchman in his early thirties, with a small mustache, who spoke English well. He did not hide that it had been a slow night and that eavesdropping had provided him with entertainment. He had served the couple before and knew who they were, which added to his interest.

Point by point, Dan drew out the waiter's detailed recollections of the couple's argument, including both Amelia's futile demand that Peter marry her and her assertion that he was involved with another woman. The jury laughed along with the witness at the very French irony that Amelia was sure her lover was still in love with his wife.

*   *   *

"Pretty good start," Dan proclaimed as he, Susan, and Cal settled into a banquette in the rear of Hi, Johnny's for lunch. Rick had gone to the pay phone. "What do you guys think?"

By tacit consent, the press now left them alone at lunch in return for Dan's willingness to be interviewed during adjournments.

"Desmarais put some more doubt in the jurors' heads," Cal said. "You could see them thinking, 'If Boelter was in love with his wife, why would she need to kill him? She would have gotten what she wanted, anyway.' "

"We've given them another suspect to focus on; that's the important thing," Dan said.

But then Cal expressed to Susan the full extent of the pessimism he was feeling. "It doesn't help, though, that Mrs. Hildreth remembered hearing you and Peter battling in the kitchen. Huyton can argue that Amelia was mistaken about Peter's feelings for you and you killed him during the quarrel."

"Maybe we could show that quarreling was normal for him," Dan suggested, "that it didn't indicate lack of love. He was a volatile guy. Unpredictable. There's no doubt about that. Maybe we put one of the servants on the stand or some employees at the paper who can confirm it."

Susan was concerned about the deeper problem. "But how do you show that I didn't end our argument by killing him?"

"That's what Mallory's testimony will prove . . . that either Peter died accidentally or, if it was homicide, it could just as easily have occurred after you drove away."

"If I'm acquitted," Susan unexpectedly inquired, "will Gil then try Amelia for the murder?"

"You can't be sure," Cal said. "Probably not. Too embarrassing for him to have to admit he tried the wrong person first."

"Good," Susan said.

Dan glanced questioningly at her.

"I just meant that I wouldn't want her to have to go through what I'm going through. Especially over a bastard like Peter."

The others at the table were silent until Dan threw out for discussion, "When should we put on Vinnie Briggs?"

He and Cal had gone back and forth about the right time to reveal to the jury that the anxious, angry union leader had gone to see Peter that afternoon.

Cal theorized, "He could have been the one Amelia heard picking up the phone in Peter's house, or else Peter was still alive then and answered the phone while meeting with Briggs.''

"Adding Briggs makes Susan only one suspect out of three," Dan said. "More doubt in the jury's mind. He could have seen Susan leave before six and then gone inside and killed Peter. Amelia testified the door was unlocked when she got there.''

The union leader's lack of an alibi for the time would provide Dan with a nice scenario to present to the jury in his summation. Amelia and Briggs were as likely as Susan to have killed Peter if Kieffer's time-of-death finding could be discredited.

"We hold off awhile and keep Briggs slotted in where we already have him," Dan decided. "We want to get Mallory on the stand early. That's always been our plan: to have Mallory refute Kieffer, who's their key witness.''

"And ours was Mallory," Rick said quietly.

Shock on his face, he stood regarding the three who were seated.

"What is it?" Dan asked him.

"I just called Mallory's office. You know, to tell him to fly down tomorrow, so we can prepare his testimony and put him on the next day.''

Dan sensed a scheduling conflict. "He promised to hold himself available.''

"It isn't that," Rick replied, clumsily shaking his head. "He's dead.''

The three on the banquette gaped at him, trying to make sense of his statement.

Rick went on. "He . . . he was killed in a car accident yesterday going home after work. No one knew to call us.''

Involuntarily, the three men shifted their gazes toward Susan. None of them could think of anything to say.

Her eyes had never left Rick's. She did not move. But after a while, her mouth slowly began to open into an O and her hands to rise up at the same slow pace to cover it and stifle the terror that was about to turn into a scream.

28

When court reconvened after lunch, Dan and Cal requested a conference in chambers with the prosecutors. Explaining what had happened, they asked Vellarde for a two-week adjournment to find a new expert witness to replace Alan Mallory, backtracked to a week, and were granted two days. The trial would resume on Friday, with other witnesses' testimony, which would give the defense a couple of extra days over the weekend to locate a new forensic pathologist.

"We need more time, judge," Dan argued. "Our entire case rests on the defects in Kieffer's autopsy findings. We have to find someone who can study the case thoroughly and has the credentials and guts to challenge him."

"I intend to keep this trial moving. Too long a recess, and the jurors' memories start to grow hazy. If you need more time to find your witness, put him on at the end of your case."

"Give us a break!" Dan blurted out.

Vellarde flashed a sharp look at him, but with something on his mind, did not reply. "Mr. Lazar, you'll recall I originally requested that you not represent the defendant—for a number of reasons, not the least of which were my doubts about your objectivity. I hope you can be open-minded about what I'm going to propose."

Vellarde leaned forward, resting his elbows on the wide mahogany desk, his gaze circling the group to convey that his proposal would involve them all. "Right now your client is facing anywhere from mandatory life down to ten years, depending on whether the jury finds she acted with malicious intent. The prosecution has presented evidence to prove she coldly decided to murder her husband during the moments after they had sexual intercourse and he rejected her reconciliation efforts. They contend she might have been planning it all along—even brought some kind of club with her.''

He paused to drive home the point before laying out an alternative. ''But the jury would also be justified in deciding that her action *lacked* that necessary premeditation. In a sudden out-of-control rage, she might have grabbed something—a pot, a pan—and struck him. But in either case, we're not talking about a hardened criminal here.''

Vellarde slowly cast his eyes around the semicircle before him. ''I'd like you all to consider an arranged plea of manslaughter. The sentence would be shorter, and I don't think it's out of line with the evidence. The state would save considerable time and money.''

''Involuntary manslaughter, of course,'' Cal quickly said, hoping to influence Vellarde's thinking.

''Voluntary,'' Vellarde differed, shaking his head. ''A fit of rage, but she definitely intended to kill him.''

Mara was appalled. ''Voluntary manslaughter could get her out of prison in two and a half years! For killing her husband! Your Honor, we're asking she get life.''

Huyton had his own concern. ''We promised the blacks in this city that justice would be fair and equal, and that we wouldn't favor rich, white people like Susan Boelter. It's important to make an example of her and not to cave in.''

''Important for what?'' Dan caustically inquired. ''Your career?''

''I resent that, Lazar.''

''Gentlemen!'' Vellarde berated them.

His tone lowered as his attention settled on Dan. ''A five-year sentence without parole. That's the best I'll do. Mr. Huyton?''

''No promises,'' Huyton replied, ''but we'll think about it.''

That sounded conciliatory enough to Vellarde for him to direct his attention to Dan. ''Talk to your client about it. If I were making a guess about how it's going in the minds of the jurors so far, I'd say it doesn't look promising for her.''

''Do you intend to put her on the stand?'' Huyton asked Dan.

''We haven't decided,'' Dan replied.

Susan herself might insist otherwise, but he would recommend she not take the stand to tell her version of the story—and be exposed to Huyton's dogged attack on cross—unless all else had failed to undermine the prosecution's case.

"I won't make it easy on her," the district attorney scrupulously stressed.

"I already heard you give that speech on TV."

Vellarde's glare halted the spat. Mara addressed him.

"We intend to put Dr. Kieffer back on as a rebuttal witness, Your Honor. You'll remember, the defense disputed his time-of-death finding on the very narrow grounds that he wasn't aware of the exact ambient temperature in the cellar where the victim was found. Just to be sure, he went back there and took careful measurements. He's prepared to testify that his original calculations were absolutely accurate."

"Now?" Dan rejoined, directing himself to Vellarde. "After we undermined his credibility? You can't let him rehabilitate himself after the fact with some phony mumbo jumbo he throws into that voodoo formula of his."

Vellarde's expression hardened and his voice rose. "Let me be the judge of what I can and can't do, Mr. Lazar. I see nothing wrong with the chief medical examiner's clarifying his testimony. We're trying to get at the truth here." He assured the prosecutors, "You can put him on."

Dan angrily jumped to his feet. "It would help if we had only the prosecution against us."

"That's enough, Mr. Lazar!" Vellarde replied between teeth set in anger. "I'll ignore the outburst this time only because I expect you're so close to your client, you're getting carried away. Exactly what I was leery of. But I warn you: Consider here what's best for her—not what will make you look good. If she agrees to voluntary manslaughter, I'll see what I can do to convince the prosecution."

Susan was waiting for Dan on the leather sofa in his office. He gave her the bad news that Vellarde had granted them only a two-day adjournment to find a forensic pathologist who would testify on her behalf.

"What about Armbruster?" Susan inquired. "He's Kieffer's deputy. Isn't he a top forensic pathologist? He could testify for us."

Dan had already phoned Armbruster. "He won't risk refuting his boss unless he's sure that Kieffer is down for the count. And for that, we needed Mallory."

Susan emitted a long, sad sigh. "It looks pretty bleak, doesn't it?"

"Going into the trial, we could count on testimony both from Ralston, who'd confirm Peter was alive when you left, and from Mallory, who'd discredit Kieffer. We could have lost either one of them and still been in good shape."

"But not both."

"Not both."

Dan purposely injected optimism into his voice. "All right then, let's put the responsibility back on Peter himself for his death. We have the autopsy report's high blood-alcohol reading to establish that he was drunk enough to have lost his balance and fallen down the stairs. We can also get his golfing buddies on the stand to state that he started drinking heavily at lunch. And we have Karen's recollection that he was drunk, which the jury may or not believe after the way Huyton undermined her credibility. But the best evidence we have is the videotape. I'd like to show it to them, Susan. They could see with their own eyes how drunk he was that day. He's holding a glass of scotch all through it. It's very convincing."

"Would Karen have to go back on the stand?"

"Yes . . . to say she shot the tape and when . . . and to describe what we're seeing."

"Then the answer is no. Having you remind the jury about all that alcohol in Peter's bloodstream should be enough. I wouldn't have put her through that ordeal the first time if Huyton hadn't subpoenaed her. A second time would be devastating."

"That tape could be important in acquitting you."

"Dan, you didn't see her the night after she testified. She was a zombie, staring at nothing, tears running down her cheeks. She's still sunk in a terrible depression."

"Imagine how much more depressed she'll be if her mother goes to prison for twenty years. We need to show that videotape and have her explain what's happening."

Susan answered fiercely, "I won't put her through that again!"

"All right," Dan finally said, relenting, "we'll do without the video-tape."

"But you aren't happy about it."

"I wish right now you'd think more about yourself and your own problem." Dubiously, he suggested, "We could put Ben Ralston on the stand. There's always the chance the jury'd believe him."

"Things really are bad, aren't they?" Her voice was fearful.

"I've seen worse," he replied.

"But you've seen a whole lot better."

"You want me to be straight with you. Okay, things look lousy. The prosecution's got the 'eminent' chief medical examiner declaring that Peter was murdered, and that it happened when you were the only one in the house. He's even going back on the stand to say he measured the basement's air and floor temperature and hasn't changed his mind about when Peter died. I've got no scientific way of refuting that."

"No hard evidence."

"Right. No witnesses. Nothing. Just a lot of common sense that tells me a drunk lying at the bottom of a ten-foot-high stairway killed himself by accident."

"Well, then?"

"Vellarde doesn't see it that way and doesn't think the jury is buying it, either. He wants me to talk to you about pleading guilty to voluntary manslaughter."

"What exactly does that mean, 'voluntary manslaughter'?"

"To be exact, that you struck Peter while 'acting under a sudden and intense passion.' "

Despite her anxiety, Susan threw her head back and laughed full out. "Oh, how wonderfully apt! A sudden and intense passion. It always comes back to passion, doesn't it? We put such stock in intellect, but in the end, it's always our animal urges that do us in."

Dan brought her back to earth. "Shorter sentence."

"How many years?"

"Five. You'd have to serve all of it."

"Five years of my life! Karen would be a woman, and I'd be a criminal in the eyes of the world."

"The alternative could be mandatory life in prison."

"Dan, I won't plead guilty to a crime I didn't commit. You don't really believe I'm guilty, do you?"

"No."

"And you aren't giving up?"

He gripped her shoulders. He wanted to reassure her. "I love you, and God help me, I'm not going to lose you. I don't know how, but somehow or other I'll get you out of this."

"And if you don't," she replied, the fear back in her voice, "I could be in prison the rest of my life."

She was staring across the room at a small brass statue Dan kept atop a cabinet. It depicted Justice in the traditional pose: as a woman holding a scale in one hand and a sword in the other, blindfolded.

By Thursday evening the defense lawyers had located two forensic pathologists who had agreed to look at the material being sent to them air express. The lawyers also had convinced a retired professor in California with whom they had already spoken several times to review the material and reconsider. None of the people sounded eager to participate.

Dan did not leave his office until well after eleven o'clock at night. He had not eaten supper, but food was the least of his concerns. With a lot to think about, he decided to walk home instead of taking a taxi. After a block or two, despite wearing a suit and tie, he broke into a trot, hoping to muster the energy to jog the rest of the way, but his knees hurt, and he was too discouraged. Only months before, he might have welcomed the opportunity to slip into a mindless run to nowhere. But too much was now at stake, and he had too little to fight back with. Everything solid had crumbled.

"Someone waiting for you, Mr. Lazar," the doorman said as he pulled open the lobby door.

Scott Feller was seated on a bench in the lobby. He stood as Dan approached.

"I called your office. Someone said you'd just left for home."

Dan nodded. He had left Rick there, still trying to reach potential expert witnesses by phone.

"I have something for you," the reporter said.

"You could have left it with the doorman."

"I didn't want to take the chance."

Feller's arms were wrapped around a thick manila envelope. He thrust it at Dan.

"What's inside?" Dan asked.

"You'll see. A cop gave it to me. He thinks you should have it."

"Part of your exposé."

Feller nodded. Both men knew that by choosing to have the package delivered by a reporter, who was protected by the state Shield Law from revealing his sources, the anonymous cop was cleverly insulating himself from discovery. The source could be anyone on the force from Stallworth or Bascombe up to the commissioner. No one would ever find out.

Dan warned, "I don't intend to be used by the police in a vendetta to make Huyton look bad."

"Read it," Feller repeated, as he moved off. "Carefully."

Only when he was upstairs and alone in his apartment living room did Dan open the envelope.

Dan recognized the contents: Peter's phone log. His spirits plummeted. He had already examined the list of phone calls made from Peter's house.

But this log was much thicker. It listed nearly six months of calls— nearly the entire first half of the year—instead of only calls made during one week in June, the last week of Peter's life. That meant it listed both the calls made from Peter's new number at the Walker Drive house in Chestnut Hill and those from his old number at the Albemarle Street estate in Dellwyne.

"Carefully," Feller had urged him, and Dan stared at the thick sheaf of papers. He realized then what else was different about the log. The one the prosecution had submitted into evidence during the trial, like the one it had delivered to him, had been a photocopy; this one was a printed original.

With little enthusiasm, he dropped into an armchair and began to skim the calls made during the final day of Peter's life. If some cop thought this list would be a big revelation, then that character did not know much about the pretrial discovery process.

Suddenly Dan was brought up short. At 6:06 P.M. on Saturday, June sixth, a call was made from Peter's phone. That final call had not appeared on the shorter version of the log.

"Yes!" Dan yelled in jubilation. "Yes!"

Assuming Amelia and Briggs were telling the truth, only Peter could have made that call. That meant he had to be alive at 6:06 P.M., a time when Susan was purchasing groceries fourteen minutes away. If he wasn't alive, that had to mean that Amelia or Briggs made the call and lied about the time they arrived at Peter's.

Dan had the proof he needed that Susan was innocent.

His first impulse was to phone her, but the manipulation of the phone log had made him wary. For all he knew, her line was being tapped. Now, every sort of skullduggery seemed possible. Instead he phoned Rick at the office, telling him only not to leave. He was taking a taxi back. They might have to work most of the night.

Waiting for the elevator, Dan reviewed the possibilities. The most likely was what he had always believed, that Peter Boelter had simply tripped and fallen down the stairs some time after using the phone at 6:06 P.M. An accident. Even if Amelia and Peter did have sex just before then, that did not mean she killed him. Either way, however, Dan knew Susan was safe.

But he now knew much more than that. He had recognized that last telephone number Peter Boelter called.

Early the next morning Susan was adding sweetener to her coffee when her phone rang.

"You were right!" Dan exclaimed the instant he heard her greeting. "That feeling you had about photocopies!"

He wished he could reach through the phone and hug her. He had grown so used to the document exchanges between prosecution and defense that he had discounted what her intuition was telling her. Still afraid to reveal anything over the phone, he said only, "The worry is over. We've got the proof we need."

"Oh, God! You aren't joking. You're sure?"

"I'm positive."

"Dan, I love you."

"Sounds wonderful." He had another reason for the call. "Susan, did you ever tell anyone that Feeney was still under suspicion and that I was tailing him? It would have been around the middle of August."

"Wait a minute, let me get my appointment book."

A minute later she was back on the line. "I remember now. It came up when Midge and I were having a budget meeting with Fred Moore. Fred brought it up."

"In what way?"

"We were going over editorial-side expenses, and Midge questioned what it was costing for Scott Feller's investigation. Scott hadn't worked on another story in weeks. Fred explained that matters were beginning to break. Just so we'd understand how big the story might become, he told us in confidence that Tim Feeney was still a suspect as the Phantom Rapist and was being followed by the police."

She hesitated. "Did he do something wrong?"

"Susan, I can't go into the details on the phone."

"Can we meet in your office?"

"I've got a lot of things to do before court opens this morning. One of them is to see Vellarde."

"Dan, can't you tell me what's happening?"

"In the courtroom."

29

The large man raised his right hand to take the oath. An unexpected witness, Irwin Hollings was a manager at the telephone company.

Dan lifted the phone log out of his briefcase and had Hollings identify it for the court.

Vexed, Huyton objected. "We already have the phone log in evidence, Your Honor."

"Then you won't mind another copy, Mr. Huyton," Vellarde sharply replied.

Confounded by the unexpected force of the rebuff, Huyton sank back into his seat.

"What period does the log cover?" Dan asked, handing it to Hollings to examine.

"From the beginning of the year through the first week of June . . . almost the first six months of the year. In late January Mr. Boelter had us transfer the phone from his house in Dellwyne to a new location on Walker Drive in Chestnut Hill. Calls from both phone locations are contained in the log."

"That meant a new number when he moved, right? From one with a Dellwyne exchange to one in Chestnut Hill?"

"That's right."

"Thank you. Would you please tell the court what each entry sets forth?"

"The number that was called, the date and time the call was made, and the length of time the caller was on the line."

"Even local calls?"

"Yes. Mr. Boelter's phone bills were sent directly to the *Herald,* so we used the same billing system we do for the company's offices. We detail every call, regardless of whether it's local or long-distance."

"Thank you. No further questions. Your Honor, I move that this phone log I've marked Defense Exhibit Eleven be accepted into evidence."

Huyton declined to question. As far as he could tell, this new exhibit was a waste of time.

Dan's gaze slowly slid downward from Huyton. "As my next witness, Your Honor," he announced, "I call Mara Szarek."

Shocked, Huyton rushed to object. "I don't know what Mr. Lazar is driving at, but Your Honor knows an attorney at a trial can't be a witness. This is totally out of—"

Vellarde cut him off. "Overruled."

"Your Honor," Huyton persisted, moving around the table as he spoke, "my co-counsel can't possibly provide any testimony that bears on the case. I request an offer of proof from defense counsel as to—"

Vellarde interrupted again. "Please be seated."

"But, judge—"

Vellarde slammed down the gavel to cut Huyton off and, ignoring him, leaned forward.

"As of now, Ms. Szarek, you're no longer on the prosecution team. Take the stand."

The spectators' murmur crackled like radio static during a thunderstorm. Vellarde's glare silenced it and then shifted back to Mara, daring her to decline.

Huyton's bewildered glance tried to catch Mara's as she rose, but she appeared to be oblivious of him and her surroundings. She drifted slowly toward the witness chair like an apparition, as if all substance had left her. The oath was taken with the merest movement of her lips.

Dan held the phone log out to her. "I direct your attention to the final phone call made on the day Peter Boelter died. What time does it state that the call was made?"

"Six minutes after six in the evening."

Another gasp from the crowded courtroom, a sharp intake of breath.

"That would be after the defendant left the house, would it not?" Dan asked to obtain clarification.

"Yes," Mara answered.

"Do you recognize the phone number that was called?"

"Yes."

"Whose number is it, Ms. Szarek?"

"It's mine."

The spectators' reaction surged up as a wave of startled crackling.

"Now!" Dan's voice boomed out the word like the shattering roll of a firing squad. "I show you the copy of the phone log entered into evidence some time ago by the prosecution as People's Exhibit Forty-one and direct your attention to that same page. Do you see that same phone call listed?"

"No . . . no, I don't."

"Would we be correct in assuming that you covered over that last phone number—using correction fluid or a strip of paper, something—so that photocopies of the log would not display that particular phone call?"

Mara was gathering her strength. "That doesn't make any sense. I wouldn't have done anything like that. I must have received an incorrect copy from the phone company."

"For your own good, Mara," Dan quietly warned, "don't add perjury to suppressing evidence and tampering with a public document. I'm sure your office is going to be thoroughly searched before you're allowed back into it."

Mara glanced up plaintively at Vellarde and then at Dan. But every door was closed to her.

"I altered the phone log," she confessed. "I covered over the call to my house."

"And delivered to defense counsel only the portion that reported calls for the first week of June, the week before Peter Boelter's death, correct?"

"Yes." She tried to smile at Dan. "I didn't think the earlier calls were significant."

"Please turn your attention to calls made on January tenth, at the beginning of the year."

Dan flipped the pages back for her and pointed to the place where she should direct her attention.

"That's also your phone number listed there, isn't it?"

"Yes."

She did not bother to glance down. The spectators were utterly silent, transfixed.

"In fact," he continued, "that was only the first of numerous calls that Peter Boelter made to your home . . . dozens of calls could be found here that were made to you, isn't that so?"

"Yes."

"What prompted the first phone call?"

Too much was coming out too quickly for her to hide behind lies or evasion or claims against self-incrimination. Only candor could save what little of her life might still be salvageable.

"I was still working for your law firm," she said, "and you had just taken on Ricardo Montano's defense, but you were away on vacation at the time, remember? So I did a lot of the early work and represented Montano at the preliminary arraignment. Peter and a reporter for the *Herald* showed up in court."

"That was on the tenth of January?"

"Yes. Peter said his newspaper was interested in the case. He and I went to a coffee shop and talked for a long while. He phoned me at home that night."

"Didn't it occur to you that he was attempting to extract confidential information from you about the Montano case for his newspaper?"

She shrugged. "After a while it did, but by then I didn't care. I was in love with him."

That was a time when Dan had been dizzy with love for her, certain that she loved him also. His tone was as cold and cut as perilously as a knife blade.

"Would you agree that Peter Boelter was a man whom women invariably found attractive—charming, good-looking, wealthy, powerful?"

"Yes."

"And you, as I recall, are a woman who seizes such opportunities. You were privy to a lot of information few others had about the case. So, at a time when I was worried that adverse material about our defense was turning up in the *Herald,* he was getting it from you?"

"Some, probably."

"I assume you wasted no time in commencing an affair with him. What day precisely?"

"I'm not sure. A week or so later. I made dinner for the two of us at my apartment."

"The night of my birthday, wasn't it? . . . when you turned up hours late, claiming you'd been stuck in York County working out a plea bargain on another case?"

"Yes," she mumbled.

"And your affair with Peter Boelter continued up until his death?"

"Yes."

"Am I right in assuming that Peter Boelter was the one who first introduced you to his good friend the district attorney?"

"Yes."

"And did you advise your employer, the district attorney here, that you were secretly having an affair with the most powerful newspaper publisher in the state?"

"No. I . . . I couldn't let him know about that."

Too dazed to react, Gil Huyton appeared carved out of stone. Dan had promised not to disclose Huyton's affair with Mara. He saw no need to break that promise. He himself knew all too well the seductiveness of Mara's allure and how deeply she could burrow it into a man. She had kept a lusting Gil Huyton on a hook to advance her career, while pursuing her love affair with Peter Boelter.

"Peter Boelter kept no servants on duty at his house on the weekends. I take it the reason was because you spent many nights there and wanted that kept secret."

"Yes."

Dan's gaze refused to allow Mara's to escape from his as he elicited the logical conclusions for the jury. "And after Peter Boelter's death, so no one would suspect you'd been having an affair with him, you erased your phone number from the log and hid all but that one week in June?"

"May I speak," she said quietly, her gaze now beseeching Dan's. "Just in my own words."

"Yes."

"Everything you've said is true. Peter and I were lovers. He was as in love with me as I was with him, I know he was. We had to keep it secret until his divorce came through. But he told me a dozen times that he wanted to marry me. That's what we were waiting for."

"You were the other woman Amelia Boelter suspected he was seeing."

"I didn't care about her. We laughed about her. Peter needed her vote, but he could never love her. He needed a woman as strong as he was." She zestfully smiled at the recollection. "We were a match."

Dan flung back a dollop of reality. "By that, I take you to mean he had money, power, and prominence, and you were greedy for all three?"

Mara bit her lip. "I admit that last phone number on the log is mine, but I never spoke to Peter on the day he died. I wasn't even back in the city yet. I had been in San Francisco for almost a week at a criminal justice conference. I flew out there the previous Sunday, the last day of May. Because I never knew when I'd be in my hotel room, I would phone Peter."

"Which explains why the log shows no phone calls to you all week."

"Exactly. When the conference ended on Saturday, I took a plane back here and arrived at my apartment very late at night. There were a few messages on my answering machine, but none from Peter. There was a hang-up, too, I think, but it could have been from anyone. The next morning, when I picked up the paper outside my door, I learned Peter was dead."

Her face crumpled, the emotion as vivid as that day. "For a moment I thought Peter might have been playing a joke on me, that he had run up a few copies of the paper as a hoax. That was his sort of humor. He could do something that would give you a heart attack and then laugh that you had fallen for it. I ran to the radio. But the news was the same. He was dead. I loved him so much, and he was dead.''

Her voice and expression hardened into ferocity. ''I vowed to make his killer pay. A life for a life. Within days I was convinced his wife had murdered him. Everything pointed to her. There wasn't a speck of doubt in my mind.''

The two women stared at each other, the wife facing murder charges and the mistress on the witness stand. Hatred seared the air between them. Dan recalled that the most savage antipathy toward Susan had always come not from Huyton, but from Mara.

Dan pushed her further. ''The problem was that when the phone log arrived from the phone company, you suddenly noticed the last call from Peter's house had been made to you. Isn't that so?''

''That was incomprehensible, a colossal mistake. Susan Boelter had killed her husband because she couldn't keep him, because he loved me and not her. She had destroyed my life. Yet she'd go free because of a mistake on the phone log.''

''And your career would be ruined,'' Dan reminded her and the jury.

''So, I whited out that last listing with correction fluid and ran off copies on the photocopier.''

His face red with anger, Vellarde interrupted.

''I've heard enough, Ms. Szarek! The prosecution owes a sacred obligation to provide the defendant with all the evidence that might bear on her innocence. By concealing a call made from Peter Boelter's phone after the defendant left his house, you knowingly prejudiced her case and put her through a harrowing ordeal.''

Vellarde now addressed the entire courtroom. ''The evidence is overwhelming that Peter Boelter made that last call, probably to learn whether his lover, Mara Szarek, had returned home yet from San Francisco. He hung up after her machine, rather than Mara herself, answered. His death a short while later was most probably an accident—but it certainly occurred after six-oh-six, when the defendant, Susan Boelter, was miles away purchasing items at a supermarket. And I so find!''

His irate glance focused again on Mara. ''Ms. Szarek, I'm referring the transcript of the trial to the state attorney general to determine whether criminal charges against you are in order.''

Finally, Vellarde's gaze shifted to the defense table. ''Mrs. Boelter, you should never have been put through this. My most profound apologies for the anguish and disgrace the state has wrongly inflicted on you.''

''Thank you,'' she quietly said.

He allowed a small smile to crease his austere face. "I imagine, though, that the news of your acquittal will get prominent front-page display in the *Herald.*"

His gavel snapped down a moment after he declared, "Case dismissed."

Susan threw her arms around Dan and ardently kissed him. People rushed over, hands slapped the couple on the back, voices clamored for statements, but the man and woman might have been alone on an island for all their notice of the others.

"Thank you, Dan," she whispered, her face against his. "You did it, you saved my life. Thank you."

"I love you."

"I love you, too. You saved me. You saved my life. You were wonderful. We have to celebrate."

"Tonight," he happily replied. "I have a few things to take care of right now."

She kissed him again. Then they turned to Cal and Rick and to the well-wishers and reporters.

"I heard it went all right," Stallworth said with a smile as he and Kate Bascombe stepped up to greet Dan on the sidewalk outside the Herald Building. "Congratulations."

"I have a feeling I have one of you to thank—or someone on the force for that phone log," Dan said, then asked, "He upstairs?"

Bascombe nodded, and handed Dan several pages to read.

After a couple of minutes Dan grimly looked up. "That's it, then. Let's go see him."

The three visitors moved through the reception area without responding to the secretary's queries. She tried to stop them, but Stallworth flashed his badge and kept moving.

Midge Boelter was sitting at his desk, with Fred Moore across from him on the visitor's side.

"That's great news about Susan," Midge said to Dan. "Fred just came up to tell me."

Moore stood up to shake Dan's hand. "My God, we were all worried sick. We knew it had to be a frame-up. Congratulations."

"Thanks," Dan replied.

"Can I get someone up here to interview you—your comments on what happened? We'll do a big sidebar to the main story."

"Not right now, Fred. Will you leave us alone with Midge?"

"Oh, sure."

Dan closed the door behind Moore and introduced the two detectives to Midge Boelter.

"You guys look serious," Midge said. "Do we have a problem with someone at the *Herald*?"

"Yes."

Dan took the armchair directly across from Midge, the detectives the two chairs flanking his. The first time he met Midge Boelter, he had viewed him as a lesser copy of his brother, subsidiary in every way. Now, without Peter to compare him to, Dan saw him as almost a smudge, a man lacking any personality of his own at all. But he fathomed that deep beneath the formless surface, strange urges boiled furiously from vents and fissures, nourishing creatures of dreadful anatomy.

"I want to show you something," Dan said, extracting the thick phone log from his briefcase. He handed it, open to a rear page, to Midge, and explained what it was.

"Mr. Boelter—" Stallworth started to say, only to be interrupted by a nervous Midge.

"Call me Midge, officer, please. Everybody does." Midge's anxiety made his effort to emulate the ingratiation Peter naturally affected sound servile.

"Midge," Stallworth agreed with a nod. "Are you familiar with a man named Timothy K. Feeney?"

Startled, Midge turned wary. "I know Feeney. He was a delivery driver for the *Herald*."

Dan pointed to the phone log. "Look at January eighth. Two phone calls were made from Peter's home to yours that night. The first one lasted almost half an hour. The second lasted three minutes."

"Yes," Midge confirmed.

"But right in between those two calls, your brother made another one . . . to Tim Feeney's number."

"I remember that," Midge said, appearing relieved. "Peter was really hot to play up the Cassy Cowell case. I mean it really energized him. He kept saying that getting the *Herald* out front on this story could really boost circulation. He learned that Feeney's truck route went past where she was murdered and that Feeney saw the killer running away . . . you know, the man the police were questioning, that Montano. Peter phoned Feeney to convince him to go to the police."

Stallworth stepped in. "Feeney says different. Feeney says your brother called him to offer him money to identify Ricardo Montano as the killer. We were interrogating Montano at the time, and somehow his name and picture suddenly showed up in the *Herald*."

Faced with the evidence of Peter Boelter's phone call to him before he went to the police, Feeney had finally cracked; he had confessed that the Boelters bribed him to make the identification. Now the detectives were here to get Midge's version.

The newspaper executive glanced from one face to the next, weighing his options.

"I remember now." The worried attempt at an ingratiating smile reappeared. "Peter told me to give Feeney five thousand dollars as a bonus. He said Feeney wasn't really eager to come forward and get involved without being paid for it."

"And this payment was supposed to be kept secret?" Bascombe asked.

"Except for a hundred dollars we gave him in the newsroom. A kind of award."

"For good citizenship," Dan sardonically explained.

"No one was supposed to know about the rest of the money," Midge said. "Peter thought it might look like Feeney wasn't doing it as his civic duty."

"Did you personally deliver the five thousand dollars to him?" Stallworth asked.

"Well, yes, for Peter."

"And you delivered additional money to him, right?"

"Yes."

"When?"

"Feeney came up to my office . . . I guess it was two days before he testified against Montano. He said he wouldn't testify unless we paid him more. I went to Peter's office to tell him. Peter said the *Herald* would get a terrible black eye if Feeney pulled out now because of all the publicity about his association with the *Herald*. He told me to pay the guy another five thousand dollars."

"And you did?"

"We didn't have that kind of money in petty cash. I cashed several smaller checks that day at the bank. Early the next morning he came to my office, and I gave him the money."

"The day before he testified?" Dan wanted to know.

"Yes."

Dan's voice rose. "Did you consider it a bribe?"

"Peter said it was just another installment on our good citizenship award. Look, this was all really Peter's doing. I didn't know what was happening. I just got the money for him because Peter told me to." Midge lowered his gaze. "I'm sorry, Dan."

"Oh, you mean because I was charged with a bribe you gave? Think nothing of it." Dan's tone flayed the other man with scorn. "I can see how someone else's getting arrested for something you did could slip your mind like that . . . even though we all had dinner together that night.''

"Peter assured me that those were two different payments," Midge replied.

Dan ignored the excuse. "You continued to make payments to Tim Feeney, didn't you?"

"Yes."

"How much?"

"Twenty-five hundred dollars twice a month."

"Was he employed by the *Herald* at that time?"

"No." Midge glanced away from Dan to give his answers, then forced his gaze back for the questions. "Peter was worried. Feeney was threatening to reveal their arrangement. Peter thought that would be messy. Especially at a time when he was negotiating to sell the paper."

Midge explained that he arranged to meet Feeney on his way to work on the first and third Monday of each month and give him an envelope with the cash. When he learned from Moore at their budget meeting with Susan that the police had Feeney under surveillance, he stopped the payments.

"Besides, Peter was dead," Midge asserted. "He was the one who'd made that deal with Feeney. I didn't want any more to do with it. I figured Feeney would be hurt worse than the *Herald* if he tried to say anything."

Dan stared at Midge for a long while before he finally spoke. "This story you're telling us, Midge, that isn't the way it happened, is it?"

Midge was startled. "Sure. What do you mean?"

"It wasn't your brother who originally located Feeney, was it? Feeney came to you himself—before those calls were ever made on the night of January eighth."

"No. Why would he come to me?" Midge seemed terrified.

Stallworth answered him. "Because Tim Feeney didn't see Ricardo Montano come out of the alley on Twelfth Street that night. He saw someone else . . . someone he'd seen several times before at work, so he didn't need much light to recognize him. The man he saw was you."

Midge remained silent, his eyes white circles of fear.

Bascombe interjected. "Your apartment is just a few blocks from the parking lot and the alley where all three women were found."

"It wasn't anything like that," Midge bleated.

Dan hammered away. "Feeney demanded that you pay him blackmail money to keep quiet about seeing you come out of the alley. You ran to Peter. Peter thought it over. The police were about to release Montano for lack of evidence. So when he called Feeney from his house to agree to the blackmail, part of the deal he made was that Feeney had to go to the police and claim he saw Montano, not you, coming out of the alley. That way you'd be safe.''

"No! Jesus, no!" Midge implored them to believe. "It was Montano. I swear it.''

"How do you know?"

Midge's face dropped into his hands. "I saw him do it.''

"You saw him?" Stallworth incredulously repeated.

Midge raised his head. "I was in the alley that night."

"Why didn't you come to the police?" asked Bascombe.

"I couldn't, that's all. So we got Feeney to go instead. And you're right, we paid him. But after the first time, he kept coming back for more money, saying he'd tell the police we bribed him to testify. It was never enough.''

"Why did you pay him in the first place?"

"We didn't want a killer to go free. I figured one of our trucks must have gone by around that time of night, and sure enough, Feeney's had. So we paid him the five thousand dollars to go to the police and say he saw Montano come out of the alley." Midge's face contorted. "If you could have seen what Montano did to her . . .''

"Tell us," Bascombe urged.

"You know the way the alleys crisscross in that block? I was in a doorway, in the shadows. Montano was in a hurry and went right by without seeing me. Cassy Cowell was coming from the other direction. He wouldn't let her pass. He started to harass her, you know, to try to kiss her and hug her. She turned to go back the way she'd come, but in a flash, almost like some kind of commando, he swung his arm around her neck from behind and threw her to the ground. He kept that arm pressed down on her throat with all his weight, so she couldn't scream, even when he smashed her hard in the face two or three times . . . and then he raped her. Then he pulled her body behind a dumpster and ran out of the alley. The whole thing took maybe two, three minutes.''

"That's how we reconstructed it," Stallworth confirmed.

"I went over there, but she was dead."

"You son of a bitch!" Bascombe raged. "If you'd tried to stop him . . . or just come forward when it happened—before he killed again."

"I couldn't. I just couldn't."

"No one would have given a damn that you were with a hooker," Dan declared.

Anguish harrowed Midge. "I saw Montano. I recognized his photo in the paper. There wasn't any doubt. Feeney wouldn't have been lying that Montano was the killer. I . . . I just couldn't come out and say anything myself.''

Awareness dawned on Stallworth's features. "You were with a hooker, all right, but it wasn't one of the girls, was it, Midge? You're a goddamn chickenhawk. You were nailing one of those pretty little teenaged boys who hang around there, right? That's why you couldn't risk your precious family reputation by coming forward to ID Montano yourself."

"You'd have wanted to know why I was in the alley and who was with me. It would have come out."

"So you just stood there in the shadows, with this kid's mouth clamped to your cock, watching a woman get murdered. Like a sick stage show."

"Look," Midge tried to explain, "I'd had too much to drink that night. I get like that sometimes when I've been drinking, but that's nobody else's business. Peter and I didn't have to pay Feeney to name Montano. We could have just forgotten the whole thing. But we wanted to stop Montano. We were doing a public service. It was our duty."

"You were trying to protect *yourself*!" Dan shouted at him with contempt. "That's why you and Peter were pushing so hard for Montano's conviction. You wanted to stop the investigation before the cops got around to interviewing the male hooker you'd bought that night."

Dan quickly spun out the rest of the scenario. Peter might even have helped convince his friend the district attorney to bring the charges against Montano and used his newspaper to influence the outcome. He attended Montano's preliminary arraignment to make sure nothing went wrong and seized the opportunity to become friendly with Montano's lawyer, first with Mara and then with Dan, who took over for her. He became Mara's lover, and after he helped induce Huyton to make her his deputy, maybe even induced her to cancel an investigation that might have incriminated Midge. He might even have loved her, as she wanted to believe.

Dan grimaced. "The fine, upstanding Boelters! This fiancée of yours, she's just a cover."

"Look, I'm trying with her, you know. She's a nice woman. I'm really trying. But it's hard."

"Midge, no one would have cared that you're gay."

"I'm not gay!" Midge snapped. "It's just that sometimes I get these . . . these urges. They're wrong! How would it look if people knew?"

For an instant Dan glimpsed the little boy whose mother had leaped naked out of her bed, yelling at him like a Fury, and crushed the bird he had brought her.

"Michael Boelter," Stallworth declared, "you're under arrest. For bribing Feeney, as starters."

He began to read Midge his rights.

Suddenly the detective remembered, "Montano's still out there."

He turned to Dan. "Now that you know Montano's a dangerous killer, for God's sake tell us where he is. You can do that now, can't you?"

"If I knew where. But I don't. He's on the run and could be anywhere."

Stallworth's hands dropped helplessly to his sides. "Christ! Who knows how many more women he'll attack? And we had him in our hands. We fucking had him."

"You told me yourself you didn't have a strong case," Dan argued. "Feeney was lying. It was perjury."

"Who the fuck cares? Only you. Montano's a serial killer and a rapist. But you had to figure out a way to free that piece of shit. Some justice!"

Dan had always thought of himself as being one step ahead of everyone else. Now his cleverness and his blind, maybe even arrogant, pride in his professional integrity had killed one woman and injured another. Somewhere among the millions of people in America's cities, a killer was hiding. Some night when Ricardo Montano got high enough and angry enough, he would attack again. For the first time in Dan's life, he was ashamed of what his skill had caused.

30

Lunch at Hi, Johnny's was intended to be an exuberant affair. Despite his distress, Dan tried to enter into the mood.

Cal insisted that he eat a walnut raisin sourdough roll in honor of his starting a new life after having been cleared of all suspicion of bribery. To tease Mary Alice, he ordered the deluxe bacon double cheeseburger with an egg on it and fries on the side, but Johnny brought him the chef's salad, to which he had surreptitiously pointed on the menu.

As they ate and reflected on the morning's astonishing events, Cal suddenly glanced up at Dan with a sly smile of relief. "That was a close one, partner."

Dan nodded in agreement. "I've been thinking how Mara worked everything out so she'd marry Peter and have it all—money, power, position. All the things she accused Susan of killing him for."

Mary Alice, who had always disliked Mara, cynically remarked, "And then he fell down the stairs . . . which saved him from a fate worse than death."

"Fate's a good word," Dan agreed. "Mara just couldn't believe that fate could take Peter from her. She grew up in a country of conspiracies, where the authorities staged accidents to cover up assassinations. She had to blame Peter's death on someone."

Rick continued the reasoning. "And who was a more likely culprit than Susan, the wife she had despised for months, who was standing

337

between her and the marriage she wanted? So when she saw a phone call on the log that would have cleared Susan, she erased it."

That comment reminded Cal. "You checked her flight back from San Francisco?"

Rick nodded. "Her plane didn't land in Philadelphia till late that night. The airline even pulled up the ticket voucher for me to make sure she was on it."

"You know what's crazy?" Dan said. "John Boelter wanted to establish a dynasty. So what did that very smart man do? He chose a wife on the basis of her pedigree and looks, the way he would choose a brood mare. Two people who were ill-suited from the start. They barely paid attention to each other, and less to the children. The result? Derelict parents produced three alcoholic children: two who killed themselves in drunken accidents and another who'd rather pay a bribe than admit that when he falls off the wagon, it's into some guy's arms."

"John Boelter was perceptive in one way, though," Cal observed. "Susan was the only one in the family whose character he ever really trusted, and she ended up carrying on what he built."

The booth fell silent.

"You're thinking about something," Cal observed.

With an abashed grin, Dan admitted, "About Susan."

"You two have gone through a lot together."

"You warned me, but I didn't realize how tough it would be to represent a person I . . . I cared about . . . how it would tear me up."

Cal started to joke that Dan's forgoing the close-to-half-a-million-dollar fee for defending Susan had torn *him* up, but he stopped, perceiving his friend's somberness.

"I sometimes didn't know what to think," Dan said. "It was so easy to believe she wasn't telling the truth. But her character was as solid as a mountain. She's quite a woman."

"So what are you going to do about it?" Mary Alice asked.

Awaiting Dan when he returned to his office was the answering service's message from Gil Huyton. Dan returned the call.

"Dan, I don't know how to say this in a way that will convey how badly I feel about that bribery charge," Huyton began. "You have my deepest, most sincere apologies. I'll personally go to the Disciplinary Board and clear the matter up. That was a god-awful mess I put you through."

"Thank you, Gil. This hasn't been an easy day for you."

"I appreciate your saying that. I've been sitting here and thinking about Mara, what she did, all the lies, her affair with Boelter. You just don't know how desolate I feel."

"I know."

"Just between us," Huyton went on, "thanks for not involving me . . . you know, my personal relationship . . . when Mara was on the stand."

"No need even to mention it."

"About Susan, though . . . without that last phone call to Mara on the log, all the evidence was against her. The autopsy report. The witnesses. How could I know she wasn't guilty?"

"You couldn't."

"I was so sure she killed Peter. And I'll be honest with you, Dan . . . even now, after all the things that came out at the trial this morning, I still believe she killed him. Oh, I know it's not rational. But deep in my bones, I'm absolutely sure she murdered him. And now she's gotten away with it."

Dan's only reply was to say, "This was a tough phone call for you to make, Gil. I appreciate it. So long."

"Good-bye."

Dan held the receiver in his hand for a long while after Huyton clicked off. Whether because of Huyton's remarks or his own uneasiness about having defended Ricardo Montano too well, Dan was now beset by a foreboding that in the rush to save Susan, he had let some loose ends remain. He mentally reviewed the phone conversation. When he came to the part about Huyton's being so sure about Susan's guilt and that all the evidence had pointed to her, Dan suddenly halted—and remembered what was still unexplained: the blood on Peter's thigh and Kieffer's claim that Peter had sex just before he died.

Dan had grilled Kieffer about body-handling procedures to demonstrate how easily a dab of blood could be inadvertently deposited by the medical examiner's employees. But he knew how careful those people were. And although he had produced scholarly opinions that *rigor mortis* could cause postmortem ejaculation, in his gut, he didn't find that the most plausible explanation. As Cal liked to put it, his theories had been defense lawyers' tap dancing.

Now that all the jubilation was winding down, Dan was left with a growing apprehension.

Instead of going directly to Susan's house, he drove the red Mustang to Chestnut Hill and parked in front of the real-estate office that was rerenting Peter's house. All the way out, his suspicion had been increasing that he had missed something at Peter's he should have seen.

A woman broker drove him over to show him the Walker Drive house. Thinking he was a potential buyer, she described its wonders, while carefully omitting that until that morning, the authorities had considered it the site of its most recent occupant's murder.

She unlocked the door, and Dan walked through the house, trying to take in everything.

The all-white kitchen was as clean and uncluttered as always. Nothing on the counters except the drain board, a small toaster oven, and, near the windowsill, the clock radio. The chairs were tucked carefully under the breakfast table near the glass doors that led out to the rear patio.

He opened the cellar door and turned on the light. The broker shuddered as he did. She swiftly declared that she would wait for him at the front door.

The concrete steps and floor had been scrubbed clean. Like water that has become still again soon after a stone has plunged into it, they held no visible reminder of Peter Boelter's death. But Dan knew that the turbulent emotions the man had aroused would roll outward for years, causing other people's lives to wallow and pitch, and some to capsize. Rest in peace, Peter Boelter.

Dan came back along the central hallway to Peter's office and stopped just inside the door. He tried to clear himself of preconceptions and let his gaze simply drift from one object in the room to the next. He would let whatever might come to mind make its own connections, hoping to spur subconscious thought into awareness. His eyes moved slowly along the books on the shelves to an armchair and then to another armchair and then to the desk lamp and then to the set of pens on either side of a clock set on marble and then to the phone . . .

"Oh, God, no!" he suddenly realized.

He stared at the phone. A moment later he was hurrying toward the front door.

"But you haven't even looked at the upstairs," the broker exclaimed.

"I've seen everything," he told her.

Dan hurried from the real-estate office to the supermarket and then around to its parking lot in the back. Near the supermarket's rear entrance, on the white-brick exterior wall, was the pay phone he was looking for.

He stared at it for awhile, then lifted the receiver and called Irwin Hollings, the phone company manager who had testified for him that morning.

"Irwin, I'd like you to check something for me," Dan said, when Hollings came on the line, "some calls made from a pay phone in Dellwyne on June sixth, just a few minutes after six P.M."

"It isn't a private phone or anything."

"No."

"No problem then."

"I expect you'll find three calls were made, all to the same number." Dan gave the telephone company executive that number, as well.

"It'll take a moment to bring it up on my computer. June sixth, you say?"

"Right," Dan confirmed, and repeated the time of day.

Several seconds later Hollings said. "Here they are. Three calls from that pay phone to that other number, all made between six-oh-five and six-oh-six in the evening."

When he heard no response, Hollings inquired, "Would you like a printout?"

"No, thanks. The barn door's already closed."

Susan saw the red Mustang pull up and ran to greet Dan at the door. "I heard about Midge. It's so sad."

Dan marched past her toward Peter's study.

"What's wrong?" she asked, following him.

"You were so clever. I could never see what was there, and never realized what wasn't."

Dan closed the study door behind them and confronted her.

"I expect you threw away the videotape after I asked to show it in court."

"Yes."

He walked to the wall shelves and pulled down the last of the seven identical golf trophies Peter had won at the country club, a tall, abstract sculpture made of stainless steel. He hefted it for a moment to feel its considerable weight. Then he looked at the inscription on the plate at the base.

" 'June sixth,' " he read aloud, and remarked, "The trophy that wasn't where it should have been: at Peter's house. How did it get here?"

"Peter asked me to bring it back and put it with the rest of his trophies."

"You said you were arguing with him when you left his house. Why would you do him a favor? In all our discussions about what happened, you never mentioned bringing back the trophy."

Dan ran a finger along the most prominent of several sharp ridges near the angular top. "I would say that little projection there is just about three millimeters long. A heavy object like this would make a very effective murder weapon, wouldn't you say?"

His stare shifted to Susan, and his voice demanded an answer. "Wouldn't you?"

Her brow was knotted with apprehension, but she remained silent. Dan began to spin out his reasoning.

"Karen lied for you on the stand, didn't she? She never told Peter she wanted to live with you. She was captivated by him. You used to tell me how hungry she was for his love and fearful that if she didn't live with him, she might lose it. But later, when a murder conviction would have taken her other parent from her, she lied about what she'd said, so the jury would believe you had no murder motive."

Susan's eyes, always unreadable, were fixed on Dan's. It occurred to him that what he had always considered her composure was really ruthlessness.

"You were desperate when you sent her out to the car so you could be alone with Peter. You were terrified that the divorce would leave you without Karen and without a dime. All my clever theories about time of death and Peter's stumbling drunkenly down the stairs were hogwash. Kieffer's autopsy report was right on the button all along."

"Don't do this, Dan."

"And so was Gil Huyton. After you sent Karen out to wait for you in the car, you seduced Peter, hoping to win him over—on one of those pool chaises or maybe on the kitchen floor. You're dynamite on the floor."

As acute as his sarcasm was the pain in Dan's voice. "A quick fuck was fine with Peter. Hell, it was even convenient—he only had to slip off his bathing suit. He was probably too drunk to notice that you were having your period—or to care. Knowing him, he probably got an added kick out of your groveling to save yourself. But right after he came, he told you to get lost and turned his back on you.

"You'd played your last card, and it came up a deuce. You were frantic. You were about to be ground into dust. So, the way I see it, to get rid of him, you reached for the first weapon that was handy: the golf trophy he'd left on the breakfast table on his way out to the pool, the same golf trophy I might have noticed in Karen's videotape if you hadn't erased the end of it. I should have realized that no one turns off a video camera while they're panning or tilting. They end a shot only after it comes to rest on something."

Dan gripped the trophy with both hands, like a baseball bat. "You slugged Peter with the trophy as hard as you could. He looked dead, and just about was. Then you dragged his body to the cellar door and pushed it down the stairs. You even went down there and arranged his head on the bottom step to make it look like he'd landed there. You probably had to wipe some blood off places it shouldn't have been."

Dan's thumb and forefinger drew thoughtfully at his chin. "But the kitchen was a mess. You had to clean up the blood. And you had to make it look like Peter was alive when you left the house. My guess is you turned on the clock radio nice and loud to an all-talk station and began to yell back at the guy who was on it. Mrs. Hildreth had come back by then to Peter's side of her property. She heard what she thought was an argument you and Peter were having. When you were about to leave, you set the radio's timer to turn off after a minute or so, and you stood on the front step yelling inside until it did, as if Peter were still alive. The problem was Mrs. Hildreth couldn't see or hear you from there. But a stroke of luck! Ben Ralston drove by. Too bad it later turned out he wouldn't have made a very credible witness."

Dan chuckled caustically. "Something else I never noticed should have been there: the sponges you cleaned up with and the maid's rubber gloves you wore so you'd leave no fingerprints anywhere. When the maid came back to the house a few weeks later, she was annoyed because she couldn't find her cleaning things. A commotion over a minor matter, I thought. Absentmindedness."

Dan pondered for a moment. "The gloves and sponges could have gone into your handbag. You could have held the golf trophy away from observers—or even under your skirt."

He smiled thinly. "Who'd have thought that such a genteel woman could do so many tricks under her skirt?"

Susan flinched and turned away, as if the accusation had been a fist. Dan grabbed her arm and twisted her to face him.

"I've never met a liar as good as you, Susan, not a single one among all the killers and thieves and scum I've represented. That wonderful well-born WASP coolness, that self-possession. You look and sound like a duchess. I was overwhelmed."

"I'm innocent, Dan. You have to believe that."

"Because I was in love with you, I did. That made me a perfect sucker. I kept telling myself that your honesty was the one sure thing I could count on; it swept away all my doubts."

Dan set the trophy on the coffee table and surveyed the study, still lacking a phone unit, since Peter took his system to the new house.

"The phone, that was the truly cunning part. It provided you with the perfect alibi."

"You have the same kind of phone in your office," she said. Her tone echoed her long months of apprehension that he would make the association.

"When I saw the phone just now at Peter's house, that's when everything finally clicked together in my mind." A rueful smile appeared to soften his face. "You could make it look like Peter was alive even though you were miles away. I figure you came up with the plan while you were driving back toward Dellwyne. You'd buy something at the supermarket and get a receipt to establish the time you were there. Oh, yes, and chat with some of the employees, so next day, they'd remember having seen you there.

"But first, first you'd make three calls to Peter's house from the pay phone outside the supermarket. Because his phone system had once been in this room, you knew the code to punch in that would activate the call-forwarding function in his equipment. So the first phone call you made to Peter's phone in Chestnut Hill was to punch in the code that would signal it to forward incoming calls to another phone number. But that other number had to be a likely one, a phone number Peter had called before. You chose the one you caught him calling the night he invited me to dinner here, a number you'd never been able to forget. You didn't know who the woman was he'd called that night, and certainly not that she was a deputy district attorney. But you were pretty sure she was his girlfriend and that other calls to her number would show up when the police checked the phone logs."

"The second call?" Susan asked, but with neither pride in her shrewdness nor a show of denial.

"That second call to Peter's house caused his phone equipment to dial Mara's number automatically and forward the call to her phone. On his phone records, though, it would show up as if the call to Mara had actually originated from Peter's own phone at six-oh-six P.M. . . . when you could prove you were miles away, at the supermarket in Dellwyne. Mara's answering machine picked up. You held long enough to make it appear on Peter's phone log that he had spoken to her, and then you hung up. Mara said on the stand that she thought there might have been a hang-up when she checked for messages late that night."

"And the third call?"

"That was to turn *off* the call-forwarding function. Now, no one would ever be able to discover that the call to Mara on the phone log had been made from anywhere else but Peter's phone."

"Has it occurred to you that I might have been calling Peter from the supermarket to continue our quarrel . . . or to make up . . . or to arrange a divorce settlement? It could have been anything. He could have kept hanging up on me, and I could have kept calling back to try talking it over with him."

"That's what you'd have wanted me to argue if the prosecution had stumbled onto those calls. Do you think Vellarde would have bought it the way he bought that call on the phone log to Mara?"

"Amelia heard a couple of phone rings inside Peter's house around then. He could have been answering my phone calls."

Dan ignored her excuse. "You had everything figured out. All you had to do was wait for the prosecutor to examine the phone log, and you'd be cleared of suspicion. But something went wrong: That six-oh-six P.M. call wasn't on the phone log the DA's office sent over to us. You couldn't believe it. Your alibi was missing. You pressed me to obtain an original log instead of a photocopy. I didn't pay any attention."

"But the autopsy findings, you said yourself they were inaccurate. Our pathologist, Mallory, would have refuted Kieffer's findings and cleared me."

"Not 'inaccurate,' Susan. The term would have been 'not medically certain beyond a reasonable doubt.' And a reasonable doubt in the jurors' minds was all you needed for acquittal. But when Mallory died, your case was in trouble. One thing after another had gone wrong. You needed hard evidence that would clear you. So you told Scott Feller to obtain an original copy of the phone log from the police. Huyton had given the police nothing but grief. They were happy to help a reporter who was ripping him apart in the *Herald*. Once I examined the original log, your problems were finally over. All you had to do was sit back and wait for me to clear you of a murder you were guilty of."

"You've made up your mind about that?"

"All the evidence is there."

"You once said you believed I was innocent."

Susan had appeared to him to be a woman incapable of deception when, all the time, she had conceived the most heinous of deceptions. He had loved her and trusted her. But she had never loved him. Just like Mara, she had used him until she no longer needed him, until he had gotten her acquitted.

"Gil Huyton and I," he reflected, "I never thought we'd have anything in common—love blinded both of us and made us fools."

"Not blind and never a fool, Dan."

"For the first time in my life," he admitted, "I'm sickened that I saved a client."

"I love you. I've never lied about that."

"After all your other lies, really big ones, what's one little one? God, you were nerveless. You really do have the kind of mind and guts that can run vast companies. You were even able to show anger toward me because I was worried about being in love with a murderess."

Disgusted by the layers of her deceit, by the evil he was certain he had glimpsed in her depths, Dan lurched away from her toward the door. Susan reached out to stop him.

"We love each other, Dan. Just believe I'm innocent. Is that so hard?"

Unexpectedly, the door opened. Karen had just returned from riding. Noticing Dan, she smiled.

"I saw your car outside."

Her eyes fell on the trophy sitting atop the coffee table. A scream burst from her throat and slivered into sobs like falling glass splinters. Overwhelmed by memory, she blurted out what she was now sure Dan had figured out.

"You know! You know I killed him! I killed my daddy!"

Susan ran to her and clapped a hand over her mouth. "You don't know what you're saying!"

Dan pulled the hand away and drew the girl into the room. He helped her to a chair as Susan closed the door.

"Karen, tell me what happened," he said.

"He was so drunk, Dan . . . drunker than I ever saw him." Karen spilled out the phrases between sobs. "I really did become afraid to choose him to live with. I tried to talk to him about it. But his breath was all liquor-smell, and his eyes . . . they were like pieces of ice. For a second I thought he was going to hit me. I didn't know what he was going to do. But then he started crying."

"Crying?"

"Tears ran down his cheeks. He said I was deserting him, that he loved me, but I was cold and heartless and deserting him. I tried to make him understand I wasn't. It was just that I didn't know what to do when he got drunk like that. I wanted to cry, too. He was so sad. But when I tried to explain, he got real angry. He began yelling that I was ungrateful and if I left him, he never wanted to look at me again. I was scared. So I said I wouldn't ever leave him and I'd live with him."

"And that's when I arrived," Susan interjected. "I told her to go to the pool house and change out of her swimsuit. Peter asked me into the kitchen to talk."

"About what?"

"He was . . . the only word for it is 'exultant.' And abusive, too, like at the courthouse the day before, only now there was no one around for him to worry about or to stop him. He told me Karen was going to live with him, so he'd finally beaten me all the way around. He said, 'You can't do anything to me anymore.'

"Suddenly he swung a punch at my head. I threw my arms up to shield my face, so he hit me in the body. He could be cruel when he was drunk. I couldn't get away. I screamed for him to stop. But he had this big smile on his face—he was enjoying how helpless I was, that I was afraid. He kept telling me how powerless I was, and then he'd throw a punch and laugh.''

"And then he raped you," Dan realized.

"Actually, raping me seemed almost an afterthought, like frosting on the great feeling that dominating me was giving him." Susan glanced worriedly at Karen. "We don't have to go into the rest of this, do we?"

"Going into this is long overdue. What happened then?"

Susan was still watching Karen. "He threw me down underneath him and yanked up my skirt. He pushed my panties aside—and the sanitary napkin. That must have been when he pulled down his swimsuit—I don't remember. But he was on top of me and forcing himself into me. I was screaming.''

Dan said to Karen, "And you heard her and came back in."

Eyes wide and unfocused, back in that kitchen once more, Karen displayed a panicky fear for her mother's welfare that was as vivid now as when she came upon her being brutalized on the floor. So, too, was the conflict that gripped her then over taking one parent's side in preference to another's.

"Daddy was naked, and he was punching Mommy over and over like a maniac. She had her hands over her face. He would curse at her and then swing a fist at her.''

"What was he saying?"

"Some things were about you." Karen dropped her eyes. "He said Mommy was a . . . a whore . . . because she was sleeping with—" Her voice fell to a whisper. Her eyes, lifting, begged forgiveness. "—a dirty little kike. I thought he was going to kill her.''

"The trophy was on the kitchen table," Dan finished for the girl. "To stop him, you grabbed it and hit him.''

Karen collapsed once again into sobs, her head bobbing up and down in affirmation. Susan enfolded her daughter in her arms.

"I don't know whether he'd have killed me or not," said Susan softly. "But Karen thought so."

Hysterical, Karen had swung the trophy with all her might. A strong athlete, she had shattered Peter's skull.

Now, finally, Dan understood. All along, Susan had been covering up for her daughter, the person she loved more than anyone in the world, the person she would give her life for.

He told her, "You could have explained to the police that Karen killed Peter to protect you. Justifiable homicide.''

Susan smiled sadly above her daughter's head buried in her chest. "But how do you justify everyone's knowing for the rest of her life that she killed her father . . . that she found him battering and raping her mother, so she bludgeoned him to death? A million times better for me to go to jail than for her always to carry that guilt. Bad enough that she'll have to live with the memory. How much more terrible never to be free of the disgrace." Her voice begged him to understand. "She loved her father, Dan. I couldn't let the world know what a monster he was—and what she did to him."

Susan's single-minded priority became sheltering her daughter from the twin dangers of a possible trial and certain notoriety. Thinking clearly, as always in adversity, Susan told Karen to go out to the car with her belongings while she straightened up inside. Even though she ached from his punches, she pulled Peter's swimsuit back on him and dragged him over to the cellar steps, letting him somersault down. She quickly arranged the body to make it appear as if he had died in an accident. After cleaning up, she took the sponges, the rubber gloves, and the trophy, argued with the sound of the radio voice until it switched off, and then left.

Still weeping in Susan's arms, Karen was mumbling, "I killed him. I killed Daddy."

Dan knelt beside her.

"It wasn't your fault," he gently assured her. "You had no choice. Liquor made him violent and dangerous. It can do that to some people. You loved him, and he loved you. But you had to help your mother. He was killing her."

"Now, though . . ." Her voice dwindled into alarm and self-loathing.

He put his arms around both of them. "You're safe now. No one will ever know."

Karen's head lifted, her eyes finding Dan's. "*You* know."

"It will always be our secret. I'll never let anyone harm you."

Relief flickered for an instant on her face. She had grown to trust him in the months since he had been defending her mother and, in some small ways, had even allowed him to replace her father. Because he had assured her without being obligated to, she began to believe she might be safe.

Eventually, Karen went up to her room to shower and change. All the while, Dan had been deep in thought. In this family of secrets, Karen's had been savagely forced upon her very young. His heart was torn by her ordeal and awed by Susan's fierce maternal urge to protect her child, no matter the risk to herself.

But a stronger emotion surged up within him: his need to protect himself from hurt and to preserve the integrity he guarded, like a tiny, perfect diamond at the center of his soul. He had always been proud that he would do anything legal to win a case for a client. The adversary system demanded no less as his moral duty. This trial to save the woman he had risked loving had challenged his integrity down to the very meaning of his life. Yet, all the while he was desperately flailing for an opening that would exonerate her, he had actually been playing out the scenario she had written for him.

She had conned him. She had conned the guy who prided himself on being smarter than every con man going, the street fighter who knew all the tricks in the book, who was one step ahead of everyone else. At every turn, she had outfoxed him and even made him love her while doing it. Not only was he tormented by her dishonesty, his pride was hurt.

After Karen left, seeing his anguish, Susan reached up to touch his cheek. He yanked his head back.

"You lied to me!"

Sad agreement draped her words. "You knew I would. You told me I'd lie to save myself."

He had warned her that love depended on the truth, but that truth and adversary justice were not necessarily reconcilable, that a defense depended on raising doubts about guilt, not on seeking to reveal truth; that truth could get twisted and stomped on and left for dead in the struggle for acquittal. She had told him she had nothing to fear because she was innocent.

He had tried to make her understand that even innocence might not be enough to preserve the truth and, with it, their love. And she *had* been innocent, as she had claimed. But only of killing Peter. Her lies about what happened that Saturday in June—and the lies she had coached Karen to tell—had betrayed his trust in her and the love built on that trust, the only kind of love he wanted, love that sustained and opened up the soul, love that was nourished by truth and shriveled before deceit.

"Why couldn't you trust me?" he entreated her for an answer.

"You were my lawyer . . . and my lover. I couldn't let you be implicated."

His eyes condemned her. "You thought I'd sound more convincing about your innocence if I believed it."

She had done everything for the best of reasons, Dan realized: for her daughter's and her own welfare—and even for his. Those ends justified the means to her, but shattered his faith in her.

Shattered also, as totally as if her falsehoods had been concocted to hide her passion for another man, was his love for her. Never again could he trust what she might tell him, what she might do. Like Peter, he had tried his best to win. And in winning, like Peter, he had lost everything.

"I loved you too much to settle for less than we had," he told her.

"Dan, you expect too much. If it hadn't been now, sooner or later I would have disappointed you. But you would have disappointed *me,* too. No one can be as perfect as you want them to be. When that illusion dies, that's when real love—and the real work—begins.''

"All I wanted was for us to be honest with each other. No lies. Love built on honesty, on trust. I'd been through enough lies with Mara. And I lied to myself when I married Hannah. No more." He shook his head, murmuring the last words to himself. "No more."

It occurred to him that two incongruous people, two people who were total opposites, had come together for a short time because their needs intersected. And then their differences—the essential inner differences—had finally gathered the strength to drive them apart.

He stood up and, slowly, as if pulling his feet from quicksand, walked out of the room.

Susan watched his figure disappear beyond the door lintel. Suddenly realizing the finality of his departure, she cried out, "Dan!" and ran after him. She caught up with him outside on the portico.

"Where are you going?"

"Somewhere new, I guess."

"Dan, how can you leave the place where you're loved?"

He stared at her. "I don't even know for sure who you are."

"I'm the same person I've always been. I'd never lie about that. You're the one who's still lying, Dan. You're lying to yourself."

"Me?"

"Now that all the barriers between us are finally down—no husband, no murder charge—what you really want is an excuse to run and not have to blame yourself for it."

He shook his head. "It's over."

"Then let's start again. And when we fail, let's start over once more. Because we'll fail a lot. That's what people almost always end up doing."

He started toward the Mustang, withdrawing his car keys from his pocket.

"What will I tell Karen?" Susan cried out. "That the man who just said he'd never let anyone harm her—who claims to place so much value in honesty—lied to her and ran away."

He stopped. She spoke to his back.

"There are lots of reasons why you shouldn't love me. We're very different. To begin with, we have careers that can put us at odds. And I sometimes just do things on my own, so you'll get angry because you didn't have a say. And once in a while, you become sulky and refuse to let me know what's bothering you until I want to shake you."

She thought she discerned another doubt harrowing him. "And maybe, deep down, you're worried people will think less of you because I've got the *Herald* and a lot more money than anyone has a right to have. It's that, too, isn't it?''

Very slowly, as if wrenching his entire universe around, Dan turned to face her again.

"Oh, yes," she remembered, "I'm not Jewish. That's a big one. And I don't want to be. But if you ever thought of giving it up for me, I'd walk out faster than you're trying to do."

She had his attention and was frantic to hold on to it. "Our kids really like each other, Dan. They really do. And they like *us*. That says a lot for us—and for what we have together."

"It just isn't enough."

She was crying now—she wanted so much not to lose him. "Then *nothing* can ever be enough."

She tried to form a single thought that would encircle him like a lasso. "Don't you understand, Dan? *It's enough that I make you happy.*"

After a long moment he admitted, "That scares me."

"Being happy?"

"Compromising my happiness because I have to be responsible for yours. Starting out a life together having already sacrificed my principles."

"Oh." She thought about that. "There are some things I won't yield on, Dan. Peter couldn't take that. You can. But I don't expect you to yield on what's important to *you*. I love you because you won't."

She grasped his hands, enclosing them in hers. "We know going in that there'll be those times—we're prepared for it. But, for God's sake, don't throw away the ninety-nine percent of life in between."

A movement above caused Dan to glance up. The curtain had been pulled back from a second-floor window. Karen was peering down at him from her bedroom, her face shadowed and grave. Their gazes held for a long while.

Finally Dan offered a little wave and let his gaze descend. His other hand was still in Susan's. He closed his eyes and heard the clash of emotions and principles and compromises within his brain. And he heard his voice telling him he would have lied, too, if his child's welfare had been at stake. But the loudest cry from within came from his heart, from its loneliness and its yearnings; if he walked away now, he would miss Susan forever. When he opened his eyes, they were on her.

"Let's give it a try," he said.

He dropped the car keys into his pocket, put an arm around her, and started walking back with her toward the house.

About the Author

Joseph Amiel, a lawyer, was graduated from Amherst College, where he studied English and creative writing, and from Yale Law School. He now devotes himself full-time to writing. *A Question of Proof* is his fifth novel. He is married and has two children, to whom he has dedicated this book.